THE BEAST OF BRIDDE PLACE

THE BEAST OF BRIDDE PLACE

A. L. WATERS

BRANOC
BOOKS

The Beast of Bridde Place
Text © 2023 A.L. Waters

ISBN: 9781739388188

This is a work of fiction. Any resemblance to real persons (living or dead), events, entities or things, is entirely coincidental.

Cover Design: Jackie Tee

Editing & typeseting: Laura Kincaid,
Ten Thousand | Editing + Book Design
www.tenthousand.co.uk

Printed and bound in Great Britain
by Clays Ltd, Elcograf S.p.A.

For All Comers

BRIDDE PLACE

A house of indeterminate period and comfortable aspect, Bridde Place stands alone in its windswept hillside north of the Pennines. Georgian windows in their limestone jambs smile down upon the weary traveller, seeming to congratulate the visitor on having come thus far, while the Elizabethan door, rising to a point, invites him to enter and rest, and put off going any further.

Bridde Place is notable as much for its situation as its aspect. Standing in front of the house, one hears already the howling wind of Bridde Pass on the far side of the rise, known locally as Devil's Pass. With the irony of names, though a path leads to the edge of the gulch, any means to cross it has long since been swallowed by the misty deep. Twin pairs of stone pillars on either side are all that remains of what must once have been a bridge. On the far side, unreachable, stretches Bridde Forest, dense and seemingly endless, the black silhouette of a bird rising occasionally above the canopy. Ancient and infamously treacherous, Bridde Forest is little explored even today. Perhaps unsurprisingly, a substantial body of local folklore has grown up around it, encompassing also its namesake house, with references to the so-called Beast of Bridde Place *being recorded as early as 1723. Readers may be familiar with the popular folksong known as the* Bridde Lament, *which references the same.*

Ed. Note 3rd Edition: Bridde Place burned down in the winter of 1871. It has not been rebuilt.

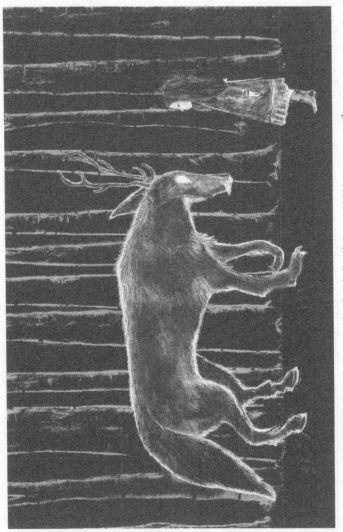

Woodcut discovered in Bridde Church demolition in 1919, provenance unknown

Farewell my bird of Bridde
Fly well my Bridde lass
The Beast appears behind you
To drive you to the Pass

He walks behind the shadows
He waits beneath the stair
And coming he will drive you
Into the calling air

— Folksong, unknown

I

Nora fought the waking.

Even as the nightmare collapsed around her, she resisted, clinging to the taste of ash in her mouth, the snap of teeth flashing in the light of flames. Some part of her, the part which even sleeping had caught the scream, warned her to remain where she was, safe with the Devil she knew. If she could only surrender, let the beast take her and drag her down the burning stairs to the darkness waiting below, then there could be no call to open her eyes.

She must not, on any account, open her eyes.

There was no help for it. The dream was broken, flames fading as lunging jaws disappeared in a puff of smoke, leaving her at the mercy of the sickening pain in her head, the knowledge that the sweet tang which hung about her could not be anything but blood.

Inch by sticky inch, she became aware of herself. The mattress was sodden beneath her, the gore soaking her nightgown and clinging to her skin, coating her hair, her lips, her eyelids, gluing the lashes together as it congealed in the unaccountable breeze.

Reflexively she made to wipe her eyes, and it was then she noticed the weight. It pinned her in place, pressing her hand to her chest like a flower as it sprawled across her, solid and familiar and dead.

Horrible understanding came suddenly, with a violence that tore her eyelids apart before she could remember to keep them closed. The pain in her head spiked with the force of it so that for a moment she could only lie wide-eyed and gasping, staring up at the canopy which had once been white.

As the moment passed, she found herself glancing down to see Victor lying across her. His face was hanging over her shoulder, a lock of his hair inches from her cheek as his forehead rested on the pillow beside her. With detached curiosity, she noticed that blood was still leaking from the shredded remains of what had been her husband's throat.

In the distance, she could hear the questions clamouring, the who and the what and the why. They made her head ache. She looked away, letting her eyes drift into the room beyond the bed. There was the dainty rosewood table with its China vase, there her lacquered chiffonier, there the door to her dressing room, the brass knob polished and gleaming. All just as it should be, just as it always was, and she might almost have persuaded herself all was well. Then she came to the windows.

There were three of them gazing out onto the London night, and the third was not as it should be. The pane was broken, letting in a draught of cold night air. Outside, the branches of Kensington's plane trees waved, raggedy in their autumn dress. Nora shivered as she watched them. It occurred to her that Joan must have forgotten to draw the curtains again.

The screaming had not stopped. The knowledge seemed to arrive suddenly in her mind, and yet she realised it had always been there. All this time it had been going on, a high keening without beginning nor hope of end, filling the room so that she could no longer imagine it silent. An inhuman sound, and yet the voice was familiar. Nora tried to turn towards it, to lift herself to see, only to find herself held down by the weight of her husband's corpse.

Oh. She had forgotten about that.

The thought made her head throb and the world quiver, so Nora very deliberately did not think about anything at all as she put her hand to the shoulder and pushed – hard. The bulk yielded easily, falling back onto the soggy mattress with an obliging squelch. She shuddered, another spike of pain piecing her skull as she sat up, making her vision slosh like water in a glass. It was a moment before she recognised her audience.

The household staff stood assembled just within her bedroom door, butler and housekeeper and cook flanked by all manner of maids and footmen. They crowded together in their various states of undress, petty daytime spats forgotten here in the dead of night as they clutched their candle ends. The flames flickered in the draught, illuminating faces drawn tight with horror as they stared, as one, at their mistress sitting up in bed.

"Please draw me a bath."

Nora's voice sounded strange to her own ears, all but swallowed up by that never-ending scream. She searched the assembled faces for Joan, who was responsible for curtains and baths and all such comforting luxuries. The little maid standing furthest inside the room, a little apart from the rest of the group. The moment she found her, Nora knew the girl was beyond any earthly comfort. Her spattered nightgown dripped upon the carpet as she stared towards the bed, her mouth hanging open in that awful unending scream.

A bustling of the crowd drew Nora's attention, and she watched as the cook – *Sharpe*, a distant voice in Nora's head reminded her, *Mrs Sharpe* – stepped forward to take the maid in charge. Without a word the massive woman turned her bodily and marched Joan out of the room, candle in one meaty hand as she guided the unresisting girl with the other. The scream trailed after them down the hall, and long after they were gone Nora could hear it, dashing itself hopelessly against the rafters of the servants' quarters far above, like a fly in a jam jar.

In the end it was McNeal who came to her mistress's rescue, stepping over the mess with her dainty housekeeper's tread to bundle Nora out of bed and into her dressing gown. As Nora allowed herself to be led away, she could hear Alcott taking charge behind, giving instruction to send for the police with the same solemn, butlering dignity he used to order the silver polished.

~

Scotland Yard arrived at the same time as her bath. The fire drew leaping shapes on the copper tub as she listened to the men piling into the great house. The thump of their boots echoed upon the cold marble floors below before being muffled by finest Axminster pile as they traipsed up the stairs and along the corridor. Closer and closer they came – far too close.

In between sluices from McNeal's water jug, Nora heard them stalking about her bedroom, watching the dance of their shadows beneath the dressing-room door. They were arguing about the date – was it yesterday, or was it tomorrow? – and the final answer, read aloud as it was scratched at the top of a grubby pad, caught in her head: *1 November 1896*.

The date flickered a moment and was gone, McNeil's nimble old fingers distracting her as they tugged at her hair, separating black curls from the crusted chunks which ran to red under the jug. Staring into the tinted water that swirled about her in the copper tub, Nora was dimly aware that some of the blood must be her own. She flinched as the scalding torrent from McNeil's jug struck the tender spot at the crown of her head. The housekeeper exclaimed in dismay.

"Madam, you're hurt! Your head, it's—"

Nora was already reaching up, fingers probing gingerly at the gash in her scalp. She squeezed her eyes shut in the effort of remembering, but nothing would come, nothing but the flames and the heat and the confusion as she struggled to evade the snapping jaws. The beast had pinned her down, and she had tried to rear away—

"The headboard," she heard herself murmur, remembering the flash of pain before the jaws had been on her again. "I suppose I must have struck it when—"

The thought was swallowed by a wave of nausea, and McNeal did not press.

"Looks worse than it is," she said, returning to her work. "Only superficial, and the bleeding stopped already. No cause for alarm I shouldn't think, though no doubt the doctor will wish to make his own assessment."

Nora nodded vaguely, hardly noticing as McNeal scrubbed diligently at the hollow of her throat, around her ears, down her arms, under her nails and in the creases of her long, bony fingers.

The housekeeper sluiced again, and Nora shuddered. There were shadows in the corners still, distracting in the way they leaped in time to the fire in the grate, to the pulse in her aching head. She forced herself to look away, focusing on the voices beyond the dressing-room door. Assassin or burglar, that was the question, they told each other. Jewellery missing, just the one piece, a knife found amid shards of glass on the path outside, but the state of the body suggested—

"Madam?"

Nora looked up to find McNeal was no longer behind her but at the door, having evidently been there long enough to conduct an entire whispered conversation. "Mr Alcott and I wondered which of the guest rooms you might like to take."

Nora blinked. "None of them. I am not a guest."

"No, Madam," McNeal agreed. "But under the circumstances…" The housekeeper trailed off, wringing her hands. She was still in her dressing gown, her grey hair tied back in haste. She must feel herself at a terrible disadvantage to Alcott, Nora realised vaguely, who no doubt had changed into full uniform the moment he had left her bedroom, all the better to receive the police. She ought to allow McNeal to go and change too, Nora thought, and then realised the housekeeper was watching her, awaiting an answer.

"The circumstances do not make me a guest, McNeal."

"No, Madam." McNeal hesitated. "Perhaps, then, the old music room might do for a spell? It's on the ground floor but quite tucked away so you wouldn't be disturbed, and it has a lovely view of the garden."

Nora gave a nod of assent, to the housekeeper's visible relief.

"Very good, Madam. I'll ask Mr Alcott to arrange for furniture to be brought down directly, and might I suggest one of the smaller rooms in the passage for Joan—" She broke off, remembering in the same instant Nora did. As one, their eyes travelled to the ceiling. The screaming had finally subsided, and the rumble of police about the house almost drowned out the eerie silence left in its wake.

Dragging her gaze away, Nora found McNeal looking at her, a question written in the lines of her tired face. Realising that in another minute the old woman would have no choice but to give voice to the thought, Nora pre-empted the discussion with the easiest choice available to her: "You can attend me until Joan is well enough to resume her duties. I see no reason to disrupt the household further. Now help me dress, and then you can go and dress too."

Pending the arrival of proper mourning apparel, McNeal had delved into the wardrobe and produced a high-necked day dress in dull black silk. Pulled tight across her angular frame, it did Nora no favours, bringing out the shadows cast by her brow and in the hollows of her cheeks, her skin taut over the hard bones in between. Only her eyes caught the light, staring back at her from the one mirror left uncovered, pale and colourless as water in a glass.

Nora had never been a pretty woman, but neither could she rightly be called plain. With her hooked nose and sallow complexion, *distinctive* was the word that had followed her through London's ballrooms in the early days of her marriage, murmured in corners and behind unfurled fans as the great and the good – and especially their wives – attempted to puzzle out just how such a match had come about. She'd looked thirty before she was twenty, and she knew that was true because, when she'd said as much to Ambrose, he'd made no attempt to deny it. Brushing her distress aside, her old friend had only smiled and told her not to worry, that her figure was tall and straight enough to carry it, and anyway, she'd be pleased when she was his age and had barely gained a day.

Ambrose. Now there was a name she hadn't thought of in a while. Well, he'd been right: on this day, when she found herself widowed at twenty-eight, the face staring back at her in the glass looked hardly any different than when last they had met, a full decade before.

She allowed McNeal to cover the mirror with the heavy mourning velvet Alcott had brought before dismissing her into the bowels of the house. The police were still there, swarming like an infestation, starched uniforms creaking and boots heavy on groaning floorboards. Now they whispered and now they forgot to – or saw no reason to bother – now they remembered or were reminded again. Snatches of conversation came to her, seeping through the gaps under doors, the cracks in the wall, carried by pipes and the hidden passageways of rats and whispers. They spoke of locked doors and broken windows, bloody handprints and filleting knives in bushes. They knew it was a filleting knife, one explained to another, because the cook Sharpe had helpfully identified it as such, and of course they were speaking to the staff, one after another, speaking to *her* staff—

Hers alone now. The thought was dizzying, and she put a hand to her forehead, willing the nausea to subside. She supposed they would be asking for her next.

~

Pale daylight seeped into the blue sitting room, only to be embarrassed by the fire. From the blackened innards of the hearth, the flames seemed to lick at the white marble surround, their flicker reflecting in the corners of polished wood, the edges of bright silk upholstery, the brass buttons on the young policeman's uniform. He struggled to rise as Nora entered, the overstuffed sofa proving almost a match for him. The man beside him managed rather more gracefully as he bowed, ignoring his struggling junior. Nora's impression of the man was all in grey: clothes, hair, eyes, even his expression seemed to be cut from the same plain grey wool, well kept and neatly worn.

"Detective Inspector Edmund Ritter and Constable Paul Wilcox of the London Metropolitan Police, madam," Alcott announced as Nora took her seat opposite the pair, ordering tea poured with a careless wave.

"Let me begin by offering our most sincere condolences, Mrs Bancroft."

As Ritter retook his seat, Nora found his voice matched his appearance perfectly. It was a voice which had offered many sincere condolences to many unhappy widows over the course of a long career; the voice of a man who, while considering that perhaps a young, wealthy and not wholly unattractive widow might not be deserving of the very fullest of his sympathy, was nevertheless sorry for his role in making her sit here, fighting the urge to hunch her shoulders protectively around her neck, an impulse resisted in no small part thanks to the restrictions of her undergarments.

"Thank you," Nora began, only to find herself immediately interrupted.

"Yes, most dreadfully sorry, madam," the constable burst in, breathless in his earnestness and barely controlled nerves.

He was young, she realised, looking at him properly for the first time; tall and strapping, with broad shoulders and a square jaw, and terribly, terribly young. Too young, she thought, irritation twisting her mouth unpleasantly – far too young to be deputising on such an important case, on *Victor's* case, when—

"I asked Constable Wilcox to join us specially," Ritter said, reading her mind, or at least her face. "He grew up in Chilting – isn't that right, Constable?"

"Yes, sir." Wilcox's eyes were wide and boyish beneath his thatch of strawberry hair. "Not two miles from the big house – I mean, your late husband's estate."

"You see, madam," Ritter went on, "in my experience, a bit of local knowledge can make all the difference, so I had the clerk look up anyone who might be useful in that regard."

The beginnings of panic gripped her. How could he know? But she knew at once it was ridiculous, panic and question both. Because of course he had been briefed. If his own general knowledge had not yielded sufficient information regarding the country seat of some of the nation's grandest gentry, some clerk would have been sent to pull out Burke's. How long had it been since the police had been alerted? Five hours? Six? Plenty of time to read the Bancroft family pages, to picture the red-brick country house in whose chapel she had been wed, where she had spent her first married winter hiding from the freezing Hampshire fields, oppressive in their endless openness. She wondered whether it mentioned that she had stayed in town ever since.

She pictured the policeman leafing through to her maiden Dallaway family entry, those grey eyebrows rising in surprise at finding only a line or two, a damning indictment of her father's stature in comparison to her husband's. She wondered whether Ritter knew just how far she had fallen short and hated him suddenly for not realising that Victor had fallen just as short, and shorter still, for he, after all, had at least had the benefit of upbringing. She hated herself, for having spent all her guile obtaining a position she was lost in, but most of all she hated Victor, for being decent, and undemanding, and fool enough to get himself murdered.

The silk of the cushions squeaked as Wilcox shifted uneasily, and Ritter shot him a sideways glance as he asked Nora the question she had been dreading, the question to which she had no answer. She had been asleep, she told them, or unconscious – it was hard to tell which – and remembered very little.

"What you do remember then," he pressed. "Take your time."

Nodding made her queasy. She picked up her cup, put it to her lips, drank nothing, set it back its saucer, picked up the saucer with cup and all and held it before her.

"I was dreaming," she began, feeling as though she were doing so again. In the cup, the tea swirled and she stared into it, as though it might be made a prism through which to focus the fragments of memory.

"I think some aspects of reality must have mingled with it, but I cannot tell which. There was – there was fire, all around, and I was held down, unable to move. I knew only that I was in danger – terrible, mortal danger I must escape at all costs – and then there was the gleam of something – something sharp, silver even amid the flames—"

She looked at Ritter, willing him to release her or at least guide her through. He nodded encouragingly and offered no help whatever.

"Something hit the back of my head," she went on. "There was a scream, I remember – it might have been my own, or Joan's – and then the sound of breaking glass." She could hear it now, the shrill, cold chattering like crystal teeth, filling her head and the room, unrelenting. "There was the fire and the weight and the screaming, and then darkness, and then I woke up, all covered in— And Victor was—"

The chattering in her head filled the room to bursting, and she watched in wonder as, very gently, Ritter reached over the low table between them and took cup and saucer from her hands. Instantly, the noise ceased, the china still and silent as Ritter set it back on the table.

Nora closed her eyes, giving herself a short, sharp shake, like a hunter flicking blood from his knife, and feeling the shadows retreated to distant, more manageable corners. "Forgive me."

"Not at all, madam. We do not pretend to imagine how difficult this must be for you. Now, did your husband have any enemies? Debts perhaps? Rivalries of any sort?"

Nora retrieved her cup, finding comfort in the ordinariness of the now tepid tea. "None that I'm aware."

A glance at Ritter's expression told her that further explanation was needed: to a policeman's mind, a rich man without enemies must be an absurdity, an oxymoron.

"You must understand that my husband was not an excitable man. He enjoyed the entertainments available to men of his class, and frankly he did not care to exert himself beyond them. I never knew him to overindulge or involve himself in any situation which might threaten his comfort. To speak bluntly, I've heard him called passive to a fault."

Here she had to bite her lip to stop the lump in her throat from trembling; she had never found Victor Bancroft's docility a flaw – indeed, quite the reverse.

"The only time I ever saw him truly passionate was over—" But that was too much. Something tore in her chest, breaking off the sentence even as she saw, no, *felt* the policemen tense like hounds catching a scent.

"Do please finish your thought, Mrs Bancroft. In cases like this, even the most trivial detail can be of significance."

Nora composed herself. "Then I defer to your experience, Detective Inspector, though I'm sure I can't imagine how it could," she said, even as she hated them. Surely they didn't need to know everything; surely some things – the small, unimportant things – she might still keep for herself, but Ritter's gaze was unrelenting and so she gave him even that.

"My husband collected balls."

She took a savage satisfaction in the ripple of surprise which disturbed Ritter's impassive face. "What sort of balls?"

"Oh, all kinds." Nora shrugged within the confines of her dress, making an airy gesture she did not feel. The movement distracted her as she watched her own long fingers twirl in the air, as though her hand were trying to escape the tether of her wrist. "Ones used for games mainly. Cricket, tennis, billiards, polo, that sort of thing. Foreign ones too: he had contacts with dealers abroad and they'd send him anything of the sort they happened across, modern as well as antique. He'd show me sometimes – when he'd received something particularly unusual, he'd invite me up to his library and tell me about it, all those little details which could be of interest to no one else."

The memory brought a wry smile to her lips. They had been happy in those times, almost friends.

"Was that all?"

"Yes, that was all." She sipped her tea, letting the moment pass and becoming matter-of-fact because it was easier than being anything else. She was tiring; it was growing harder to keep the flames in their corners. "Those occasions were the only times I ever knew him to excite himself emotionally, about anything. You must understand, Detective Inspector, that my husband and I did not know each other well. In the main, he had his pursuits and I had mine, and rarely did they overlap."

"I see." Something passed across Ritter's face, a suggestion, she thought, that perhaps he did not, in fact, entirely see, but he let the subject alone and moved on.

"I understand a telegram arrived late last night, for Mr Bancroft's hand only. Would you know what it might have related to?"

"No, I'm afraid this is the first I've heard of it. I suppose whoever was on duty must have directed the runner to Pimlico, where Victor kept his mistress. Mrs Nailard, I believe her name is. You might ask her."

It was only in the look which passed between the policemen that she realised they knew exactly where the telegram had gone but had not expected her to. The young constable especially could not hide his pity for her, nor his disgust, and in her distraction she felt a rush of tenderness for his innocence, that he did not yet realise how many arrangements people might make, how much better their lives could be for them.

"Very well," said Ritter, closing his notebook with a snap. "Thank you, Mrs Bancroft – you've been most helpful."

In her clouding mind, it was not until he rose that she realised he considered their interview at an end.

"What of my necklace?" she asked, anxiety gripping her suddenly. "McNeal says it was stolen…"

Ritter glanced at her and, seeing that she was in earnest, sat down again. "Forgive me, madam – we understood from your staff that the necklace was of little value."

"It is," Nora agreed, the point of his statement eluding her. "It's a silver disk, slightly twisted with a hole in the middle, so that it may be used as a whistle. The design is traditional to the village of Bridde, where I was born, but not much known elsewhere."

She found herself speaking too quickly, breathless suddenly.

"To my knowledge it has no value beyond the weight of the silver but belonged to my great-aunt Virginia. I was raised by my father's family from the age of three, after my parents died when our house burned down, and that necklace is all I have left of my mother's side. I was wearing it the night of the fire—"

At the memory, her hand went unconsciously to her throat, which seemed to tighten and choke with remembered smoke. The pressure of her starched collar, hardly felt a moment ago, was suddenly unbearable, and she tugged roughly at it.

"I'm sorry to hear that," Ritter said, and indeed his grimace was sympathetic. "Did you wear it much in recent years? Did anyone know of your sentimental attachment?"

Nora shook her head, fingertips still resting at her throat. "I don't think so. I haven't worn it in years, not since I left school—"

A thought occurred to her, a sudden flash of understanding; from the way Ritter sat back from her gaze, she knew it must have shown on her face. "Don't you think it strange, Detective Inspector, that a thief would have chosen such a plain thing, with so many more enticing pieces in that same box?"

"Indeed, madam, very strange. I would even venture to say unheard of." Ritter smiled gently. "In my experience with thieves, you see, they generally take the whole box. But do be assured that we will pursue every lead, however slight."

As he rose a second time, Nora looked up at him with the plaintiveness of a child. "I would like my necklace back," she said. Then she stood, her skirts rustling abruptly as she went to the bell pull.

Alcott was at the door in a moment.

"Ensure the gentlemen have all they require," she told him. "I am not to be disturbed."

She did not stay for the policemen's thanks, nor Ritter's plea to call on him at Scotland Yard with any new information, at any time convenient. She felt his questioning eyes upon her

back as she swept out but did not turn. The shadows were closing in, tunnelling her vision into a long dark corridor which
admitted neither left nor right. The pulse in her head drowned
out all other sound as she fumbled to the music room and
navigated to the newly installed bedstead by feel alone. Her
fingers caught the bed linen, and something in the softness of
it was comforting in the moment before the dream flooded her
entirely.

II

The repetitive rasp of steel over coarse stone filtered from the kitchen into the passage beyond. Though no stranger to grand houses, Ritter thought he would never cease to be amazed by the multitudes they contained. They seemed to him whole communities within a single building, distillations spanning the whole gamut of the social order, highest to lowest, and with all the divisions and interdependencies that entailed.

Not ten minutes before, he had been sitting in a gilded world, neglecting his expensive tea in favour of observing the widow, the lady elegant even in her distress, sitting taut and thrumming as an overstrung violin, her long hands twisting white shapes against the black of her skirt, eyes too bright as she perched rather than sat upon her seat, not sinking in an inch, as though she might take flight at any moment. And yet, the effects of shock aside, she had belonged in that room; or rather, the room had belonged to her. Ritter had watched as she presided and instructed and accepted unquestioning obedience as her natural due. Inconceivable that another woman should rule in that same roost, and yet, not a hundred paces from that fine room, they might be in another world.

The butler had handed them over to the housekeeper, whose office was set aside for police use. She had led them through the grand entrance hall to the discreet entrance of the servants' staircase, and, down it, through the passage to the cavern of a kitchen.

It was a vast space, giving the impression of shadow even as daylight filtered through the row of small windows high upon the wall. Cupboards lined the walls, tall and short, deep and shallow, one with open shelves displaying jars of colourful substances which Ritter could not identify. On rods suspended from the ceiling hung a vast array of ladles, forks, colanders, pots and pans, and there on the wall in pride of place was an enormous copper fish kettle shaped like a turbot, its scales gleaming in the dull light. At the end of the room, a huge iron stove held court, belching heat and steam which brought out the myriad flavours of the air, and in the middle stood a great slab of a table, the scrubbed wood covered in stains and burn marks and a mass of scrapes and gouges.

Behind the table, dominating the room with her presence, stood its unmistakable queen. A woman of immense proportions, as wide as three of her maids and as tall, Ritter was convinced, as strapping Constable Wilcox. He watched as, over and over, she lifted her powerful arm thick as a ham and brought it down again in a perpetual cycle, running the keen edge of her knife over the whetstone to produce the continuous rasping which filled the room. A mass of short, wiry black curls had escaped her white cap and she glanced up through them as the group filed in, regarding the interlopers with bright pinprick eyes set deep in her vast red face.

"Mrs Sharpe," the housekeeper began, but whether by way of introduction or address, Ritter was never to know.

Spying Wilcox's uniform, the cook's eyes flashed, cold as the blade she had not troubled to set down.

"I already told them everything I know," she said, jerking her great head to indicate some unspecified past interaction in the depths of the kitchen, or perhaps in the door-lined passage Ritter could see leading off beyond it. One of those doors, he thought, presumably led to the housekeeper's office where

Jameson and his men had conducted the staff interviews in the early morning, and where Jameson waited now, ready to brief Ritter on the results.

The housekeeper whose office had been so appropriated batted not an eyelash in the face of the dragon before her, perhaps not finding in it anything out of the ordinary.

"Dot," she said soothingly, even kindly. "I'm sure the gentlemen won't want to be wasting their time. They surely won't trouble you more than they need to."

Dot Sharpe did not take her flinty glare off Ritter. "And my girls neither?"

"Only if we have questions not yet answered," he agreed, making himself the very soul of affability.

Behind him, he heard Wilcox's starched uniform creak in barely suppressed outrage and made a mental note to teach the boy the value of not making unnecessary enemies, particularly in people you might shortly be wishing to make you tea.

Dot Sharpe, satisfied or remembering herself or both, pressed her thin lips together but gave a curt nod. "As you say, sir."

So dismissed, they followed the housekeeper down the length of the kitchen and into the passage beyond.

"I would ask you both to excuse Mrs Sharpe," she whispered confidentially, once they were out of earshot. "She is a forthright woman at the best of times and it has been a trying day for everyone, but for her perhaps especially..."

Trailing off, she selected without looking a large iron key from the bunch hanging from her belt, held together by an improbable combination of metal hoops and frayed twine. Ritter wondered whether it was force of habit, a nervous tic or simply exhaustion, or whether she had really locked Jameson in the office. If so, Ritter thought, it might well have been for his own safety.

Before he could find out, however, a sudden commotion distracted him – raised voices coming from upstairs and the slam of a door so heavy it could only be the front one, as though the responsible footman had been distracted in his duty – or disabled from doing it. Even listening intently, he could make out nothing but the general shape of distress – frustration, he thought, or even anger – the actual words left muffled and unintelligible after their tumble downstairs.

Without a word, Ritter left the housekeeper by her office and doubled back the way they'd come, Wilcox close on his heels. As they passed, Ritter noticed the cook frozen in her work, the knife hovering over the whetstone as she listened too, her face dark and lips pressed so thin they all but disappeared.

Taking the servants' staircase one floor up, they stepped out into the entrance hall. From the marble floor to the sweeping walnut staircase to the crystal chandelier suspended fully two floors above, the place was an exercise in magnificence. No trapping of pomp and circumstance had been spared.

From the carefully selected bronzes on their pedestals to the gilded clock and hunting scenes chosen in the best of taste, no visitor privileged enough to be admitted via the front door could be left in any doubt as to the nature of the household they had entered, and in the centre of the polished floor stood a man fully in keeping with his surroundings. Though he could be no more than thirty, there was a weight to his presence, a dignity which many men twice his age would have been pleased to command. A dignity, and an arrogance, Ritter thought, for though he was a handsome man, well built with good strong features beneath a mop of curling dark hair, there was no mistaking the sneering lip, the superior flash of his eye as he looked around for someone to address, someone of greater consequence than the bullied footman cringing before him.

"Alcott!" he barked, holding out a rolled newspaper with an air of being unable to decide whether to throw it down or thrash someone with it. "Is it true? Is Victor dead? Speak, man, speak!"

Crossing the marble floor noiselessly on felt soles, the butler bowed his grey head. "I'm afraid so, sir. My most sincere condolences." He sounded deeply tired, and there was a husk in his voice to which Ritter suspected the formal old throat was entirely unaccustomed.

At the butler's words, a succession of emotions blew across the newcomer's hard face, too quick to disentangle. They left behind an expression hard and smooth as flint.

"My sister-in-law," he said. "Where is she? I must see her at once."

The butler lifted his head, just slightly, out of the depths of grief and into its more conventional attitude of subservient granite. "Mrs Bancroft is not at home to callers at present. May I take a message, sir?"

It was at that moment that the flint faltered, dissolving in an acid so bitter that its source must surely run deep, far deeper than could possibly be dug in a single grief-filled morning.

"Yes, Alcott," he sneered, proud jaw working as though veritably chewing on his own venom. "Why don't you tell Mrs Bancroft that I await her invitation to enter the house I was born in."

After spitting out the widow's name as though it, especially, wronged him, he turned on his heel, the footman leaping to open the door, that the gentleman might make his exit without the smallest break in his stride.

"The younger brother, I take it?" Ritter asked, remembering the note in his morning briefing of the family.

"Indeed, sir. Mr Christopher Bancroft." The butler frowned. "I was not even aware he was in England – we have not seen him back since he was barely more than a boy."

Ritter felt his eyes narrow. "I see," he said, turning to Wilcox. "Constable, run and enquire where we may call on Mr Bancroft and pay our respects. Lively now!"

~

Watching Christopher Bancroft storm out of the house, the blackest of rages twisting his handsome face, Margaret Wilcox was gripped by two opposing impulses of equal strength: to go to him, and to hide.

Opposing and impossible, they held her fast – she could not go to him because he had not invited her to come; she ought to hide so that her uninvited presence would not be a further excuse for strife, but there was nothing but the solitary plane trees to hide behind, and their slim trunks would not conceal even her scrawny form – leaving her to watch immobile as he disappeared into the waiting cab, his gaze all inward, fixed on whatever torment he carried out with him. Or had carried in with him; she had no way of knowing – by the time she'd woken up, he'd already been gone.

The cab rattled away over the cobbles and she watched it go, the regular clatter of hooves and wheels filling the street so that she did not notice the figure approaching her from the house until he was close enough to satisfy his curiosity and let her catch his incredulous "Meg?"

It was the inflexion which gave him away: boy to man, a voice will change beyond recognition, but an inflexion may remain, especially when the word has been hidden away in all the years between.

Margaret turned and looked into the face of her brother, even then peering disbelieving into hers. With his size and breadth and constable's uniform, she would not have con-nected the twelve-year-old boy she had left behind with the man before her but for that one word. She doubted he was having the same problem. She had been eighteen when she left and knew the intervening decade had not so much changed as tired her, and of course, her small frame topped with her violent hair, flaming red to her brother's gentle strawberry, made her distinctive; searching for her at the tail end of a night, Christopher laughingly called her his tiny beacon.

"Hello, Paulie," she said. Something in the corner of her mouth trembled, and she wasn't sure whether it was an attempt at a smile, or a memory of the opposite, the last time she had seen him, standing silent amid their mother's howling clamour. He'd looked numb then, as though fear and confusion had coalesced into the single definitive realisation that Margaret was leaving and he was not.

Even now, the memory stabbed at her guilt, so it took her a moment to connect the furtive glance he cast over his shoulder with the way he positioned himself in front of her, taking full advantage of his superior bulk to hide her from the curiosity of anyone who might happen to peer out of the windows of that great house.

There was nothing furtive about the look he gave her though – or numb. "What do you want?" he demanded, and Meg felt whatever the tremor had been harden.

"What do I want?" she repeated. "You approached me, Paulie. What do *you* want?"

She watched him take stock of her, of her Italian coat and tan boots, expensive once and now well worn. The wind snatched a lock of hair from beneath her feathered hat and it streamed out before her, red and crimped with tight, disordered curls. She resisted the urge to snatch it back, to appear a proper lady, the way she had managed to persuade half of Europe she was. Almost, at any rate. If her mouth was a touch too sharp, her step a fraction too quick, her hat pins that much too brilliant, they'd been ready to forgive her, for the sake of Christopher's name and her own charm.

Then she looked at her brother and realised that no amount of name or charm could make a difference.

"What do you want?" he asked again, as though she had not spoken a word. There was a crest of pink upon his cheeks, but his voice was dull and flat, the steady cadence of the young bobby on the beat, as essential to his personal armoury as his helmet and truncheon, brooking no argument by refusing absolutely to hear any.

"I don't *want* anything!"

Though he towered above her, he flinched in the face of her irritation, and Margaret instantly, instinctively knew why: she had their mother's eyes but brighter, and knew too well how they blazed.

Even as the thought softened her, made her regretful and guilty all over again, something in him seemed to harden. "Ten years it's been, Meg, ten years of disgrace and not one word, and now— If it's money you're wanting, there's none to be had. I send Mother every penny I can spare to keep her, and you remember what she said—"

That was too much.

"Do you imagine I've forgotten?" Margaret snarled. "Every word I remember, every single one, and each one makes me gladder to have got away when I did."

"I'm pleased to hear it," said Paul, and even with everything, Margaret could not deny the tiny flicker of what might be pride at how dry he managed to sound; how grown up. "Then why were you following me?"

Margaret stared at her brother in amazement. "I wasn't following you! I say again, you approached me, and on a public street no less. How could I have even known you were here?"

There was a moment, a flicker of an instant, where she thought reason might win out. Then it was gone, replaced by that impenetrable confidence in the face of all logic which he could only have learned from one person. Even now, the sight of it made her spine twitch.

"I don't know how you knew I'd be here," he said. "I've only been working in London a year, and I'll be the first to admit I don't understand how information travels at the speed it does. However, I have come to understand that clever whores often have information they have no right to, and very rarely an honest reason to be skulking about in broad daylight on one of the grandest streets in town. Where her brother just happens to be working."

There was a moment during which Margaret wondered what the methods of clever whores could possibly have to do with her, just a fraction of a second before she realised her own brother thought she was one. Her impulse was to laugh, but one look at him and it died in her throat. The policeman's superiority glared down at her, barely masking the brother's shame. Together, they combined into something like hatred.

The town house loomed above them, its regular grey stonework so different and yet of the same Bancroft cloth as Chilting Hall's crumbling red brick in whose shadow they had spent their childhoods. Even now, when she had seen so many fine residences in so many countries – come to know them familiarly, intimately, to regard them and their way of life as ordinary, even mundane, to be put out when no suitable entertainment was offered her there – she suspected she would always think of the Bancrofts' sprawling country seat as simply "the big house", lofty and superior and not for the likes of her. She had spent the early part of her life half drawn to it, half repulsed, but always aware of it, until the day she had turned her back on it – and on everything else.

She wondered how much he recalled, and how much of that had been warped by a mother's unhappiness. She supposed he remembered finding the ring, emerald and gold secreted beneath the skirts of her ragdoll, beloved even at eighteen. Did he remember he'd taken the doll in a childish attempt at punishing her? Did he remember that he'd wanted to punish her because he'd found himself saddled with her chores while she was called up to the big house for hours at a time, he for the first time not welcome to join her?

Or did he recall only the startling discovery of a jewel the likes of which the village boy had never seen, and his mother's inexplicable rage when he brought it to her? A rage which was only amplified by his sister's refusal to explain, to name the man who had made her the gift. Or paid her with it, as their mother had screamed until she was red in the face and wet around the mouth, and Margaret had left, all three of them knowing she would not return.

She supposed the assumption was a logical one – the only one, really, for a girl like her in a situation like that – and she had nothing to correct it with. Even now, she was not married, and from the righteous look on his face, she knew that nothing else would do. The temptation to ask him where, precisely, he thought the money for his schooling and the fine uniform he wore had come from rose within her, but she refused to yield; she had no wish to quarrel further.

Even as he glared down his nose at her, she felt her indignation drift away on a current of sorrow.

"I'm not here to cause you difficulties. I'll be gone as soon as I can, I promise," she said, wishing with all her heart that it could be today. What she wouldn't give to leave London this minute, to pack their bags and head to Dover in time for the next ferry, to put their backs to the smog once and for all...

But they would not, she knew. Not now. Not again.

Though it was not yet noon, the sky had begun to darken, the air grown heavier with the promise of a rain which might not fall for hours yet but, when it did, would do so mightily. It struck Margaret as fitting somehow. She wondered where in this miserable place one might get a bag of roasted chestnuts and perhaps a nip of gin at this time of the morning.

"Goodbye, Paulie," she said.

As she turned to go, she thought she saw the faintest ghost of something cross his face, there and gone almost too quick to see, something which might have been sorrow. That was her welcome back to England.

III

Though Ritter had known Paul Wilcox only a matter of hours, already he understood that a certain stiffness of back was not only characteristic of the young constable but an indelible part of his being. Nevertheless, Ritter couldn't help but feel this was a bit much: Wilcox appeared in the doorway of the housekeeper's spare but not mean office in a posture which ran almost to the concave. Twin points of vivid colour stood out on his cheeks while the rest of his face sank sickly pale into the gloom, and overall his air was that of a man attempting to crush something sharp between his upper vertebrae, and only now realising just how exquisitely uncomfortable it was.

Ritter, sitting behind the housekeeper's broad desk, waved him inside. "Come in and shut the door, Constable. What happened?"

"Sir?"

A certain rabbit-like mien took the place of stiffness as Ritter watched him apparently try to recall the purpose for which he had been dispatched not half an hour before. Finally, understanding came, though the dawn was marred by the black cloud of failure.

"He was gone, sir," Wilcox admitted, inspecting his shoes. "Driven off before I could catch up with him."

"Gone?" Ritter felt his eyebrows lift. "You've been away almost twenty minutes, man!"

"Yes, sir." Wilcox's head sank lower, broad shoulders twitching in what looked a great deal like a repressed wince. "Sorry, sir. There was a – a vagrant, sir."

"A vagrant?"

"Yes, sir. Causing a disturbance, sir."

"A disturbance." Ritter did not like to think of himself as an impatient man, nor an unfair one, and as he put down his pen, he reminded himself that really, it was no one's fault but his own: after thirty years, he ought to know better than to trust to common sense over explicit instruction.

"Constable Wilcox," he began, speaking with what he hoped was sufficient care and deliberation to prevent future repeats, "you have been pulled off street patrol to assist on the most high-profile murder this town has seen in years. As such, for the duration of this case, you may consider that disturbing vagrants and their like are no longer your concern."

Wilcox looked straight ahead at the wall behind Ritter's head, which Ritter knew to be blank. "Yes, sir. Only—"

"Only?"

"Only I thought she might have seen something, sir."

Ritter paused in the act of retrieving his pen, considering. "And had she?"

Wilcox flushed as he hung his head. "No, sir."

"I see." Ritter returned to his open notebook. "Nevertheless, good thought, Constable. Sit down.

"While you were questioning your vagrant," he went on as Wilcox drew up a spindle-backed chair, "Sergeant Jameson has been briefing me on the staff interviews he and his men conducted this morning."

He gestured to a haphazard stack of papers covered in untidy scrawl which in filing would be elevated to the status of "reports".

"Nothing of much use there, I'm afraid. The butler and housekeeper confirm everyone was accounted for in their respective beds at lights out, and I understand that there is a bell system to alert the butler or housekeeper if either the men or the women should leave their corridors before the morning. The only ones outside it are the cook in the kitchen, the coachman, the valet and the lady's maid. The valet knows of no enemies of his master whatsoever, and furthermore had the evening off to visit his father in Lambeth, not returning till five o'clock the following morning, that is to say after the murder was discovered and we were already on the scene. Apparently the victim wasn't expected back till after that time, which tells us that he changed his plans at some point during the night.

"The coachman reports that he took Mr Bancroft from his club to Pimlico – that is, to visit his mistress – only to be unexpectedly called back shortly afterwards to take Bancroft home, which was unusual. After taking Bancroft home, the coachman shared a nightcap with a couple of his fellows, during which time the murder took place. Jameson's men are checking the alibis and speaking to the mistress about the telegram and anything else she might have been privy to. In the meantime, that leaves us with—"

Ritter paused and Wilcox, recognising a test of his attention, supplied in rapid fire: "The cook and the lady's maid, sir."

"Very good, Constable." Ritter smiled. "The cook and the lady's maid. The cook was asleep in her room and heard nothing but was helpful to Jameson in identifying the knife they found thrown from the window as being" – Ritter rifled through the papers – "of the 'filleting' variety. Jameson says she showed him her own for comparison and has promised to keep her ear to the ground in case any of her fellows should complain of missing theirs. Not that most murderers are in the habit of obtaining their equipment from neighbouring kitchens of course, but in this case nothing would surprise me. In any event, the murderer interests me less than the man who paid him."

"Sir?"

Gone was the shame-faced boy of moments ago, and Ritter looked up to find instead an enthusiastic young officer, bright and keen to understand. Something in it warmed the cockles of Ritter's jaded heart, reminding him of… well, reminding him.

"This murder," he explained, "was almost certainly premeditated and almost certainly professional, and the only reason I add the caveat is because in the policeman's business there are only three absolute certainties: death, taxes and the endless paperwork they generate. Remember that if you ever intend to enter the detective branch."

"Yes, sir." Wilcox's head bobbed eagerly. "What makes you almost certain in this case, sir?"

Ritter steepled his hands in front of him. "Let's review, shall we? Jameson found no doors or windows unlocked, and no sign of forced entry – the broken window in the bedroom being too small and too high to be much use for that purpose. Thus, we know that the assassin must have entered the house at least a couple of hours prior to the event and hidden himself until Bancroft returned, which, remember, he was not due to do for another several hours. There's your premeditation. As for professionalism, this is an interesting one. You'll be aware, Constable, that a man can be killed by as little as a drop in his wine, one which might simply send him to sleep and be untraceable forevermore. With enough money, a murder can be arranged to never be discovered as a murder at all."

Seeing Wilcox's eyebrows knit together, Ritter paused and waited for the question he knew was forming. If there was one thing young policemen ought to be taught, in Ritter's opinion, it was to ask why.

Even under what Ritter hoped was an encouraging gaze, however, Wilcox hesitated. Ritter waited until finally the younger man blurted out: "But, sir, why wouldn't—"

That was as far as he got before some force felt only by Wilcox grabbed the question and pulled it back again. Still, Ritter took it, sensing that some battle had been fought and a reward was in order.

"Excellent question, Constable," he said, ignoring Wilcox's flush. "Just because a murder is premeditated and professional does not mean there can be no element of passion behind it, of personal feeling. In this case, it seems that the responsible party not only wanted Mr Bancroft dead but wanted him to know it was at the command of someone else – someone he likely knew – and, moreover, that individual wanted everyone else to know it too. Most probably someone who felt wronged by Mr Bancroft in life somehow and sought to make a joke of him in death. Mr Bancroft was subject to an exceptional degree of mutilation – poor Jameson was green about the gills, and him a Laing's Nek man – which certainly was not necessary for death. Indeed, it would be a disadvantage for the assassin: physically very hard work, and all the while the risk of discovery. Someone charged a premium for that, mark my words.

"And then there's that business with the necklace, taking only the worthless silver one and not the gold or gems, so that the papers will make a meal of it. At the rate the newsmen turn things around these days, by tonight every household in London will be talking about the contents of Mrs Bancroft's jewellery box, and what they'll be saying is that it contained plain silver of provincial design, not even stamped, according to the house-keeper. Now, does that strike you as an accidental outcome or like one impeccably orchestrated to give Victor Bancroft a humiliating death likely to be gossiped about for years to come?"

"The second one, sir." Wilcox frowned. "But what about the knife, sir?"

"Ah, the knife." Ritter could not resist a little grin. "The knife, I suspect, is where we may find our turning point. I understand from her doctor that Mrs Bancroft seems to have knocked herself insensible on the headboard somehow, but our assassin seems to have run out of luck when—"

"The scream," Wilcox finished and looked immediately startled at the sound of his own voice, as though he had not intended to speak the thought aloud.

"Precisely." Ritter, torn between irritation at interruption and pleasure that the constable could keep up, chose neutrality. "The lady's maid came in from her adjacent bedroom and screamed at what she found, causing the villain to dispose of his knife in a panic and flee, probably back into the house to hide until he could slip out unnoticed amid the commotion. Which means that..."

Ritter left the sentence hanging, an invitation for Wilcox to complete it, or to ask the question which gnawed at Ritter even as he spoke: why leave a witness? Why not just kill the maid?

For his patience, however, he received only a blank look. Wilcox's cheeks grew pinker by the minute, until Ritter took pity and finished the sentence himself: "Which means that we need to have a word with the maid. Call in the housekeeper, would you, Constable?"

McNeal, having been turned out of her office but afraid to venture too far from it in case she was needed, had settled herself in a discreet corner of the kitchen. In her lap was a woollen sock ready for darning, but it lay untouched, the housekeeper absorbed instead in the rhythmic movements of the cook still sharpening her knife. Again and again she drew it over the whetstone, until it was a wonder it had any blade left at all, and Wilcox had to call the housekeeper's name twice to get her attention.

"I'm afraid Miss Fletcher – that is, Mrs Bancroft's lady maid – is taken ill," McNeal told them when she finally came to the office. "She was always a delicate thing, and I'm sorry to say the sight this morning was too much for her. She's suffered a nasty turn."

Ritter, if not unmoved, remained unswayed. "That is unfortunate, but unhappily we must distress her a little further. She may well be our only useful witness. If she is too unwell to be brought down, then we will go to her."

The housekeeper's pursed mouth gave some indication of what she might have thought of the suggestion, but she refrained from voicing her opinion. "Very well, sir. If you will be good enough to follow me upstairs then."

It was as they crossed the kitchen that the continuous *rasp-rasp-rasp* which by then seemed to pervade the very fabric of the room itself, forming a discordant harmony with the hissing of steam and the low rumble of the stove, ceased abruptly, punctuated by a heavy *thwuck*. Ritter turned to see that the cook had jabbed her knife into the wooden work surface, where it stood perfectly upright, still quivering slightly from the force of the blow. Mrs Sharpe loomed over it.

"Are the gentlemen wanting to see Joan? Let me take them up, Mrs McNeal. You have enough on your plate, and Lord knows it's unlikely the mistress will be wanting much of a lunch today."

The housekeeper looked round at her charges, irritation chasing gratitude chasing irritation across the worn lines of her face. In the end, Ritter suspected it was reluctance to argue in front of strangers which made the decision more than anything else.

"Thank you, Mrs Sharpe," she said. "That's very good of you."

The cook nodded, satisfied in victory. "I'll just lock this away," she said, wrenching the long-suffering knife from its unnatural position.

"I can do that, Dot…" McNeal began but trailed off at the look Mrs Sharpe gave her.

Ritter watched as the cook went to a cabinet at the back of the kitchen and pulled out a key she wore around her neck from where it had been hidden beneath the high collar of her dress.

"Cooks can be a bit funny about their knives," McNeal said, and Ritter might have taken it as an apology for witnessed rudeness, except that the housekeeper seemed unduly distracted, staring thoughtfully at the cabinet even after the cook had locked it back up.

～

Mrs Sharpe led them up through the house, flight after flight of uncarpeted stairs encircled by windowless walls which bore the scuffs of daily hurry. The cook went first, her dark skirts swaying behind her, covering her heavy tread. In spite of her size and the numerous restraining contraptions no doubt employed in keeping her dress in place, she kept up a steady pace, showing no sign of tiring even as Ritter felt his own lungs begin to complain. Wilcox, young and strong, sounded entirely comfortable behind him, and something about the whole situation galled Ritter into using what breath remained to him to strike up a conversation.

"Been with the family long, Mrs Sharpe?" he called up.

The cook glanced back over her shoulder. "Near enough twenty years, ever since I lost my Thomas. Best butcher in Barking he was. I didn't fancy my chances of finding another like him, so I went into service. Not that I couldn't have married again," she added, glaring down as though Ritter had dared suggest anything to the contrary. "But my Tom and I always talked about a little rooming house in Swanage, and I've a mind to see it through. I've given a good piece of my life to this place and no mistake, but it won't be long now."

"Very adventurous of you." Ritter willed himself not to pant. "Does Mrs Bancroft know of your plans?"

"I dare say she might, if she cared to know. I make no secret of it." The cook's bright eyes narrowed down at him. "We're can't all be Geraldine McNeal, you know. She's been here so long I reckon she's forgotten she's not part of the brickwork by now. Came as lady's maid to the old mistress when that lady was married and been here ever since."

"Is that so?" Ritter felt his ears prick – metaphorically, he hoped. "She must have known the son then? The younger, I mean – Christopher?"

They'd reached the top of the stairs, and he almost walked into the large woman's broad back as she stopped and turned to him.

"I dare say a number of us knew Master Christopher," she said, sucking in her cheeks as though the memory rankled, but just as Ritter thought she might go on, she turned back to the corridor. It was lined with identical plain doors, typical service quarters, but the first was marked by a decorative brass tack.

Mrs Sharp indicated it with a jerk of her powerful chin. "Joanie's in there. We put her in Mrs McNeal's room, what with her own being so close to the mess."

She spoke about "the mess" as one might the debris following a party, but as Ritter stepped towards the door, he found his way blocked by her massive form.

"You'll be patient a moment while I make sure she's decent," she said, knocking once and disappearing into the room.

Ritter was keenly conscious that it had not been a question. Not, of course, that he'd had any intention of objecting.

He waited patiently until the cook reappeared and nodded them inside.

On a bed in the centre of the sparsely furnished room lay a young woman, scarcely more than a child. The blankets were drawn up to her chin, and the shape of the body beneath might be described as spindly. Mousy hair hung limply about her face as she stared unblinking at a plain wooden cross hung on the wall opposite, though whether she saw it or whether it just happened to fall within the line of her unseeing eyes was impossible to say. Ritter thought she looked sixteen, if that.

"Young to be a lady's maid, surely?"

"You might say that." Mrs Sharpe pressed her lips together with such force that it seemed to squeeze spots of angry colour into her cheeks. "She was one of mine first. Not a natural kitchen girl, I grant you. The work was heavy for her, but she was getting stronger. She was getting along, but then the previous lady's maid handed in her notice and the silly chit got ideas. Went straight to the mistress and begged – *begged* – to replace her. And the mistress, she knew no better than to allow it and wouldn't be set straight by anyone. Say what you will about that woman, no one can make her do anything she hasn't a mind to, and damn the consequences." The cook shook her head in disgust. "And now look at poor Joanie. She had no business being in that room in the first place, none at all."

"Surely no one could have predicted—" Ritter began, but the cook was no longer paying him any mind.

"Joan," she said, turning to the girl and addressing her loudly and slowly. "These are the gentlemen from Scotland Yard."

The girl gave no sign of having heard, and, looking at her, Ritter was not sure he had expected anything less.

"They want to talk to you about last night," Mrs Sharpe went on, and at that the girl did react, a flinch shuddering through the frail body.

Ritter approached the bed cautiously. "Hello, Miss Fletcher," he began. "We'd like to go over anything you may have witnessed last night."

But even as he spoke, he realised it was hopeless. He had thought she might be shamming, either on purpose – afraid of discussing what she had seen, perhaps, or simply wanting a day in bed – or else because she believed this was the proper way for a young girl to react to horror. Now though, as he stood directly in front of her unblinking eyes, he had the unsettling impression that she was not only entirely unaware of his presence but also of her own.

Recognising it as hopeless, Ritter let the girl alone and went back to the door where the cook still stood. "I understand you found her first?"

Mrs Sharpe nodded. "Dreadful state she was in too – screamed bloody murder till I poured a bit of brandy down her throat. She's been like this ever since."

"I see. We'll have her taken to hospital – she's plainly in need of medical care if she's going to be able to tell us what she saw."

He glanced back at the stricken girl, trying to find in her face some hope of recovering his best lead, when the cook interrupted his thoughts.

"Begging your pardon, sir – might she be taken to Great Ormond Street? She's only a mite of a thing, and them being a children's hospital, they might suit her better, I thought. And…"

Ritter was surprised to find the prickly woman hesitate.

"And I would ask your permission to visit her, sir, when my duties permit."

Caught off guard, Ritter struggled to reconcile the expression of attachment to what he had come to know of the cook's character, but he saw no reason not to agree. Great Ormond Street was as convenient a place as any, so far as he was concerned.

As they made their way back down the stairs, Ritter returned to another subject which was increasingly beginning to interest him. "Mr Alcott mentioned that Christopher Bancroft has been away for some years," he said. "Do you happen to know his business abroad?"

Beside him, Mrs Sharpe held her broad shoulders stiff as a general. "I understand he was on his grand tour, sir."

"Grand tour? Isn't he rather old for that? The man must be thirty."

"Twenty-nine, sir. Nineteen when he left."

Ritter raised an eyebrow. "Mrs Sharpe, I don't pretend to be an expert on the point, but to my knowledge grand tours don't last ten years. Do please speak frankly, madam."

"Nothing to speak of, so far as I'm concerned. He was caught in a dalliance just before he went away and it caused a row. We haven't seen him since." The massive shoulders lifted in a tight shrug. "He always was a stubborn one."

Ritter turned that over once or twice. "He was disinherited?"

"Not so's I'm aware," she said, and even though Ritter had surmised that her former young master was not a favourite, he was nevertheless surprised to hear the bitterness there.

"You bade me speak frankly, sir," she went on. "And to be frank, if you ask me, by rights he ought to have been, for what he did to that poor girl. Lord only knows what became of her, once he'd had his fun. She's not shown her face in the village since, I do know that much. But allowances must be made for the caprices of young gentlemen, I suppose."

The way she pursed her lips, however, made Ritter doubt her conviction on that point.

In the entrance hall, a tall policeman with a sergeant's uniform and an impressive moustache was waiting for them.

Ritter made a beeline for him. "What have you got, Jameson? Did you find out what the telegram said?"

"Not as such, sir." Jameson spoke in the clipped tones of one who had hoped to deliver better news. "We traced it as far as Pimlico where it was delivered, home of a Mrs Nailard, lady understood to be the gentleman's mistress."

Behind Ritter, the creaking of starched linen suggested that Wilcox had stiffened where he stood. Ritter paid him no mind, but Jameson could not resist a glance at the boy, curiosity threatening to devolve into resentment at the sight of a constable's uniform standing so familiarly in Ritter's shadow.

"You know Constable Wilcox," Ritter said, seeking to avoid a squabble and annoyed at having to do so. "One of Phipps's, but he grew up near the family seat so I've enlisted him as my dogsbody for the duration. Did you manage to speak to the mistress? Does she know what was in the telegram?"

Jameson, mollified perhaps by the knowledge that he at any rate was above being anybody's dog's anything, turned his attention back to Ritter. "We did and she doesn't, sir. She said Mr Bancroft read it in her presence but didn't tell her the contents, only that it came from his brother in Belgium. She said he became upset on reading it and left immediately, before he had even, ah, concluded his business with her." Jameson glanced at Wilcox again, the bristles of his moustache twitching with just the very suggestion of a leer. "So to speak, sir."

"Yes, all right, Sergeant." The word "brother" was buzzing around Ritter's head like a particularly fascinating bluebottle, and he had no time for anything else.

"Any sign of the telegram? Or have we got a copy from the company yet? It is imperative we know what it says."

From the look on Jameson's face, Ritter knew he wasn't about to get good news.

"The coroner thinks he might have found it," the sergeant said. "Or at any rate part of it, lodged in the victim's fist. However, the condition of the body and especially the, ah, *wetness* make it so we'll probably never know for sure, he says. We're trying to get a copy through the company, but they're saying that since it came from Belgium, we need to talk to them, which I reckon is probably going to mean a warrant over there, judging by the Montpelier case."

Ritter pinched the bridge of his nose, trying not to remember how long that case had taken. "Fine, Sergeant," he said, because there was nothing else for it. "Get it done. I don't need to tell you how quick. And in the meantime, find out where the brother is staying. He might have been in Belgium yesterday but he's certainly in London today. Look at the hotels first – a man who hasn't been back in town in a decade is unlikely to have too many friends left here."

"Sir."

Leaving Jameson to get on with his orders, Ritter turned back to the servants' stairwell. He was surprised to find Mrs Sharpe still standing at the entrance. Apparently not afflicted with the impulse of most staff of great households to get out of sight at the first available opportunity, she watched the policemen speculatively – or rather, Ritter realised, watched the police*man*, for her eyes were trained squarely on Constable Wilcox's handsome face.

As Ritter led the way back down to the office, she fell into step with the constable behind him.

"Wilcox," Ritter heard her say, slowly, tasting the name as she would a broth. "You wouldn't be Mary's lad, from the village?"

Though Ritter heard no response, he assumed Wilcox's open book of a face had given one, or else that Mrs Sharpe had been already confident in the answer, for she went on.

"I saw your mother before we came up, keeping well you'll be pleased to know, and my word isn't she proud of her boy, even if he does have to be so far from home." She spoke conversationally, setting aside even the flimsy guise of deference she'd managed for Ritter.

Wilcox answered her familiarity with brittle civility. "Thank you, madam. It is a pleasure to know she is well."

"I remember your sister, you know," Mrs Sharpe went on in a voice Ritter couldn't quite place, something which might once have been tender but had long since crystalised into something harsh. "Never a livelier girl. Such a shame what—"

"The shame is my sister's and no one else's," he interrupted, so sharply that Ritter, caught off guard, could not help but wince at the bitterness there. "She is a slut and whore who broke her family's heart, begging your pardon to use such language before a lady ma'am, but I'll thank you to make no further mention of her in my presence or my mother's."

"I beg your pardon I'm sure," the cook murmured, but nothing could dispel the weight of the silence which had fallen in the wake of Wilcox's outburst.

It was hard to believe that such venom could flow from so mild a face, and yet Ritter was not as surprised as he would have liked to be. Certainly, a sister's childhood betrayal might explain the boy's distaste for any suggestion of Bancroft's extramarital excursions, even those apparently condoned by his own wife. Explanation, however, did not make the attitude any less worrisome. For his part, Ritter had seen far lesser chips develop into that cruel contempt which a young policeman might find it all too easy to apply to those classes of people with whom he was likely to be in contact with most frequently, regardless of whether the individual concerned happened to be the accused or the victim.

IV

It had not taken Jameson long to find Christopher Bancroft, because Christopher Bancroft had not troubled himself to go any further than the first place one might expect to find a new arrival of plentiful means and no home to call his own.

The Grosvenor Hotel lay immediately behind Victoria Station, its many-windowed façade and carpeted awning making it abundantly clear that only the very best class of traveller might expect to be received by the liveried doorman, his top hat raised deferentially over watchful dark eyes.

Even on the first floor, though the doors along the corridor were no more distinct one from the other than those in the Bancroft servants' quarters had been, there was a sense here that this was on purpose, that each plane of polished wood and brass numerals were deliberately made as identical as possible, in order to better guard the privacy their occupants paid so dearly for.

Ritter followed as the snub-nosed clerk led the policemen to one door among the many.

"These are Mr Bancroft's rooms, sir," the young man said, his voice barely above a whisper, so that what Ritter had felt was a rather discreet knock sounded positively uncouth in its wake.

Nevertheless, the response from within the room was slow in coming, and he was about to knock again when brisk footsteps stayed his hand, just in time for the door to be wrenched open to reveal Christopher Bancroft, apparently in the full temper of a gentleman disturbed. "Yes?"

"Sorry to disturb you, sir," said Ritter. For the sake of form, and to set a good example for young Wilcox, he made an effort to actually sound at least a little bit sorry. "We met earlier this morning, though regrettably were not introduced at the time. I am Detective Inspector Edmund Ritter of the Metropolitan Police and this is—"

Bancroft nodded curtly. "I remember. I'm afraid I had to leave in some haste, and now I'm sorry to say you catch me again on my way out. There is a great deal to do, as I'm sure you understand."

"Of course, sir, we understand entirely," Ritter agreed, making made no move to leave.

For a long moment, Bancroft glared at him, and Ritter stared steadily back, until finally Bancroft tossed his head irritably.

"You may as well come in then," he said with bad grace, holding the door open for the policemen to troop inside. His lip curled as he eyed Wilcox's uniform. "And the next time you pay a call like this, you might consider doing it in a less eye-catching get-up."

The suite's sitting room was large and comfortable, with three grand windows letting in such daylight as remained. A sofa and matching chairs upholstered in bottle-green leather sprawled about the fireplace like lazing hounds, on one of which a coat of fine black wool had been casually tossed. The dining table was evidently in use as a desk, strewn with letters, balled paper and an open address book, One of the pair of doors leading through to the bedroom stood open, revealing a glimpse of rumpled sheets and unplumped cushions on a bedstead surrounded by luggage open and half-heartedly unpacked.

On a small buffet nearby stood a silver tray laden with a crystal decanter, amber with brandy, and three matching tumblers. Space remained for a fourth, but it was nowhere to be seen. In its place lay a single lady's glove. Bancroft, seeing Ritter note it, met him with a look of such frank defiance that it was almost mockery, the knowledge that, though he might be forced to let Ritter into his rooms, Ritter could have no say in whomever else it might please him to entertain there.

"Now," said Bancroft, once he had made his point, "what is it that you gentlemen imagine I can do for you?"

Ritter, whose personal feeling, simple curiosity aside, was that Bancroft could invite half the whores of Shoreditch into his rooms for all he cared, returned his attention to the matter at hand. "Well, sir, myself and the constable here are tasked with investigating your brother's murder, and we hoped you might be able to shed some light—"

"I can't." Bancroft had turned away and was fishing about inside the pockets of the coat left on the sofa. Nevertheless, at the mention of his brother, Ritter thought he detected a certain flinch of the proud shoulder.

"I beg your pardon, sir?"

After retrieving a silver case from the inner pocket, Bancroft went to the window.

"I can't help you," he said, pulling out a cigarette.

The snub-nosed young clerk – who, absent any instruction to the contrary, had followed them inside – darted forward to light it for him.

"Thank you, Charlie," Bancroft said, before continuing to Ritter: "I returned to England only last night following an absence of ten years. I can't tell you anything about my brother's life – his friends, his enemies, his lovers, his business relationships or what he liked to eat for breakfast. Ten years ago I believe it was scrambled eggs with kippers, but men do change their tastes, so who knows. I've had no word from him since the day I left, when he wished me a good trip."

"But he had word from you, sir, didn't he?" Ritter prodded. "As recently as last night?"

Bancroft's eyes narrowed over his cigarette, and Ritter thought he could pinpoint the very instant when realisation dawned and the guard came down like a stone. "Ah, you mean the telegram, I suppose. Yes, I let him know we had business to discuss."

"What business might that have been, sir? I imagine it must have been something momentous, to bring you back after so long an absence."

The other man's eyes had not unnarrowed but watched Ritter carefully through the haze of smoke, ice beneath the fog, leaving Ritter with a distinct impression of being puzzled out.

"I take it you haven't read it then?" Bancroft asked, drawing on his cigarette. "The fact is that I had hoped to finally set things right between us. He had ignored previous overtures by letter, so I thought it best not to give him too much notice, you understand."

He exhaled, staring at the tip of his cigarette as though the glow fascinated him suddenly. "You may imagine my feelings on learning the news this morning."

"Indeed, and may I say how very sorry I am, sir. The business which keeps you so busy now, from which we are regrettably detaining you, is newly arisen then?"

Bancroft frowned through the smoke. "I am discovering the business of death to be rather a hectic one, yes," he said, adding "thank you" as Charlie dutifully anticipated his need of an ashtray. "For a man of my brother's stature, the funeral alone is complicated enough, and then there is the management of the estate and all those who depend upon it—"

"I'm sure Mrs Bancroft is grateful to have your support," Ritter said, and though it was only the smallest of nudges, it was all that was required to bring it out in full, that shadow he had first seen in the marble hall of the Bancroft residence. It tore at Bancroft's polished features, a thing far darker than the mere thwarted will of a spoiled man, a thing cold and trapped and terribly, terribly angry, and though it was gone again in an instant, the man had to take a long, composing drag before answering.

"I have full confidence that we will come to understand one another," he said.

Ritter nodded in affable agreement. "Undoubtedly, sir, undoubtedly. I think, under the circumstances, your having been away and so forth, we needn't detain you any longer, though I must ask that you inform us immediately should you think of or come across anything which might be relevant to our investigation. Good day, Mr Bancroft, and sorry to have troubled you at such a difficult time."

"Your servant, Inspector." Bancroft's lip curled with the amusement of the spoiled youth he must once have been, secure in the knowledge that his father was rich enough to bribe any police commissioner. It was a dead boy's face, however, a feeble ghost called up to disguise the man who knew his father had exiled him, the man who kept that awful shadow behind eyes sparking cold and hard as flint.

Ritter doubted that man had ever been anyone's servant. He wondered what had really been in that telegram.

~

Margaret heard the door closed behind the policemen, rather harder than might strictly be considered necessary, but made no effort to rise. She lolled on the divan by the bedroom window, waiting for the approaching footsteps to find her.

"He doesn't know, does he?" Christopher asked.

She looked up to find him staring down at her, his brow knit in confusion or irritation, or most probably both; he hated being in the dark.

"Meg?"

Margaret shrugged, the movement reminding her of the weight of the glass in her hand. "I shouldn't think so. You told me not to tell them, remember?" She said it lasciviously, teasing the idea that she might ever have done anything purely because she was told to, but he didn't smile, didn't let the joke draw him in. Perhaps he was too tired. Perhaps she was.

"Still, I'd have thought he'd have worked it out by now." Christopher crouched down over an open trunk and began to root through a pile of formerly folded silks and linens. "Not turning out to be much of a detective, is he?"

"Can you blame him, when you didn't leave until fully six weeks after I did? And then on a trip planned anyway?" She couldn't tell if it was the brandy making her defensive, or if it had been there anyway, ready and waiting. It was this town, she thought, the soot hanging heavy in the fog, leaving even thought murky and bleak.

Christopher stopped his search for Lord knew what, sitting back on his heels to give her a level look. "You'd have preferred the life of a paupess, I take it? Because that's what would have happened. What *will* happen, even now. Victor dying makes no difference, you know – the clause is still in effect."

Though he'd barely lifted his chin, the challenge there was unmistakable. Margaret did not take it up. She did know, and he knew she knew, and none of that was the point anyway. Her head was too heavy for a fight. "You haven't told me how she was."

"That's because I don't know." With a snap, he closed the lid of the trunk which did not need closing. "She wouldn't see me. But she'll be persuaded of reason once it all sinks in. Only a fool does not know the limits of her own abilities, and of all things, I've never heard her called that."

Margaret pushed herself up to something like sitting. "What are you going to do?"

"My duty."

Christopher rose, as though the force of the word impelled him. Margaret thought he needn't have bothered. Even hunched on the floor, elbow deep in underwear, he had radiated superiority. It was not a thing he wore but a thing he was, she realised; he would have lent lordliness to a potato sack.

"First I'm going to see my brother buried in the style befitting a Bancroft," he went on. "And then I am going to make sure our tenants—"

"*Her* tenants, Kit," Margaret corrected, getting up. "Not ours."

She watched him stiffen at the reminder and felt for him in his futile pride. Margaret did not pretend to understand the detailed workings of such things but she knew enough to know that, with no title and no entail, the Bancroft fortune was now squarely in the hands of a woman who might choose to see Christopher or might not, and no amount of pride, ancestry or superiority of mind could change that. One man only might hope to control the estate during her lifetime: if she chose to remarry then naturally her future husband would naturally become—

The thought hit her harder than it had any right to, but she pulled herself together. Christopher Bancroft might do many things, she knew, but not that. Even with his plans gone so wrong, he would not marry a woman other than herself. Not after everything. He wouldn't.

Christopher followed her into the sitting room and stood frowning as Margaret refilled her glass. She ignored him. It served him right for dragging her back here. And what for?

They had been happy abroad, making their own friends, court-ing their own esteem. Abroad, they had quarrelled when they felt like it, made up as it suited them, and never had there been any doubt that they would. They had been free. And now he expected her to walk back into the net without so much as a medicinal glass to steady her nerves.

"I don't know why you're in such high dudgeon," he said, not bothering to conceal his disapproval. "When we were kids, coming to London was all you could think of."

Margaret went to the window, staring into the depths of her reflection; the night came on so quickly here. "Yes," she agreed. "And then I came."

Immediately she wished she hadn't said it. What was the use of reminding him, of reminding *herself*, of those miserable weeks?

She took a deep pull of brandy, gulping it down so that her eyes watered and the memory blurred, praying he would leave it alone. It was only when she heard the scratch of pen on paper that she realised he had not heard at all.

It was raining now, the promise of the morning made good, and Margaret watched the thick slugs of water crawl down the pane, blurring the indoor reflections with the shadows outside. When at length the scratching of the pen stopped, she did not turn around.

"I'm going out," said Christopher, and in that strange mir-ror, his face was almost as white as the envelope in his hand.

"Don't go down to the dining room, will you? I'll order supper sent up."

~

**Mr Christopher Bancroft, Grosvenor Hotel to
Head of Records, Great Ormond Street Children's Hospital**

1 November 1896

Dear Sir,

*My father was the late Henry Victor Lloyd Bancroft, whose
name you will recognise as a longstanding supporter and
patron of your institution. I write to you seeking certain
records I understand to be in your possession regarding the
health and well-being of a member of my family, whose care
now falls unexpectedly to me. Please confirm by return how
best to go about obtaining such records, and to which name
future correspondence should be addressed.*

*Faithfully your servant,
Christopher A. Bancroft*

V

Nora came awake to the striking of a clock, a single silver note ringing out from the deepest depths of the house. It was a sliver of a tone, significant now only because it was alone, the clock which struck it being itself so insignificant that whoever had gone around stopping more important clocks to mark their master's passing had forgotten it entirely.

It rang once and then not again, leaving Nora in the dark with only the spatter of rain and the creaking of old woodwork for company. It was this more than anything which told her that the hour was past midnight – the house always sounded different in the dark. Yet she thought there was something else tonight, some scuttling in the walls or scratching at a distant door just on the edge of hearing. She might have blamed the police, but surely they must be gone by now. Probably it was only the wind, catching in the chimneys.

Slowly, stiffly, she stretched herself out and felt under the pillow for matches. They weren't there of course – everything had been done in a hurry, everything in confusion, nothing where it was supposed to be.

The moment of disorientation quickened her pulse and her senses, sharpening her eyes enough to make out a table near her bedside. On it she spied the outline of a candle and beside it a rectangle of solid black – the matches McNeal presumably had not dared to nudge under her mistress's sleeping head.

Alertness flared even before the light, bubbling up until Nora felt awake for the first time that day, for the first time since the night before— Well, before. And it did not stop: if anything, the thought made the bubbles rise higher still, until they popped into a shivery giddiness which would not let her be still.

The flame flickered as she moved the candle too quickly to a table which seemed intended as writing desk and dressing table both. A large oval mirror stood with its mourning cover half slipped off, and next to it was her inlaid letter rack, still holding the invitation to the Brucknells' winter ball received the day before— Well, before.

Beside the rack lay a selection of pen and paper. Perhaps McNeal had thought her mistress might like to write a letter or simply her own thoughts. Perhaps Nora had even asked for the things to be left; she no longer remembered. The day seemed a distant thing, vague and discordant, drifting ever just beyond grasp, as though she had never fully woken up to it.

Nora sat herself at the desk, but it would not do. The glass showed her rumpled dress and hair escaping from every loosened pin, and every movement she made called her attention back to it, as though expecting to see something more than her familiar self looking back. And yet she could not seem to reach up and cover it.

Unable to settle, she rose finally with the abruptness of one acting before realising they intend to act, and, picking up the candle, stepped out into the passageway. With the staff long abed, it was deserted, not with the fleeting emptiness of the day but rather the deep desolation of night, with many hours yet to go before light and friendly faces would come again.

Somewhere outside, the wind caught sharply and howled its indignation. Within, the only sound was the padding of her feet upon the carpet, the subtle groan of the floorboards beneath. The tiny flame of her candle served only to emphasise the darkness massing around it, and yet she did not hesitate as she came to the staircase and began to climb.

The third floor opened before her, a wide landing ringed by unpretentious doors just beneath the attic servants' quarters. It had been the children's floor once, with schoolroom and nursery, and bedrooms for older boys and girls and their guests. One day, it might be so again, but for the moment it was relegated to storage, looked in on only by the occasional maid.

Most of the doors were closed, but a couple stood open, revealing here a crib stacked with a rocking horse, there a pile of hobbyist paintings topped with pinned butterflies, the frame broken. Nora made for the door at the end of the corridor, which opened onto a room directly above her own despoiled bedroom two floors below. It appeared to have once been a playroom and makeshift theatre, with runners for a curtain on the ceiling and a raised platform for a stage. The floorboards here were bare and polished, and the moon cast its light upon them, broken by the shadows of the window bars, and of the twiggy remains of what might once have been a rather fine fern still in a pot on the windowsill.

Against the walls stood a variety of wooden props, a marquee faded with age, and a number of chests and crates. Some looked like they had been made for the purpose, painted in bright colours and cheerful patterns to suit the room, but others were crude, ordinary shipping crates rudely made. These gave the appearance of having been stacked at random and in a hurry, but though shipping crates might ordinarily be intended purely for transport, the film of dust upon these suggested their travels had long since come to an end. A couple of the nearest ones stood open, revealing a haphazard array of costumes, wigs, shoes and glittering paste-work. Around them hung a mouldering smell which seeped into the musty air.

Near the window stood a shape like a sofa covered in a dust sheet. Seeing it, Nora tensed, hesitating for the first time since rising from her makeshift desk. The thing ought to stay covered, she knew. Invoking the ghosts of the past to help with the present could surely not end well, but what else did she have?

Setting her candle on a closed crate, she tore off the dust sheet with a snap that made the little flame shudder. Beneath stood a most remarkable piece of furniture: a sofa large enough for a man to lie on, its original upholstery entirely obscured by a mass of patches, a thousand or more tiny scraps of fabric in every combination of colour and texture imaginable, each one beautiful in its own right and yet too small to be of practical use to anyone other than the person who had constructed this sofa.

At the sight of it, Nora breathed in, not in a gasp but to replenish that within her which had deflated with the realisation that it was just as she remembered, except Ambrose O'Rourke was not sat upon it waiting for her. Yet even so it drew her, as though containing nevertheless some trace, some essence which was more than the sum of its myriad parts.

She sat down gingerly, like a child unsure of permission, but finding the seat soft and welcoming, she began to relax, the old springs squeaking as they gave way, until she was quite enveloped, as if held in a protective embrace. The thought made her smile as she traced her fingertips over a patch of rose crêpe.

"Hello, my old friend," she murmured, her eyes falling to half mast as memory flooded in. For a time, silence again claimed the room, broken only by the keening of the wind around the window frame.

"Victor's dead, you know," she said at length, as though speaking to one who had always been in the room. "At twenty-eight I find myself a widow. He died – was murdered, I should say – this morning. I think it was this morning at least. I don't know what time it is any more. I don't know what anything is—"

Her voice caught even as she smiled, too grim to be wry.

"The police have been of course, like flies on carrion. One of them, the one in charge, wanted to know if I knew who'd done it. If *I* knew—" She laughed, short and bleak. "I don't even know why he was in my room! I hadn't seen him in months, and he was never so rude as to call after ten. They must have thought me ridiculous, stumbling over the smallest detail. But my head was so full of ghosts, and I keep jumping at them, backing away and bumping into others, and getting so terribly muddled... Oh, I do wish you were still here."

The last came out almost as a whimper, and she stared into the empty corners of the room as though seeking something in their shadows to hold her arms out to, to be comforted by. But there was only uncaring darkness, and at length she began again.

"Lady Brucknell's December ball invitation arrived yesterday – or was it the day before? I put it aside to think of an excuse to decline – Victor never liked balls, you know, not of the dancing kind." She giggled, a sound edged in hysteria. "And I went off them once your dear Mr Vascelles was no longer there to keep me company. Yet now that I have the perfect excuse, am wholly excused for a year and a day, and Victor need never be bothered again, all I can think is that the confines of it will crush me. Already I feel I cannot abide it for another instant, and it's only been a day!"

Without warning, the giggle rose, hit its jagged crescendo and shattered into dry, heaving sobs. They overcame her, suffocating her as they forced their way out of the narrow bones which held them, contorted now as she curled around herself, gripping her chest to stop the shuddering convulsions. She rocked back against the sofa, her face twisting grotesquely, laughing even as she sobbed.

"I don't even know why I'm crying," she choked out, the words half asphyxiated as the need to speak pressed harder than the need to breathe. "It's not as if I loved him. I barely even knew him – that was the whole *bloody* point—"

Here the tears won out again for a time, all her attention needed merely to keep the pieces of herself from falling apart altogether.

When next her head lifted, sobs and laughter were gone, leaving behind only a seething bitterness.

"You were right, you know." A fury gripped her all at once, as violent as any she had known. She leaped from the sofa and rounded on it, as though it specifically were to blame. "I hope you're satisfied. You were right and you knew you were right, and still you left me to it, knowing what you knew—"

On the last word, her voice broke anew, shoulders crumpling inward as she stood trembling in the centre of that cold, empty room, on the verge of collapsing onto the very same sofa on which she had vented her rage not a moment ago.

It was a movement at her feet which distracted her, the briefest spark of life, ignited and dead in an instant. Nora stared, tears forgotten as every muscle pulled taut.

No, she realised, not life, nothing like it: across the floor, the moonlight drew its window sketch, with its glazing bars and its fern cadaver, and now again as she watched, the keening wind slipped between the casement cracks, making the tips of the dead twigs shiver. Across the floor, the spindly shadows chased each other, a ghoulish play lasting only so long as the wind cried.

Nora stared, unable to look away. All of what had consumed her mere seconds ago lay abandoned as the game started up a third time. This time, it did not stop.

As the wind howled, tips of the ancient branches stirred against themselves, snapping and chasing each other like a hydra in disarray. They darted away and dashed back in chaotic unison, and Nora's breath grew shallow as the frenzied dance played out before her.

The wind screeched louder still, became too much for the decrepit old twigs to bear. One by one they broke off, the twitching shadows vanishing into the blackness below. Nora watched entranced as the last of them fell and was swallowed up. The wind kept up its clamour and still she did not move. The pit, bottomless, fathomless, yawned before her. Just one step—

She could not draw her eyes away. The thrill of fear was in her chest. Her breath came hard as the draught plucked at her hair, and she seemed no longer to be standing in a disused old room, musty and close, but somewhere altogether different, somewhere vast and cold and windswept, on the edge of—

It was the question which made her stop. The edge of *what*? The answer felt a breath away, just on the edge of touching. Instinctively, she looked up for it, peering into the same shadowed corner as before.

This time, it was not empty.

All at once the wind rose, dashing itself against the windowpane in a vicious gust, snuffing out the flickering candle still standing on its box. Nora was left in darkness but for the moonlight and the burning eyes which gazed out from the shadows. They beckoned.

In the instant she met that awful stare, all was stillness. Her heart seemed to freeze in its beat, and she was aware only of those eyes – and of the pit gaping at her feet. It seemed to pull at her, to call to something woven deep into the very fabric of her, promising, promising, one step, and—

Never looking away from the shadow's face, she lifted one leg. Extending it experimentally a fraction at a time, she moved inch by inch, until at last the floorboard under her other foot creaked in protest at the additional weight.

The mundanity of it brought her back. She looked around – at the cheerful cases, at the abandoned props, at the dead pot plant; at all the things which were not the edge of a windswept cliff in a place she had never seen. Finally she looked down at her own extended leg, hovering over the edge of nothing. It was reality which toppled her, not into nothing but against the old sofa, her head knocking against the carved armrest as she fell.

It took only an instant for pain and confusion and fear to coalesce into all-consuming panic. It surged through her, winding around every limb as she flailed, making her trip over her own skirts as she stumbled from the room, not allowing her body to pause even to right itself.

The slam of the door echoed as she flew down the stairs, not daring to even think of the horrible eyes behind it. The answer they gave could not possibly have been true anyway.

~

Geraldine McNeal was out of bed before she realised she was awake.

She found herself standing in the dark of a strange room, with a strange smell and a strange draught and a strange carpet under her bare feet, and for the longest moment could not understand how such a thing had come about. Her mind reeling, she groped through stashes of old dreams and older memories, searching for equilibrium. Fragments of ghosts and kidnapping madmen and other ghoulish stories not thought of in fifty years were called into skittering life by the strangeness. And then, all at once, her groping mind found purchase on reality, and she knew it all for nonsense, remembering in the next that the reality was much, much worse.

McNeal had spent the day doing everything she could. There simply had been nothing else to be done. She'd looked after the mistress. She'd let Dot look after Joan before trying to talk to them both, not that it had made any difference: Joan's mind had been gone well before the police had physically removed her trembling body, leaving them to hope she would be able to find her way back again once she understood she was safe. McNeal had said as much to Dot, that for all the girl's vagueness, she had always been able to find her way, but though the idea had seemed to comfort the cook somewhat, there had been no persuading her to put her knife away. Even tonight, McNeal had been forced to leave her old friend in the kitchen, letting her grief take years off a blade whose glossy handle marked it as practically new.

Then there had been the mourning arrangements – having the clocks stopped, the mirrors covered, searching the attic for what accoutrements could be reused from previous deaths, and ordering new what could not. She had written for the dressmaker to visit Mrs Bancroft in the morning, had supervised the setting up of the mistress's provisional accommodation in as much finery as could be managed on short notice, and chosen a modest room for herself a few doors down, to sleep in in her acting role as lady's maid.

She had made herself so busy that she had hardly had time to notice the weight in her throat. Only once had it threatened to drag her down: she'd passed the late master's rooms and seen Cox, the valet, sat at the desk, writing out what she had no doubt was an application for his next position. Seeing her, he'd risen and pressed her hand: he would take the train to Hampshire, to make arrangements there; it was unlikely he would return once they were complete.

When he had left, McNeal had taken a deep shuddering breath, but then Annie had managed to cut herself on the back of a mirror she had been trying to cover and bled all over the Persian rug. Immediately McNeal had been off again – and glad of it.

Alone in the dark, a thundering on the staircase made her start. It came tumbling down the hallways at speed, very close to her own door now, and almost as close to Mrs Bancroft's. The housekeeper's first thought was that the murderer had returned, to finish the job he'd left half done, but no – this wasn't the stealthy tread of a man able to get in and out of a house of more than a dozen people without detection; this was the frantic, trampling dash of one who no longer had the wit to care whether she was discovered. McNeal's hand was on the doorknob even as the shriek rang out, calling her name.

She found the mistress halfway down the corridor, a black shape with a skull-white face contorted in breathless panic. In the dark, her eyes shone wildly, entirely without colour, so that McNeal could not help but remember how Miss Ealing, the previous lady's maid, had disliked attending her before dawn.

The thought brought an unexpected burst of empathy as McNeal fumbled for a candle: after all, it was not the lady's fault her eyes happened to be exactly the wrong shade of blue, just as it was not her fault that she did not possess the gifts which had marked her mother-in-law out even from her esteemed crowd. True that it had been a bitter pill to swallow at times, to see her walking around so erect, so proud, with nothing anyone could see to be proud of, but in the present moment, she was only a young woman in distress, a new widow frightened or even made ill by her nightmare, and McNeal found it easy to approach her with warmth.

"Whatever is the matter, madam?" She approached Nora carefully, touching the widow's shoulder to calm her agitation. "Are you unwell? Shall I have the doctor fetched?"

Nora did not appear to hear her.

"The mourning drapes!" she burst out, with such force that McNeal dropped her hand in surprise. "Why aren't they up? They must go up immediately! *I could see the branches, McNeal!* I could see—"

Here distraction seized her, her sentence forgotten as she spun round, as though trying to look in every direction at once. She lost her footing and staggered; McNeal caught her arm, supporting the terrified woman.

"What branches are those, madam?" she asked, holding firmly to a calm she was suddenly no longer sure she felt. "The drapes are airing out, and some needed mending. They'll be hung first thing in the morning."

"That's not soon enough! They must be hung now, immediately. The *branches*—"

Those strange eyes fixed on the housekeeper, wide and full of panic at things that weren't there. So earnest were they in their fear that McNeil wondered whether she too might not have been infected by the creeping shadows in the corners, had not exasperation got there first.

"The drapes cannot be hung now, madam. The staff cannot be roused from their beds in the small hours a second night running and expected to work their day."

Something in the housekeeper's steadiness seemed to catch Nora, bringing her somewhat back to herself.

"Of course, I—" She swallowed, visibly wilting as she looked about her in confusion, as though having only just realised where she was. "I don't know what came over me. I'm sorry."

Whatever fire had taken her had evidently burned itself out, and the mistress looked suddenly fit to collapse. By the light of the candle, McNeal noticed for the first time the tracks shimmering like fairy dust on her wan cheeks.

Nora did not protest as the housekeeper manoeuvred her into her makeshift bedroom, allowing McNeal to undress her and pick out the loose pins still caught in the dense black mass of her hair.

"Would you like me to fetch you some supper, or some of that tea the doctor left in case you couldn't sleep?" the housekeeper asked, before realising she would get no answer.

Nora sat before the uncovered mirror, staring into her own glittering eyes with a gaze which made McNeal start with recognition, being quite identically blank to the one Joan had worn when they had carried her out.

But Nora did not tremble, only swayed in her seat as Mrs McNeal's deft hands moved her this way and that, unhooking buttons and pulling at laces before finally helping her up, draping the loosest of shifts over her and putting her into bed.

That night, Geraldine McNeal slept the uneasy sleep of one nagged by a thought eluded, some fragment of understanding teasing just beyond reach. In images that were not quite dreams, she saw her mistress in the dark again, her long body twisted, grotesque with some strain, the long back misshapen, hunched over as though with the weight of limbs it did not have.

They kept her half awake, these flashes, with the sense that if she could only hold them a little longer, she would see the answer for herself, but it was only in the morning that she understood.

The chambermaid, having tidied the mistress's bedroom, brought the corset to McNeal in her office. The girl had found it loose and misshapen, entirely unfit for its purpose or any other, and when McNeal used her penknife to split the seams open, she was astonished to find much of the boning – finest baleen no less – crumbled to little more than powder.

With the supporting structure so disintegrated, it must have been an awkward, uncomfortable thing to wear, and in the letter with which she returned it, Mrs McNeal made no bones about telling the manufacturer precisely what she thought of their quality control.

CROFTSEND

I

Fifteen years before the possibility of becoming Mrs Victor Bancroft even occurred to her, Nora Dallaway travelled almost the whole length of the country. Escorted by a succession of porters, she shuffled from coach to train to train to coach, a note pinned to her black smock in case of mishap. In that manner, she journeyed from Bridde in the north, the remains of the ancient house still smouldering, to her father's ancestral Kent, where his relations would take her in. She was three years old and the distance incomprehensible.

Croftsend was a pleasant sort of house, large enough to keep a gentleman's family comfortable and feeling no need to be any larger. It sprawled genially on the edge of Plimhurst Green, and on the day Nora saw it for the first time, she spoke not one word. Nor did the matter show signs of improving in the days which followed. Whether it was a case of could not or would not was a matter for debate, but the end result remained the same: the child was silent, and nothing could induce her to be otherwise.

It was not the beginning the Lindup family had hoped for. Judith Lindup, née Dallaway, in mourning for her beloved brother, was quick to call in the local physician, family sage since her own childhood. Dr Cuthbert could only urge patience. Such a journey would try the nerves of the best of us, he said, but for so small a child, with only the hands of strangers to hold, it hardly bore thinking about. And it must be remembered too that it was not yet a month since the fire which had taken from her not only her parents but absolutely everything she knew, every familiar face and place and object, save the silver charm she had been wearing around her neck on that dreadful night and now would not consent to take off under any circumstances. Even at bath times she clung to it, though any vexation caused by her biting and scratching was tempered by the piteous sight of the purple flush of bruises blooming beneath the fragile skin. Spilling across her collarbone and over her tiny shoulder, they formed a series of points remembering where the little body had been seized in a wrenching grip. When asked the name of the beast responsible, however, the child only pressed her lips together and stared.

Patience, urged Dr Cuthbert, *have patience with the poor mite*, but weeks passed and bruises faded, and in the daily grind of life, it became harder to remember why. In the kitchen, the housekeeper turned to the cook and wondered aloud whether the child realised her own luck, blessed with an aunt and uncle good enough to offer her a place in their home equal to their own children. Orders were placed for new clothes, shoes and toys, from the very same shops as supplied dear Miss Violet's needs, and Master Ben's, too before he had gone away to school. The Lindups had given the child a home and a bed and even a sister – surely an improvement on her lonely state in that distant place – yet received not so much as a *thank you* for their trouble.

In the schoolroom, the governess worried over her ability to include so young a child – young in body and seemingly younger still in mind – in her lessons without neglecting sweet, willing Violet, who at seven years old was to have been her only pupil. In Miss Simmons' opinion, Nora ought to have a proper nanny, one with experience in managing difficult children of that age, but Croftsend was Miss Simmons' first post out of her own schoolroom, and though teaching came easily to her, less so did the navigation of her employer.

Judith Lindup suffered with her nerves at the best of times, but since the arrival of her niece, the lady of the house seemed stooped under a weight from which she could not wriggle out. She drifted about the house in a sickly pallor which could not be accounted for even by the unflattering effects of mourning on her peachy complexion, which even her previous pleasure of secluding herself in the conservatory with her watercolours did nothing to restore. Every time Miss Simmons asked to speak with her, determined to put forward her thoughts on a nanny, something in the lady's eyes made her fall silent: too big for her face, they seemed always now to be full of tears.

In her bed at night, Judith Lindup wrung her hands and did not sleep. Already she doubted her strength, her ability to love a child she not only had not borne, but whose very presence was a constant reminder of her grief. That this baleful child, with her sallow skin and hair black as a crow's wing over silent, glittering eyes, that this child without speech, without sweetness or charm, should be all that remained of her excellent father – of dear Stephen, who had been kind and gentle and clever, and every other good thing – seemed the cruellest of ironies.

In the rose garden, Judith lingered by his plaque on the wall and wondered at him. Bad enough to holiday in so godforsaken a place, for the sole purpose of seeing a house he had read about once in a book, which by his own account had nothing to recommend but age, gossip and a rather curious situation, but then to fall in love! To commit himself so far away, when surely there must be heiresses aplenty nearer to home, ready to fall over themselves at a chance of marrying that very best of men?

But it made no odds now. Stephen was gone and Nora was here, Miss Dallaway now as Judith had been before her, as no one else ever would be again. The last of the line, and Judith called upon to raise her as her own. It was a call she felt in every fibre of her being, and she was determined not to shirk it but to give her niece every care Stephen's daughter deserved, body and soul both.

As the weeks passed and still no word passed those pale lips to suggest what might have come before, Judith decided it would not do to take chances. There was nothing for it: the child must be christened.

It was a bright spring day when the Croftsend household set out along the lane to the village, the green-tipped branches swaying over patches of early forget-me-nots in the grass verges below. Family and staff both were in attendance – the exception old Cook, on account of her knees – joining the end of the procession over the common. The church bells rang out from their Norman steeple to welcome the baker, the blacksmith, the solicitor and all those people who together make up an English village, each with wives and children in tow. White-haired Dr Cuthbert walked in conversation with farmer Ludlow, Fly the sheepdog trotting obediently at her master's heel.

Though each member of the congregation wore their very best, no little girl's dress had as much lace as Violet Lindup and her cousin's, and no woman but Judith wore silk, for the Lindups were acknowledged as the first family of their small district. In their first attendance since the new arrival, the ladies, hand in hand in hand, wore their mourning: Judith in deep mauve, for the brother she had lost and the sister she had never known; Violet, holding her mother's hand, in soft lilac, for the uncle and aunt she had never met; and, holding her cousin's other hand, Nora head to toe in black, for the father and mother and the life taken from her. Only one speck of brightness twinkled upon her dark form: still no earthly force could persuade her to remove that silver pendant, and so it hung incongruously upon her narrow chest, catching the sunlight. Now and again, she clutched it with her free hand and put it in her mouth.

On that morning, a great many necks craned – discreetly or otherwise – to catch a glance of the little stranger, but not one of them did Nora return. As she walked, her eyes never left her cousin.

Violet swung their hands between them, unable to suppress her excitement in showing off her little cousin, very nearly as good as a sister.

With Violet's honeyed curls bouncing merrily in their ribbon, her cheeks plump and her ready laugh, the contrast between the cousins was stark, yet the girls seemed equally untroubled by it, if indeed they noticed it at all: Nora looked trustingly at her guide as she followed Violet across the common, and Violet's smile as she led Nora along shone quite brightly enough for two.

Already among the stragglers, the Croftsend party found themselves additionally delayed at the edge of the green. As Captain Lindup stooped to retie his shoelace beneath the withering glare of his wife, the staff went on ahead, leaving the family hurrying to be at their pew in time for the opening hymn.

The churchyard rooks perched in the bare branches of the old elm as Captain Lindup led his troops through the gate. The great black birds were well known to parishioners, having nested in the belfry for several seasons now and being enthusiastic participants at every church picnic, thus the family paid them no mind as the creatures took flight and landed on the worn stone lintel above the church door, their wordless cries filling the air. The birds kept up their warning as the family hurried along the path, harsh caws rising and merging into a frantic crescendo, all but drowning out the pealing bells as the birds stalked about their perch on their wicked gnarled feet like sentries, shaking their tarry feathers in agitation as they screamed.

The Lindups took no notice. Never had the creatures been known to behave badly to their loyal purveyors of fairy cakes and finger sandwiches, so there seemed no reason now to divert their attention from their rush. It was only when they reached the open door that they realised their mistake.

As the sole of Captain Lindup's boot brushed the stone threshold, the rooks launched their attack.

Leaping from their perch, they dove bodily at the family, shrieking and beating their wings about the human heads with such spiteful vigour that two birds seemed to carry in them the fury of a dozen at least. Crying out, the Lindups tried to duck away, but the confusion only made it worse: apparently losing all interest in the adults, the creatures turned their violence on the little girls, and no amount of shouting or beating of hats would make them let up.

The children now had added their terrified cries to the general mayhem, and the birds dove at them again and again, not merely viciously but with purpose. Flying at the sobbing girls with talons outstretched, they beat at them with furious black wings, relentless, blocking out the sun and enveloping the cousins in a storm of feathered black. The girls stumbled, scraping their knees in the dirt as they clung to one another, crying and seeking to shield their soft faces in each other's frock, but still it wasn't enough. Still the birds came on, relentless, like beasts possessed.

It was at the sight of her daughter's blood, torn by a stray talon from the fragile skin of the little hand which even now clutched her cousin's that Judith Lindup stopped thinking and acted. In a burst of mothering instinct, she snatched her child by the scruff and dragged her into the safety of the church. The force of it was such that Violet could not help but drop the hand she held, smaller even than her own.

With Violet out of reach, the birds made no attempt to pursue her. Instead, they turned the full force of their assault on Nora, battering her tiny form as though determined to drive the child from the very earth on which she crouched.

Captain Lindup could only watch, frozen in a horror by the monstrous sight. He had no particular fondness for his wife's niece, who did not seem to understand that children, like women and dogs, were generally pleased to submit to his bright eyes and genial smile, but truly this was horrific.

The birds flapped and screeched and tore at her, rending her dress and flying at her hair, as glossy and black as their feathers, the victim all but indistinguishable from her aggressors in the mayhem.

It was the young vicar who broke the spell.

Seeing Mrs Lindup dashing down the aisle to the sound of the organ, clutching her last-born as though at least one of their lives depended on it, Mr Cranleigh had taken it upon himself to investigate. His appearance at the doorway brought Captain Lindup back to the needs of the moment.

Snatching Nora up under one arm, he pushed the astonished vicar back inside the church, slamming the heavy door behind them just in time for the maddened birds to fling themselves against it, the dull thuds of their bodies muffled by the weathered oak. Again and again the thuds sounded, accompanied by furious cries echoing above the organ's tune. The vicar raised his eyebrows in a question, but Captain Lindup could only shrug, pulling a grim face as he bundled his niece up towards the family pew.

The girl's crying had subsided by now, and instructed to wipe her face and smooth her dress, she obeyed, silently but without protest. It was therefore not difficult for Cranleigh to return to his post and for the eyes of his flock to follow him there, assuming nothing more interesting than a child's tantrum. He was a good speaker with a strong clear voice, which he did not find it difficult to raise over the incessant cawing still echoing from beyond the roof.

By the time they came to that part of the service reserved for baptisms, he had all but forgotten the incident, being only reminded of it by the torn lace on Nora Dallaway's dress as he went to take her hand. She hesitated a moment, looking to her cousin, but Violet's encouraging smile reassured her. She allowed Cranleigh to lead her to the font and help her onto the stone step, that she might be high enough to bow her head when the time came.

In spite of her tear-stained face, Nora was now entirely calm, watching the vicar in solemn silence as he moved through the rite. It was not until they approached the wetting, the vicar pushing the little dark head gently forward as he spoke, that anything out of the ordinary occurred. At that crucial moment, not one but two unusual things took place in such rapid succession that, afterwards, Cranleigh wondered whether he was right to separate one from the other.

First, as he ran his fingers gently through the child's coiling black hair to clasp the back of her skull, the queerest sensation overcame him. Though a man of the soul, Cranleigh had never before given much thought to the sensation which came through the palm when lain upon a human head, be it for the purpose of christening, comfort or simply to stroke his wife's pale chestnut hair. It was at once impalpable and definite, the current of another soul running up through the conduit of muscle and bone to touch his own, a sensation as crucial and unconscious as that of a beating heart. Cranleigh became conscious of it only on that morning, when he pressed his palm against the skull of a little girl and found it missing. The shock of it was so sudden and so horrible that it floored him, like a physician having just discovered his walking, staring patient to be without a pulse.

Feeling his knees give out, Cranleigh caught himself on the granite font. It was from this vantage point that in the very next moment he turned, drawn by the cacophonic noise which filled the church without warning. The colossal smashing sound bounced off every surface, mingling with the discordant chorus which arose in its wake, the screams human and avian both. He was just in time to see the great black birds, having shattered the stained-glass window depicting St Peter, flying straight at him. Like murderous black arrows they came on, talons outstretched and cruel beaks open in shrieks, ruby drops falling from their ruffled feathers onto the pews below. Cranleigh looked into the polished gleam of their eyes and knew what it was to be hated.

The idea, no, the knowledge of what they might have done had he not stumbled back out of sheer instinct was one which many years later would still wake him with a shiver even on the warmest of nights. As to what could have happened had it not been for Mr Ludlow's presence of mind, he dared not imagine.

As the swooping birds turned their attention to Nora, alone and helpless by the font, beating about her head with whistling black wings, the farmer launched into the fray.

Scooping up the child in his arms, he ran to the safety of the tiny vestry, as behind them Fly the sheepdog remained on guard, barking savagely at the mad birds now circling just out of reach.

With their quarry out of sight, however, the rooks had calmed, and might have been mistaken for ordinary birds trapped by accident, were it not for the occasional ruby drop which still fell, a reminder of the deliberate violence of their entry.

With one final turn about the nave, they retreated whence they had come, dislodging what remained of St Peter's halo as they went. Cranleigh lay where he fell and watched them go, thanking God for His mercy and swearing to never mutter a single ungenerous word about dogs in church again.

As Fly's barking quieted, Ludlow reappeared, Nora still in his arms. Depositing the girl with her family, he gestured to her chest as he spoke a quiet few words to Captain Lindup. He then repeated his opinion to the vicar who, having got to his feet and laughing in sheer relief, repeated it to the congregation.

The birds, Mr Ludlow believed, must have been attracted to the child's silver necklace, standing out so wonderfully against the black of her dress. Still chuckling, the vicar reminded his flock that it was this very irreverent playfulness and sheer *joie de vivre* that God so loved in His creatures.

Relief at the existence of a sane explanation was infectious, and soon the entire congregation was smiling and nodding along with him, quietly agreeing amongst themselves that no more need be said about it.

In the week following the service, the Lindups made a generous contribution towards the restoration of the window, and some little while later the birds returned, looking a little the worse for wear but showing no further murderous inclinations. Nevertheless, the next church picnic was quietly postponed, and from then on until Nora was sent away to school, Mr Cranleigh struggled to find time to dine at Croftsend as he had in the past.

For her part, Nora was instructed to henceforth keep the necklace beneath her smock if she must wear it at all. Additionally, upon further consideration, it was agreed that she was really altogether too young for church, and that she might better spend her Sunday mornings at home with Cook.

II

It took fully six weeks following her arrival to establish that Nora was not, in fact, mute. The discovery was made one spring evening, just as dusk was melting into twilight. The girls trotted downstairs to the kitchen just as Grace, the maid, was about to empty her suds out of the back door, rounding the corner to find Grace's arms drawn back, sleeves hooked behind her bony elbows as she held the pail ready to launch.

And launch it might have done, had not the squawk startled her. She paused a moment, glancing up to see a little figure in black detach from Violet's side and fly at her. Though Nora was not large for her age, the impact was enough to knock both girl and maid to the floor where they sat, sopping wet in a puddle of dishwater.

The squawk, the clatter and finally Grace's outraged scolding drew the attention of the housekeeper, Mills. Grace had lapsed into sulky muttering, glaring at Nora as she picked herself up and attempted to wring out her skirt, but Nora remained where she had landed. Hair clinging to her skin in damp dregs like slick black feathers, she peered about her with huge eyes as she realised she had done wrong. When she found Violet, still standing on the staircase as she stared open-mouthed at the scene, Nora opened her mouth.

The sound which emerged was low and coarse and entirely unintelligible, something like a fledgling crow. The first strains of it chilled Violet: she had learned about the Devil causing people to speak in tongues from Mr Cranleigh's sermons, and surely a sound like that could be nothing less?

Horror gripped her for a moment, but then the strange noises began to resolve themselves into something like words, and she realised it was only the little voice struggling to remember itself after months of disuse. What had started as a half-whispered, half-sobbed croak gradually clarified, until the last word could be clearly understood.

"… warning," Nora said, looking out into the falling light, and though Violet knew something momentous had occurred, for a moment she could not place just what. Surely Nora had always spoken, had she not?

Mills had forgotten her anger in sheer astonishment.

"So she should, miss," the housekeeper agreed, seeming to have understood far more than Violet. She eyed Nora as though seeing her for the first time. "A warning should always be called out at dusk. One can never know just who might be passing by outside, but it's certain they'll not take kindly to getting their coats splashed. Even such coats as are not given to us to see."

Violet felt a tremor pass up her spine. Mills' people had come down from Northumberland, and she had told Violet stories of those who live among us but are seen by us only when they wish to be, of how they can twist your will like a daisy on a chain if you don't stand against them, and how they had a thousand and one tricks to make you forget you ever wanted to. The thought of them as close as just beyond the kitchen door was a thrill and a terror both.

Evidently less impressed, Grace was unable to contain a derisive snort at the idea that she might have offended the fairies with her dishwater.

Mills silenced her with a look. "I should mind my manners if I were you. 'Tis the fashion now to make mock of what has been known for centuries, but I ask you, how else but by repeated experience could such knowledge survive, long before anyone thought to write it down?"

There seemed to Violet to be no answer to that, and Grace, though she looked surly, did not attempt one.

III

As though those first words had unstopped some dam within her, afterwards Nora was silent no more. At first she addressed herself only to Violet, but little by little, as her needs dictated, her range expanded until it included the whole household. Her language was as advanced as could be expected for her age and for a couple of weeks the household enjoyed relief. Then came the discovery that with the unblocking of speech had flowed other, less desirable habits.

Precisely when the stealing had begun, no one could say for certain. It was not discovered until later when the caches were found, uncovered by chance or by smell, or when the maggots they attracted began to emerge as flies. Truly, the choice of object was almost worse than the bald fact of the theft. Biscuits or sweets would at least have been understandable – not to mention less hazardous when left under floorboards and behind bookcases – but these Nora rarely touched. Instead, she chose things for which she could have no conceivable use: cheese rinds and bacon trimmings, vegetable peelings and stale breadcrusts and solitary peppercorns all were filched and left to rot in caches along with leaves, twigs, pine cones and a diversity of small corpses or parts thereof, their long tails or webbed feet in various states of decay.

Nor could she hold on to the things given to her. Clothes she divested herself of on her own mercurial whim, and a king's ransom in shoes was wasted upon her. Personal cleanliness appeared beyond her grasp; everywhere she went, a trail of earth, leaves and bits of moss followed, no matter how carefully Violet and Miss Simmons tried to clean her up at the door.

The worst of it was that she would not deny culpability, nor show any remorse. Scoldings were taken with a silent expression of curiously ferocious woe and made no difference whatever. She resisted confinement absolutely, be it within a room, the house or even just the garden. Whatever measures were put in place, she escaped with remarkable ingenuity and no consideration whatever for her personal safety, nor indeed modesty. In these moments there was no trace of childish clumsiness about her movements, and she might as often be found on top of the bookcase or the linen cupboard as on the settee with her cousin. Once she was found perched on the roof by the weathervane, having presumably climbed out of the attic window, and on another memorable occasion, Mr Ludlow brought her home wrapped in his wife's best blanket after finding her wandering through his field at dawn, stark naked and wet with the early morning dew.

Corporal punishment proved even less successful than confinement: Captain Lindup was not a man who enjoyed striking children, and his pains seemed to have no effect upon the behaviour of anyone other than poor Violet. In some misplaced attempt to compensate for her cousin's deviance, she would whip herself into a veritable fever of cringing obedience for days afterwards which her parents found quite terrible to watch.

Dr Cuthbert, in his wisdom, could make no suggestion other than continued forbearance combined with gentle education, and so for more than a year the household muddled on, foreseeing and correcting as best they could. Locks were placed on the kitchen bins and Nora's dresses buckled where she could not reach. Miss Simmons did what she could in the schoolroom, and all the while the Lindups held long discussions in the dining room after supper, which left Judith with wet eyes and a headache, and the captain murmuring about business in town.

The morning of the fair began as pleasantly as any Violet could remember. Ben, home from school and feeling magnanimous, had offered to take the girls and give his parents a day of peace. At fourteen, he had his own room now and ate with the adults, but in honour of the occasion, he consented to breakfast with the girls in the nursery.

Afterwards, Cook helped them pack a basket with chicken and ham sandwiches, Scotch eggs, great slabs of cherry tart and a flask of apple juice from their own orchard. So fortified, they set out towards the green, Ben carrying the basket in one hand and holding his sister's in the other, and she in turn clasped Nora's on her other side. Nora looked to Violet and Violet looked to Ben, and Ben, warm in the glow of their admiration, looked to the responsibility he undertook.

The sound of the fair drifted down the lane, mingling with the birdsong which wafted on the summer breeze. Distant at first, an indistinct hum of excitement and promise swelling like a balloon as they drew closer, it finally popped as they rounded the last corner, its constituent sounds bursting into individuality like so much confetti as the green came into view, decked out in all its glory.

The stalls, orange and yellow, purple and green, fanned out from the central point marked by the helter-skelter striped in red, blue and white, like the church steeple of this marvellous new village of fun which had sprouted up miraculously in the very midst of the old one. The hawkers in their gaudy waistcoats stood by, ribbons and feathers in their hats distracting from their grizzled features and beady eyes. They called out, inviting and cajoling, their hoarse voices rising to a collective pitch, rippling through the fair in the wake of anyone looking like they might be in need of a prize. Punch and Judy went rollicking through their paces once more to the sound of jeers and laughter, and even the livestock in their strawbale pens joined in, bleating and lowing along, their musky essence mingled inexorably with the sweet smell of toffee apples and the crisp hot oil of popping corn.

Children known and unknown streamed among the stalls and between the legs of their patrons, rushing from one end of the fair to the other and back again, their small bodies unable to contain the excitement of the day. When they finally collapsed from lack of sustenance, the rich produced a warm penny from a grubby pocket to hand over in exchange for sweets, and the poor fell to mother's bread and butter, to fortify themselves against another headlong rush. Through it all the punters wandered, half the village in their Sunday best and more yet to come. They breathed in the concoction as they handed over ha'pence for a go at the coconut shy, or lined up for a picture at the daguerreotype booth, or glanced out of the corners of their eyes at the fortune teller's tent tucked discreetly away near the back, the deep blue flap embroidered with black birds and silver stars.

It was the porcelain doll which started the trouble. The top prize at the shooting booth, Ben had noticed his sister's adoring eyes upon it, and after lunch, as he led his troops back into the fray, he announced his intention to win it for her.

Being the best prize the booth had to offer, the doll required a large number of points to win it, and Ben promptly set to. Though he was an admirable shot, the endeavour was not a quick one. Violet, seeing that the gentleman down the row was attempting the same feat for his daughter, watched the contest with mounting anxiety. The gentleman was not so good a shot as Ben, but he had the benefit of a substantial head start, and they were neck and neck. Violet trained her mind on her brother's bullets, her knuckles clenched white at her sides as she willed them to fly straight. She was sure there could not be a second such doll in all the world, let alone in the back of so dingy a caravan.

It was at the moment when Ben turned to his sister to place his prize proudly in her arms that he glanced behind her, to where Nora's small dark head ought to have been bobbing but was not. His eyes grew wide and his mouth slack, and in that moment Violet wished she had never laid eyes on the stupid doll.

Perhaps it had been the gunpowder which had frightened her, or perhaps she had simply grown bored with the wait. They did not know, and it did not matter: call as they might, she did not come. Enquiry followed frantic enquiry, but there were so many children running here and there and everywhere that no one remembered any of those who had not tried to reach into their pockets.

Finally, one woman thought she had seen a little black-haired girl hovering about the fortune teller's tent. On questioning, Madam Petra agreed that Nora had been there, standing so close to the entrance flap that they had both of them had quite a scare when Madam Petra had stepped out for a breath of fresh air. She could say for certain that it had been Miss Dallaway – those were not eyes one forgot in a hurry – but the girl had fled, and Madam Petra had seen nothing of her since. Being at least an hour ago, closer to two, and with no other sightings since, the unfortunate Ben had no option but to run all the way home and tell his parents.

The search went on for hours: every tent, every house, every garden, every crevice of every shed, but Nora could not be found. Nothing so awful had ever happened in the village, and even the carnies felt it. There was even talk of dredging the duck pond, but it was not until Captain Lindup was on the verge of riding for police assistance in the neighbouring town – Plimhurst Green being too small and too peaceful a place to warrant its own constabulary – that Mrs Ludlow, poorly in bed, happened to glance out of her window, spying on the roof of her husband's haybarn a most peculiar silhouette.

How Nora got up there was to remain a mystery. The building was of brick, agreed by the assembled crowd to be unscalable without equipment. The pitched roof on which she sat was intended to be accessed only for repair, for which was required a very long ladder indeed. It took Ludlow and his man until after dark to fetch that ladder and get her down. By this time, the events of the day were telling on poor Ben: fearing every minute that his little cousin should fall and hurt herself, or worse, and he alone to blame, the brave stout boy finally came apart completely, sobbing into his mother's arms.

Violet cried too, for Ben and her ashen-faced parents and their perfect day spoiled. She did not cry for Nora. Nora, she knew, would come back just as she always did, meaning no harm and not understanding that any had been caused. This much was perfectly plain to Violet, and indeed, it was an ongoing source of confusion that it did not seem to be to anyone else. Thus, when finally Captain Lindup carried her cousin upstairs to bed, with Mills close behind bearing plates of warm bread and milk, Violet tucked into her snack contentedly, certain that all was now well.

IV

On the morning after the fair, Ben was cheerful again, laughing and playing with them and evidently bearing no grudge, so it did not occur to Violet then that anything had changed. Indeed, in the weeks which followed, even the drawing-room conversations ceased, so she came to believe that her parents had at last accepted that Nora was as she was, and that was all. Only later did Violet understand that the conversations had ceased not because her parents had admitted defeat but because the decision had finally been made; that, with Nora's aberration on full public display – and, worse, implicating poor Ben – it had been an inevitable one. So it was that, shortly after Ben left on his holiday, Dr Virgo descended upon Croftsend. All because Violet had seen a doll at a fair.

He had been with the family nearly a month when, on that Sunday deep in the dull heat of August, Violet slipped away from her parents as they lingered after the morning church service and ran down towards the woods alone. Dust clouds rose about her feet as she bounded over the baked earth, the yellow dandelions and dainty cow parsley nodding serenely as she passed. Thistles half again as tall as herself scraped their prickling spines against her bare arms, but Violet paid them no mind. Even the fat pods of sweet peas weighing down the curling vines which escaped Mrs Ludlow's kitchen garden could not tempt her, for though she had no way to tell it, Violet knew time was short.

Even so, she found herself slowing as she came to the Greenman Oak. It stood at the far edge of a bit of land behind Ludlow's farm, just at the point where scrubby wasteland turned to woodland proper. The name came from a knot of scarring on the near side. Once a branch had grown there, and when it had fallen, it had left behind a protrusion which time and weather had smoothed into the uncanny likeness of a gnarled face. The Greenman peered out from behind the ragged bark, with knowing eyes and a crooked smile for all those who would pass.

Mr Ludlow said that a long time ago, before his father's father had even thought of building their farm, the forest had stretched all the way to Croftsend. In those days, the Greenman had marked the point which only the most daring – or the hungriest – hunters crossed. Beyond it, the forest grew dark and too dense to be useful, the brambles crowding thick and impenetrable, hiding pockets of nettles and treacherous hollows just waiting to snatch hold of a careless ankle, so a man would struggle to walk even a hundred yards beyond the Greenman with his shoulders straight. Now that the edge of the forest had moved back, it was no longer nearly so dark, and little girls had little shoulders. Even so, Violet did not like to rush past the Greenman. It didn't seem respectful.

As she crossed the threshold, which always seemed to her more of a physical barrier than the gradual replacement of grass and weeds with weeds and brambles would suggest, a cow lowed in the fields behind her, as though calling her back to civilisation. Violet did not heed it: this was not the first time she had been to fetch her cousin and she knew her way well enough. Nevertheless, clambering over the rotting remains of a beech and feeling the soft press of bright moss supple and other-worldly beneath her palms, the hem of her dress catching on a spur like a dagger, she could not silence Mills' stories whispering in her ear, drawing shadowed pictures between the trees: witches and trolls lying in wait to gobble up naughty children gone astray, fairies with golden smiles persuading you to forget their diamond eyes, and the Devil himself, whose ire Mills said had long ago caused the depression in the forest floor.

Truthfully, Violet wasn't convinced about that last one. As the ground began its gentle descent beneath her feet, it was difficult to imagine anything so dreadful having created it. Here, the undergrowth opened up again, if only slightly, and the sunlight trickled like rain between the slender forms of birch and hazel, giving life to ferns unfurled like fans, and gilding the copper curl of last year's leaves. They crunched beneath Violet's feet, dry even as the smell of damp earth and growing moss hung in her nostrils.

Violet tried to step more lightly, wishing she could be quiet. Without her clumsy tread, there was only the birdsong to be heard, and the flutter of the leaves swaying on branches above. It was a still sound, like the inside of the church when even the vicar has stepped outside, but she knew deeply that this was not *her* church, that she was a visitor and had no right to disturb its peace.

In the centre of the depression was a circular hollow, the gentle slope giving way suddenly to steep sides, as though the crust of the earth had been scooped out, like clotted cream with a teaspoon. In the centre of the hollow was Nora.

She sat with her back to Violet, black hair loose over her shoulders. Around her danced the dappled shadows thrown by the canopy far above, the shape of the hollow giving the impression that the shifting light had formed a circle especially for her amusement. Chattering in her childish way, she reached out her small hands and passed them through the dapples moving around her as if to stroke them, giggling softly as she did.

"Nora!" Violet called, seeing no point in delaying the inevitable. Her voice cut the stillness, sharp and human.

The little shoulders twitched in startled response as Nora fell silent, drawing back her hand.

It was then that Violet saw it – or thought she did. It was not in the light that Nora had been giggling at but rather in the space between, the barest suggestion of... something.

Directly in front of her cousin, there was the merest whisper of a shape flickering in the shadows, behind them, between them, of them, a thing without substance, without breath. In nothing but the faintest allusions, Violet made out the horns curving up, the great wings dark and heavy upon the back, and the eyes, the eyes which were not a shadow or a whisper or anything Violet knew, eyes like fire made solid, without pupil or soul, eyes which should not be, which could not be and yet which were, watching her across the stillness she had broken. In that instant, Violet knew nothing but that those eyes were eternal, and that they would follow her until her dying day.

And then it was gone, in a fraction of a moment, the heartbeat it took for Nora to turn around and see her cousin. She smiled, so Violet had to smile back, and when she looked back to where the apparition had been, there was nothing to be seen, only the twisted roots of birch pulled up in a storm, and the sun catching on the copper leaves. The feeling, too, had evaporated like morning dew on radish leaves, eternity there and gone in a breath. Violet all but forgot about it the moment Nora scrambled up the bank to join her.

"Where's your ribbon?" Violet scolded half-heartedly, feeling in her pocket for the spare she now carried as a matter of course. "Come along – if we don't hurry we'll be late."

Nora's smile grew reluctant at that, but she put her hand in Violet's without protest.

Violet's heart hurt even as it swelled, knowing her cousin loved her enough to allow her to lead her back to a place she would rather not be, and that she had no choice but to do it, for Nora's own sake.

V

From her desk in the schoolroom, Miss Simmons heard the patter of little feet upon the landing, hurrying across to the nursery. She remained where she was, giving Violet a few minutes to tidy up the little one before joining them, sitting down at the small table laid for three. Thanking Mills for the tray of poached salmon, green beans and jam pudding to follow, Miss Simmons served the girls and then herself. It was not her job but a matter of practicality: with no nanny, she did not want Violet to find herself responsible for her cousin's table manners along with everything else. Not that Nora lacked table manners as such; Miss Simmons watched as the little girl fixed her peculiar eyes on Violet and proceeded to copy her movement for movement, bite for bite. It was a charming sight in its way, pretty Violet with her loyal shadow.

It lasted until the landing creaked with clipped footsteps beyond the nursery door. Then Nora froze, her food forgotten as she transferred that unerring attention from Violet to the door. Miss Simmons made no effort to press the issue: experience told her that not one more bite could be forced now. At best, the attempt would wind up a stain on the nursery wall; at worst it would end on the ground in a puddle of the rest of the girl's lunch, as the little stomach clenched itself against what it feared to come.

Precisely what that was, Miss Simmons had thus far failed to ascertain. She found Dr Virgo to be a dispassionate man rather than an angry one. Firm yes, even rigid, but not cruel. Indeed, for all that Nora vexed him day after day as he attempted to apply his methodology, Miss Simmons had never heard him raise his voice. Rather, he seemed in his element when the girl was at her most awkward, utterly sincere in his desire to help difficult children and their families. There was something almost religious about him, taking satisfaction as a priest might in the thankless work he felt called to, applying his unique skills where they were most needed. Miss Simmons did not dislike him, and yet, as even the sallowness drained from Nora's morose little face, leaving it a ghostly grey, she was sorry for her, and for her own inadequacies, which had left her unable to help Nora before it had come to this.

Inevitably, the door opened, revealing the lean upright form of Dr Virgo. He nodded to Miss Simmons, who, knowing her cue, rose from her seat. Virgo immediately took her place, crumpling his long legs under the small table, his torso fully twice the height of Nora's, who watched him as he watched her.

When Violet rose to follow Miss Simmons, neither Nora nor Virgo noticed her. They appeared to be sizing each other up – he impassive and she inscrutable. There was fear in the girl's eyes, Miss Simmons thought, abject terror, yet there was more too. It seemed to her for an instant that Nora was poised on the edge of something which might equally be flight or a leap at the man's throat. It was only the eyes though. Otherwise, Nora barely seemed to breathe.

Virgo, for his part, did not seem to notice either his pupil's eyes or her breathing. As Mills cleared away the dishes, her face carefully blank, he placed an object like a coiled leather belt on the table. It chinked with hidden metal as he set it down. "Now, Miss Dallaway," he said, "we must discuss your disappearance this morning."

It being a Sunday, Miss Simmons decided they would make a start on *A Midsummer Night's Dream*, on the basis that if Violet must be contained to prevent her sneaking back into the nursery, it was only fair that she be occupied by something she might actually enjoy.

Violet was half-heartedly trying to tell Hermia and Helena apart when her efforts were interrupted by the scream. It echoed through the house, rattling windows and bouncing off floorboards as it shook the drowsy afternoon rudely awake. Immediately following, there came a litany so obscene that Miss Simmons regretted that, in covering Violet's tender ears with her hands, she had none free for her own.

Dr Cuthbert was sent for as Virgo made his way gingerly down the stairs, cradling his right arm as he groaned and yelped, as though every movement caused him fresh agony.

Mills put her head round the schoolroom door with instructions to remain strictly within. Miss Simmons did her best, but Oberon and Titania were as nothing in the face of the distraction consuming pupil and governess both. They muddled on until just after three, when Violet claimed a call of nature.

Watching Violet dash down the stairs, knowing full well she would not be back, Miss Simmons went to look in on the nursery. It was empty now, with no sign of strife save the small chair overturned upon the floor, an uncoiled snake by its side. Approaching, Miss Simmons recognised it as the leather belt-like contraption which Virgo had brought in. It was too long to be a belt though, and, picking it up, she found it to be too heavy as well.

Downstairs, the drawing-room door was firmly shut. Miss Simmons hesitated as voices drifted through the keyhole.

"The child is dangerous!" That was Dr Virgo, his voice distinctive even as pain rippled the calm surface. "She must be where she can be properly restrained and studied without risk to her carers. I shall take her today, just as soon—"

"My dear man, you're in no state to do any such thing."

Cuthbert, ever genial, spoke in a tone Miss Simmons recognised as the one he used to soothe his youngest and most dramatic patients.

"I'll remind you that you're in a great deal of pain, which along with such relief as I have already dispensed is well known to play tricks on the mind. Now if you'll come along—"

"She *broke* my *arm*."

"Certainly your arm is broken," Cuthbert agreed placidly. "However, do consider what is more likely: that a little girl found the strength to break the arm of a full-grown man, or that the restraint you were applying backfired accidentally? Now do be sensible and come along to the surgery, while the narcotics are at their best effect. You'll thank yourself for it; that road is not one I should like to be travelling in your condition."

"Is harmless…" Virgo protested, but his voice was weak now, beginning to slur under the effects of whatever he had been given.

There came the sounds of people getting to their feet. It was as Miss Simmons turned away, thinking that she had better leave the "restraint" with the rest of the man's things, that a breathless presence pushed past her skirt and flung open the door.

Miss Simmons turned back just in time to find all eyes on Violet, who ignored them all as her frantic gaze swept the room.

Not finding what she sought, she looked helplessly at her mother. "Where's Nora?"

"Why, in the schoolroom with you," came the automatic reply, but even as Judith Lindup spoke, Miss Simmons watched her eyes grow wide with realisation.

Even with Cuthbert's ministrations, Virgo's cries could still be heard with every bump encountered by the physician's trap as they clattered down the lane, yet at Croftsend his suffering was all but forgotten as the household turned itself upside down. Every nook was searched, every cranny; chimney stacks and disused cellar checked. In the end, it was Mr Ludlow once again who came to the rescue: seeing a tiny black figure sprinting through his field, he'd sent Fly to give chase, offering toffees from his pocket until Nora could be persuaded to let him lead her home.

Dr Cuthbert had barely been given time to return to his surgery before being called back again, but though he pronounced her hale in body, Miss Simmons had her doubts about other parts.

Lying in bed that night, she recalled how the normally agile child had climbed the stairs following her retrieval, starting violently at every sound, her gait halting and awkward, as though her legs were no longer quite as she remembered them. Miss Simmons was in no doubt that, whatever had happened in that room, intentional or not, whoever's fault it had been, it ought not to have.

The clock in the hallway struck eleven, and Miss Simmons stopped trying to keep her eyes closed. She reached for the Bible on her nightstand, running her thumb down the grooves of the lettering, feeling the grain of the leather, well used and lovingly cared for. She did not need to read it to know herself remiss.

Pulling on her dressing gown, she tiptoed to the nursery and slipped inside. As her eyes adjusted to the darkened room, she heard the soft snuffling rising peacefully from Violet's bed on the left. Turning right, to where Nora's bed stood beneath the window, she saw the last sight she would ever see.

The figure on the bed was so large that it completely obscured Nora, if indeed Nora was still there at all. The curtains stood open, silhouetting the thing against the light of the crescent moon, so Miss Simmons could only make out the outline: twisting horns curving up and out, ending in vicious prongs; wings folded in rest but moving lightly, a gentle rhythmic twitching, as though in mockery of the breath it had no business drawing. Moonlight caught the claws like scythes on the front legs, the cloven hooves gleaming behind, and still poor Miss Simmons might have kept a sliver of wit about her, had it not been for the eyes; the eyes which were not eyes at all but holes gaping into a burning abyss, a bright empty glow of nothingness into which she stumbled and could not pull herself from.

Her last thought was of her pupil.

"Violet!" she screamed, even as madness took hold. "The Devil! He has your cousin, child! Run – run before he takes you too!"

It was then that her lungs collapsed, and Miss Simmons with them: in her terror, she had forgotten to keep breathing.

Cuthbert was summoned for the third time that day, though nobody expected him to do more than confirm with authority what any fool could see. What remained of Miss Simmons lay on the nursery floor until he arrived, twitching slightly as the last vestiges of life drained away. Nora would not be dragged from her bed, clinging tearfully to the headboard with each attempt, and so finally Violet got in with her, pulling the covers over both their heads until arrangements could be made to move the dead governess downstairs.

When it was done, Mills brought them cups of warm milk. After she left, Violet lay awake, unable to turn from what she now understood. The governess's last words still sounded in her ears, the dream through which they had come combining them inextricably with memory, with the horror of the thing in the forest. How she had not known it then she couldn't think, when the truth was so clear, so obvious, so inexpressibly awful. But she must not turn from it, not when poor dear Miss Simmons had died to speak it, to warn her...

"Nora," Violet whispered into the darkness, feeling her mouth suddenly dry as cobwebs. "Did you hear what Miss Simmons said? Before she— Did you hear her?"

Beside her, the little body moved, hair rustling against the pillow and tickling Violet's cheek as Nora shook her head.

Violet looked to find Nora staring up at her. Though there was hardly any light in the room, her eyes seemed to glitter, and for the first time, Violet felt the faintest twinge of discomfort. Refusing to acknowledge it, she looked away, calling up the image of her cousin in daylight, her upturned face so eager to please.

"She said the Devil had you," Violet said quietly. "Have you seen the Devil, Nora?"

When she looked again, Nora's eyes were round as pale saucers in the dark, little moons bouncing side to side as her head shook no. They could leave it at that, thought Violet, go to sleep and forget the absurd day and its awful questions forever. Then she remembered Miss Simmons and knew they could not.

"I think—" Violet swallowed. "I think perhaps you have."

Beside her, Nora stiffened.

Violet took both her hands in her own, clasping them tightly, willing it to be enough. "I think perhaps I saw you with him, in the woods this morning. He was in front of you and you were talking to him, stroking him. Do you remember?"

Nora said nothing, but there was no need. As Violet spoke, the little body had begun to tremble. Nora's mouth opened, moved, but no words came. Violet found that she was shaking too and felt the hot pinpricks of tears forming in her eyes. She summoned her resolve and did not let them fall, holding Nora close to her and trying to pour every drop of comfort she could muster into the embrace.

"It's all right," she whispered. "No harm will come to you, I promise. Only tell me what happened."

Though her body still trembled, Nora appeared to draw strength from Violet's assurance.

"He is not bad," she begged, in words that were barely more than breath. "He only wants me to follow him."

Her eyes were huge, pleading with Violet, with the world, with the thing that plagued her, so that Violet's fear was overtaken by an anger hot and deep, such that she had never felt before. That any hateful fiend should presume to ensnare her own dear cousin, darling little Nora, who looked to Violet so absolutely. It was not to be borne.

"No!" Violet clung to her newfound ferocity. "My dear, he is lying to you. The Devil always lies – it is his nature; it is all he is capable of. Remember Mr Cranleigh's sermons—" But of course, Violet realised, Nora could not remember, for she did not accompany the family to church.

Above the shining eyes, Violet saw the little white brow furrow and cursed her parents for their lack of foresight. Now she must do what she could.

"Think!" she insisted. "If he means no harm, why can he not show himself openly? Why must he lead you away to where not a soul comes? Or come in the night, when good folk are soundly at their rest?"

"He thinks the houses are too loud," Nora whispered, but there was doubt in her voice as her young mind tried for the first time to rationalise the irrational, to make sense of the senseless. "He says I belong there, that we belong there together. He says I must come, that I have no place but where he brings me."

"He is *lying*! Houses are loud because they are full of people, good, kind, cheerful people, such that God loves and the Devil cannot abide. Your place, dear Nora, is among them, among *us*. Promise me that you will turn from him when he comes and follow him no more!"

Nora stared up at her cousin, eyes wide and unblinking in the darkness. Violet willed her to see it, the fear in her own heart that was all for her.

Slowly, the little girl nodded, and Violet hugged her close, kissing her in relief.

"I will sleep with you," she whispered, feeling the ridge of Nora's necklace pressing into her own breastbone through two layers of nightgown. "Tonight and every night, and protect you always, if you only promise never, ever to entertain the Beast again, not for one moment. If he comes, turn your head, avert your eyes and run home, or to church, where he cannot get you. Do you promise?"

Snuggling close, Nora nodded. "I promise," she whispered, and with that, Violet could breathe again.

The next morning, she put it to her parents that Nora must now surely be old enough to join the family in church on Sundays. Neither could find the wherewithal to object, and if Judith Lindup fancied that the rooks watched her family a little too closely for comfort whenever Nora was with them, there were no further incidents to speak of. Nevertheless, the subject of a christening was never again raised.

~

Mrs Nora Bancroft, Kensington to
Mr Ambrose O'Rourke, Far From London

6 November 1896

My dear Ambrose,

The strangest of days. This evening my husband is buried and I find my hands curiously empty. You might argue that they have been empty since our wedding day, and to that I would have no counter except to say that I am sure they never itched then as they do now. I think it must be this wretched dress: the crêpe scratches so, it is hard to sit still. The dressmaker claims it is to honour Victor that I must be uncomfortable, but I call that strange – he never required my discomfort in life.

The house is as muffled, every window blotted, every mirror covered, every clock stopped. I find myself wandering about the space which is left, passing from room to room as though in a dream, yet unable to settle. Sleep has become a distant concept.

I was dreaming the night it happened, and sometimes I wonder if I ever truly woke up. Though I can no longer remember the face of it, it is as though the nightmare was not dispelled by daylight but simply pushed into the shadows, and is lurking in the corners even now. I think perhaps it was always there, only I'd grown used to it, put it away as well as I could, as one puts away and no longer notices the irritants of the city rush, or the eternal whispering bell in one's ears, always calling. Only now that things have changed, that everything is raw and immediate, is it aggravated, prowling about and clamouring for attention in this new darkness. I will not give it, I say. I made a promise long ago that I would not, and I shall keep it. I shall.

See, I have blotted my page, for the sake of a dream and a shadow. You see how anxious I have become, how my nerves itch with it and will not let me rest. Admittedly I do not help myself: the physician sent a sleeping draught and it remains untouched, in spite of McNeal's best efforts at persuasion. Poor woman. I don't doubt I add unfairly to her burden, but not even that can induce me to take it. I was administered such a potion once at St Clare's, and nothing in the world can make me repeat the experience. The blackness was worst of all.

So instead I wander the halls and dally in the rooms, feeling a stranger in my own house and frightening the servants with my appearance. They look at me strangely from behind the cover of their bows and curtsies, thinking I don't feel their eyes pricking the back of my neck as I pass. It saddens me sometimes, and sometimes, I admit, it is amusing. Nevertheless, this is an exceptional day of uncommon demands, by the dead, the living and Mr Alcott, and they must be allowed to get on with their work in as much peace as they can muster. Thus I force myself to sit still, and ask you to be my anchor once again. No doubt you would love the solemn spectacle of it all, so I will tell you about it.

Christopher Bancroft – my estranged brother-in-law; no doubt Em can tell you the gossip about him – arrived early this morning to take charge, and God help me but I let him. He has been here ever since, upstairs and down, bending his head close to Mrs Sharpe's in the kitchen as though they were old friends, discussing with quiet urgency some dish or other, keeping everything so private that even I don't know what the final spread will be.

No sooner had he left Mrs Sharpe than I heard him pressing Alcott on the number of mourners. I am given to understand that we have a very respectable amount, with no shortage of takers; apparently the notoriety makes it quite a desirable job in that sombre profession. Christopher has given strict instruction that there is to be no drunkenness or other nonsense during the procession, on pains of dealing with him directly.

I will not be attending of course – feminine nerves and so forth; apparently they become more delicate in direct proportion to the size of the dead man's purse – but truthfully I would have preferred to dispense with the procession. It seems to me they are becoming old-fashioned at any rate, and for our event in particular will surely only invite more talk. Though I suppose there will be talk regardless, and Christopher is set on having every bit of pomp and circumstance. He went on and on about "lifting my burden" and "doing right by Victor".

Whether or not his devotion is to be trusted, with Alcott and McNeal hovering about like anxious children to see whether they would be allowed their treat, I did not feel I could rightly refuse. They have both of them served this family for longer than I have been alive – it is only natural that they should have a personal interest in seeing that the name gets its public due, the sort of due they remember from their early years. They have already had to dispense with the public lying in wake of course, as well as any hope of getting him home to Hampshire: the police made it clear very early, and in terms only slightly more discreet, that the body was fit for nothing more than to be placed in the ground as quickly as possible. You should have seen Christopher's face when I told him! It was quite like a lemon, though perhaps it was only the effect of having to ask permission at all. He does not strike me as a man used to doing so.

Poor Victor. I do wonder what happened. I suppose perhaps men of his stature cannot help but tread on a few toes when they are not minded to look where they are going, but if I never knew him to be altruistic, neither did I ever see him do deliberate harm to anyone. For all your warnings, he was not a bad man, nor even a bad husband, in his way. Certainly no worse than I was a wife.

I do not think the same can be said for his brother. For all his supposed helpfulness today, I sense he has his own agenda. Though he has not made his complaint explicit, when he sees me, he can barely keep his civility in check. He seems to resent my very presence in what he rather plainly considers to be HIS house. I suppose he will get used to it, if he remains in England.

In any event, here I sit in the midst of it all, letting the preparations go on around me, absurd though I must find them. Earlier, I actually found one of the maids stood among the wreaths which will not stop arriving, going over each individual white lily to ensure that the yellow stamen had been fully cut out, lest its colour render the arrangement too cheerful! Perhaps I am a poor judge: I've never been able to find anything cheerful about hothouse flowers at the best of times; no amount of colour can take away the fact of their slowly creeping rot, without earth to return to.

Still, I am resigned. Better to have it done as quickly as possible, I think, for everyone's sake. Living like this is enough to try anyone's patience.

You know, I actually heard McNeal squabbling with Mrs Sharpe just now? It was after Christopher had left the kitchen and was inspecting the ballroom with Alcott. I was in the hall when I heard raised voices down below, McNeal protesting Mrs Sharpe's apparent intention to run some errand at this crucial time, and Mrs Sharpe rather fiercely insisting that she must and that McNeal ought to mind her own affairs and leave those of others' alone.

I can't tell you how surprised I was, not only that two such stalwarts would be caught having words where anyone might hear, but because I rather thought they were friends. In all the years I have known Mrs Sharpe, I have only ever seen her lower her hackles for two people: McNeal and poor Joan

Fletcher. That being the case, you can imagine my surprise when McNeal rejoined, in a low voice which I'm sure she didn't realise the stairwell would echo as well as it did: "He used to be your favourite as I recall, once upon a time."

At this, based on solid footsteps which sounded below, Mrs Sharpe returned from where she had been leaving to express her indignation. "Don't confuse pity with affection, Geraldine," was her reply. "I felt sorry for him, and so did you. So might anyone, for such an angry motherless little mite, and I thought I might teach him to put it to better use than some. I can only say now I ought to have known better, and will thank you to leave it at that."

I lingered shamelessly, but no more was said. I can only suppose they were discussing Christopher. I know his mother died when he was a boy, not long after Mrs Sharpe joined the household, and as for his temper, though he wishes to hide it, he does so poorly. I do not pretend to like him, yet for today at least I cannot but be grateful for him, for providing me with a co-host this evening, and one whose very presence is likely to draw at least a little of the gossip upon himself.

I confess I am not sure I should have managed without him. I find now more than ever I struggle to keep focused on matters at hand. My mind wanders and on the smallest provocation is liable to turn to strange thoughts. I am not sure how I could be expected to get through such an event, with all its niceties and expectations of form, when I can barely manage to stay alert in the day to day. I lose track of time, of myself, and I am not sure I can even blame the darkness we presently live in. In a peculiar way I like it: without daylight to illuminate, without time to press, without mirrors to prove my own existence, I drift, and in drifting find the comfort of eternity, the promise of never reaching shore. The physician tells me it is only shock.

Poor McNeal does her best with me, but when she asks what I would like, of food or dress or activity, I find I have no answer to give her.

She wants to fit my room up more suitably: though my old bedroom upstairs has of course been cleaned, the servants are still shy of it and so she has not pressed me to return. Nevertheless, it grates on her that Mrs Bancroft – whomever might happen to bear that name at any given time – should sleep in such a hodgepodge of a set-up, so obviously assembled in haste. She wants new furniture to be ordered, and though a month ago I know I would have agreed emphatically, now the very thought of it is exhausting to the point of pain. I can't even find it in myself to decline the Brucknells' invitation. It sits in the rack, a reminder of "before", taunting me, unanswered. No matter. They will know I cannot come.

I feel I can hold nothing clearly in my head, and then suddenly some inconsequential thing strikes me, lodging there and refusing to be removed. It seems to me then to be of the very greatest importance, and yet even as I feel it with all my heart, I could not for the life of me tell you why.

One such thing is my jewellery box, the one which was robbed. It's a pretty thing, Japanese lacquerware inlaid with gold and mother-of-pearl cranes, but I can't rightly say I gave it much thought prior to Victor's death. It was one beautiful thing among the many in this house, and in my eyes it had no more value than any other. Why, then, should it be that it was that particular box I wanted so badly after Victor's death?

Even after I understood that it had been left in a singularly gory condition – McNeal told me this and yet as she said it, I found I already knew, having most likely caught a glance of it when she ushered me out that morning, half insensible as I was – I found myself insisting with unaccountable vehemence that I must have it.

She offered first to have the remaining contents moved to a clean box, but I could not have it; the very idea seemed to me grotesque. I told her she must bring it down immediately or else I would fetch it myself, and so the good woman went and wiped it down as best she could.

It sits on my dressing table now, the wings of the cranes marked forever with the faint sinister rosiness of that gruesome stain. McNeal averts her eyes from it when she can, and I know I ought to put it away for her sake, but I cannot. When she is gone – and I call on her as little as possible – I find myself opening it and gazing into the velvet depths, not at what lies there but at what does not.

She came in one evening, or morning perhaps, and caught me like that. A powerful shame came over me then, as though she had caught me doing something faintly unclean, but as we looked at one another, she softened noticeably. She made some tactful remark about the many fine gifts my husband had made me, and I averred, for certainly the contents of the box attest to Victor's generosity, with row upon row of precious trinckets lying neatly on a base of red velvet. She seemed somehow to like me better for admiring those baubles, and I realised that she thought me mourning the loss of the man who had given them to me.

I know I coloured in the face of her warmth, ashamed that nothing had been further from my thoughts. Indeed, I had not been looking at any of those fine things but rather at the place where a much less fine thing had lain; in other words, at the empty space where Aunt Virginia's necklace had been, tucked away in an unassuming corner. To this spot, my eye returns again and again. There is something about the velvet there which is almost hypnotic, so that as I stare into it, I almost fancy there is a message there, something of the utmost importance, if only I could decipher it. It pulls and pulls at me until

I must draw back for fear of overbalancing, and look about instinctively for something more useful to occupy my time.

You may raise that arch eyebrow at me and point out that writing letters with no address is a poor interpretation of useful, but I tell you it is not. Though you may never read this, writing it is a comfort. You must know you grounded me like no other person has, and it is that grounding in which I feel myself in dire need of now.

Though I admit I have avoided dwelling on the past as best I could, thinking of you now, you stand before me clearer and more distinct than any person actually present. Indeed – and you will laugh at me – I even went to sit on your sofa the other day. I had it brought from the Young Bess after you'd left. They must have thought me the most eccentric creature to want such a thing, but it has always been a comfort to me to know it was there.

The night I went up was the first time I'd been to see it. It was the night after Victor died and had been such a strange twenty-four hours that by then I was quite turned about. Consequently, the particulars are in consequence so muddled in my mind that I can no longer make them out, but what I do remember with absolute clarity is the feel of that sofa. Even now, it is comforting to think of. I do miss you ever so, even though we parted angrily. I must go down now, but no doubt I will have cause to write again later. I find it a comfort to speak to you, even if you will never hear.

Yours ever with love,
Nora

VI

The coffee house was small and stuffy, the air by the window clammy upon Margaret's cheek. The teacakes were satisfactory, however, and the young waiter amused her. Feeling his eyes upon her – on her dress, too fine for his establishment, and on her hair, pinned up carelessly, evidencing a lack of the maid one might expect to accompany such a dress – she met his curiosity with her own forthright gaze. Her manners, she knew, and knew he felt it too, were at once too fine and somehow never quite fine enough, not scrupling to order for breakfast a meal designated for the afternoon.

Allowing him to watch her, she tore off a piece of teacake and dipped it absently into her cup. Lashings of butter swirled in the milky tea like slick oil, and immediately Margaret regretted her distraction; the continental fashion intended for twice-baked almond biscuits to be dunked in coffee thick as treacle, and was entirely unsuited to the spiced buns of England, soft and delicate under their crisply toasted crumb.

Still, the flavour was not entirely drowned. The candied peel released its tang as Margaret chewed, mingling with the warm cinnamon and lively sultanas, all joined together in their buttery robe of sweet tea-soaked bread, and suddenly she was back there, back in the dark of the tiny shuttered shop at Waterloo, barely able to support her own weight as the shadow of Edna Stovell loomed over her. Back, Margaret supposed, to where she had wanted to go.

He'd been right of course: she hadn't always hated London. Once upon a time, in a life barely remembered, when Chilting village had made up all of the known world and Christopher Bancroft had been nothing but the vague shadow of a younger son living in the big house on its edge, the city had been the sole object of her desire. St Paul's, Piccadilly, the Houses of Parliament; their very names had filled her with a wonder and longing already fading in other areas of life. In a place where names like Paris were rarely uttered and the likes of Marrakesh not at all, London had seemed to contain the very spirit of the world, and she'd dreamed herself there as she went about her chores, discovering the endless marvels of the museums and the libraries, and walking in the glow of the Burlington Arcade, gazing at displays of velvet gloves and Italian shoes, and thinking herself blessed just for the opportunity of looking.

She'd grown up, become a young girl insisting she was a young woman, but even as everything had happened, as Christopher Bancroft had become Kit and then a world unto himself, the city had still been there, a childhood promise waiting for her at the end of the railway line. She'd told him of it as she'd told him everything, and he'd been thrilled to indulge her, bringing her postcards and sketches and books to pore over, and promising to take her as soon as they were married.

On that fateful night, when everything had changed and left so much broken beyond hope of repair, it had sustained her. Hovering on the terrace, peeping out from the rhododendrons at the edge of the glazed library doors, it had warmed her as she shivered with cold and shock. Through the blur of her tears, she'd watched the tall proud shape of him standing by the mantelpiece, glowering at his father in the armchair, responding to his son's argument with a dispassionate glance.

She could name the precise moment Kit had spotted her, and the one immediately following, when she'd realised he was not going to open the doors, to introduce her as the woman he loved and intended to marry. His expression had remained entirely unchanged as their eyes met, and he'd given the faintest shake of his head, intimating to her to stay where she was, out of sight and out of consideration.

She'd hidden in the bushes until the father chose to turn in, until the library was dark, the fire banked. Then Kit had appeared from around the edge of the house, a coat under his arm.

"You can't stay here," he'd said, once she'd explained she could not go home. "You'll have to go to London. Take the first train."

In the darkness, she had not been able to read his expression, but the purse he'd pressed into her hand had suggested that her sudden appearance had told him enough.

"This should be enough to keep you amused for a while."

"Until you come and marry me?" It had been the only question in her head, the sound of it almost crowding out the sudden flex of his arm across her shoulders.

"Yes," he'd said, just a heartbeat beyond the automatic. "Of course. It shouldn't be long. I'll bring my trip forward."

She'd known he meant his grand tour, so often discussed and planned, on which she would join him as a matter of course, because he loved her. And just because he loved her, he'd promised they would begin it with a week in London.

Before they'd parted, he'd pulled her close for a moment. "Don't worry," he'd murmured. "Everything will turn out well. You'll see."

It had been enough. Young and infatuated, it had been easy to believe not only in him but in the world. As the first rays of early twilight had broken across the fields, she'd set out with a full heart and a spirit giddy with love.

She'd kept them under her coat like hot coals warding off the cold air of the platform. The inside of the carriage had proved colder still though, and when finally the whistle had blown, the surly glance of the conductor had told her what she'd already known: her coat did not fit, being meant for a woman taller and stronger than Margaret, and every minute the heat was leaking out through the gaps she could not fill. The conductor had looked at her ticket once, and then a second time, making sure she saw.

As he'd left her, the first houses had begun to emerge through the fading night: squat, cramped dwellings with mean little yards backing onto the railway line. Raw-boned dogs had barked on the ends of rusting chains as little girls in grubby pinafores appeared carrying pails for raggedy chickens, watched by the rheumatic eye of an ill-favoured old goat.

Margaret had felt the dream breaking up then, but still she managed to hold the pieces of it, those gilded imaginings, until the train clanked into the station. Stepping onto the platform, she'd stood beneath the arches of Waterloo and beheld a city as far from her fairy-tale imaginings as it could be: a city real and ugly and never-ending.

Around her, her fellow passengers had poured off the train with hardly an inch between them. They were like the city they flocked to, grey and unfathomable, intent on their own business, with no thought for one another and less care. They had hurried off with their backs to her, and yet she'd felt there could not be one smile, one gentle feeling among them as they streamed out through the exits of that vast, porous cavern they called a station to join the tumult she could see beyond.

Impossible to imagine how one could find a single soul amid so much chaos, she had thought, and once she had thought it, she could not stop. The weight of the purse in her pocket had become oppressive suddenly: enough to survive in this place for a time, for time enough until she forgot her way back, and then who would know, in this place where no soul would ever be found again? Because in that place of relentless reality, it would be impossible to hold on to any shred of fantasy; the idea that in a world like this even a younger son would really marry a village girl. How could he, when he'd never know where to find her?

In fairy tales, a heroine might die of a broken heart. Reality was infinitely crueller, however, and so Margaret had not died. However much she might have wished to collapse where she stood, dragged down by the unbearable weight of the purse until the hurrying feet of the world found it convenient to crush her, self-preservation would not let her. It was a strength she had not reckoned with until that moment – less the will to live in victory than an absolute refusal to die defeated.

It was that which had dragged her across the tide to an empty apple crate, and then, when the responsible clerk appeared like a genie with his fist raised, to the darkest alcove in view. There she'd collapsed in her grief, slumped amid the roar of the trains and the whistles of their conductors, the smell of the smoke and the horses and the endless people washing over her, hour after hour, a fallen wretch insufficiently interesting to make it worth the moving on. There she'd remained until the glass panes of the ceiling had begun to darken through their crusts of grime and pigeon shit, and grief became a less immediate force than hunger. Sitting up, she'd spotted through the thinning crowd the bustling shape of Mrs Stovell.

Whether it was the board she carried, chalk scrawl advertising the best spiced buns on the South Bank, or the twinkle in the good woman's eye, the only spark of warmth to be had in all of that frigid cavern, Margaret had not cared to wonder. She had simply risen in a daze and scuttled across to follow the board or the twinkle or both, and when the board had been carried inside, the twinkle vanishing behind the single shuttered window, she had experienced a misery so great that the howl it produced had cost her the last of her strength.

The next thing she knew, she'd been within the darkened shop telling the gist of her story between enormous bites of a stale bun. The room had been tiny, with room only for the counter which during the day was piled high with sweet, sticky buns, and the squat stool Mrs Stovell sold them from. It was there that Margaret had spent one of the most valuable hours of her life.

Chewing with a relish only hunger can know, Margaret had told her story willingly, as though the telling would set her free. She'd spoken of all that which could not now be undone, and as the words had left her realised that, even in her anguish, there was a thrill in being unable to turn back. Even if the blow had weakened her, even if she stood on the lowest rung, she was there and she was her own: the future was hers to make.

Even now, a full decade later, with clothes and manners and experiences the village girl could barely have imagined, Margaret still remembered that fierce certainty, felt the ghost of its blaze flicker in her breast. And not just in her breast: she had believed herself to be walking aimlessly, thinking vaguely that perhaps a trip to Liberty's was in order, but evidently some part of her had had other ideas.

Drifting around the bulk of Spitalfields, the human stench of Shoreditch reached her even through the sweet rot of bruised apples and fallen cabbage leaves which permeated the market. It tasted bitter on her tongue, twisted her mouth into an ugly shape, but she made no move to turn back. There would be no point: evidently she must see it – see it and remember.

Behind the doors of the shuttered bun shop, Edna Stovell, rightly judging Margaret too foolhardy to get on the morning train home and forget her little adventure altogether, had taken it upon herself to furnish the girl with an education. She'd told Margaret first of a boarding house her cousin ran, in Shoreditch but respectable, and almost as cheap as the ones which were not, making sure Margaret memorised the address and directions. Then she'd spoken at some length of the proper way to deal with unwanted advances by those who would not care whether a girl was respectable or not, of that particular balance of confidence and cocky good humour which would engender their respect while not threatening their pride, and of the signs that it was time to simply run – correct management of such instances, the good woman had emphasised, with a gravity which made Margaret suspect she spoke from experience, was of the utmost importance. A single misstep could spell ruin or worse.

Mrs Stovell had then discussed the question of money, and the work which would bring it, crushing in the mentioning of it any hope that she herself might have work to offer. Without reference or introduction, Mrs Stovell had said, it would be difficult to secure a steady position. Margaret must therefore content herself with day work, in the factories at first, but once she had saved enough to buy stock, she might consider moving onto flower selling to see if it would suit her better. An industrious girl could buy a dozen bunches of whatever might be in at Farringdon or Covent Garden – primroses, carnations, moss roses and lily of the valley in their seasons, and hothouse violets when the winter cold forbade any flower blooming naturally – and with a few gathered leaves and a ha'penny for paper could make up eighteen or twenty posies. These might be sold at a penny a piece on the streets of Highgate or St John's Wood, to gentlemen for their ladies, or to ladies for their parlours, pretty balms on nagging consciences. In that manner, the energetic worker might earn enough for bread and shelter, and even put a little by to cover those days when the weather was too wet to sell. And, of course, as Margaret established herself in her new home, she might take on work for those neighbours a rung or two up from herself, as a charwoman or taking in laundry and mending work, or anything else she might have skill enough to persuade others to part with their money for.

At the end of the lecture, Margaret, stiff with the armour of her determination, had taken out a coin to pay for her dinner with fingers still sticky from the eating of it. It was then that Mrs Stovell had chuckled, and in it had been a note of sorrow which Margaret would remember in the nights to follow.

"You're an honest girl," the baker woman had said. "There's not many round here as'll thank you for it, but you're an honest girl nonetheless."

Pulling out a bit of old newspaper, she'd wrapped a second bun, shaking her head sharply as Margaret's pride had opened her mouth to protest.

"And now I'll thank you to allow me the honest thing in return, and give you a second into the bargain, for they are all hard as a ram's skull now and not fit to be sold at full price. Keep it for your breakfast – you'll need a solid start. And you can come back here of an evening and get another two for the same – you'll find it works out about the price of bread, with a good deal more nourishment in them – and I won't hear a word about it."

Seeing Margaret's sharp chin lifted in planned protest, she'd softened. "I've a daughter myself," she'd added. "And I cannot pray that someone will do for her what I will not do myself."

It occurred to Margaret now, for the first time, that she had never thought to ask about Mrs Stovell's daughter.

Before her, the rooming house looked as it had always done, a tall narrow construction of bricks the colour of horse piss, its roof slumping forward like a crooked widow on her cane. Margaret gazed up at it, taking in the same weather-worn door which had greeted her that night, as the same windows, their casements grey with the same neglect, looked hungrily on. From the gutter, the same odour rose to harry her nostrils, the potato peels rotting in the same human filth, and out of the corner of her eye, she saw as she had tried not to see then the same sunken-eyed women, lurking in the same doorways.

Within the house, Margaret had no doubt that the smallest attic room still crouched beneath the ramshackle roof, the same damp patches spreading over the same iron bed with the same mattress, flattened still further by another ten years of desperate girls. Descendants of the same yellow-toothed rats no doubt still scurried, their chief accomplishment the further enlargement of the same rat hole in which Margaret had spent the better part of an hour nerving herself to hide the purse, whose weight seemed to her then snare and saviour both.

Sitting in that meagre room, the walls bowing in around her as though fit to cave, Margaret had begun her London career. In the washstand on legs so rickety that it must be approached like a nervy colt over the loose floorboards to avoid calamity, she had washed her face in the cold water, scrubbing her wool stockings as hard as she dared before hanging them over the fireplace – little more than a hole in the chimney breast and smoking with a pittance of coal.

In the cold grey of morning, the city had proved every bit the incomprehensible warren it had promised to be, and Margaret had found herself setting to with the vigour of one who must make the best of a thing or else drown in it.

Beginning the day with a stale currant bun washed down with tea from the downstairs tea urn, impossibly both too weak and powerfully bitter, she'd set out through the drizzle to make her fortune. At the factories, she'd taken what day work she could get, boxing matches or sorting rags for pulping as she sat among the other women, listening to their gossip and opinions, storing them carefully away to be distilled for usable advice that evening as she'd sat in room.

On days when there was no work to be had, she'd wandered the streets until her feet blistered and her head spun, watching, learning. Sometimes, if her head began to swim too much to take anything in, she'd found she could charm certain of the chestnut vendors into letting her have those too burned and shrivelled to sell, and then she would sit on a bench to peel them, the delicious heat burning her fingers as she relished the taste of salty char and sweet nutty flesh. As she ate, she'd watch the passers-by, seeing who bowed to whom and trying to work out why.

The flower girls in particular had interested her, and sometimes she would follow ones of her own age at a distance, watching how they changed their manner for each potential customer – playful with the younger gentlemen, sweet with the older, and with the ladies pitiable, though never without spirit. One day soon she would join their ranks, she'd promised herself. Then at least she would be out of the choking dust and smoke of the factories, but first she must learn the trade as best she could, to avoid squandering money on stock she did not yet know how to use.

Each day would finish with a walk to the tiny bun shop at Waterloo. There she would help close up the shop in exchange for finishing the dregs in Mrs Stovell's tea urn with the first of her two stale buns, and if there wasn't much to talk about between them, the company of a friendly face would make up the lack.

In the evenings she would sit upon her bed in the attic room, counting out her earnings and stashing what she could beneath floorboards and loose skirting, keeping her back to the grimy dormer window and those women in the doorways far below. The window was too high up, and too opaque with cobwebs and filth, to see much out of in any event, but the knowledge of those women, of their very existence so close to her own, had repelled her, frightened her in ways she did not fully understand.

The bolt on the door had comforted her, as had the leathery cry of the landlady denouncing whichever of her tenants had had the lack of foresight to come home drunk, loudly denying the wretch even the scant comfort of a bed until the cold night had chased the sin from his blood. Or hers, as the case might be. When she'd heard it, Margaret had found herself torn between gratitude that one such as Mrs Ruskin stood between her and all the villainy of the world, and pity for the poor soul she condemned. Underneath it all had been a profound sadness with something of the incomprehensible note inspired by the women in the doorways within it, but Mrs Ruskin's raucous cry had all but drowned it out, allowing Margaret to sleep in something akin to peace.

The cry which shook the house now was not Mrs Ruskin's. As Margaret listened, there came from within the roar not of that old dragon, whose fiery breath alone had guarded the last remains of that respectability which had led Edna Stovell to recommend it, but a different sort of shriek altogether. It culminated in a broad, echoing clatter, sounding uncomfortably like someone being thrown down bare wooden stairs, before the door was wrenched open with such force it was a wonder it did not come off its hinges.

Margaret watched in horror as a man emerged, his long face twisted with rage and effort as he dragged the struggling woman out onto the stoop by her greasy yellow hair, her dress too threadbare to stand up to such rough handling. Her face was gaunt, with that pinched look which speaks of a hunger never sated – and a determination to carry on regardless. She snarled and cursed, contorting wildly – fighting, Margaret understood with a start, not to get away from her assailant but to remain within his house.

"No rent, no roof, and you know it!" The landlord heaved at the woman as she clung to the dilapidated door frame, spitting like an angry cat.

Margaret found herself unable to tear her eyes away as the struggle went on.

Finally, the landlord got his knee into the woman's back and, with a final groan of effort, dislodged her, sending her flying into the street.

"And good riddance, ye shameless whore!" he shouted after her as she landed in the gutter. "No rent, no roof, Elsie Smith, and don't you forget it!"

Without so much as pausing for breath, the fallen woman picked herself up onto her knees, twisting around to scream back at him with all the impotent, murderous hate of her soul: "If you paid me like everyone else, I could pay you your bloody rent, you ugly bastard!"

Her only reply was the slam of the door, hard enough to rattle the windows in their frames, as the landlord disappeared back into the dingy depths of the house Margaret had once called home.

She could not remember precisely the moment at which it had become so. In the course of six weeks, her life had changed so completely, her eye become fixed so firmly on tomorrow, that she'd barely remembered yesterday, let alone what had come before. New dreams had taken the place of old, and she had not compared them, only let them fill her head and draw her forward, day after day, hardly noticing as life shifted around her, the yellow house becoming home and the miserly bed quite her own.

The instant at which they had stopped being so, however, *that* she recalled, in all its abrupt and colourful detail.

She'd been on her way to the bun shop, the station clock chiming six overhead. Experienced now, she'd woven through the thronging crowds without a second thought, eager to share the excitement which threatened to bubble over at any moment. She had spent the morning at Farringdon watching the flower trade, and from there had gone to Green Park to see what greenery might be had, think it all over properly and finally conclude that, all in all, she could well be ready to try her hand at street selling.

Running through her plans for the hundredth time, to check for soundness and simply to enjoy the feel of them, she had repeated to herself where she would sell, how she would combine her flowers to stand out to their best effect, what time of day and what class of patron would be most suited to her style. The station and its denizens had floated away, irrelevant, until a single shout had brought them back even as it had dismissed them entirely, itself suddenly the only thing in the world: "Meg! Where in God's name have you been?"

She had looked up to see him striding towards her through the crowd, a figure imposing even at nineteen, yet all she had been able to see was the boyish peevishness of his expression, fondness bubbling back up as naturally as if she had never so much as wished to send it away. She had smiled up helplessly even as he'd frowned.

"Where have you been?" he had demanded again, once he was close enough to take her by the arm. "Six weeks and not a single word, not one hotel knowing your description. How on earth did you expect me to find you? I thought—"

His hand on her arm had squeezed too tight, anger wrapped around fright until she had kissed away the need for it. And that had been that. A lifetime brought into being for want of a letter, gone in instant. They'd taken the first of the waiting hansom cabs and left six weeks behind, like so much dust in the street.

Margaret had never looked back for it, had averted her eyes even, yet some part of her had always known it remained always where she had left it, waiting. It seemed to her suddenly to be lying there in the very gutter, mingling with the filth in the gutter which stained the fallen woman's skirts, and all at once Margaret could no longer look away. She watched as the woman looked about her for the least awful place to push herself into standing, or perhaps only for something to throw at the door closed so rudely upon her. Instead, she came upon the toe of Margaret's boot.

Margaret loved her boots. They were Italian leather, bought in Milan that first year, the first purchase she had ever made by herself, for herself. No asking permission, no worrying over her purse, she had simply seen them and loved them and so she had bought them, the cobbler bowing, calling her *signora* and taking her fully for the lady she wished so badly to be.

Now soft and supple with wear, Margaret was acutely aware that her boots were worth more ten years old and standing in the dirt than every item the woman before her wore taken together when new.

The woman, too, was plainly aware of it. The fall, or perhaps the door frame, had cut her across the cheekbone, and the long thin gash dripped red into the gutter. Slowly, as if she would rather not, her gaze left the boots and travelled up, over the wool coat, the velvet glove, the emerald pin, until finally, most reluctantly of all, it came to Margaret's face staring down at her.

Whether it was the expression the woman found there which defeated her or something within her own self, Margaret had no wish to know. The woman hung her head, returning to Margaret's boots.

"Begging your pardon, ma'am," she mumbled. "I'm never normally late; he knows I'm not, only my little one's dreadful poorly and them doctors need paying, and—"

The woman went on speaking, but Margaret no longer heard her over the rushing which filled her ears. Reaching into her purse for a coin to protect herself with, she found herself staring at the reflection they cast in the unwashed windowpane.

Framed in bare, worm-eaten wood, they made a social tableau worthy of a Dickens plate, the grand lady unable to conceal her revulsion at the poor wretch shrinking at her feet, afraid to even lift her head, aware that the mere fact of her existence was enough to give offence.

The picture could not show that Margaret barely saw the woman on the ground, that the true source of her revulsion was the coin between her own gloved fingers and the knowledge, ineffaceable, of precisely how much bread and rent it could buy, down to the ha'penny. It burned her, and she thrust it at the woman, who stared up at her with such a confusion of hopeless pride, of resentful gratitude, that the recognition of it almost made Margaret cry aloud.

"Attic room, rat hole behind the dresser," she heard herself snap, a sharp disgusted sound, more to purge her own past than bolster this woman's future. Tossing the coin down, she turned before the clatter fully died away, the echoes against the slimy cobbles pursuing her in her escape.

Margaret no longer heard them: her only thought was to find a bottle of gin, the strong kind with the bathtub aftertaste, to soothe her nerves and help her while away the day. Then she could pretend she did not know exactly where she would be by evening, this evening like no other, when her lover would lay his only brother to rest.

VII

The house cast its glow onto the street beyond as the guests streamed in, exactly as for a ball. Only the crêpe-covered wreath upon the door suggested the grimmer nature of the event, and the glossy black noses of the horses waiting discreetly at the side of the house. Glancing into the dim alley which served for the yard, Ritter spotted twin pairs of gleaming black eyes above the muzzles, and behind them another and another, for a total of fourteen pairs of enormous blinkered eyes staring out from the darkness, each matched with a pair of sleek ears above, swivelling without ever quite matching up. A hearse and six then, Ritter worked out, to be followed by two coaches and four carrying the choicest guests.

Ritter, wishing to arrive after the majority of the guests had settled in, thumped on the front of the coach to slow it. He leaned back in his seat to allow Annabelle a view over him, and together they watched the confusion of characters who would make up the funerary procession.

Wandsmen, their long scarves about their shoulders and weepers trailing from their hats, held their black-draped boards as they ambled about, attempting to stay warm. They bowed their heads towards each other, all the better to ignore the mutes, those men without ceremonial duties, whose only purpose was to make up the numbers in the best mourning wear they could afford. A little apart, the featherman guarded his great tray of ostrich plumes from the mud and the nibbling mouths of horses alike, in order that it remain pristine when he carried it aloft at the head of the march. Atop the steps of the hearse perched the undertaker himself, the ringmaster, waiting for instruction from the house. He kept his beady eye on every one of his actors, threat and promise both, should any man threaten the smooth running of the act and cost him even a penny of his fee.

No doubt about it, Ritter thought, handing his wife down from their carriage: the pageantry of Victor Bancroft's send-off was certainly going to rival the drama of his death.

In the ballroom, the chandeliers dazzled, reflecting off the glittering crowd. It was amazing, Ritter thought, how spectacularly people dressed entirely in black could contrive to sparkle; all it seemed to require was sufficient purse and a complete lack of personal interest in the man who had died. Salacious curiosity did not count of course.

He watched as now the lady with the faceted onyx headpiece, now the gentleman with the brocade waistcoat straining at the buttons wandered, as if by accident, towards the heaps of lilies and black ribbons which hid the coffin beneath. There they paused, imagining themselves to be giving the impression of paying their solemn respects; perhaps imagining that they truly were. In the minutes before they were displaced by the next set, they stared openly at the polished oak, as though they could see through to the mangled body within, find the answer to the question which had Scotland Yard itself at a loss.

Officially at a loss that was. Ritter did not like to promote his hunches to theories until they had earned it.

Officially, therefore, his presence this evening was purely social, a mark of respect for the victim whose murder he was in charge of solving. He'd even brought Annabelle, in case there should be any doubt: no one thought twice about a man with a wife, especially a pretty one, and Annabelle could usefully bend anyone's ear with her pleasant conversation on the folkish history of England, delivered with the total earnestness of the academic mind.

As intended, they had arrived late, just as the other guests had settled into the merriness of their mourning, no longer keeping one eye on the door to see the new arrivals. A quiet word in the butler's ear ensured that the names of Detective Inspector and Mrs Edmund Ritter would not be projected across the crowd in the typical stately fashion, and so the Ritters were allowed to arrive unobtrusively, tucking themselves in discreetly among more illustrious mourners.

It was the two figures at the end of the room who interested Ritter the most. Side by side, they were handsome in their proportional height and matching black, solemnly greeting the steady stream of curious faces which passed before them. The casual onlooker might take them for a pair, but Ritter knew better. With long experience in the minutiae of people, he saw the space between them, tenuous and wary. Their gestures not of individuals working together, he thought, but rather of two people each performing the same task while pretending the other was not there at all.

And yet, Bancroft was not fully master of himself: the side-long glances he cast his widowed sister-in-law were brief but unmistakable, though they seemed to be not at the woman herself but the place she stood in. Watching him, Ritter found himself wondering – not for the first time – what had really been in that telegram. It might be a coincidence of course, but in his experience it so rarely was. He wished the Belgians would hurry up.

A footman with a tray passed by, distracting Ritter, and when he turned back, Bancroft was alone. Ritter hardly had time to look about when the call rang out, urgent and imperious from across the room: "Inspector Ritter!"

He turned to see the widow approaching through the crowd, bearing down on them with an intentness which impressed Ritter with a sudden impulse to get out of the way.

Black skirts stood out behind her as her pale eyes glittered in the light of the chandelier, and Ritter found himself remaining where he was purely out of the knowledge that there was nowhere to run: the room was packed and already the widow was upon them.

"Mrs Bancroft," he began, "allow me to introduce my wife—"

"Mrs Ritter, of course."

The widow's neck struck Ritter as just a fraction too long as she craned it in Annabelle's direction. Annabelle freed herself from his arm to curtsy, but even separated he could feel his wife's nerves, already drawn over the sheer grandeur into which she had been dragged, now rattled further by the concentration of their hostess's attentions. Nevertheless, he did not divine what form her anxiety would take until it was too late.

"Mrs Bancroft, do accept our condolences," Annabelle began, and from the way she clutched convulsively at her shawl, Ritter knew his wife was fully aware that there she should have ended. As the widow looked at her with those strange colourless eyes, however, he saw Annabelle's mouth open in spite of herself, her mind retreating to the safety of her beloved bookshelves.

"My husband tells me your people are from Bridde," she said. "A most fascinating legend. Many out-of-the-way places have their peculiar and often quite frightening tales of course, but the Beast of Bridde Place is considered chilling even beyond the ordinary. Most monsters of the sort are equipped with a key, you see, a grove to stay away from after sunset, a posy to hang above the door, or some such. But in the Bridde tale, there is none. The maiden is simply marked from birth and her fate plays out accordingly. Even in the folksong, the narrator makes no attempt at rescue but accepts his sweetheart's demise as a foregone conclusion, mourning her even before the tragedy has occurred. You know the song of course, 'The Bridde Lament'?"

Annabelle sang softly, tunelessly, with the wide eyes of one horrified to find that she was doing so, and yet unable to remember how to stop.

Farewell my bird of Bridde
Fly well my Bridde lass
The Beast appears behind you
To bring you to the Pass
He stalks behind the shadows
He waits beneath the stair
And coming he will drive you
Into the calling air.

As she mouthed the lyrics, she looked at her husband with such abject misery that if Ritter had not already been looking for an opening to bring the awkwardness to an end, he would have been compelled to begin immediately.

As it was, he was ahead of his wife in wishing to save her from her own marvellous brain, and as soon as the final sylla-ble had left her lips, he forced a chuckle. "My wife is a great adherent of Lady Wilde, you see," he offered in apology, then realised he needn't have bothered: as Annabelle finished, the widow had already turned from her, with the utterly blank expression of one having chosen not to hear.

Instead, Ritter found himself suddenly the whole focus of her attention, with every bit of that rapacious intensity with which she had first fixed him from across the room.

"I've been meaning to come and see you," she said, bending her head towards him in a curve which seemed to involve the whole length of her back. "What news? I know not everything can be put into letters, particularly if it is not definitive, but I am sure that by now you must have something."

There was something feverish in the way she spoke, eyes shining as her hand eagerly found his arm.

Ritter cut her off with a shake of the head. "I'm afraid not, madam," he said, sorry to be unable to give a widow, even a peculiar one, better news. "I can assure you that in the event of any developments, you will be the first to know. I will even call personally if it would give you comfort—"

Her hand on his arm distracted him enough to glance down. From the gentle pressure of a woman's hand, it had increased steadily as he spoke until it might have been an iron talon clamped there. When he looked back at her, the widow's eyes were brilliant with a fanatical element which alarmed him.

"But you must have *something*!" she burst out, all discretion forgotten in a rush of passion. "There must be some clue you've overlooked, something which will lead you to it? It was my aunt's, you know, precious to no one but myself. It is most important that I have it back."

She was rambling now, and Ritter was grateful when Annabelle broke in, bewildered. "Surely it is the apprehension of your husband's assailant which concerns you, madam?"

There was something in the way the widow stared at her then, fixedly and with such blank incomprehension that it made Annabelle shrink back, and Ritter forced to quash the impulse to step in front of his wife as needlessly provocative.

It was too long before the eyes began to move again, to flick towards a laughing woman and follow a hurrying footman across the room. Ritter watched as something in that strange hard face drew together, so that he could note the precise moment at which Mrs Bancroft recalled her position, and then herself. It seemed to send her reeling.

"Of – of course," she managed to get out, as Ritter reached instinctively to steady her. She all but leaped from his touch.

"You must excuse me – I'm afraid I'm not myself. Pray do excuse me…"

Ritter could only bow in astonishment as she turned and fled, not into the crowded ballroom but out of it, through the double doors which led into the depths of the house.

~

The merriment chased Nora down the passageway. The clamour of voices bouncing off the marble floors, the click of two hundred heels or more stepping in counterpoint, the subtle swish of the service doors as footmen hurried to and fro, the sweat of all those people and the perfumes of the guests, the odour of plates arriving and plates left to stand, all came together in a pell-mell of human amusement, entirely indistinguishable from the balls she had hosted as a young married woman. The only difference was in herself: then she had been intent on doing her duty; now she could barely remember what it was.

Movement caught her eye and made her pause and turn to a parlour door left ajar. Within, a gap in the heavy mourning drapes exposed a sliver of glass doors leading onto the terrace, the cool silver of the reflection cutting through the haze of the house. As she approached, it threw back at her her own silhouette, her face no more than an inky blankness against the lamplight of the corridor.

Only when her nose was inches from the glass, close enough to smell the night beyond, did she notice the rapid pulse of her heart. For a moment, she tried to remember why that should be, but then the frail panes trembled in their painted frames as her knuckles curled about the brass handle, clenching around the chill seeping through from the other side. She pushed down and, just like that, she was in the cool night air, the terrace before her as the darkness stretched all about her, as though it were the very simplest of things.

It was the first time she had been outside since Victor died, but more than that, she realised standing there, it was very likely the first time she had been outside at night since she'd married him. Quick steps from front door to carriage and back again hardly counted, under the coddling portico with its blazing lanterns and attentive faces waiting to shield one from a single drop of rain, the faintest puff of breeze. It left the darkness one could see from within a barren thing, flat and sterile, so that, standing in those little pockets of protective artifice, it was hard to remember that there was such a thing as Night at all. Yet here she was, waiting patiently in a Kensington garden.

A faded moon shone down, casting the lawn in a thin silvery light and leaving the shrubbery in darkness. At the bottom of the garden, a grand old column of yew presided, the wind shivering through its pliant branches as Nora stepped out, whistling as through in greeting.

Nora drew a breath, tasting the smells: the freshness of the grass, even in its dormant season, tempered the faint tang of the newly fallen leaves, and underneath it the rich dampness of mouldering soil, soaked with the morning's rain. From within the branches of the yew an owl hooted, sending the tiny souls in the undergrowth rustling for safety. Through the crisp air came the swish of a bat in its darting chase, and the silence of the fox was betrayed by a single scrape of claw on stone. Beneath the crust of earth, roots quested even now, reaching into soil turned by the worms, inch by laborious inch. If it was strange to think that such a place could be in central London, how much stranger that central London could exist in such a place as this.

Nora's eyes fluttered closed, opening in time to see the traces of her exhaled breath, touched silver by the moonlight.

It floated before her, an undulating path of her own vitality drifting down into the quickened darkness beyond. Without thought she followed it, drawn by those impulses which whispered on the breeze, calling on her to run, to jump, to scream into a night which belonged to her.

It was with surprise that she felt beneath her sole not the soft floor of ancient forest but the stone of the veranda, carefully lain and utterly unyielding. The sensation brought her back to herself, girdling her feelings with something like relief as she saw before her not the ancient forests of England but her own back garden.

The smoke of the city tickled her nostrils as her eyes adjusted to the moonlight, bringing into focus the lunging monkey puzzle and the dandy rhododendrons. In their ancestral memory lived an entirely different night than that which stirred in the creeping ivy and the scrappy hawthorn, and yet here they all grew happily together, joined in this place by the ingenuity of man and a tidy square of his lawn. Even the yew, ancient and venerable, was covered in the acrid city stench, smoke and soot clinging to every needle.

All around Nora rose the evidence of human existence, driving out the rest, until she could not imagine what had caused her back to tense like that, her knees to flex ready for the spring, full of a bone-deep understanding too absurd to be grasped: voices floating out from the house, increasingly bolstered by champagne, combining with the creak and stamp and whinny of the waiting procession massed just on the other side of the garden wall. Even as whatever knowledge, whatever strength had been momentarily within her grasp drained away, she was comforted. Here, in her own little garden, she was safe; here, humanity would hear her if she called.

Lulled by the thought, she descended the stone steps as the final echoes of tension ebbed away. A path of hard-packed sand ran around the edge of the lawn, separating the grass from anything the gardeners wished to grow taller. In the silver unreality of the moonlight, she followed it round, letting her limbs fall into a gentle, lilting gate which drove all but peaceful emptiness from her mind.

It was at about the three-quarter mark, coming to the corner where the yew held court, that she noticed it; realising by slow degrees not what was there but what was not. A shadow of impulse reformed, whispering even as she walked to listen, listen beneath the racket of the world, *listen*, LISTEN, until finally she could not but obey.

Beneath the mighty tree, she listened beyond the clamour of civilisation and heard nothing. Hidden in those great boughs, the oldest in the garden, the largest and home to the most creatures, she found only silence, deep and fearful, the breath drawn before the scream.

Reflexively, she stopped there, steeping herself in the silence as her muscles tensed and her nerves flexed on instinct, reaching out beyond her to probe the darkness for the source of such fright. And there it was: hidden in the undergrowth, as close to the base of the tree as size would allow, there crouched a nightmare, a confusion of pain and fear muddled into snarling, unkempt fury straining to pounce at its source, restrained only by its own lack of comprehension, its own inability to see what that might be. Then it found Nora. The threat roared out in every direction, yet as Nora turned in fright to face her dreadful assailant, she found there was nothing to be seen.

She stared into the darkness, feeling the chill on her neck as the darkness stared back. Stillness stretched around them, Nora and the nameless, faceless thing screaming silently for her blood, reaching into eternity and then broken in no time at all.

"Nora, is that you down there? What in God's name are you doing?"

The call came from the veranda, shattering the silence until it seemed impossible that it could ever have held anything at all. Catching her breath, Nora turned to see Christopher Bancroft storming across the lawn towards her.

"What on earth are you doing out here?" he demanded, approaching her. "I've been looking everywhere for you! We're about to set out – come and see us off."

"I…" Nora faltered, mired in her own confusion. The anger his demands inspired in her bubbled up, hot and potent. She wanted to fight him, but equally she wanted a witness, some-one else to look and to *feel*, to know that she was not mad.

She turned back towards the yew "Do you see…?" she began, pointing vaguely, but of course there was nothing there.

"See what? You're tired. Come back inside."

He did not bother to hide his impatience, nor wait for a reply as he took hold of her arm and led her across the lawn. Nora had no choice but to follow, stumbling in her skirts as she twisted to look back over her shoulder. On the dewy grass, the moonlight turned the tip of the yew into a black arrow, pointing them back towards the veranda.

It was as she felt the stone of the first step under her sole that the wind picked up. With a sudden gust, the yew shud-dered, needles shivering together on its spiny branches, so that all at once the black arrow on the grass came apart, a thousand pinpricks of silvery green piercing it until the edges frayed and the centre dissolved, revealing it to be no arrow at all.

Nora froze, no longer mistress of herself. Two steps ahead, Christopher, still dragging her by the arm, did not anticipate her sudden immobility and by the force of his own momentum was yanked stumbling back down towards her. She heard noth-ing of his protests, her senses fixed entirely on the flickering shadows. There, where the shivering dark met the shimmering light, empty eyes burned in the night. They held her, and she could not look away.

The terror came in a flood, washing away her petty fears of angry darkness in the swell. But it was the dread siren call which truly chilled her, that awful compulsion too much for any poor nursery promise to quash. It was all she had though; with Christopher's shouts echoing after her, Nora did as she had long ago promised she would – and ran.

VIII

Ritter strolled through the deserted streets, hat pulled down and hands thrust deep into his pockets. Occasionally, a cab passed him, the driver pulling up his horse invitingly in the hope of business, but Ritter waved them off. The night air was bracing, his pace comfortable as he passed from the light of one gas lamp to the next, and he needed time for a good mull.

From a curious beginning the evening had only grown more peculiar, until he could only be glad that Annabelle had gone home early. The widow's outburst had unsettled his wife exceedingly, so that even when he had explained it away as the behaviour of a woman reeling from tremendous shock, overwhelmed by the obligations she was reputedly ill-equipped to meet at the best of times, her mind grabbing instinctively to some lesser piece in order to avoid being swept away by the devastating whole, Annabelle had nodded, and agreed, but even after several slugs of wine had been unable to stop eyeing his arm, still tender where the widow had gripped it.

It was true that Ritter had not expected that, but then fear was known to give a brute strength even to the most feeble, and if ever he'd seen a frightening murder it was this. Just the memory of the corpse, the way the limbs had been pulled from their sockets and all the senseless *tearing*, was apt to put him on edge if he thought about it too long. He suspected embarrassment at her own *faux pas* had played a part in his wife's reluctance to remain, but whatever the reason, he had not been entirely sorry to escort her from that particular house. Neither had he been quite ready to leave himself however. There was something there, he sensed, some clue, as the widow had said, just waiting to be unearthed. It called to him, cajoling him, so once he had seen Annabelle home safe, he had asked Jackson to turn the carriage back towards the Bancroft residence. This time, however, rather than being deposited by the front door, Ritter had got out at a darkened corner a little way away, from which he could amble, easily and to the interest of absolutely no one, into the narrow yard which lay alongside the house.

~

When he'd arrived, the waiting procession was still milling about, horses tossing their plumed heads impatiently as wands-men and mutes stood thicker than ever, thin coats pulled tight about them as they stamped their feet and puffed on their threadbare gloves. Off to one side, a fire now burned in a rust-ing metal grate, but it was a puerile thing, entirely inadequate against the vast chill of the night, its feeble flames hardly worth the fuel they ate.

Nevertheless, the men clustered around it, staying at the front of the yard and shunning entirely the other end, though it was both warmer and more sheltered. In an instant, Ritter saw both why it was warmer there and why the shivering men did not so much as glance in that direction: at the end of the yard was the service entrance, a large, plain door set in the una-dorned stonework of the side wall, immediately beyond which lay the kitchen. The door was open now, pumping the auxiliary heat of the iron stove into the freezing night air – and in the doorway stood its keeper. Silhouetted by the light within, the figure rose out of the darkness like a mountain, only the faint glow of a pipe slung between unseen lips to suggest that it might possess such a thing as a face. Nevertheless, Ritter recognised her immediately as Dorothy Sharpe, the Bancroft cook.

He did not begrudge the woman a quiet smoke after hours working to feed all those insatiable mouths above. Equally, he did not blame the men around him for giving her a wide berth. Something about her encouraged nothing less – something less to do with her size and more with those steely eyes, cold as the blade of the knife which even now Ritter's mind saw gripped in that mighty fist.

It was not a universal impression, however, or else some men simply became impervious, through exposure, or their own arrogance. This was the only explanation Ritter could imagine as the shape which had been approaching rapidly down the internal corridor brushed past her as it stepped out into the yard, materialising into none other than Christopher Bancroft.

He looked about furiously but evidently did not find what he was looking for; Ritter and the mourners were dismissed without a second glance.

"Where is she?" he demanded, turning back to the cook accusingly, as though he suspected her of hiding whoever it was under her ample skirts.

The cook removed the pipe from her mouth. "Where is who?" she asked, her tone placid and containing not a single solitary note of deference.

Bancroft closed the distance as far as he could without making it obvious that, though he was a tall man, he wasn't quite tall enough to tower over her. "*Her*," he thundered. "That woman who thinks she can—"

"If it's the mistress you're referring to, I'm sure I don't know where Mrs Bancroft is. And if I did, I certainly wouldn't go telling a guest without her leave."

The cook spoke with outward calm, but Ritter knew an undertone when he heard one. It made the back of his neck tingle.

Bancroft either did not hear what Ritter had heard or did not care.

"Don't pretend your loyalties lie anywhere in that house," he scoffed, and Ritter had the sudden impression of witnessing a conversation which had been going on for much longer, and was about much more than the words presently being exchanged.

The cook puffed on her pipe. "I won't if you won't."

Bancroft's lip curled at so open a display of insolence, but urgency evidently distracted him. Without another word, he stormed back into the house. The cook remained looking after him, finishing her pipe with a frown which looked to Ritter almost like concern. He lingered, hoping for some indication as to what might concern a woman like that, but at length she tapped out the pipe and disappeared back into her kitchen domain, leaving him alone with the waiting mourners.

The order to make ready came down shortly afterwards. Under the practised direction of the undertaker, the procession formed up, the featherman with his billowing tray taking his place at the front, followed by hearse and coaches and finally the lowly foot mourners forming the disorderly tail. Ritter considered joining them, but it would be difficult to remain anonymous in the smaller group going to the church, especially without the convenient camouflage of Annabelle and the other wives.

It was as he was leaving the throng, crossing to the opposite pavement to avoid the clattering hooves, that he was brought up short by a most extraordinary sight: from that side of the house opposite to the one from which he had just emerged, the side down which led the garden path where the famous knife had been found, there burst without warning the figure of a woman. Her face chalky white in the darkness, she shot out at full gallop and raced down the street ahead of him, black hair tearing from its pins as her skirts flew out behind her.

In the blink of an eye she had turned a corner and was gone, too quick to even give chase. With the commotion of the procession to distract them, no one else appeared to have noticed anything amiss, and Ritter was left to stare after her in solitary amazement: though he had only seen her for a moment, he was quite sure it had been Mrs Bancroft.

~

Nora burst into the coffee house as a storm does, with a blast of cold air and no delicacy, reason or control whatever.

Throwing the door open, heedless of the glass pane slamming against the coat rack behind, she half ran, half stumbled between the tables and their eclectic collection of patrons. They leaned on arms clothed in velvet coats worn bare at the elbows, and shirt sleeves patched with gold thread and stains which would never come clean. With their feathered hats and brocade caps, not one among them could walk a daylight street unremarked, but here they blended together in vaudeville mundanity, their individual remarkability rendered unremarkable by the whole.

At the end of the room, the solid wall finally ended Nora's flight. Pressing against it as though she sought either its dissolution or a comforting embrace, her legs gave way, not all at once but slowly, so that she slid down inch by inch, her bombazine skirts creaking as they crumpled beneath her. In the midst of the black puddle they made, she sat with her eyes closed, clenching and unclenching her hands in the smooth fabric, a keening whimper leaking out with every ragged breath.

Nobody rose to help her. Indeed, few so much as glanced at her. Even with her eyes closed she felt it and was comforted. Partly it was the familiarity of it, the casual boredom in the face of the blatantly strange which was part of the very essence of the George. Though she had not known she was heading there until she had arrived, it pleased her to see the place unchanged. Mainly, though, the comfort lay in the knowledge that if no one approached her, then no one could ask her what the matter was. Even just the thought of the question dragged her back, made her remember…

But of course, she remembered regardless; so long as she cowered here, trapped within herself, she would never forget. To pull herself up, to banish the dangerous thoughts from her mind, she needed help.

With an effort, she hauled herself up and took a table near the wall. Behind the counter stood a slight man in clothes made for someone larger, his shoulders lost entirely in the depths of his florid waistcoat. As he wiped a greasy cup with a greasier cloth, Nora felt his gaze on her as she rose, passing from her hair, pulled loose, damp and wild from exertion, to her dress, which, even splattered by the stagnant puddles she'd had no mind to avoid, nevertheless suggested the presence of an ample purse within it. She caught his eye.

"Tea," she called. "Sweet. And pen and paper."

Her voice trembled with the continued quivering of her lungs, but the man acknowledged her with a dull nod. His air suggested plainly that she was not the first madwoman he had served, perhaps not even today.

The room was warm, the smell of cooking fat and burned coffee beans combining with the low hum of conversation and murmur of life outside in a blanket which seemed to cover the world, to muffle the harshness of it all to a more manageable degree. Nora wrapped herself in it and the gentle memories it stirred, yet still her mind was not fully soothed, twitching as her eyes flicked instinctively this way and that.

The waiter placed the cup and two sheafs of yellow writing paper before her, offering her the pencil from the pocket of his gigantic waistcoat. Her hand shook as she reached up to take it, feeling the wood flimsy and liable to snap in vice of her grasp. Nevertheless, she put it to paper, pressing hard, raising her concentration as a shield around her on every side.

6 November 1896

Ambrose,

You will never guess where I am sitting. I would not believe it myself, could I not see it with my own eyes. And yet these eyes have deceived me once tonight perhaps.

No. No more.

Begin again.

Looking about, I recognise none of the faces here, yet the George remains just as we knew it, down to the bottle-green paint and the coffee-stained copy of last night's paper.

Would you be pleased to hear it, I wonder? Or would you scoff at such stunted ambition? You always encouraged mine, until I contrived to fulfil it so completely. But I won't dwell on what is passed.

Neither will I on what has brought me here. I had thought myself insulated, unreachable in this space I forced myself into, but now—

No. I will not speak of it, even to you. It will do me no good, and if you ever read this letter, you would think me mad and have Emil write to Bedlam for their first available bed. And I would be forced to agree with you both: after all, who but a madwoman would dwell on a nightmare so persistent that she dreams it only when waking? And allows it to disturb her so much that her breath tightens, squeaking against the cage of her ribs, threatening suffocation, so that she can hardly hold her pencil to write, nor even read the words she scribbles too frantically?

Only a woman in the grip of madness would, and I give my word that I will resist it with every creaking breath.

Once, when I was ill at school and liable to wake in a fever-induced panic, the matron taught me to chase away phantoms by recalling those ties which bind me to the waking world. It proved unexpectedly effective.

There, you see? Even consummating the thought into words on the page has helped. I begin to be able to read my own letters. Surely that must be a start in the conquering of one's own mind? I can even lift my cup safely. The tea is hot and full of so much cheap black treacle that it sets my teeth on edge. It helps, and so do you.

As I write to you now, at school I wrote to my great-aunt Virginia. I don't believe I ever told you about her, which is a shame. I think you would have admired her, but when you and I knew each other, I was so intent on the future, hardly daring to glance back at the past. And yet she was one of the principal supports in getting me even as far as that, and there is hardly anything I regret more than the loss of our connection.

That being the case, you may be surprised to learn that I remember meeting her once, on the day she gave me the pendant now stolen. That meeting is my earliest memory, treasured without context in the mind of a child, without beginning or end, though I know now that it must have come the morning after the fire.

Very early she arrived, so that when she pulled open the door to the stairwell where I had sheltered from the blaze, it was to reveal the dawn breaking upon the lingering mist. The new sunlight caught upon her dress, black as a raven's wing, as she bent down to speak to me.

I cannot rightly say how old she was. I know only that her face was worn in a way that seemed to me not old but ancient, as though each line was not the flaw of a failing body but a mark of pride, a path she had walked to its end and back again. I remember thinking she must have walked a great many paths, more than I could imagine. Equally, I do not know how tall she was, but when she bent towards me, I had the sense that she was coming down from an immense height.

I cannot remember what she said. In truth, being only three years old at the time, I am not certain I wholly understood it. I knew only that she was my family — I suppose I must have seen her before that day, but I do not recall it — and that I expected her to take me with her when she left. That is the moment I remember most vividly, the sorrow when I understood that she would not — and the fear. For the first time, I knew myself alone. It was then that she reached up and took from around her own neck the necklace now lost, placing it around mine. Her fingers were long and gnarled, and dry as old roots where they brushed against my skin. The necklace felt heavy to me then, but it was a comforting weight, and when I smiled, she smiled back, her eyes glittering above her hooked nose. To this day, her eyes are the only ones I've ever seen which look like mine.

The pendant made a whistle, she gave me to understand, a design unique to Bridde, and indeed I have never seen another like it. I remember blowing on it as I watched her depart, the moss on the hem of her dress trailing behind her through the ashy ruins of what was once Bridde Place.

I never saw her again, but from the age I was able to read until I went to school, she wrote to me every year on my birthday. I would find her letters on my bedside table in the morning — my aunt Judith preferring to keep any evidence of my mother's family out of sight — and though they were not long letters, they were dear to me, full of words of comfort and assurance.

One particular theme of hers, I remember, was the concept of a path laid out for me, which, if walked with determination and fortitude, would lead me where I must go. In later years, I own that I resented her absolute conviction on the point, the conviction of a mind too old and too removed to realise that such a path, if ever it had been lain, must surely have burned up along with my parents and home. Then, though, before I was able to search and find it gone, the idea filled me with a profound calm. I treasured it as I treasured her letters, safe in their hatbox under my bed.

Years later, when I fell ill at school, she wrote to me again, and though I was too muddled to remember much of what she said, the mere proof of her existence was a wonderful comfort. How I hated Aunt Judith when I finally awoke fully enough to find she had taken my box and all it contained! And yet, I must find some gratitude for her too, for she at least allowed me the birthday letters she did not approve of and must have provided my address at school when I was too unwell to even feed myself. Though she disappeared my father's money and curled her lip at my mother's name – and for that I will never forgive her – at least she allowed me Great-Aunt Virginia.

I may yet need her to repeat the favour: Inspector Ritter came this evening, but when I pressed him on the question of the necklace, he seemed as before to think me afflicted with hysterical sentimentality. He is wrong, I am sure of it; the more I consider the question, the more sure I become. Consider it: Victor's life threatened no one, and his death benefits only myself and a handful of minor legatees. It is a senseless thing, and in the midst of that senselessness, there disappears a piece of jewellery which is at once worthless and entirely unique. How can one think anything but that the necklace is involved *in some way, if not actually the object of the whole loathsome exercise?*

I do not see that one can, and it plagues me. I see the necklace before me in my dreams, calling to me. The police may think me daft, but I will not deny the facts before me. Aunt Judith may still have Virginia's address, and I have determined to write and ask with the first post. Once she sends it, I can write to Virginia and ask her the true significance of the necklace, those details incomprehensible to a young child.

I would even think of visiting her, if circumstances allow. Based on his treatment of me tonight, I begin to think Christopher Bancroft imagines he will step into Victor's shoes, evidently meaning to make me a far more demanding husband than Victor ever was. You may laugh and I would too, only he does not strike me as a man used to being gainsaid. I suspect we may yet come to some challenge over the matter, and I had better gird myself against it, which may mean staying in London for some time. Perhaps I had better write to Em's brother – Hugo, I believe? – and hope he will bear out Mr Vascelles' parting promise to me.

In the meantime, I suppose I had better get home before he tries to declare me drowned in the river and starts a legal battle over the definition of "next of kin". Truly, I would put nothing past him. There is an arrogance about him, a level of conviction in the rights of his very existence.

But no matter. I will not think on him tonight. Thank you, dear friend, for keeping me company and distracting me from myself. When I am home I shall burn these pages and imagine you reading them, wishing you both safe and well together. It is my dearest hope that it should be so.

Love always,

Ever Your Nora

IX

She ought not to have gone. Lying in the dark in a bed she had not paid for, Margaret knew it now as she had known it then, and yet she had gone anyway, and given the chance knew she would do so again. For her sins, she was left with the vision of Nora Bancroft's eyes, moonlit and horrible, pinning her in place with their accusation of her, their knowledge.

Trapped by the prickling undergrowth and her own shame, burning her cheeks even now, she'd had no choice but to watch the scene play out. Kit had appeared, and the widow had submitted to his urgency before being seized by a sudden turn, fleeing as though the very Devil himself were upon her heels. Black skirts flying behind her, she had disappeared down the side passage and over the garden gate – the same gate which had been six foot high and locked when Margaret had shredded a charming new pair of French gloves scrambling over it – apparently without breaking her stride. Indeed, at the crucial moment, the shadows seemed to endow her not with skirts at all but great black wings.

Yet it was not the widow's caprices which kept Margaret awake, listening to the church bells tolling hour after hour, trying not to watch the door which did not open, but rather the man she had left behind.

Following the lady's extraordinary disappearance, Kit had called after her in astonishment, even chasing her a few paces before realising the futility. There had been a moment then when he'd been confused and annoyed, jolted out of focus by sheer bewilderment, and Margaret had been seized by a sudden urge to rise, to show herself, to confess and be forgiven.

Too quickly had it passed. In an instant, he was once again the man who had first walked out into the garden to command the woman who owned it. She'd recognised it, that obstinate set of the jaw, the squaring of the shoulders, that sharp toss of the head, the impatient little snort, the flint eyes which sparked as if to say "we'll just see about that". And not only had Margaret recognised it, but she'd loved it, as truly and deeply as any part of him – had done since the very first time she'd seen it. Of course, it had worked in her favour then.

"Look, Meg, I can't marry you."

That was what he'd said to her, and even as he'd said it, the first inklings of that stubbornness had suggested themselves in the jut of his chin, the straightness of his back. They'd only grown as he'd told her of his pompous old goat of a father threatening to disinherit his younger son entirely should he marry the woman of his choice, or even stoop to cavorting with her on British soil. The old man had loathed the very idea to the extent that he had made a legal fact of it, and yet all of the bad news had washed over her as she'd realised the important thing was not the words but the way he'd said them.

"What then?" she'd asked, when at last he'd finished. She hadn't really needed to: she'd heard it rising in every syllable, and when he'd turned to her, it had not been with defeat but with furious defiance.

"Then," he'd flashed, "we play his game. He wants to force me to take you away until I get bored, then leave you there when I want to come home. But there is no home for me without you, and I defy anyone to grow bored with the world at their feet, even the world less one stuffy old island. What do you say?"

Margaret had looked up at him then, at the face so familiar and yet ablaze as she had never seen it before, but brighter, sharper, fiercer, stronger, his natural gifts forged by the heat of burning resolve into something more. He'd stood before her no longer the boy she had known, and she'd risen to meet him with relief, for she too had changed, had stepped beyond the girl who had loved that boy.

They'd gone to France first, where a doctor had stoppered up the last potential impediment to her freedom, almost at the cost of her life. To recover they'd gone to Milan, and then to Venice in time for Carnevale. Through Florence and Rome and Naples, Margaret had kept her Italian primers always within reach, making him quiz her in the privacy of every carriage and train, so that before long she had caught him up in the rudiments and they were both making strides towards fluency. When Italy began to lose its lustre, they'd crossed the Mediterranean, passed through Tunis, Algiers and Casablanca until they came to Marrakesh, with its labyrinthine old city full of heat and spice and coloured awnings brilliant in the North African sun.

So many wonders had they seen, and experienced, and lived, that it was baffling to Margaret how they – how *she* – should have ended up right back where they had begun, under a sky so shrouded in smog that one might look upon the sun with impunity and mistake it for a particularly insipid gas lamp. She, who had friends from Barcelona to Constantinople, who wintered in Italian vineyards and dazzled the most fashionable Parisian ballrooms, the whiff of scandal around her lack of vows only enhancing the wit of her conversation and the brilliancy of her jewels in the eyes of the beau monde, at least when reflected in the proud regard of the undeniable breeding close at her elbow. How was it that she found herself back again, stuck in this awful town in this miserable country, the grit of it wearing through her polish a little more every day? And all because a chance remark in an Antwerp salon had led to the discovery of Dr bloody Virgo.

Outside, the church bells clamoured, agreeing by and large that the hour was four o'clock, though without any comforting assurance that all was well. The old poem rose in her memory, with its oranges and lemons, and its chopper with intent on your head.

Her thoughts were scattered by the rattle of a key in the lock – an awkward, distracted sound, as though the primary attentions of the rattler were required elsewhere. When the bolt did at last relent, Margaret watched the door open to the hall light, first a fissure of it and then a chasm, in which was silhouetted a tall figure, familiar even in its distortion.

Waving away the clerk with a gesture which seemed to rely as much on gravity as any strength of his own, Christopher stumbled into the room, all uneven shoulders and haphazard steps.

Blinded by the darkness which followed the closing of the door, Margaret heard rather than saw the unhappy figure stagger across the room. Faint tendrils of whisky fumes preceded him, and when her eyes adjusted, it was to find him leaning heavily against the frame of the bedroom door, as though unable to trust his legs to take him any further.

"Vic's dead." His voice was thick with drink and grief, and in his face was a mute appeal so forlorn that for a time all else was forgotten as she got up to help him.

She lit a lamp and helped him to the bed, undressing him and pouring as much of the contents of the water jug down his throat as he could hold, taking upon herself responsibility for his bodily needs, that he might be left free to wrestle with those of his heart, the ones he could only allow himself to grapple with in the throes of drunkenness.

"D'you remember Paris?" he asked, lying in bed and looking up at her as she went to turn out the lamp.

They had been to Paris more times than she could count, but Margaret did not need to ask him to which of those innumerable occasions he was referring. Nevertheless, she did not reply. The usual answer, the one they had agreed on so long ago that, in the sober light of day, it would never have occurred to him to ask, was that she did not remember. It was largely the truth: the greater part was lost to her, the context of journeys and conversations and worries and resolutions. Only fragments remained, short staccato bursts which lingered in her mind. The gracious mansion block with its faded dignity on the avenue lined with trees and potholes; the incongruousness of the apartment within, the genteel pink and polished rosewood of the reception rooms and the bare walls of the surgery beyond; the bright winter light beyond the windows as she lay on the table, the silver instruments gleaming in their tray.

The lined face of the lady had come and gone, floating above Margaret like a balloon, smiling first, with pleasantly accented English, and then abruptly fearful, muttering in a language Margaret did not understand as those bright, bright eyes looked where she could not see. Then there was Kit, a disembodied voice beside her, all propriety forgotten as he'd shouted in that same unknown language. It was then and only then that she had felt the pricking of fear, wondering what could be frightful enough to chase his voice to such unnatural heights. It had been too difficult to hold on to any such thought, however, and soon she'd let go, drifting back into the fog. By the time he'd appeared before her – was it later? How much later? – she'd felt only profound peace, and as he'd clutched her hand, pleading through uncontrolled tears, her only feeling had been regret that she could no longer move or speak, wishing she could explain things to him so that he would understand and know that all was well.

Later, when she had woken up in the hotel bed stiff and sore, exhausted by the overwhelming effort of lifting her head, only one question had been in her mind. The physician had been beside her, and with herculean effort she had grabbed at the sleeve of his white coat. "Did it work?"

Watching the man's pink little mouth thin in distaste, for an awful moment she'd thought he might refuse to answer her. Finally, though, medical responsibility had won out against personal morality.

"The object is placed where Madame wished it," he had said, refusing to look at her as she'd struggled to catch the words through the drugs and the unfamiliar accent. "For my part, I suggest you may as well offer the Blessed Virgin a wax cucumber as accept a discredited midwife's mischief. It would be safer for you, and likely make as much difference. I must tell you that I urged Monsieur to let me remove it before you awoke, but he would not give permission. Therefore, I can only say that you ought to have the *bêtise* removed as soon as you no longer have need of it, and within fifteen years at the absolute most, though it is my fervent hope that Madame think better of her choices before so long."

Yes, Margaret remembered Paris. And the doctor had been wrong: the midwife's *bêtise* had worked, and worked splendidly.

The look on her face as she brought the lamp to the bedside table must have been answer enough, or else Christopher was continuing a conversation which existed only in his head as he went on.

"When Mother was sick I tried to bargain, with God, you know, swearing I'd be good forever, that I'd never misbehave, or be wicked or quarrelsome or unkind again, that I'd eat what Mrs Sharpe made and always mind my manners if only He'd save her. Boys' stuff."

He gave a short laugh and then grew thoughtful, looking up at Margaret. "That was the worst part about Paris. I kept trying to bargain again, would have given up absolutely anything, only there was nothing I could offer. I knew if I promised to play by the rules from then on, you'd never forgive me."

He smiled wryly, and she touched his hair as she blew out the light.

As she climbed into bed beside him, she heard him murmur wonderingly to himself: "I'm not sure what I would have been prepared to trade for Vic."

Beneath the covers, she reached out and found skin. Instinctively he rolled towards her, draping himself half across her in a pleasant weight which soothed them both.

"We were just kids," he mumbled into her shoulder, and, too tired suddenly to wonder at his meaning, she found herself giving voice to the one thought which had hung in her head every hour since their return.

"Let's go home, Kit," she whispered. "Please let's just go home."

Immediately it was said, she wished she could take it back. Why press, why now, when she knew full well that if there was any possibility of them going, they would already be gone?

Beside her the covers shifted, the warmth breath on her skin making her shiver.

"We are home, Meg," he said, the words perfectly clear even in his drunkenness. "And the sooner she understands it, the better."

X

Following the longest night it had been subjected to in years, the Bancroft house was sluggish. The footmen blinked owlishly in the mid-morning light, the maids drooping as they carried out armfuls of limp foliage in a shuffling procession which scattered as Nora swept through the halls.

She found Christopher in the blue sitting room, inspecting the elaborate clock which stood on the mantel above the fire. The funeral now over, the shutters were open and the drapes gone, bathing him in a cool grey light.

Hands clasped behind his back, he did not look round as she came in "My grandfather bought this clock, you know," he said. "He had it sent over from Venice, after he saw a similar one in a house he took there. Then, later on, he had the fireplace built to put it on, and the room decorated to match, all because my grandmother did not find it was shown off to its best advantage in any of the existing rooms. So he built a room for a clock, to please her, and in return, she showed the clock and its room to all those who called upon her. A great many people called on my grandmother, you know. She was quite a figure."

Nora swallowed her ire as best she could and perched herself on the overstuffed sofa as she called for tea. "So I am given to understand. What is it that I can do for you, Christopher?"

At this he did turn, joining her. She was appalled to find him choose for his seat not the armchair, decently removed on the opposite side of the coffee table, but the spot on the other end of her own sofa – the place of a friend, an intimate, a confidant.

Nora fought the impulse to rise – or, better yet, chase him off – as he bent his proud head towards her.

"Well," he said, in the low tones of familiar concern, "you can begin by assuring me that you are quite recovered after yesterday. That must have been a nasty turn you suffered, to keep you not only from seeing off your husband's procession but from receiving the mourners on their return. We were all most concerned for you."

"Thank you, but I'm sure there was no need." Nora inclined her own head, a suitably demure gesture which excused her looking away from his eyes, like flint, and hiding her own in turn. "I am quite recovered now, as you see. It was the shock catching up with me, no more than that."

"I'm relieved to hear it," he said in a tone suggesting he was more concerned than ever. "Though – forgive me – I must admit I have my doubts."

Surprised, Nora looked up to find him watching her, cool and impassive. The more she looked, the less forgiving she felt.

"I'm afraid I don't take your meaning."

"Only that I'm afraid my brother has left you with a heavy burden, one which would be a challenge for any woman to bear – or man, for that matter – but in your case—"

"In my case?" Nora no longer made any effort to disguise her irritation, and Christopher had the good grace to look briefly abashed.

"I'm afraid we have not had the opportunity to become acquainted as brother and sister as I would have liked, but accounts of your health are far-reaching—"

"My health is impeccable, I can assure you—"

"—and frankly they call into question your ability to manage an estate of this size, which takes so prodigious an amount of effort, skill and a lifetime of learning merely to avoid running into the ground, let alone making necessary improvements."

He was managing to inject a note of actual concern into his condescension, and a sudden perversity tempted Nora to answer it with callous honesty.

"And if I do?" she asked, taking up the cup which had appeared before her and looking at him levelly over the rim. "Run it into the ground, I mean. What concern is it of yours?"

Though Christopher controlled his face impeccably, he could not prevent the sparks flying behind his eyes.

"Whatever stubborn foolishness passed between myself and my father" – though his voice remained low, it no longer held so much as the pretence of concern, at least not for her – "whatever apathy my brother inherited on that score, let me be absolutely clear that my first loyalty has always been to this family, and to our estate—"

"*My* estate," Nora interrupted, taking a certain pleasure in the words, in the effect they had. "Mine to run into the ground if I so choose."

A snort of laughter escaped him – a grim, mocking sound without warmth or amusement. Nora thought it matched his face.

"You understand, I take it, that *your* estate supports upwards of a thousand people, all told?" he asked. "That it is their livelihood and their well-being whose fate you mock? But perhaps you don't. I don't think Victor ever really did, so I don't know why I should expect better of the woman who tricked him into marriage."

Nora's outrage flared hot and furious. "I did nothing of the sort!"

Christopher smiled at her, though only the upward points of his lips distinguished his expression from the blackest scowl. "I can't speak to what you did, though it is my lasting regret that I was not there to prevent it. What I can do is assure you that this will go no further. No nameless, childless wife, who has proven so totally unequal to the demands of the position she courted, will be permitted to make a mockery of the name which is my responsibility, my *birthright*, law be damned."

Nora did not trouble to pretend her scowl was anything less as she met his glare. "You can damn the law as much as you like, but you cannot will it away."

"Perhaps not," he said. "But I can ask questions. For instance, how does a three-year-old girl managed to survive a fire which kills her whole household without a single scar to show for it?"

Again that awful grin, as though he had swallowed something ugly but would keep it down willingly, if only he could cause that look upon her face. Nora felt it and could do nothing. She had not expected him to know, had not imagined that *anyone* knew, and the way he said it, drenched in a threat she could not fully grasp...

"I hid in the stairwell," she heard herself say, in a voice she could not recognise as her own. "It was all in stone, with the door a foot thick—"

It was not his grin which sent her reeling: she saw again the door before her, the grain of the wood ancient and petrified, the sheer weight of it...

The acrid smell of smoke was in her nostrils as she fled the room, letting him drive her from it with the threat of truth.

A sudden brilliance cut through the corridor, and she whirled, startled, to find a flash of glittering eyes flung back at her, full of her own fright.

Atop a rickety stepladder, the parlour maid tugged at the black stuff still covering the mirror as big as she was. She dropped it and dipped into a precarious curtsy as Nora rounded on her, seizing her fury with both hands. "What do you imagine you are doing?"

The poor maid trembled hard enough to wobble the step-ladder over the carpet. "Beg pardon, madam. Mrs McNeal said to take down the shrouds, now that the master's been laid—"

"Your master is still dead, and this is still a house of mourning," Nora snapped. "You would all do well to remember that. Leave the shrouds and go and close the shutters in the sitting room. I have not ordered them opened."

"Yes, madam." The maid clutched at her wooden perch to still its trembling, or possibly her own. "Only Mr Christopher, he said to—"

The very name coiled itself around Nora's guts and squeezed. "That man has no authority in this house. He is no longer to be admitted even into the hall without my express permission. You may tell Alcott that I am not at home to callers, least of all Christopher Bancroft!"

She did not wait to hear the maid's stuttering apology but continued to what was now her bedroom.

Relief turned to utter paralysing shock as she opened the door: the curtains had been opened in her absence, the shutters beyond them unlatched and put aside. Enormity opened up before her. The window was too large, disproportionate to the small room. Above, garden greenery still hung with morning fog, the sky expanded, endless grey whirling upon itself, vast beyond comprehension.

Teetering on the edge, Nora groped for the bell pull. McNeal's hurrying footsteps were drowned out by the flap of great black wings rising from the misted branches of the yew.

"Close the shutters," Nora hissed in the breath before she fell. "And nail them shut."

~

Mrs Nora Bancroft, Kensington to
Mr Hugo Vascelles, City of London

7 November 1896

Dear Mr Vascelles,

You may perhaps be aware that I knew your brother before he left London. Though I only knew him a short time, his friendship was dear to me, and while I was never formally a client of his, he advised me on financial matters of a personal nature in that capacity. Upon his departure, he invited me to speak to you should I find myself with a similar need in his absence. To be blunt, I now find myself with not only such a need but one I fear is acute. I would therefore be greatly obliged to you if you could make time to see me at your earliest possible convenience. Please confirm the time and place by return.

Yours with sincere gratitude,
Nora Bancroft (née Dallaway)

PS: As I have reason to believe there are forces actively working against me, I must ask that you tell no one of our correspondence or intended meeting.

ST CLARE'S

I

St Clare's School For Girls had been designed with a particular effect in mind. Beginning life as a convent in the latter half of the fifteenth century, it had been saved the worst ravages of the Reformation by filling a very particular niche – the need of rich men for a place to send wayward daughters not diminishing regardless of who headed her father's church at any given moment.

The school stood on forty acres of marshland, though the boundaries were no longer maintained, as no one had the slightest inclination to encroach upon them. The moors stretched as far as the eye could see, and even the peat was known to be poor, tempting to no one. A single wide road, cut as straight as the boggy landscape would allow, led to the school and not beyond it, so that it seemed to the girls arriving in September of every year that St Clare's might well be at the very ends of the earth. They watched the scrubby gorse and windswept grasses from behind their carriage windows, and, as she came into view, could not take their eyes off the solemn grey edifice which marked their journey's end. Ancient and austere, weather-beaten and yet with her steeple as erect as ever, the impression she made upon her future inmates was most effective.

It was the lifelessness of the place which struck Nora most deeply, on that journey in her thirteenth year. Not a movement was to be seen but the carriages rolling one after another through the massive gates, depositing their young charges in the maw of the beast in an exchange by which St Clare's understood to chew them into the shape of young ladies, in return for the young lifeblood needed to sustain her for yet another generation.

So Nora perceived it and found herself torn. Looking at the tiny windows with their iron bars and the squares of kitchen garden arranged in militant precision, she resented them already, so that she clenched her teeth and only a glance at her uncle dozing opposite prevented her from baring them. And yet, if suddenly he had awoken and repented – if he had seen anything to repent for – and offered to turn the carriage around with immediate effect, she could not say with any certainty that she would have accepted. For what did she have to go back to?

She had been allowed little time to prepare for her departure. Whether the decision to send her to school had been a sudden one, or whether her aunt Judith had simply preferred not to mention it, to stave off whatever reaction her niece might show, Nora could not decide. Knowing the temperament of her aunt, both seemed equally likely in their turn. Regardless, it was undeniable that, with Violet gone up to town for her first season in April and married by the end of it, barely eighteen and full of excitement at her new life, Nora had become an anomaly at Croftsend. Without her cousin to root her there, to want her and to make room for her in her own place, there had been nothing to disguise the bald truth of it, that if Nora was not precisely unwanted, she had no place in that house. She herself had felt it as keenly as anyone.

Though she had not been aware of her uncle's arrival late the night before, immediately she saw him at breakfast that morning, she'd understood. Over the years, business had conspired to detain him in town with increasing regularity until his presence at Croftsend was more of a rarity than not, and in the main it did not seem to Nora that her aunt was overly displeased with the arrangement. Still, certain tasks continued to require his efforts as head of the household, and so there he had been at breakfast, chewing his bacon uncomfortably as his wife looked fixedly out of the window over her plate of congealing eggs. Nora had felt very little as she'd watched her trunk carried down the stairs.

Going up, she'd looked in on the schoolroom one last time, for form's sake. Already it had acquired the dusty, desolate air of a room long disused, though she had sat in it to go over her French verbs not a week before. The nursery had been more cheerful, but even it had carried the sense of a thing packed up and put away lovingly for the benefit of future generations to which she would not contribute. Here her throat had tightened as she'd run her fingers over the little dining suite, too small for her now, the varnish on the wood worn thin and flaky. She'd picked up a favourite bear, a beloved storybook, petting and thumbing through the pages until the lump in her throat had grown too heavy. She had sat on the little bed which, stripped to the mattress, was Ben's again, or Ben's future children's at least, and cried.

Even then, though, she had known she was crying for sentimentality, for the childish sake of it, for childhood and for Violet even, so distracted by the thrill of her new life that even letters were breathlessly short and far between. Without Violet, the room could no longer produce those laughing, ridiculous, joyful moments her cousin had pulled from it, and without them, there was nothing there to regret. That in itself was a grief, in its own way.

It was Mills' knock at the door which had caused her to get up and wipe her face, pausing only to retrieve the faded hatbox from its place under her bed. Cleansed by the relief of tears, Nora had found she was able to take her leave of her aunt with a cool dignity which made Judith look away, a feat it secretly pleased Nora to have accomplished.

Standing in St Clare's assembly hall with the rest of her cohort, Nora could no longer feel pleasure, nor anything but the incessant draught which crept through the cracks in the venerable stonework, taking every advantage of the identical smocks in which the girls were already attired, worn thin and colourless by the unfeeling mangle. Such a smock each girl had found to welcome her on her dormitory bed, and left just enough time to change into it before being rounded up by the house matrons and herded into the great hall. There they stood, scrubbed floorboards creaking beneath their restless weight, row upon row of girls in various stages of formation, the oldest at the back, almost ready to be released into the world and the youngest at the front, preparing to be shaped in their turn.

On the stage before them stood those women tasked to carry out that transformation. Even in the moment, Nora could absorb very little of them. They seemed to her an uncertain mass of stern faces over shades of sober grey and solemn black, a grim hydra behind the headmistress as she spoke in front. In the gloom, even their skin took on an ashen tone, so that the only flash of colour among them was a strip of angry orange, hanging from a hand near the centre of the mass as naturally as though it were an extension of it.

It was a cane, Nora realised with a shudder, a yew cane polished to high gloss, and in the moment that the word hooked in her mind, the headmistress intoned gravely around "a school of the highest moral character", so that the two, the cane and the phrase, became inextricably linked in Nora's mind, a recollection as sharp and bright as the rest of that first day was a blur.

II

In the beginning, Nora sought protection in that old fortress of hers, silence. She spoke when called upon and not otherwise. It was not intentional, only she found that, with the strain of listening, she had no time to think of anything to reply. She listened to the buildings, to the bustle of the dormitories, the clamour of the dining hall and the hush of the corridors, empty as classes went on all around, to the tread of lone footsteps and the distant crash of a faraway door in the wind, so sudden and frightful that she started in her seat and was surprised when no one else seemed to hear. She listened to the wind itself, sweeping in great sheets across the moor and shrieking its fearful protest at any who dared stand against it. Sometimes, it seemed to Nora that the cry was just beyond the window, close enough to tap. Then she had to muster all her powers of concentration to ignore it, and on those days she was first out of her seat at the end of one class in order to be the first arrival in the next, to be sure of a desk as far away from the window as possible.

She listened to the teachers and the matrons and to the other girls, who had begun to make themselves at home. They giggled on the playing fields and gossiped in the common room, and crowded together on the centre bed after the matron made her last round, telling stories harvested from older girls, of long-dead nuns whose dreadful wraiths walked the passages on stormy nights. Then Nora crept to the edge of the group and huddled there, for warmth and for comfort.

There she was on the night Marit Hansteen shyly got out her treasure for the first time.

Marit had spent the first decade of her life in her father's homeland of Norway, first in the family's town house in the shadow of the Egeberg, and then, as her father's illness had progressed, increasingly with her grandparents at their country home. Upon his death, the family had removed to her mother's ancestral England, where the widow had married again to a gentleman with a residence in Harley Street. Concerned for her daughter's future prospects, she had insisted Marit stay in England, but the girl's heart would not be dislodged from her grandmother's house overlooking the fjords, and never would she allow the family to forget it. Thus, by mutual consent, she had removed to a place where she might brood in peace, and to St Clare's she had brought the treasure she now showed.

It took the form of a large picture book of Norwegian fairy tales and folklore, gifted to her on the occasion of her christening. In exquisite detail, the book discussed the many strange and fantastical creatures said to roam the fjaelds and make their homes in the dark pine forests and deep, still lakes of that strange and distant land. By candlelight, the girls would gather about Marit in a corner of the common room and thrill with delight over the spritely elves and playful *nisser* in their pointed red hats. They marvelled at how the stocky dwarf's beard was so carefully picked out it looked soft to touch, and recoiled in gleeful horror at the hairy trolls and frightful *nyk*, with hair like drowned weeds and eyes just above the waterline, lying in wait for unsuspecting children to tempt with its beautiful, treacherous tune. Every evening they pored over pictures of furry, bear-like horrors and women with wings and talons, listening to legends like the changeling children, infants left by these dreadful denizens for unsuspecting human parents to love and raise as their own.

Sitting on her bed at the centre of the group, Marit held the book on her lap and turned every page almost reverentially. She permitted no one else to touch the pages as she translated the incomprehensible text but allowed the girls to gaze at the fantastical illustrations as she spoke, magnificent woodcuts enhanced by her grandmother in delicate watercolour. Nora, on the outside of the group, caught only glimpses, but the work was so skilful that even at a distance, the strange and terrible characters seemed to peer out at her, curious, questioning, inviting her to peer back. She thought she might have done, had she been able to get closer, but equally could never quite be sure she wanted to. Something in their eyes gave her the same queer feeling as the dreams gave her, and without the waking to wash it away, it was harder to forget.

She did not think it was that which so fascinated the other girls though. Rather, inspired by Marit's own adoration of her treasure and longing themselves for something to fling their childish feelings into, they flocked to it, so that even a few older girls began to take notice, and readings became a common-room affair. The group would gather about the hearth, Marit allowed the biggest armchair by virtue of her supreme position as storyteller, while the others gathered on smaller chairs, settees or horsehair cushions spread about the flagstones, to gasp and sigh over stories they by then had heard a dozen times.

Not everybody was enthralled however.

One evening after supper, Nora, torn between listening and not, wandered along the edge of hearing to where a girl she recognised from the dormitory across from her own sat reading alone on a threadbare loveseat. Glancing up, she saw Nora approaching and smiled, moving aside to make room. A pat on the worn seat cushion was all the invitation Nora needed.

Though they had never spoken, there was a certain strength in the way Louisa carried herself, an ineffable conviction in the way she held her head even when reading, and though some rigidity of neck was perforce required to maintain the posture, there was something comfortingly certain even there.

They sat in companionable silence, Nora not quite realising the question hovering in her mind until it was on her lips.

"Louisa," she said, running her fingertip along a ridge in the velvet, "do you ever have the same dream more than once?"

Louisa's reply was silent, the mere setting aside of her book in order to listen more attentively, but still Nora felt encouraged to go on.

"I have a dream sometimes, that I'm standing at the edge of a great chasm, or ravine of some sort. It's nowhere in particular that I know of, certainly nowhere I have been, and yet it is always the same one. On the other side, there is a dark forest which seems to me endless and dreadfully old, but though I am standing right at the edge of the chasm, there is no way across. This dream I have had all my life, I think, and never gave it much thought, but lately…"

"Lately what?"

It was not until Louisa prompted her that Nora realised she had trailed off and drawn her knees up to hug them. She was embarrassed to find herself in the position of a child, but Louisa did not seem to notice, only looked at her warmly until the words came.

"Lately, I am not merely standing. Lately—" Nora broke off, considered, tried again. "Lately, I feel I am being pushed. Though I do not turn around, I sense there is something behind me, something sentient closing in, deliberately driving at me, and I…"

Worry was starting to creep into Louisa's brown eyes, mingling with the warmth, but though the sight made Nora swallow, she could not stop.

"And though there is no way across and I must necessarily fall to my death, I have the most powerful compulsion to jump. There seems to me to be no other choice, and in the dream jumping does not seem so very bad—"

"But it is!" Louisa broke in, impassioned suddenly. "It is! You mustn't think of such things, dear Nora – you know that, don't you? Why, the very idea, when it's in one's head, who knows—"

Nora was suddenly, abruptly conscious of impropriety. "It's only a dream," she offered weakly, looking away. "Silly really. I just wondered."

She knew her apology had been accepted when Louisa changed the subject.

"I thought I might take a turn about the yard," she said, getting up. "I find a little fresh air before bed helps me sleep."

She lingered in polite invitation but could not quite disguise her relief when Nora took up the book she had left on the seat, declining further company.

It was a treatise on prayer from the last century, and so busily did Nora attempt to interest herself in it that she did not see what led to the altercation across the room. A cry jolted her from her reading and she looked up to see Louisa paused by Marit's reading group.

"Blasphemy!" she cried, staring at the assembled girls with eyes wide in horror.

Marit, at the centre of the group, stared steadily back. "I beg your pardon?"

"You know perfectly well!" Louisa's voice was a sort of overloud whisper, as though, even as she could not risk staying quiet, she feared the very words in her mouth. "I heard you, telling stories of Christian souls being lured to drowning by evil music, as though it were a farce! I always felt that book must be sinful somehow; the pictures alone make it plain, but I never expected— To speak of such hellish fiends with such ease, such *enjoyment*—"

She broke off, unable to hold the terrible thought in her head, her eyes pleading with Marit to tell her she was mistaken, and though Marit was quick to oblige, very likely the other girl would soon wish she had not. Perched like a queen in the midst of her courtiers, the storyteller glanced around at her audience, waiting with bated breath to know where this delicious turn of events would lead.

"A nyk isn't evil," she replied in a voice whose calm was belied by the colour rising in her cheeks. "Any more than a lion or a wolf is evil. And how can any creature be hellish, if it is not a creature of God? Not everything is, you know. Take a walk through the Marka and you will soon understand. Only total arrogance could fail to, and that I'm sure *is* sinful. Even here, you know, in your very own England, there remain things outside the realm of God."

As Marit's colour had risen, Louisa's had drained, and now she looked at her adversary with an expression that suggested she beheld no less than the Adversary.

"All things are of God," she whispered, not in a voice of retort but reassurance, meant for herself and perhaps any of the other girls who felt as she felt, knew as she knew, a truth to cling to as she fled with backward steps. And it was true that some of the girls were looking distinctly uncomfortable themselves.

Louisa did not turn her back to Marit until her shoulder hit the ancient door frame, and as soon as she was gone, Nora watched the group begin to shift, loudly remembering the time, their essays, their evening walks and last looks into the gardens. One after another they dispersed, until only the reader and a couple of her most devoted – or obstinate – adherents remained.

Though Marit put on a brave face, she could not quite keep the quaver from her voice as she took up her story again. Nora was sorry for her, but too preoccupied to feel it much. The book lay open in Marit's lap and there was room now in the circle, close enough that one might see…

Even as the thought drew her, pulled her bodily forward so that her back stretched and her neck arched, something weighed her down, a weight in her lap pushing her into the cushion, keeping her there no matter how she strained.

And then it was all for naught: in came Miss Jackson, and Marit did not need more than a flick of the history teacher's prim head to follow her out.

When Marit next appeared, it was without her precious book. She returned to the dormitory with her head down, and no one asked for a story that night. Nora, buttoning up her nightgown ready for bed, thought perhaps it was for the best.

III

By the end of the first term, the youngest girls had begun to glean what previous generations had realised before them, that the staff of St Clare's had grown overly reliant on the initial terror inspired by the place and in themselves become complacent, making no effort to reinforce it unless roused to do so. This they preferred not to be, thus an unspoken pact had formed, whereby the mistresses would not look for infractions if the girls would not show them any. Thus St Clare's had evolved from punitive beginnings into a school whose playing fields were muddy and gardens more so, and no girl permitted to shirk her turn in either, but whose mistresses by and large had no object than to have their students learn the day's lesson, being predictably pleased when they did so and proportionately irritated when they did not. Said irritation they expressed primarily in the form of the solemn passing around of the demerit badge, accompanied by assignment of lines no longer than might reasonably be completed without too much encroachment on free time, in order to save both girl and mistress the need for further unpleasantness on the morrow, and if Miss Pendle's cane might have been an evil thing in other hands, in hers it was simply a convenient compensation for her lack of height vis-à-vis the maps in her Geography room.

Furthermore, though the buildings were draughty to a one, the groundskeepers were eternally at work stopping the worst of the gaps, and the coal supply was generous. The uniform smocks proved not entirely intolerable once the girls had dug out their own petticoats and warm underwear from their trunks, and though the food was generally under-seasoned, it appeared in sufficient quantities, at regular intervals, and generally at the appropriate temperature.

The youngest girls slept four to a room, which was not so very different from the nurseries most of them had left behind and could even be convivial when it suited them. Even the hoary corridors were disappointingly free of ghosts, unless one counted the exhausted matrons walking their nightly rounds. In short, while there was as much for the girls to complain of at St Clare's as might be found at any school – and complain they certainly did – for true horror, they were forced to make their own.

For Nora's cohort, though the stories in Marit's book had been an amusing distraction, for most they had in truth been only a slight improvement on the Alice books of their nurseries. While the details might be grimmer than the girls were used to, and in places gruesome enough to turn the most brazen arm to gooseflesh, they remained safely upon the page, pinned there long ago by people far away. They could not hope to satisfy the adolescent craving for immersion in their own immediacy.

Thus it was the disappearance of the book which set the tone with its adherents more so than the book itself. Though Marit had openly admitted that her treasure was locked away in the headmistress's office, where the owner might read it if she wished but show it to no one else, the rumour mill took no notice as it ran along its merry way. In the corridors and on the corners of the playing fields, whispers of burning could be heard, which soon turned to combustion, first in the headmistress's grate and then in her very own hands. The chaplain was thought to be looking pale, very likely due to an attempt at exorcism which had only been partially successful, and when poor Marit tried to point out that she had held the book only that very afternoon, she herself was discarded, no longer required in the face of bolder personalities and livelier imaginations.

With the primary function of St Clare's now being as a sort of holding place for girls whose families did not desire their daughters to be punished or even particularly uncomfortable, but who nevertheless could not or would not keep them at home, it was usual for a sizable contingent to remain in residence through the holidays. Not everyone did however, and as the girls who had left for Christmas were returning that January, it was impossible not to notice in particular the heightened profile of one Henrietta Nichols.

Henrietta, with her commanding presence and flair for the dramatic, had been the natural successor to Marit as the High Priestess of Strange. That January, under the cover of blankets and giggling darkness, she showed her most devoted acolytes their latest relic. Where precisely she had obtained it, nothing could make her disclose. Intimations were made to grimy bookshops in Covent Garden, and other such low sources, and looking at what she lay between them, the faithful could well believe it. A small shilling primer bearing the title of *The Gentlewoman's Guide to Explorations Beyond the Veil* lay upon the sheet, its pages curling with damp and age, positively begging to be tried out.

The appointed night was a bleak one. As wind howled about the dormitories and the rain lashed the rattling windows, five girls waited in the dark for the matron's last round. Then, one by one, they rose and left their sleeping dormitories, creeping down the corridor to the old storage room at the end, each clutching the supplies she had been tasked to bring. One girl brought thirteen candles and a box of matches; another carried bunches of sage from the garden. The third had a handful of salt and the fourth coal for marking, and Henrietta Nichols brought mainly herself, the primer clasped beneath her nightgown.

Amid the lighted candles, they sat together on the floor, the cold flagstones nipping through flimsy nightgowns as they joined hands and began the chant. Three times they called upon that which they did not understand. Three times the candles flickered and the wind howled, and three times they were stoic in their disappointment and did not admit their relief.

Only Henrietta seemed to feel their failure. Each time the invocation reached its crescendo, the scream of the wind seeming to rise in sympathetic unison, only to die away without a whisper, her head drooped forward, as though dragged down by the weight of despair. With each defeat it sank further, until on the third and last attempt, her head fell so suddenly and so deeply that her companions privately wondered if she had lost the use of her neck.

Her hair hung loose and thick about her face, obscuring her expression, and something in the air, something their own chanting had brought into being, momentarily prevented speech. Thus the girls remained in their places with their hands joined, peering in anxious silence at their leader.

Finally, Henrietta raised her head. With her hands detained by her fellows, she made no move to push the hair from her face as she looked slowly around the circle. As her hidden gaze passed from one girl to the next, each girl in her turn suffered an impression of being scrutinised wholly and deeply, and found wanting. It was an impression made no less unsettling by the way the head moved upon its neck; stiffly, as though with long disuse.

Then, in the very moment the last girl had had her turn, Henrietta loosened her grip on the hands which held her. She fell forward with a groan which in seconds became recognisably her own, a soliloquised complaint on the subject of her poor bottom being quite frozen to the floor. The others, released thus from the oppression they could not have named if they had thought to try, realised in the same moment that they had their own complaints. They chimed in with enthusiasm, so that the party broke up amid emphatically whispered grumblings, each girl making her own impassioned contribution. In that way, there was no pause in the conversation into which other subjects might creep.

Within twenty minutes, each girl was snug in her bed, drifting peacefully off to the snuffled breathing of her classmates.

Within an hour, Henrietta got back up.

With movements awkward as though forgotten, as one waking from a sleep deeper than any girl of fourteen can rightly conceive, she rose from her bed. Without so much as a glance at her sleeping mates, she made her ungainly way into the corridor, staggering as a calf does, still struggling to understand the shape of its limbs.

Whether it was the unaccountable clatter produced by the awkward, shuffling gait which woke Louisa in the next room, or whether some deeper call, even she could not say. She knew only that as she emerged into the corridor, there was no room for doubt. The apparition wearing Henrietta's face over her billowing nightgown continued its grotesque procession towards Louisa's door, towards the girls still sleeping soundly in the room behind her, and towards the many others in their rooms beyond. It was in the realising of this that Louisa knew true fear, and in it found the courage of her convictions.

Leaving the safety of her doorway, she planted herself in the middle of the passage, spreading her arms wide to bar the way.

The thing which was not Henrietta gave no sign of noticing. It lurched on, jerking the limbs which did not belong to it, until Louisa could see beneath the tangled hair the glow of eyes lit by too many lights and breathed a heartfelt prayer for strength.

Only when they were nose to ghastly nose did the creature stop. Somewhere in its throat, Louisa swore she could hear a hitching, a sort of catch, creaking with the effort of breathing. Then she realised that the thing was trying to speak.

"Stand aside," it ground out, but though Louisa recognised some shadow of the voice she knew to be Henrietta's, it was the rest of it which chilled her. To give shape to its words, it was as though the creature brought to bear all the sounds of the lonely moor beyond the walls, drawing up the keening wind, the whispering grasses, the bare branches creaking like bones, warping them all to its will, into words which chilled Louisa to the bone.

Henrietta's mouth twisted into a mockery of a smile, as though the thing felt Louisa's fear and approved. "You are not the one I seek," it groaned. "Stand aside."

At the force of it, Louisa felt her knees weaken, trembling with the impulse to run fast and far. Then she thought of the rows of sleeping innocents behind her and did not move.

"I will not," she said, raising her voice. "In the name of God, I will not!"

At the invocation, there came over the creature an air which Louisa had not expected but could not help but recognise. She knew it at once for the air of the headmistress, which she herself had been subjected to following the book debacle. It was the unmistakable air of a woman girding her patience as she persisted in trying to reason with a girl too foolish to know it.

"I have no quarrel with your God, child," said the Henrietta thing, still with this air about it. "Nor He with me."

But Louisa's bravery had reached its limits and was breaching into a hysteria she could not hope to control.

"You shall go no further!" she screamed, and, not daring even to pause for breath, she launched into a recital of the Lord's Prayer at a volume heard to the rafters.

In the space of a minute or less, every soul on the floor was awake. As door after door was flung open to what all the racket was about, Louisa stared into Henrietta's stolen face. Though it lasted only an instant, the look of defeat she saw there would keep her brave for the rest of her days.

Realising that it was beaten, the fiend withdrew its talons and Henrietta's face was her own again, flooding with confusion in the moment before she collapsed into Louisa's arms.

In the excitement which followed, with girls crowding around their fallen comrade until the matron pushed them aside, shouting for anyone with the wherewithal to listen to fetch the nurse at once, nobody noticed Nora trailing drowsily after her dorm mates, clutching reflexively at the pendant around her neck.

"Aunt Virginia?" she called softly, looking about as she rubbed the old silver.

It was Marit, standing in her place at the edge of the group to which she was slowly growing resigned, who turned to her. "What was that?"

Nora, still blinking owlishly, shook her head as she woke up a little more. "Oh, nothing," she said. "It must have been a dream, that's all. I only heard my aunt calling."

IV

Friendships begin in all sorts of ways, and that was the sliver of conversation which began that between Nora and Marit. It was a gentle, undemanding sort of friendship, consisting primarily of sitting side by side in the dining room, quiet conversation in the common room and long walks across the heath, as far as they were permitted to go. They talked about lessons and books and gardening, and what they intended to do after they finished school. Marit, of course, never varied, and spoke at length about her plans to get on the first train, boat or eight-legged horse able to take her home to her grandparents. Nora had no such certainty but rather a vague idea that she must go for a governess unless she could manage to marry well.

As the years rolled by, the latter seemed increasingly unlikely even as the former grew ever more unappealing. What had become of her parents' money, of which there must certainly have been some, she did not know other than the Lindups had been responsible for it and now there was none. Without it she could not be an heiress, however, and knowing herself to have insufficient personal charms to compensate, she turned, reluctantly and not without some bitterness, to thoughts of remaining at St Clare's to teach. Here, at least, there was the heath, and no Judith Lindup or her equivalent to worry over a home and children she could not control. Between them, Nora thought, the two might perhaps just about make up for a lifetime of trying to corral girls like herself.

The years passed with peaceful regularity. Once or twice, Nora visited Violet, now Mrs Gordon. The journey was long, and the bustle of the city and the demands of Violet's young family proved a rude awakening after the quiet retirement of the moors, and ultimately no regularity was established.

Her own prospects after St Clare's being generally unenthusing any way she looked at them, Nora preferred to go walking on the heath and let her friend point out the migrating brent geese which reminded her of their white-faced Norwegian counterparts, wondering aloud how year after year, they could know where to go. Marit said the young ones followed the old, and

Nora supposed that sounded sensible, and tried not to imagine the fate of chicks orphaned before they could be shown.

It was in their final year that the pair discovered the copse. With age and tolerable behaviour, restrictions on their walks had been lifted to such an extent that, so long as they reported to classes, meals and evening curfews on time, they might walk as far as they were able. This, for two fit and vigorous young women enjoying the fresh air, was rather far indeed.

The copse covered a patch of lowland a brisk morning's walk northward from St Clare's. Here the stunted birch and stringy ash of the moors became denser in number and, pushing through the mass of brambles and ferns which guarded them, one found that in the centre, the trees began to grow straighter, prouder, at once protecting each other from the ravages of the wind and competing ferociously for a meagre portion of sun, so that for ten or fifteen acres, one had the sense of walking in something like woodland.

It was in truth nothing so very exceptional, but for those who had had nothing but heath to look upon year in and year out, it was a treat. Moreover, having never heard anyone else speak of the place, the two girls were able to think of it as quite their own, which, in a school of over a hundred girls and half again as many staff, was a luxury indeed.

It was this promised solitude which drew Nora's steps that morning towards the end of her final Lent term. Marit was in bed that day, laid low with the influenza which had been passing through staff and students alike. Nora bid her feel better in the morning and for once did not regret her absence.

The day was a mild one but blustery, suiting Nora's mood. As the end of childhood drew nearer, dated with such precision by the end of term in early June, she found herself increasingly aware that teaching in one form or another was really the only answer for her, and equally that she really did not want to do it.

Attempts at reconciliation had only brought further bitterness, and so that morning she left them behind, striding out without so much as an apple in her pocket, as though she could bend the world to her will with nothing but her own vigorous pace.

Soon, the smoke of the school chimneys fell away, leaving nothing but the wind on her cheek, the stonechat with its curious, almost crow-like croak at her side. The pungent gorse caressed her coat and the pale grasses lay willingly down beneath her boot as the copse loomed ahead, safe behind its fortification of brambles and stinging nettles.

Nora found she had no need to pause, nor even break her stride to traverse them. She had never walked this way before. In a pair they walked briskly, but there was conversation and observation and discussion of where to go. Now there was only Nora, and the world in which she existed. Her very bones seemed to unhook themselves that her limbs might swing more freely, so that the creepers fell away and the stalks bent aside to let her pass, respectful of her passage.

Behind her, they closed like sentries, leaving her in the dim closeness of woodland untouched by human hands. The air was cool and earthy, the ground soft and mouldering beneath her step. She felt it through the sole of her boots, breathed the sweet rot of life and death and life again, felt the creak of the old branches in her own blood.

The wind crept in carefully here, as did the sun, gilding a leaf here, dazzling a mossy cushion there. The trees stood dense and massive, reaching to impossible heights even as their fallen limbs littered the floor around them, feeding clusters of tawny inkcaps and creeping white lichen. There was no path here but the one she chose. The satisfaction of walking it, of knowing it with utter conviction, was a pleasure striking deep in her very bones, a rightness profound and absolute, comparable to nothing but the last time she had walked it.

In stages and by degrees, it came to her that in fact she had never walked this path before. That she could not have. That having entered a copse composed of a few stringy birches and some scrawny ash, the open moors never more than a hundred yards in any direction, she now walked in true forest, deep and ancient, left alone by the foresters not because it had no use but because none had yet found his way in.

She knew suddenly with absolute conviction that she walked a path never trodden by human feet, and, what was more, she did not walk alone. Indeed, she was being led.

She could not say precisely when she had come to a standstill. As primal awareness took over, the very air about her seemed to slow, every muscle straining, every nerve twitching. The thing in front of her turned to look back.

It stood between the shade of the trees, obscured and shifting, and yet Nora knew it would have been still harder to see in the plain light of day. There was a rough impression of four legs, something like an enormous wolf, but while the iron-grey coat and slinking tail agreed, what then of the wings, and that crown of jagged horn bristling upon the head...?

Her mind balked, cowed at the prospect of untangling the details, sorting claw from cloven hoof from glistening sharp-toothed jaw. Though the hair upon the nose grew dense and wiry, vapour rising from the nostrils, there was about the muzzle the undefinable, unmistakable shimmer of dry bone, as though the thing was at once wholly alive and dead so long the skull had been picked clean and polished white by the weather of ages.

And then there were the eyes, which were neither. Blazing bright in the darkness, they watched Nora without pupil and without soul, a thing entirely outside of God, beyond the realm of Christ and the reach of any church known to humankind.

They drew her, those eyes, hellish prisms promising another world. That was what truly frightened her, ramming the cold spear of panic into the small of her back and twisting it there. Even as she saw the thing, even as she recited to herself the knowledge of what it was, nothing could negate that over-whelming impulse to follow.

It was an urge she knew well, had awoken time after time dazed and longing in the moments before remembering the abyss she longed for and shivering with the thought. The promise she felt at the edge of that crumbling precipice, the promise of peace and lightness and freedom, was repeated a thousandfold in those eternal eyes, and knowledge was not enough to resist.

Instead she held to another promise, the memory rising unbidden and clear as the day it was made, the earnest assur-ance of one small child to another, to remember always, always the lie. For lie it must be. Certainly there could be no flight in falling, no lightness in the dark, no freedom so confined, and even as she could not make herself believe it, she clutched at the memory like a talisman, an anchor, a mast to which she bound herself.

As though watching her own actions from afar, as a disin-terested onlooker might, Nora saw her right foot lift slowly beneath her skirt. For an instant it hung in the air, and even then she could not say what she meant to do, could not even say what she hoped for. She dared not ask, for fear of what the answer might turn out to be.

Finally, she felt the curve of the muscle, the tug which pulled upon her entire body to turn her back the way she had come. Still the thing watched her, and she held its ghoulish eyes with her own until her neck could support the strain no more. It was as her gaze tore away that the fear, lapping at the edges all this time, at last swelled up to engulf her.

Driven before it like a fox before the hounds, she plunged through the undergrowth of that place which could not be, hardly noticing the fallen branches which barred her way as they had not been before, the brambles tripping her up, wrapping around her ankles in cables like steel, leaving her to pull free with a strength she had not known she had.

Thorns shredded her skirts as branches lashed at her face, yanking her hair from its pins until it streamed in long black tendrils behind her. Nora felt nothing of it. She existed only within her flight, and in the very core of it recognised its futility, the utter hopelessness. With those walls which protected her mind brushed aside in the rush, she knew in those moments that the thing she fled was bound to her and she to it; that no matter how fast or how far she might fly, be it to the very ends of the earth, it would follow her, forever nipping at her heels in mind, body and soul, for the rest of her God-given life.

V

Nora awoke to the sterile walls of the school infirmary room. Memory was fleeting – snatches of a desperate race across the moonlit heath, depleted and gasping without thought of ever slowing, but the fever burned away any context or sense. She recognised the form above her as her own house matron and understood dimly the gist of what was said: that she had broken curfew, staying out many hours more than the distance she had covered ought to have required. Only after midnight had she been found, one of the groundskeepers coming upon her streaking across the moonlit heath as though the Devil himself were chasing her. The man had caught her as she collided with him, appearing not to see him at all until she was held fast in his arms. Then, beyond the reach of any assurance, she'd fought his grip like a woman possessed, screaming like a banshee, and though he was a sturdy man in the prime of his life, in her distress she had succeeded in dislocating his shoulder. It was the sound of his yelp which had brought her to her senses enough to know him, at which point she had collapsed in a dead faint, so that he had been forced to carry her back, slung over his uninjured shoulder.

When the fever did not break with morning, the diagnosis was influenza. Nora lay in the infirmary, the other worst-affected girls in beds all around her. Dreams and memory came and went, mingled and became one, sometimes clear in front of her and other times vague, twisting shapes, taunting her even as they evaporated the moment she tried to fix them. Sweat soaked her sheets as she struggled and fought, never knowing whether she sought to flee the visions or hold them to account. The nurse listened to her pleas and cries, branding them delirium as she prepared a sleeping draught.

When finally Nora shook off the blackness, she knew she must still be dreaming, for Marit did not share her dormitory, and yet there she was, watching Nora from under drooping eyelids from the next bed.

When she saw Nora was awake, she reached a weakened arm across the divide. "What is it hounds you over there?"

"You must not go back to the woods!" The force of Nora's conviction made her lurch up in her sickbed. She squeezed Marit's limp hand until she felt the knuckles crack and give beneath her grip, not for malice nor for comfort but to make her friend hear. "Do you hear? Never, never again!"

"Why's that?" The fever brightened Marit's eyes even as it weighed her voice down, made it slow and dreamy, full of the disinterest of the invalid to whom the world beyond the sickroom has become vague indeed. There was nothing vague about the flinch as she withdrew her arm however.

"I saw the Devil," Nora whispered, hardly daring to hear her own words. "And He called to me."

"How do you know it was the Devil?" Marit asked mildly. Her stricken hand lay at her side, curled into a claw, but she appeared to have forgotten it. "There are many things in the woods which are not for the likes of us. Don't cross them or heed their call, and they'll do you no harm."

"Have you seen them?"

Marit shrugged against her pillow, a small gesture which seemed to cost her a grave effort. "Only the will-o'-the-wisp," she murmured. "Outside the window at night. Just two burning flames where no lanterns hang, waiting."

Nora held her breath. "Waiting for what?"

"For someone to follow them of course. But only a fool would do that, or a man too drunk to know better. They'll lead you through the moors and off the edge of a cliff, if you're not careful." Marit chuckled. "Terribly pretty though."

Nora could not answer, Marit's words squeezing the very breath from her lungs. *Twin flames, under the window. Waiting to lead you off the edge of a cliff.*

"What's the matter?" Marit's voice drifted in the darkness, too weak to hold its own course. Then she seemed to rally, propping herself up to peer across at Nora as though seeing her clearly for the first time.

"My dear, did you know your eyes have too many lights behind them?"

Nora remained silent. She knew not what she knew. Her own fever rose, chilling her and made her teeth chatter, so that she could not ask Marit what she meant.

Marit, in any case, was rapidly slipping beyond answering. Nora could do nothing but watch, extending her own trembling hand. Though Marit made no move to take it, she smiled across at Nora with half-closed eyes. In that manner they fell asleep, Marit never again to wake.

Nora knew it the moment she opened her eyes. The bed beside her was empty, stripped down in readiness for the next girl to need it. When the nurse appeared on her rounds, Nora could hardly see her through the film of tears, but all she said was: "Please bring me my box – the striped one beneath my bed. I should like to have it here."

They were, she understood later, the first sensible words she had spoken since she'd been found raving on the moor. Her fight was not over however, and yet the illness had its claws in her still.

In the weeks which followed, she was sensible only of brief spells of lucidity so entirely isolated one from the other that they might have been separated by minutes or days, and she too exhausted to care which. Weakness, lethargy and abominable headaches plagued even those, so that her only pleasure during those days was in the letters arriving from Great-Aunt Virginia, the first since her last birthday at Croftsend. Now the venerable old lady wrote incessantly, pages full of comfort and assurances to her bedridden niece. Each time Nora awoke from the doctor's liquid stupor, there would be a fresh letter waiting upon her bedside table.

Nora kept them in her box, refusing to let it be put away. She read them continuously and without discrimination, beginning again with the first as soon as she had finished the last, any time she was well enough to keep her eyes open. Again and again she read them, until the ink smudged and the corners bent and darkened with use, over and over and over, hardly glancing at any other mail she received, not even the letters from Violet, offering a home in which to convalesce.

The nurses and matrons who came and went muttered together in the corridor, wondering and with increasing concern, until one day Judith Lindup appeared at Nora's bedside. Perched primly on the plain infirmary chair, she chatted about ordinary things: Violet's latest arrival, what a charming and suitable match Ben had made, and how delighted they all were with her, how Mills was struggling with her rheumatism again, and so on, until at length Nora began to doze. When she next awoke, there was a pile of oranges on her bedside table where earlier pen and ink had lain, and the striped hatbox was nowhere to be found.

It was April before Nora was deemed well enough to travel. Violet herself was to come up and fetch her home to London, and it was as Nora waited for her in the common room that the headmistress put her head around the door, holding a large rectangular parcel wrapped in brown paper. Marit's mother had declined to take it, she said, being too distraught to bear the reminder. Nora's name had come up in her daughter's letters on occasion though, and so the bereaved woman had suggested that Nora might like to take the old book for a keepsake. The headmistress had been reluctant to hand over so evocative a work until Nora was through the worst of her nightmares, but now that she was bent on leaving them... She hadn't finished her sentence, only held the parcel out until Nora took it with muttered thanks.

She felt nothing at the touch of it however. That chapter of her life which contained the book, and Marit and her stories, and everything which sanity would not allow her to think on was closed, and must remain so.

With nary a look she put it away at the bottom of her trunk and banished it from her mind. Her thoughts now were only of the future, of London and the room Violet offered there, right in the heart of the only place Nora knew to be vast enough, to be chaotic and utterly human enough to be impenetrable, safe.

XI

Nora awoke in some confusion to find McNeal standing over her. The good woman hovered, oil lamp in hand, evidently in a state of internal debate concerning how best to rouse her mistress without being allowed to open the blinds. It was not a conundrum which, in the weeks since the funeral, she had yet been able to solve.

Nora stared up at her. In that state of unreality, the woman seemed little more than the sum of the lines on her face, furrows worn into the flesh by age and care, thrown into shadowy relief by the flame of the lamp as McNeal hesitated.

"Good morning, madam," she said at last. "Will you take breakfast? A glass of juice perhaps? Mrs Sharpe says the oranges are in from Italy early this year and as sweet as she can ever remember them."

Nora gave no answer. The brisk ordinariness of the question was jarring, confusing her, so she merely watched McNeal bustle about the room, a bobbing light in the darkness, and tried to puzzle out if the housekeeper was really there at all.

Sometimes, she wondered if any of them were. When she walked the corridors, unable to sleep and yet only half awake, they scurried out of the shadows like ghosts, haggard figures with weary faces. They bowed and curtsied when they remembered to, and startled when they did not, as though she were the one to fear. She gave no orders, approved no menus, and yet food appeared; not as it had done, not at any particular time or on any particular table, but materialising at her elbow apparently out of thin air: sweet almond biscuits, stewed apple in a dish, cold ham with chutney and white bread, slices of spiced fruit cake laden with dollops of brandy butter; meals suited to taking a nibble here, a spoonful there, and unlikely to spill with too much mess or putrefy too quickly when set aside and forgotten. The bulk of these preparations were undertaken entirely by the junior kitchen staff, Mrs Sharpe absconding daily on visits to the hospital. And why not, when there was no one to eat what she prepared? Nora was glad someone was with Joan at least.

She heard no conversation and yet words were spoken, drifting out of empty corridors or down the stairs, whimpers of legends and childhood stories dimly recalled, complaints of a white head too independent from the proud shoulders on which it perched, eyes glittering in the darkness. Tears and sharp words would follow, reprimands for silly maids upsetting themselves with superstitions, with wicked stuff and nonsense, and over a poor woman in mourning at that. And then at night, when they all lay breathing in their beds high above, poor little Joan Fletcher screamed out from their dreams and rang in Nora's head.

Nora heard every breath and every whimper – could not remember how she had ever stopped her ears before – but she did not listen.

The wind whipped around the corners and whistled in the chimneys, dashing itself against the house until the fires leaped and the gas lamps hissed and flickered, and all meaning was drowned out. The clocks stood still, and even the church bells of the city blended together within the Bancroft walls to a single cacophonous entity. Day had blown into night and night into perpetually darkened day, the only marker of passing time the pile of unopened envelopes teetering upon the tray. There they remained unopened but not unconsidered, having been dismissed on the basis that the sender was unlikely to be in possession of any intelligence concerning old women or stolen necklaces. The Brucknell invitation remained alone in the rack, unanswered.

Nora watched in abstract wonder as, without a single twitch of her composure which might in any way hint at disapproval, McNeal rearranged the pile of letters into two stacks, thus preventing calamity. "I hope you slept well, madam?"

It was not the question but rather the rasping shuffling of paper against paper, card against card, which recalled Nora to something like the present.

"Not at all." She shook her head, as much to clear away the shadows as anything else. The shadows went nowhere of course but consented at least to reorder themselves a little, to let her have a sliver of clarity in their midst. "I don't think I've slept a wink in weeks."

Was it weeks? She could hardly tell, only that—

"I am sorry to hear it, madam. What a shame, and with your appointment this morning too." There was a note of suppressed giddiness in the housekeeper's voice, a sort of excited anxiety which must not be expressed, and yet Nora caught it and felt its echo.

Her appointment. Yes. Hugo Vascelles would finally see her this morning. They would have their appointment and she would tell him about her fears, about the doorstop visits, the indignation and barely suppressed rage to which she listened from where she hid deep within the house, about the cards which arrived multiple times a day now, one with every post, and which she would not open, lest their threat permeate even here. She would tell Hugo Vascelles all about Christopher Bancroft, and Hugo would advise her, help her, as his brother had before him.

A thought occurred to her.

"McNeal," she said, glancing at the piles of unopened envelopes, "pick out all the letters from Mr Bancroft and put them in a bag for me to take. I should like Mr Vascelles to see them."

~

"Do please accept my apologies for having been unable to see you before now." Hugo Vascelles leaned back in his leather chair, comfortable behind a desk the size of which ought by rights to have dwarfed him yet was fully commanded by his small frame. Through the window filtered the distant hubbub of Threadneedle Street below. "I'm afraid family business kept me in France – my aunt, you know – but I do regret your being left alone, even for a matter of weeks, with such a burden on your mind."

He gestured to the pile of letters he had finished looking through.

Nora shrugged, tearing her gaze away from the pair of portraits behind him. "It's not as though I'd read them."

Hugo Vascelles regarded her with eyes warm and congenial and alarmingly bright, reassuringly familiar as she felt them take gentle but meticulous measure of her. They pried into her, firmly and with the greatest of care, digging and parting the cracks, uncovering the living fossils in places she had thought dead for years. Or perhaps it was not him at all; perhaps she was only attributing to the present man the effects of the distant one.

Even with her own averted, she could feel the eyes of the portrait upon her, dark where his brother's – painted opposite as well as seated below – were light, but otherwise identical in every respect. Hung side by side, the faces too might be mistaken for mirrors, but for the complexions: fair on one side, dark on the other. Otherwise, the same straight noses and fine bones recurred in both, the angle of the brows and a certain firmness about the mouth all that kept them from delicacy. The portraits were good without quite managing to be great, the artist lacking the skill to capture the more idiosyncratic traits of his sitters. On the fairer, he had failed to capture the air of quiet studiousness which hung about the man before her, and on the darker, Nora was left to superimpose from memory the certain daring about the eye, the boyish quirk of mischief about the agile mouth, though the subject could not have been less than forty-five at the time of painting.

Hugo was watching her, waiting, and Nora forced her mind from the ghosts of the past to the villains of the present. "What does my brother-in-law say?"

Hugo grimaced politely. "In words, not a great deal. But then one would hardly expect him to. His reputation has him stubborn to the point of absurdity but far from a fool. Of course, that only means one is obliged to read between the lines to know his true meaning. His general theme is rather monotonous: he wishes you allowed him to help you run your estate, which he refers to as 'the family estate', and begs that you see him at your soonest convenience to discuss practicalities. In his earlier letters" – Hugo drew out a sheet from the bottom of the pile, glancing at the date – "those from a couple of weeks ago, the request is couched in general civilities, asking after your health and so forth, but as the days go on, those rather fall away, leaving his central message to stand out more clearly."

He put the letter he'd been holding back in its place near the bottom and spread the whole pile out, like a fan depicting the progression of one man's insistence. Though the words were upside down to Nora and she resisted the temptation to try to read them, it was impossible not to see how the paragraphs grew shorter, the sentences more abrupt as initial civilities and endearments fell away one by one until the most recent were addressed simply to "Sister".

Catching herself reading the word and not wanting to be drawn in further, Nora looked away.

Hugo's concerned eyes found hers. "Are you well, madam? It's a distressing business for you, to be sure."

For a moment, he looked as though he might well reach over the desk between them and put a hand on her arm. He didn't, but just the idea of it put a lump in her throat which made it impossible to speak. To clear it, she forced herself to laugh, a strange spluttering sound containing no amusement at all.

"Ridiculous, isn't it?" she asked as Hugo looked at her questioningly. "To be so distressed by offers of help from a 'brother'?"

Hugo frowned. "I wouldn't say ridiculous, madam. I wouldn't say ridiculous at all. In fact, I'd say rather prescient to realise that, even where the words are kindly – or at least, not explicitly offensive – genuine offers of help rarely come with every post, nor do they wind up reading as though the writer were barking instructions at a rather feeble-minded reader. You have done well in coming to see us."

He was right, she knew. The Vascelles brothers had made their name dealing with cases like hers. Both brothers were Oxford men, but though they employed both lawyers and accountants, they themselves were neither. Rather they had turned their father's modest foreign fortune into a vast English one by creating a firm to which the cream of society could turn when their own legal and financial representation balked at the crisis facing them. The Vascelles' artistry – for so it truly was – lay in some combination of Hugo's ability to consider every possible eventuality from every conceivable angle and Emil's brazen delight at recombining these in ways never before conceived of, until even the most apparently hopeless of situations was made to dance to his jaunty tune.

It was touching, Nora thought, that even now, years since that singular tune had last been heard within these walls, Hugo still kept both portraits in equal positions and referred to himself as "us". It seemed to her that the younger brother felt the loss still, though he must have known it to be inevitable. To build so extensive a fortune from so modest a beginning in barely twenty years was remarkable enough, but to do it on the basis of nothing but their joint wit, ambition and perfect refusal to stand on ceremony where it got in the way of business was nothing short of provocation.

Indeed, it might be said that the greater surprise lay in how long it had taken for the hammer to fall. Perhaps it was that, after a short while, there was nary a notable family in the country who had not sought the brothers' expertise or wished to have it available should they need to do so. Perhaps it was that, through charm and marriage, the Vascelleses had found themselves in the very social circles whose highest members they served, new money gilding old names and old names dignifying new money. The Mr Hugo Vascelleses were a quiet couple, content in themselves and unlikely to offend, while the Mr Emil Vascelleses were charming, vivacious and able with the greatest good humour to crush any suggestion against them, so much so that it was only years after the wife of that pair had returned to her ancestral home and her husband to the life of a cheerful bachelor that, by that gentleman's own actions, the social circle remembered that Emil Vascelles was not a man they wished to call their own. And even then, though no denial of the distasteful rumours was ever made, it was a mark of respect that Emil Vascelles was nevertheless permitted to depart under the dignified guise of expansion abroad.

"How was it you said you knew my brother?"

Nora started and realised her gaze had wandered back to the portrait on the wall. "I didn't," she said, colouring. Then, to soften the words which had rushed out too sharp, she added: "We met through a mutual friend. You might say he introduced me to my husband. To tell you the truth, I think it rather amused him."

She found herself smiling.

Hugo snorted. "He has always had a most peculiar sense of humour."

The words lingered between them, hung with private memory.

Aware, perhaps, that the moment had grown too personal, Hugo took up the letters with a flourish, as though wishing to brush it away. "Now, as to your situation, while there is no overt mention of any particular intention contained in his letters, the manner in which they are sent tells us that what Mr Bancroft is seeking is control."

Nora nodded, as much to herself as to Hugo. Though she had not thought to put it into so many words, visions rose before her of Christopher walking into her house as though he owned it, holding forth on funeral arrangements, directing her staff and scolding her as though she were an errant child under his charge. There could be no doubt about it – control was exactly the word.

"Can he get it?"

Hugo's brow furrowed over steepled fingers. "In principle, not unless you give it to him. I haven't seen the paperwork of course, but nothing you've told me gives me any cause to doubt the validity of your husband's will, nor his ability to make it. The assumption must therefore be that you are the right and proper owner of everything Mr Bancroft refers to as 'the family estate' – including, I might add, the allowance it pays him every quarter. I think this must also be his view. If it were not, he would have made his challenge in the courts before now."

"You said in principle," Nora reminded him. "What of practice?"

The corner of Hugo's mouth twitched at the question, but it was too grim a thing to be called a smile. "In practice, you know as well as I do that the power differential between a woman married above her station, without family name or children to support her claim, and the younger brother bearing so respected a name, does not follow principle."

He looked suddenly grave. "I must tell you, Mrs Bancroft, that there are large segments of the population, in every strata of society, who, given the facts of this case, would deem it only right that he should inherit what his father had before him and judge the law a damnable nuisance in frustrating it."

Nora sat very still, her fingers curling around the polished wooden armrests. She saw Hugo glance at them, distracted, before going on.

"What I am driving at, madam, is that while you have the law on your side, he has the lawmakers – or enough of them to make a difference – on his. Even they cannot change the law, but they can bend it. You would be amazed at how flexible the law can be in the hands of an expert."

Here Hugo could not resist a little grin, and Nora knew he was counting himself foremost among that category. She did not begrudge him: who would not twist the world to suit them, if they could? And anyway, she needed him to.

"What will he do? And how can he be prevented?"

Hugo shrugged, a precise movement within his well-cut sleeves. "The obvious thing for him to do is to try to have you put under guardianship, with himself as guardian. For that, he will need to prove to – or at any rate persuade – the Powers That Be that you are unable to manage your own affairs. Naturally there are rules – he will need the sign-off of two independent physicians and so forth, but suffice it to say the obstacles are far from insurmountable for a man of means and determination."

Here Hugo paused, presumably to see how his client was taking his assessment. Though her bodice had seemed to wind tighter with every word, Nora inclined her head for him to proceed; nothing she had heard surprised her.

"Once granted guardianship," Hugo went on, "he would be free to take any action regarding your estate and person which he could justify as being in your best interests, and I feel obliged to inform you that in such cases, almost all actions by an affectionate guardian are so justifiable in the eyes of those with the power to prevent them. A 'good' outcome for you in such a scenario might be a quiet existence in a secured wing of your own country home – in Hampshire, I believe? – under the care of private nurses. A bad outcome would be—"

"Bedlam," she finished for him, cold and flat. Hugo flinched at the name.

"Well, given your position and his it would probably something rather nicer, or at any rate more discreet, but that's the general idea, yes."

He cleared his throat, as if to cleanse it of some foul flavour left behind. "As I said, this path is the most obvious for him to take, the one we most commonly see when a man or family of means wish to remove a woman's agency – or anyone's, for that matter. It's highly effective and, sadly, entirely legal."

The armrests were hard beneath her grip as her face twisted, a release of tension in what Nora was sure was a perfectly monstrous grimace. "And here I thought he just wanted to marry me."

"Ah." Hugo smiled, a little timid suddenly in the face of her expression. "I suspect he might prefer that too. There is more dignity, not to mention power, in the role of husband than that of guardian. It is, however, illegal for a man to marry his brother's widow. The law considers it to be incest, you see. Which is not to say that most of the population take the slightest notice, or are even aware of the prohibition – you see, you yourself were not – but where it concerns so large an estate as yours, I am sure he would want to do everything irreproachably in the eyes of the law. Although" – Hugo cocked his head to one side, with the fascinated air of a scholar considering some newly discovered conundrum – "I suppose, with the right connections, it might be possible to obtain some sort of dispensation, particularly if he combined the two and framed it as doing you a kindness, sacrificing his conjugal rights for the fraternal love of a mad-woman— Forgive me, madam, I only meant—"

Hugo broke off, flustered at his own words, but Nora shook her head. It was as much as she could manage at this point, but it was enough to bring a return of his business sense.

"At any rate, our work remains the same. We must discover whatever ammunition he intends to use against you and dis-arm it before he can. You will forgive the question therefore, madam, but I must ask, is there anything in your history which could be used to bolster a claim of mental infirmity? A deliri-ous illness, an imprudent love affair, anything at all?"

Nora felt the grain of the armrest stark beneath her finger-tips. Some part of her had expected the question, while another had refused to consider its existence. Now that it was spoken, she could not conceive of it, groping in the dark for answers to a question her mind could not hold.

"When I was a child, there was a doctor— and – and at school, when I was ill, I heard the nurse whispering—"

She looked up at that kindly face all concern, and suddenly unable to remember that it had once been a different shade, she pleaded with it like a child: "He knew about the fire."

Hugo Vascelles's voice came to her from very far away. "Pray do not distress yourself, madam. We will arrange for research to be undertaken, and if there is something to be discovered, we will uncover it and prepare for it. You needn't think on it again. Come now—"

Lost in the mire of her own mind, Nora understood she was being spoken to only barely. It was a single word which caught her attention, a flare in the fog, bringing her back and lighting her up with purpose.

"I wonder," she began, the question tripping over her tongue in its haste to get out, "while you're looking into my background, conducting 'research' as you say, might you see if you can obtain the address of my great-aunt Virginia? My aunt Judith Lindup, in whose house I was raised, has it, or had it, but she has not answered my letters, though I have sent several on the subject."

Hugo's head bobbed in acquiescence as he retrieved his pen to make a note. "Certainly, madam. And the lady's surname?"

"I…" Again the fog, threatening to close in. Only the power of the flame kept it from enveloping her. "To own the truth, I'm not certain. She's on my mother's side, born at Bridde, as I was."

He was looking at her, Nora realised, with something dreadfully like concern; seeing her own mania reflected in his mild eyes, she remembered herself, feeling the heat rise to her cheeks.

"Pray do excuse me. It's been such a trying time, and this awful fabric, it scratches so damnably at one's nerves."

She pulled viciously at the stiff tulle of her sleeves in a burst of sheer frustration as Hugo rose, coming round the desk to offer her his arm. She took it automatically. The shape of it, the weight, the size were all so familiar, even the cadence of the voice beside her, offering her every assurance, yet as he led her away, it was all but drowned out by the realisation that he was not his brother after all. For one thing, she thought, glancing back, Emil would never have let a client sit in a chair in that condition, so entirely out of keeping with the otherwise impeccable office – such deep, ugly gouges marring the armrests.

XII

Ritter sat on a bench in the southern tip of a triangular bit of grass and gravel too small and awkwardly shaped to build anything worthwhile on, which had therefore been designated a "park". In front of him, he held the morning's *Daily Chronicle*, occasionally reading a word or two by accident.

Within the rather grandly titled Lower Grosvenor Gardens, he was alone save the ubiquitous pigeons and a single fat bruiser of a squirrel. On the other side of the iron railing, the bustle of Victoria Station went about its day. Cabs and omnibuses vied for space, horses snorted and tossed their heads, getting in each other's way as they were pulled up short, or spooking as a harried clerk darted into their blinkered field of vision, a leather satchel clasped under his arm as he took his life in his hands. Ejected from the commotion of the street, his sudden appearance on the pavement upset a pair of ladies in walking dresses, the snuffling Pekes at their heels launching into a frenzy of congested yapping. Across the road, their racket caught the scabbed ear of a mangy cur as it slunk, tail down and ears pricked, ever watchful of the dogcatcher's net, as it headed to whatever chophouse the porter's boy was known to be most generous at.

Not a one of them so much as glanced into Ritter's fenced refuge. Even as the wind, rising since the morning, tore ferociously at the handful of red and yellow leaves still managing to cling to the spindly trees, the park remained entirely uninteresting to those outside, which was precisely why Ritter had selected it.

Behind, in a quiet side street chosen for its easy access to the main road, a vehicle looking precisely like a hireable brougham lingered discreetly, every bit as though the driver were taking a quiet moment to wash his lunch down with a swallow from his flask, just enough to keep the blood flowing. The carriage gave no sign whatever that it in fact belonged to the London Metropolitan Police, nor the driver that having a nip of any-thing remotely interesting where Detective Inspector Ritter might see was more than his job was worth. Ritter, it was well known among the men, could spot a delinquent policemen through steel plate if it came to that.

For his part, Ritter did not discourage tales of his reputed powers, and indeed more than once had rather wished they were true, especially if they could be made to extend beyond the remit of mere constables drinking on duty. Since they did not, however, Ritter contented himself with readjusting his newspaper, that he might better keep his eye on the main entrance of the Grosvenor Hotel diagonally across the street.

In the weeks since the murder, a representative of the London Metropolitan Police had been assigned to every entrance of that hotel every hour of the day, to watch for the emergence of Christopher Bancroft. When his distinctive fig-ure appeared, they followed him whither he might go until he returned, following which they wrote up detailed reports for Ritter to pore over. In Ritter's opinion, the man's sudden return to England alone, timed too conveniently to be acciden-tal, mandated nothing less, to say nothing of the astonishing behaviour he himself had witnessed on the night of the wake.

In the beginning, things had promised well. On the day following the funeral, Bancroft had been followed to the fam-ily home in Kensington and seen to leave with, as the report eloquently observed, "a face full of thunder". The following morning he had returned, only to be turned away at the door. According to that report, at the moment of refusal, Bancroft had had such an expression that the officer on duty had been fully prepared to break cover in order to prevent a second murder within those walls. That comment had prompted Ritter to remind all personnel assigned to the case that, murder aside, on no account whatever must Bancroft be made aware of Scotland Yard's interest in him until said interest could be substantiated.

In the event, however, he needn't have been concerned: in a moment, the report stated, the man had had himself under control again, and had left without another word to return to the Grosvenor.

Since then, there had been nothing. Once a day, Bancroft strolled around St James's Park. He chose the afternoon visiting hour for his outing and thereby found the paths reliably deserted by people of a rank to know him. Four times he had lunched out, always alone and always in establishments offering thoroughly decent fare but with a clientele unlikely to recognise a Bancroft. Letters went out to his sister-in-law with increasing regularity but invariably went unanswered. This helped Ritter to breathe a little easier – when he recalled the abject terror on the widow's face the last time he had seen her, it was hard to reconcile his decision not to call upon her directly. Nevertheless, he stood by his reasoning that, if she was of sound mind and at liberty to communicate with him, then she was fully capable of doing so, and if not, any meddling of his might well do more harm than good at this delicate stage. None of which did anything to answer the critical question of what was Christopher Bancroft *doing*?

Or, more precisely, what had he *done*? Ritter had his suspicions of course – had had them since he had first watched those cool grey eyes glance around the hall of one of the finest houses in London with an air of absolute proprietorship, and nothing since had done anything to dissuade them.

Accounts of the man's life on the Continent had been gathered, describing a glittering social circle of the Bohemian elite. At least a handful of these acquaintances were known to be at this very moment in London, and yet he sent them no letters and received none. A red-haired woman shared his rooms and there had been some discussion around picking her up for questioning. As yet little was known of her however, and though investigations were ongoing, nothing had yet been uncovered which might inspire her to switch her loyalties away from the man whose money she threw about her like water. With her removal more likely to alert Bancroft than not, Ritter had reluctantly backed away from that line, keeping the woman aside as a potential useful witness later on, once the events needing witnessing had been more firmly established.

That left Ritter waiting, and wondering, nursing his suspicions even as he pointed out rather tersely that suspicions did not make convictions every time the police commissioner ground his teeth at the delay.

And then, suddenly, word had come in that Bancroft had ordered a landau for two o'clock that day. Though the bells of Westminster Cathedral were only just striking half past , Ritter had not been able to resist coming down and relieving the sergeant on duty early, for the sheer novelty of the thing. Anyway, the wait need not be idle: indeed, the informality of the busy street and the bracing, gusty breeze might prove conducive to more organic conversation – always the most useful kind in Ritter's opinion, especially with subordinates.

The whine of unoiled hinges distracted Ritter from his thoughts, and he glanced back to find Constable Wilcox struggling with the reluctant gate. The thing, perverse to the last, caught the constable square on the ankle as he passed through, so that he stumbled and almost dropped the newspaper-wrapped bundle he was holding. For a moment, all attendant hearts were in their affiliate throats – Ritter being as fond of his lunch as any man – but after a gravity-defying fumble, the day was saved.

"Mrs Sloane's was closed, sir," the constable reported red-faced as he approached Ritter's bench. "But there's a new place just opened behind the cathedral, so I went there instead."

Ritter took the parcel from Wilcox, indicating for the young man to join him as he surveyed the glistening grease splatters already leaking through the paper, making the personal ads run. "Fine, Constable. You never know, perhaps holy mice improve the flavour of the cat."

"Sir." Wilcox, busying himself with tin cups produced from within his coat and a flask filled with what he no doubt referred to as "coffee", sounded as though he was not entirely certain whether the inspector was making a joke or not. Truthfully, neither was Ritter. It had been some time since he had had a meal like this, a luxury typically reserved for those ranks of the force who passed their shifts out of doors and on foot. Unwrapping the disintegrating paper to reveal the steaming meat pies within, Ritter was appalled to find himself rather looking forward to it.

They tucked in with all the satisfaction of a hot meal on a blustery day, and for a time the only voices heard were the pigeons cooing hopefully at their feet, Ritter nudging away any with the temerity to hover their bobbing hindquarters in the vicinity of his shoes. Only when the pies were gone and the "coffee" no longer hot enough to compensate for its flavour, to say nothing of texture, did Wilcox venture to ask the question which, from the sound of it, Ritter suspected had been on his mind for some time.

"Sir," he said, and Ritter, noticing that it was now less the address of the deferential subordinate but rather the 'sir' of an uncertain schoolboy, glanced across to see Wilcox watching the same entranceway which Ritter had kept an eye trained on since sitting down. "Sir, do you really think he did it?"

Ritter crumpled his empty wrapper thoughtfully before replying. "Do I think," he began, choosing his words carefully, "that Christopher Bancroft personally butchered his own brother? No. In fact, I know it to be impossible, and so do you, Constable. Remember, the stationmaster at Dover put Bancroft and his companion there less than two hours before the murder was discovered. Bancroft may be capable of many things, for all we know, but I'll stake my reputation on his being earth-bound like the rest of us."

"But you do think he was behind it?" Wilcox pressed. "Hired someone, I mean? They're a fine family, the Bancrofts, the very finest my mother always says. It's hard to believe—"

"Constable, without wishing to impugn on your no doubt admirable mother's estimation," Ritter interjected, gently but with sufficient firmness that, even as the boy tensed in instinctive defence of the parent he himself had invoked, his mouth remained respectfully closed, "we as policemen are fortunate in that we are not called upon to 'believe' anything. Rather, we review the facts before us, and make our assessments accordingly.

"For example, it is a fact that Dr Wallis, with his years of experience of all manner of human death, expressed surprise that no large, distressed animal, such as a bear, was involved in this one. We know also that, when presented with the fact that no evidence of a bear or other large predator was uncovered at the scene but only a simple kitchen knife, he opined that, based on his experience, any man able to cause such damage with so crude a weapon must not only be strong but skilled, and with a good knowledge of anatomy. We note then that the killer must also be skilled in other ways, to enable him to disappear in a house full of servants, without leaving behind so much as a footprint. Is this a reasonable summary of the facts as you understand them, Constable?"

Wilcox eyed his superior with the air of one uncertain of whether there was some joke afoot of which he might find himself the butt, but he nodded. "Yes, sir."

"Good. So, on the basis of those facts, Sergeant Jameson is attempting to locate any individual known to this police force or any other who may fit that description. Unfortunately, his efforts have not yet borne fruit, but we continue to hope that they will do so. Hope, however, like belief, is no basis for good police work, and so we continue our search for facts in other areas of the case, to whit, the victim's personal situation. Through extensive questioning of all persons with whom he was known to associate, we know Mr Bancroft to be a man of good standing in all areas of his life. He paid his debts, did not cheat at cards, returned invitations to sport, did not bother with other people's wives, mistresses, sisters or daughters – nor with their husbands, lovers, brothers or sons – and generally was not known to involve himself in matters which did not concern him. Indeed, one or two sources suggest that he was frequently delinquent even in those which arguably did. Thus, not only do we have no evidence that any of the man's enemies were possessed of the skills noted by Dr Wallis, but we have no indication that he had any enemies at all.

"Thus, we begin to seek unknown enemies, that is to say people who were known to bear him a grudge, or stood to benefit from his death. We come across only one, an estranged brother who was known – again, factually, through our colleagues overseas – to express bitterness over his situation. In particular, he resented the victim's refusal to return his overtures at reconciliation, even as he disapproved of the victim's marriage and stewardship of the family name and estate.

"We know that, on at least one occasion, he responded favourably to flattery that he himself would be more suited to the role of family head. We know for a fact that this brother could not himself have committed the murder, certainly for want of time and likely for want of skill. We know also, however, that men possessed of skills of any kind may often sell them for profit, and that skills of the kind required here may be purchased, often through an intermediary of questionable but not actually reproachable record. Further, we know that, less than a week before the murder, Christopher Bancroft transferred a substantial sum to a disgraced English doctor living in Antwerp, who so far has told our Belgian colleagues only that it was 'payment for information'. I understand they are in the process of arranging for him to be forced to tell precisely what information, on pain of perjury—"

"And the telegram too, sir, the one Mr Bancroft sent. Sergeant Jameson says they're expecting to have it to us within a few days." Wilcox's brow furrowed, a picture of boyish confusion. "But, sir, why would a man about to have his brother murdered send him a telegram?"

Ritter, forgiving the interruption in favour of encouraging an enquiring mind, smiled the wry smile of the educator, proud that his student has thought to ask a question to which he himself does not yet know the answer.

"Ah, now you're on the right track, Constable. Unfortunately, the mere fact of being police officers does not furnish us with facts we have not yet earned. Your mother is given her beliefs by the mere fact of asking for them, but you and I, lad, we must go out and dig. And there are still plenty of facts to be unearthed in this case. The telegram is one, that locket the widow is so sentimental about another. Why does a man known to enjoy socialising stay holed up in his hotel for weeks on end, in the wake of a plan perfectly executed? Even the murder itself raises questions. Why make – or pay for – such an effort, which significantly increased the risk of discovery, when a simply cut-throat would have produced the same result? And if the maid was indeed a witness, why leave her alive and risk her speaking of what she saw?

"We can speculate, you and I, draw on our collective experience and hypothesise that some of it may be red herrings to throw us off the trail – not unsuccessfully, I might add – or the product of a young man's mind, left to stew in its own bitterness too long. It is easy to imagine such a character in such a situation becoming so focused on concocting a murder as humiliating as it is bloody that he fails to take into account that, without entail or will to the contrary, the family fortune is now the legal property of the widow, so that he now finds himself scrambling to take control before she can recover her senses and realise it.

"Do you know, in some countries it is entirely legal to marry one's brother's widow, and in those cases, the courts here, with the right encouragement, have been known to accept the situation as a fait accompli?

"As Wallis knows his field from experience, so I know mine, and experience tells me the likelihood of all of this. Without facts however, it's none of it of any use. And remember that we are not just interested in the facts we expect to find. At any moment, some new information may appear which wholly alters our understanding of the situation. We must be prepared for it and welcome the challenge to our previous assessments. Do you see, Constable?"

"Yes, sir."

The look on Wilcox's face suggested that he did indeed see and was struggling to parse what he saw. Ritter, recognising the signs of a mind laboriously reordering itself to accommodate the suggestion of a new perspective, left him to it.

The question, when Wilcox finally formulated it, was a surprising one. "Do you feel sorry for her, sir? For Mrs Bancroft, I mean?"

Ritter did not have to think about it. "Certainly I do. I can't say I like her much, but waking up like that, and then to find yourself faced with a man like Christopher Bancroft, who based on reports bears about as much resemblance to his brother as a wolf to a petted puppy… Even if she is putting up more of a fight than he might have expected, in my experience, when a man unaccustomed to changing his plans meets a woman unwilling to accommodate them, the result is usually very unpleasant, especially for her. My wife tells me there are whispers that she has taken leave of her senses entirely, and though I don't know it for a fact, I can hardly blame her if she has, given the circumstances. In other words, Constable, yes, I do feel very sorry for her."

"So do I, sir."

There was something forceful in the way he said it, as though bolstered by Ritter's support against some unknown contrary position.

"My mother never liked her," he went on, revealing exactly who that contrary position belonged to. "She'd wanted him to marry a proper lady, with a title, like the last Mrs Bancroft. She was terribly upset about it."

Ritter was about to agree, or at any rate to say something agreeable, when suddenly the boy's face changed, became confusedly defensive, as though realising he had said the wrong thing and must protect himself and the injured party both.

"My mother has been very ill, you know," he said, rebutting an accusation Ritter had not made, but at that moment, Ritter's attention was required elsewhere: across the road, the door which in all their conversation Ritter had never taken his eye off opened, and none other than Christopher Bancroft stepped into the waiting landau.

~

On the box of the police brougham, Constable Moore didn't need telling his job. He followed Bancroft's landau nimbly through Westminster and north along Victoria Embankment until they turned off by Somerset House, taking the Strand onto Kingsway and then Southampton Row. The narrow lanes of Holborn followed, through the legal district and into Bloomsbury, where Moore pulled the horses up hard across from the red-brick frontage of Great Ormond Street Children's Hospital.

Out of the window, Ritter saw Bancroft emerge from his landau, collar turned up against the fat raindrops just beginning to fall, and disappear inside. He considered his position. As a younger man, he might have been tempted to follow Bancroft in; indeed, he might not have realised there were other choices available to him. Now, though, he shook his head as Wilcox reached automatically for the door.

His own children having never needed more than the odd visit from the family physician, Ritter's only association with Great Ormond Street was recent and conducted at a distance. Upon the cook's request, he had ordered Mrs Bancroft's stricken maid cared for there, with two sentries posted on her door at all hours until such time as she either regained her senses or he found some other way to identify her master's killer. Thus, he knew nothing about the place specifically, but over the years, duty had called him to enough bedsides to give him a fair idea of hospitals generally. In his experience, they tended to be great hives of activity, heaving with busy people in white coats or pinafores who knew exactly where they were going, and distressed people milling about in confusion, too upset to know where they were, much less care.

Though one might not think it, a couple of men fitting into neither category – still in their greatcoats because they had no designated place to hang them, nor had they been in the place long enough to colonise some little corner of the overwhelming whole for their own – going about peering into rooms at random would stand out to people, especially when one of them was a great strapping lad like Wilcox. In particular, Ritter had no doubt they would stand out to a man who surely at this point must have at least an inkling of being of interest to organisations most people would prefer to be ignored by.

At this stage of proceedings, the last thing Ritter wanted was to stand out to Christopher Bancroft. Rather, what Ritter wanted was for Christopher Bancroft to believe himself if not undetected, then at least discreet, and able to go about his business with impunity. If such a man ever deigned to glance over his own shoulder, Ritter wanted him to see Scotland Yard toddling along far behind, patiently turning over one meaningless rock after the other, a bumbling, unthreatening presence, until the moment Ritter had gathered enough rocks to clobber him with. But that could only happen if Bancroft felt secure enough to be careless about at least a few of his rocks, metaphorically speaking.

Thus, Ritter remained where he was and waited.

He did not have to wait long. Barely a quarter of an hour after Christopher Bancroft had disappeared into the hospital, he re-emerged into the street. The rain had set in properly by now, darkening the sky already drawing into night, though it was not yet four o'clock. It poured down in sheets which ran off the roof of Ritter's brougham and down the windows in dense streaks, obscuring the view. Nevertheless, it was impossible to mistake the tall, dark figure, the way it stepped into the street to summon the landau with the command of an imperious hand.

It was the other hand which interested Ritter though. Bancroft held it clasped to his chest, holding something under his coat to protect it from the weather. The shape of it was unyielding however, the flat rectangle of a document wallet clutched over Bancroft's ribs as though he had just traded it for his firstborn.

Ritter only had a moment to be intrigued, however, before Bancroft surprised him again: the landau had pulled over, but rather than get in immediately, he turned away, making an impatient gesture towards the hospital he had just left. In the next, another figure appeared from within. Picking up her skirts to avoid the worst of the puddles, she hastened across to join him, and though she wore a large bonnet of the old-fashioned kind tied about her face, Ritter knew her immediately. The very size of her, and the way she carried her bulk not awkwardly but with purpose, as though she knew exactly what it could do and how to do it, belonged unmistakably to Dorothy Sharpe, the Bancroft cook.

She reached Bancroft in a matter of seconds, and as he handed her in, Ritter gave sign to Moore, wrapped in his oilskin on the box, that the chase was to begin again.

The rain turned the passing streets to watercolours, bleak greys and browns running with the merry glow of shop windows and gas lamps. Bit by bit, the shops fell away and the lamps grew closer together, the streets growing wider and the houses grander until Moore pulled a hundred yards away from one particular grand house Ritter was coming to know especially well. Bancroft's landau had stopped in front of it, not in the middle where the columned portcullis offered shelter but off to one side, where Ritter knew the side alley leading to the kitchen lay. The landau door opened and Mrs Sharpe stepped out, holding on to her bonnet as she hurried down towards the kitchen door Ritter had seen her in the night of the funeral.

In other words, Bancroft had taken her home.

The man himself did not follow her however. He remained in the landau, which moments later was in motion again.

On they went, and though Ritter could not find it in himself to be surprised when they rolled down Buckingham

Palace Road, past Lower Grosvenor Gardens, from which Ritter's former pigeon companions had long ago taken their leave, no doubt going to their roosts snug under the roof of Victoria Station. Nevertheless, as he watched the landau come to a halt in front of the Grosvenor Hotel awning, that Bancroft might go to his roost without being subjected to the indignity of even one more drop of rain: a whole afternoon for that.

He put it aside without too much trouble. While it would certainly have been nice of Bancroft to lead them to dinner with the killer, preferably at a table in the window of some easily observable chophouse, as it was he had by no means been ungenerous. Leaning out of the brougham window, Ritter gave hurried instruction to Moore. He was keen to get back to Great Ormond Street before memories faded and shifts changed.

Tracing Bancroft's steps within the hospital did not prove difficult. In a reception hall brimming with a confusion of mothers in shabby coats and reedy, sallow-faced children crying in rickety chairs, or chasing each other between the legs of harassed nurses pushing trolleys laden with gleaming metal and half-empty bottles, a well-dressed gentleman must inevitably stand out. The nurse on duty nodded in recognition before Ritter had even finished his description.

"I know the man you mean," she said, stepping automatically out of the way of a pair of children in leg braces screeching with laughter at the sound of their metal legware clattering across the tiled floor. "Came to pick up some documents from the records department. Impatient to get them, he was – said he couldn't wait for the post."

Because he knows we're watching his post, Ritter thought, but what he said was: "I'll need copies of everything he got – immediately if you'd be so good."

The look she gave him told him just how soon "immediately" meant in a place like that, no matter how good she was, but he held her gaze levelly until she huffed.

"I'll see what I can do, sir."

As she marched away, Ritter found himself unexpectedly solitary. Glancing about, he spied Wilcox some distance away, making his way towards a row of chairs filled with waiting patients. The particular chair he was intent on contained a woman Ritter didn't recognise, though the ostentatiousness of her bonnet and the contrast it made to the pinched, sallow look of her cheeks, the left side split by a long, thin cut, gave him some idea. It was the manner of Wilcox's approach, however, back stiff and face hard, which told him what he needed to know; that and the way the woman glared up at the constable, as though she too was aware, and if she did not precisely invite it was nevertheless fully prepared.

She stood up and gave an ironic little curtsy. "Constable," she said, and Ritter might have said there was ice in her voice, if he'd believed she could afford such a thing.

Before Wilcox could respond, Ritter was at his side, a warning hand on the constable's elbow.

"Madam." Ritter inclined his head to the woman and felt Wilcox's arm tense in objection to such politeness.

In response, Ritter tightened his grip but smiled up at the young man. "Friend of yours, Constable?"

From the way Wilcox jerked round at the very suggestion, Ritter had a sudden suspicion that only his hold on the lad's arm, and the lad's existing respect for him and his rank, had saved him from having to explain a black eye to Annabelle.

"Certainly not, sir." He lowered his voice. "Miss Smith is a resident of Gropecunt Lane, sir. I recognise her from my beat."

Ritter almost laughed. Under different circumstances, he might have done, at the sound of an old woman's euphemism for prostitution in the mouth of a young man, which somehow managed to be infinitely more vulgar than the word itself. There was nothing funny about Wilcox's face however.

He glared at the woman, as though her very existence personally insulted him. It was a look Ritter had seen before, at the beginning of the investigation when they had been discussing Victor Bancroft's mistress, and later when the subject of Wilcox's own sister had come up. It had been less blatant without a person actually present to direct it at, but it had been there, twisting the handsome young face into something profoundly ugly. Ritter thought he had gleaned enough to understand something of its source – a wayward sister, a mother made ill by her ensuing distress – but frankly he did not care: it was not a look appropriate for a man to direct at a woman he was duty-bound to protect, and Ritter intended to deal with it.

"Not a very pleasant place to live, I shouldn't think," he said, because this was neither the time nor the place. He tipped his hat to the woman. "Good day, madam. With me please, Constable."

Wilcox came, because Ritter left him no choice in the matter, but his arm was taut in Ritter's grip.

"Sir, I know that woman," he protested. "She's known to be pox-ridden – she can't possibly afford—"

Ritter cut him off with a look. He'd had just about enough of this, but the nurse with the clipboard had reappeared – Wilcox's private fixations would have to wait.

"I'm afraid Records is closed for today, sir," the nurse told him. "But I left a note on their desk with your request."

Ritter nodded in thanks. He would send Sergeant Jameson over first thing in the morning to make sure they read it. In the meantime: "Did Mr Bancroft do anything else while he was here? Request anything, or speak to anyone?"

"Only to find Miss Fletcher's room, sir. I told him, and then later he left with the woman who always visits her, a large woman—"

"Mrs Sharpe," Ritter finished for her, remembering Bancroft's companion. There was something there he was sure, something important, some connection beyond the obvious which permitted her to speak harshly to a man so far above herself and still be invited into his carriage...

He was yanked from his thoughts when a white-coated gentleman collared him, begging a word.

"Did I hear rightly that you are Inspector Ritter, who signs the orders for Miss Fletcher?" he asked, drawing Ritter into a discreet corner. "I have been hoping you might come by so that I might speak to you directly. I'm sorry to say that in spite of our every effort, Miss Fletcher's condition remains entirely unchanged. We gave her sedatives initially, understanding her to be suffering from severe nervous shock, but she has not had any for weeks now, nor any other medication, and yet she continues to give every appearance of an individual under heavy sedation. Frankly it has us baffled. The fact is that there's not much more we can do for her here. She needs to be somewhere more suited to long-term care, where appropriate steps may be taken..."

He trailed off, looking to Ritter for an answer to the question plain on his face, the request to take a hopeless case off his hands and give him back a bed.

Ritter considered. In his experience, it was not unusual for a shock to the nerves to cause unexpected and sometimes difficult behaviour. It was, however, practically unheard of for it to cause someone to enter a total catatonic state lasting for many weeks. Additionally, if someone behaved as though they were taking a specific substance, it was typically because they were, whether or not they or anyone else were aware of it. And though someone taking the trouble to give the maid tranquilisers under the very nose of her doctors did not answer his question of why she was still alive, it told him that at least there *was* a reason. Taking the trouble to continuously sedate someone was infinitely more trouble, not to say involved far more risk than either killing her or leaving her be. That meant someone was equally keen to keep the girl alive as to keep her quiet. Within the privacy of his brain, Ritter grinned: Now he knew more than he had a moment ago. Now he knew that his question was not *why not* but *why*. This was progress, and a positive was typically easier to answer than a negative.

"I would be grateful if you could keep her here another week or so," Ritter told the doctor. "If you will kindly direct me to her room, I need a word with the men on her door."

Having received directions from the disappointed doctor, Ritter turned to find himself almost walking into the solid breadth of Constable Wilcox. The young man stood loyally at heel, though his attention was somewhere else entirely.

Ritter followed his line of sight to find it squarely back on the woman who had been his target just moments before, yet as Ritter gritted his teeth to keep from barking at Wilcox in frustration, he noticed she looked almost a different person. Rather than glaring at the world from under her deliberately conspicuous bonnet, at once inviting remark and daring anyone to make it, she seemed now to have forgotten the world altogether. Crouched on the floor made slick and dirty by the rain tramped in, she appeared to have eyes for nothing and no one but the child now being led into the reception by a nurse.

Seeing the woman's outstretched arms, he gave a squawking cry and flung himself at her, and though the bodily strain of lifting him was written upon her face, so too was the fact that she would not have given it up for the world.

It was not her face which interested Ritter however. Unnoticed by either of the pair, Wilcox was watching them with an expression Ritter suspected he did not realise he was allowing anyone to see.

As the woman thanked the nurse and departed with her boy safely in her arms, Ritter put a steadying hand on the young man's shoulder, knowing that now was both the time and the place: impressions held better in softened wax, no matter the source of the heat.

"Sometimes," he began, "the facts are the most important thing in the world, but most days they pale in comparison to everyone getting on as best they can. A good copper knows the difference, and a great one defers to it. Remember that. You might need her one day, or her lad. And even if you don't, they will always need you."

For a moment, Wilcox gave no sign of having heard. Then, his throat moving as though he had to force the word out over something rough, he said, very quietly: "Sir."

Ritter left him to it as he went to give Miss Fletcher's sentries their new orders: effective immediately, the visits of every doctor, nurse and fellow officer were to be recorded discreetly by the men on duty, including name and time, and the log provided to him by the end of each shift.

The men took his orders in stride, but as Ritter turned to go, the senior man piped up: "What about visitors who aren't doctors, nurses or with us, sir?" he asked. "Only, that cook comes by daily now, and just this afternoon Mr Bancroft himself—"

"Keep them out." Ritter wasn't sure what was going on with the pair of them, but something was, and he had no desire to make life easier for them. In any case, he was about to embark on a tedious process of weeding out potential suspects, and the less muddy he could keep the metaphorical waters of the search, the better. "No unessential visitors to be allowed in, on my express instruction."

XIII

"I found it in the nursery." Violet offered up Marit's old book, half because it was the nominal reason she had come, and half for the sake of breaking the increasingly stretched silence. "I can't imagine how it got there. I suppose Nanny must have found it at some point and put it away, thinking it was the boys' – when you were staying with us, before you were married."

It felt ridiculous to add that last bit – when else could it have been, when they had barely seen each other since? – and Violet found herself wondering which of them she had added it for. She thrust the wrapped book at the cousin she barely recognised. And that, too, was ridiculous, when Nora looked practically identical to how she had then, in those months she had made her home in Violet's best guest room after leaving school. Rather, Violet felt she was seeing her differently. Nora was the same, her features as sharp, her eyes as pale, but Violet was only now capable of seeing just how sharp, just how pale. But surely it was only the setting, the mourning dress and the colossal silence of the dark house. This evening was the first time Violet had been invited in: she could not picture it in daylight.

"I hope you haven't missed it," she went on. "I ought to have brought it sooner, only…" She trailed off, the impulse to talk stemmed by the feeling that there was no one listening.

Nora, perched on the edge of the blue-and-white-striped settee, which Violet had thought utterly charming until her cousin had sat upon it and rendered it simpering with the harsh black of her dress, had unwrapped the book. In the act of running her fingers over the faded cover she paused, a crease in her brow and a small, pensive curl at her lip. It was an expression which might equally have run to a smile as a frown, but she sat unmoving, suspended between the two.

Violet found herself at a loss. It was an uncommon experience for her; indeed, friends often beseeched her to join parties promising to be awkward, specifically to make use of her talent for brightening the dullest conversation, breaking the tersest silence. Now, not only had she not been invited to break it, she had not been invited at all, yet the stiff old butler had not quite been able to conceal his relief at her arrival as he'd left her standing in the entrance hall to find out if madam was at home.

The light of the chandelier had been brilliant of course, but it had carried with it a sense of contrast, an impression that it was so brilliant because every other part of the house lay in darkness. The place had the air of a stage about it, lit up where the audience needed to see and not an inch beyond. Even the great staircase seemed to rise into gloom, and then out of the darkness Nora had appeared, arms outstretched in greeting as her eyes glittered in the sudden brilliant light...

Violet gave herself a little shake, knowing it was her own guilty conscience casting shadows on the wall. For if there were any artifice at play, it must surely be her own. She could not but be acutely conscious of it, that the very premises on which she presented herself were false: of course she had not come to return an old book, discovered and forgotten again multiple times over the intervening years, nor even to mourn with a dear cousin, once almost a sister.

The bundle of letters burned in her pocket. In the Italian fireplace, the flames seemed to sense her discomfort and answer, leaping too high, their shadows mocking as they danced on the walls.

Violet shifted uncomfortably in her seat, making the heavy silk creak in protest. It was the sound, she supposed, which told her that Nora had been recalled to her presence, even before she looked round.

"Thank you." Nora lay the book aside, covering it again with the cloth Violet had brought it in, protection from the rain even now drumming savagely against the windowpanes. A gust of wind shrieked somewhere within the chimney, making Violet jump.

"Truthfully I haven't thought of it in years. It was a present from a school friend who died. I can't read it of course. She was Norwegian."

Nora smiled at the memory – a small, wistful smile, entirely human. It warmed Violet to see, and she returned it instinctively.

"We did wonder," she said. "It certainly has some marvellous illustrations, quite fantastical. It's a good thing the boys never looked at it – they would have had nightmares for weeks. They have such imaginations. Even as it is, Mills will insist on telling them stories whenever we visit Mama, about fairies and changelings and I know not what. Frightened poor Toby half to death a couple of years ago. Even after his father assured him that the city is too noisy for fairies to visit, he still made Mills draw him up a list of rules to memorise – only of course she calls them 'good neighbours'. Really, you should have seen it: never offend a good neighbour, never accept anything from a good neighbour, never put yourself in their debt in any way and never let them think you have; a good neighbour may look human at a casual glance but they can never get it quite right, especially the eyes, and so on. The same stories she told us when we were children, I suppose, only I never noticed then how ridiculous it sounded at the time. You do remember old Mills, don't you?"

"I do."

Something about the way Nora said it dismissed further conversation on the subject out of hand.

"To tell you the truth, when Alcott said you had brought something of mine, I was expecting something else entirely. Have you heard from your mother lately?"

Though the question was ordinary enough, the way Nora looked when she asked it was anything but. Violet found herself glancing away. "No," she said. It was not a lie: the letters in her pocket were not from her mother.

"You will stay to supper of course?"

It was only the abrupt change of tone which told Violet that she had been heard at all. Indeed, in that instant, the entire atmosphere of the room seemed to change, as though the very air danced to its mistress's tune. Violet looked up to find herself met with a smile so broad and so empty that it was little more than a gash across the sallow skin.

Violet had not thought about it until that very moment, but all at once she knew absolutely that she did not want to stay to supper. But she had not yet discharged her errand, and Nora just kept smiling at her, eyes like diamonds looking through Violet as though she were nothing, as though she were not there at all.

Violet caught herself and took herself in hand, as resolutely as she would her own son, had she caught him behaving in so disgraceful a manner. Fancy reading such horrors into her own cousin, letting her own nagging conscience colour her every move – her very house! – with the sinister, when quite plainly there was nothing there not attributable to ordinary mourning and grief. Why, had not Violet's own mother behaved a good deal more oddly than this following the death of her only brother? And had not that tainted her feelings towards his daughter, to an extent which persisted even now? So much so that simple letters, requests from her niece for the address of a relation, caused her enough distress that her children must become involved? For that was what had happened, and that, Violet reminded herself firmly, was all that had happened: Nora had written to request the address of a relative on her mother's side, which she believed Judith to have. In her grief, she had made the request several times and at the last rather forcefully. That alone had given Judith such a turn that Ben had had to be sent for, and he in turn had sent the letters to Violet in London on the basis that she and Nora had been close once, and she might therefore reasonably ask Nora to desist.

That was what had occurred – that was all that had occurred, Violet reminded herself firmly, and her own discomfort at being involved was no reason not to accept an invitation to dine and give comfort to a cousin obviously struggling with her own grief in this big, lonely house.

"Of course I will," she said, shame making her emphatic. "I should be delighted."

The dining room was smaller than Violet had expected, or perhaps it was only that the walls were taller. Lined with narrow windows curtained in impenetrable swaths of velvet, they stretched to the distant ceiling, as high as the room was wide. The table was immense, however, and the hunting scenes which lined the walls fractionally too big for their allotted space, so that on the whole, there was a curious sense of disproportion about the room, nudging Violet off balance even as Nora's eyes met hers over the steaming almond soup and pinned her to her chair.

"Tell me all," she said, and Violet had the distinct impression of being asked an earnest question by a smiling mask.

She seized it nevertheless and began conscientiously, trying to remember all that had happened since their last meetings, which had petered out shortly after Nora's honeymoon. It was a long list: Ben's children arriving of course, and her husband finding a publisher for his books, and her own attempts to balance the bringing up of her boys with the needs of the various societies to which she belonged. She was just at the point of explaining how she was trying to carve out at least an hour of practice on the piano every day, to learn the latest tunes so that she would not disappoint the company when she was inevitably asked to play, when outside the wind caught itself against the house and howled in outrage.

Nora, who had been listening to Violet with every appearance of absorption, cocked her head as though for a knock at the door, if the door had been where the windows were. There was nothing to be heard now but the raindrops drumming in counterpoint to the crackling fire, but even as Nora looked back for Violet to continue, Violet had the impression she was still listening for something, straining for it at the expense of all else.

Violet was halfway through a litany of the boys' petty illnesses before her empty soup bowl was noticed and Nora rang the bell. Not that Violet could claim herself any more observant: only as the footman appeared to clear away the dishes did she realise Nora's was still full.

There was turbot to follow, a beautiful fish expertly poached, served with leeks and a delicate velouté, but Violet could enjoy none of it. Outside, the wind had risen, whipping itself up to the precipice of a storm which would have made Violet fear for the chestnut tree in next door's garden, had not Nora absorbed her attention so completely. They were not significant, her gestures, not at first; a tremor of the hand holding the fork which never seemed to rise to her mouth; a short, sharp shake of the dark head; an irritable glance back, as though at some impertinent fellow patron. Only, of course, there was no fellow patron.

There was only Violet, apparently quite forgotten now, and the fire dancing across the hunting scenes, and the windows, and the howling wind beyond.

"The wind is terribly loud," Violet said, because she had to – absolutely had to – say something. Anything. And yet it was almost a surprise when Nora looked up to find that she had heard.

"It is?" she asked, every bit as though she had not been twisting to its very tune, jerking to it like a puppet on a string. "I own I hadn't noticed. I'm afraid I've been rather distracted lately. It's been difficult…"

She speared a bit of fish with a wry smile, apologetic even, and Violet was surprised at the force with which she found herself seizing on it, all but choking on the rush of sympathy those words brought. Sympathy – or relief. "I cannot begin to imagine—"

"They took my pendant, you know," Nora went on, intent suddenly, as though Violet had not spoken at all. "The police claim it's a coincidence but I'm sure it can't be. I wrote—"

"Is that the one you had as a child?" Violet interrupted.

Her voice was too loud in the room, yet she hardly cared. She knew only that there was something unwholesome about that intensity, and she must stem the flow before it could become something more.

"I recognised the description in the paper. I remember you always wore it, even in the bath. You'd whistle on it, and it would make a sound just like the wind." The words were in her mouth before she knew what they would be, and though she tried to keep them in, they tipped out anyway, pushed by sheer momentum. "You'd tell me you were calling your dog."

The very air seemed to rustle against itself as Nora smiled.

"Perhaps now my dog is calling me," she said as the wind moaned outside, and it was a joke of course; she was smiling in amusement at her own nonsense joke, but Violet couldn't laugh, couldn't look away from those impossible glittering eyes...

It happened quite suddenly. All at once the wind rose to a howl, a plaintive, almost pitiful sound, a sound which Violet could quite imagine coming from some creature ignored by its mistress. It was not the sound which fixed her horrified in her place however but her cousin's reaction to it.

Nora whipped round in her seat, but this time she did not content herself with a glare at the covered windows. She rose, pushing her chair back so that the legs scraped cruelly over the silk carpet, already turning towards the offending cry.

It was at that moment that Violet saw it: the twist of the overlong torso hinging sharply at the waist as it turned away entirely independent of the hips below, while above the head remained perfectly level, too preoccupied with the unseen intruder to trouble with any disguise.

Nora stalked over to the window, her shoulders drawn up like hackles, still bent slightly at the waist, as though in her distraction she had forgotten to fold herself back to human proportions. If she sensed Violet's eyes upon her, she gave no sign. The rustle of her skirts mingled with the persistent keening of the wind as she took up the satin curtain pull and gave it a yank of such ferocity that the mechanism shrieked in its tracks. Violet fancied she heard the dull thud of fixings straining against their plasterwork, and for a moment worried that the curtains were about to come down on top of her cousin, pole, pulley and all.

The fixings held however, and as the curtains opened, Violet could only stare: revealed behind the heavy velvet was not the lamplit Kensington evening, nor even a storm so fierce as to obscure everything beyond it. She could hear the drum of the rain against the glass, the cry of the wind as it rocked the window in its frame. Neither glass nor rain were visible however, and she could see only the barest suggestion of frame where it peeked out behind the rough planks nailed across it, obscuring all the world beyond.

Even Nora seemed taken aback for a moment. She stared at the construction, crude and vulgar amid the elegance of the room, with a look of such confusion that Violet was ready to grab onto it as a sign of continuing kinship, to use it to insist on her own ridiculousness. Only it was not ridiculous. Even as she sought to deny it, she knew the truth. Whether it was new or had always been present in some infant form, a form she herself had been too young to know, she knew it now undeniably.

"Do excuse me," Nora said, turning back towards her. "I'd forgotten I ordered the windows boarded up. Not all of them have shutters, you see."

It was the way she said it as much as anything, with a smile of bashful realisation, as though admitting to some minor personal eccentricity rather than the ordering of her home blotted entirely of natural light. For that was what she had done. Violet saw it suddenly with perfect clarity: nothing else could have forced an entire house in the middle of town into such complete darkness.

Outside, the wind howled and the rain drummed, and inside there was only Nora. Her shadow fell upon the boards behind her, twisting in a way not entirely accounted for by the leaping firelight. The flames flashed golden white on her canines as she smiled, and all at once the room was too small, the walls too high, shutting Violet in with this, this—

She could bear it no more.

Knowing thought to be her enemy in this moment, she snatched up her glass and drank it off in an ugly gulp, fortifying herself enough for a single outburst. She pulled out the letters and held them out: "I'm afraid my mother cannot help you. I would ask you to leave her be, and all of us."

Whether she managed some thanks for dinner or excuse for her departure, she never knew. She knew only that, as Nora opened her mouth, she tossed the bundle on the fire and fled, clattering through the vast darkened house, her own nightmare nipping at her heels.

It was that nightmare which prevented Violet ever going back. Even in the calm rationality of daylight she remembered it, peering out from the darkness, its eyes like the drawings in that awful book, confirming every nameless fear her mother had ever had.

XIV

It was the look on his face which told Margaret for certain what for weeks she had refused to understand.

Christopher looked up at her from the dining table with an expression which might have been called beatific, if not for the determination which focused the joy into something hard, something almost like dogmatism.

"It's here!" he all but laughed, looking in glee at the documents spread out before him. "It's really all here, every bit of it, just as Virgo said it would be. She's certifiable on this alone, and with her recent behaviour, well…"

Margaret made a noise which she hoped conveyed sufficient enthusiasm and went to the bedroom, to find a coat capable of standing up to the rain. It beat against the window in sheets, but was suddenly preferable to remaining in this room a second longer.

She was pulling on her boots – the ones from Milan, from better days – when Christopher came in, leaning against the door frame, a handful of papers clutched in his hand.

"Did you hear what I said?" he asked as though he really imagined Margaret could have missed it. "She really is mad as a March hare. Virgo recommended that she be sent to his school – remember I told you he had an institution out near Wembley at that time? – after she broke the poor man's arm when she was a child, but her family were too sentimental."

Margaret paused in the act of tying her laces. "I thought he treated her when she was very young?"

"He did. His records put her at four at the time." Christopher frowned. "Are you going out?"

"Just for a walk."

Margaret fetched her green poplin. She wished he hadn't come in, but now that he had, she might as well put on a sturdier dress as well.

"What on earth did he do, to give a four-year-old girl the strength to break a man's arm?" she asked over her shoulder as Christopher stepped forward automatically to help her.

"Nothing," he said, distracted by the buttons. "He just tried to treat her. I told you, she's mad."

They'd never kept personal servants, preferring to save the money, look after each other and damn the world. As he finished the work though, Margaret turned back just in time to catch the veil of irritation lifting from his face. It was a faint thing, and perhaps in his concentration he had not even noticed it himself, but there it was: irritation, that he had to be involved in such an operation. Irritation, because such work was not what he was made for.

The realisation struck her like a blow. Her first instinct was to claim ignorance, but what would be the point in such a lie? She knew him as well as she knew herself. Better even. And she knew that, for all the man's obstinate refusal to bend to it, he was still the product of his formative years. Whatever he might pretend to himself, he bore the stamp of a boyhood he not only had not forgotten but, deep within some place secret even to himself, had not wished to forget.

She was under no illusion that the father had intended the estrangement to be anything but temporary: nothing she knew about Henry Bancroft, whether his private affections or his public deportment, suggested he had intended to permanently exile his younger son. What the end result might have been, whether capitulation or perpetual stalemate between two men equally and in equal parts stubborn and aware of their place in the world was never to be known. Death delights in making mock of human design, and Henry Bancroft had died within a year of their departure, thrown from his horse during the last hunt of the season, his head cracking open against the rocks like a liver-spotted egg.

They'd been hard to find during that first year and in consequence had only heard about it the following spring.

That discretion, their movements not quite secret but not so far from it as to make the difference, had been largely on Margaret's account. She had feared pursuit, reprisal even, and none of Christopher's assurances that his father would do nothing to invite scandal could assuage her. It was a relief, then, when the old man died, a horrible, evil relief, to be squashed up and buried in some dark and hidden place, never to see the light of day. She had been punished for it anyway though, and with the greatest of irony, for it was then and not before that Christopher had begun to glance homeward.

It had been subtle, at first, just the faintest twist of the head in moments of distraction, helpless, as though pulled on a string. On those occasions when he caught himself in the act, the disgust which filled his face had been comfort enough. And in any case, she could hardly blame him, not when she'd been writing letters home, and sending money every quarter even when she got no response. Even when she'd stopped bothering with the letters, she'd kept up the money, a steady flow enough for her mother to keep the cottage and keep Paul in good stead and education. If Christopher had ever asked her about it, she'd have told him the truth: that it was money she needed to spend to pay off her conscience and buy her freedom.

News of Victor's marriage had followed before the end of that summer, and for three months together, every tongue they encountered seemed to be wagging on subjects including his choice of bride, the involvement of the elder Vascelles brother, whose machinations were said to have put her in his path, and whether it was true that, though admitted to be gently born, the lady in question had been in circumstances so much reduced that she had been living in an attic room on the sufferance of a cousin until the day she was married. Some even whispered that she had gone to school, and in general it was wondered what on earth could have possessed Victor Bancroft to make such a perverse choice, when it was said he did not appear to even be particularly attached to her.

It was a question pondered in salons across Europe. The presence of Emil Vascelles in the situation added additional spice, given the latter's flight from London before the marriage had even taken place, couched in respectable business but rumoured to be anything but. It was a conundrum, and one too delicious to resist the questioning of the estranged younger brother.

For three months then, Christopher had been drawn into the speculation, equally in confidential tête-a-tête and for the amusement of jovial groups, called upon to explain the conundrum and lay bare the family perversion which caused young men of so many gifts to bind themselves to women so very much beneath them.

He'd borne it as well as he could, which sometimes was even admirably; an elegant deflection, a knowing look, a smirk on a pointedly closed mouth, and always with one hand conspicuously on Margaret's waist. She'd thought the shadow drawing together under the knit of his eyebrows had been irritation then, or embarrassment, and she hadn't questioned it. Neither had she asked when long nights had resulted in letters addressed to Hampshire in the morning tray but only offered silent consolation when none came in reply. By then, she'd known the feeling.

Winter had brought new scandals to marvel at, and though still no replies came from Victor, the money appeared with the same unerring regularity as under his father. Meanwhile, the balls dazzled and the wine sparkled as much as it ever had. In the face of such gilded pleasure, it was difficult for any shadow to remain unfaded. Indeed, in that golden glow, it was possible to believe the darkness was wiped away entirely, and if, on inspection, that glow was reflected off the bars of a gilded cage, then at least it was a cage large enough that one need not see the bars if one did not care to look. More importantly, it trapped them both equally, together.

"Let's go to Paris," she begged, desperate suddenly and not knowing why. "Or Venice, or Istanbul. Let's go to Istanbul. The Zhemchugovs will be there by now. I can write directly – they always have room—"

But no, it was no good: there was no escaping it, that shadow which had never gone away, which she knew now had never been either irritation or embarrassment but concern, frustrated and impotent, until that meeting in Antwerp had armed it.

She hadn't been invited to that meeting, nor to those which followed. She'd seen the shadow growing though, every day darkening, focusing, honing that face she loved so well, until she hardly dared look at it for fear of what she might see.

She looked now and saw.

"We've been through this already," he reminded her. "I have a responsibility—"

"But you don't!" Margaret burst out. "You gave it up for my sake, remember? *Victor* had a responsibility, now she does, and after her it'll be her heir, but *you* will never be responsible ever again!"

The look he gave her was like ice over a storm. In spite of herself, Margaret felt the urge to crack it. He had never withheld himself from her, not as he did from other people; it was unfair to force it on her now.

"I have a responsibility," he repeated, folding his arms and looking at her from a great height. "Whether you agree or not."

And there it was. The tone of his voice had frozen her insides, and the look he gave her shattered them. It was a look she knew well and one she had never expected to be on the receiving end of. It left her with barely enough breath for the question. "What are you going to do?"

"What I must." He had the grace to turn away in the face of her wretchedness, marching too briskly back to the sitting room.

She trailed behind him, helpless to do anything else.

Look, Meg, I can't marry you. That was what he'd said, and she'd believed him absolutely. Perhaps he had too. Perhaps he still did. But it wasn't true, was it? It might have meant disinheritance, but he could have married her nevertheless. Then they could have forged their own way, together, as she had been setting out to do alone. As she had given up for his sake.

"Are you going to marry her?"

His back was to her, bent over the documents on the table, but she knew he'd heard her by the way he tensed. Bracing himself.

"Answer the question, Kit." She'd intended to demand, but it came out in a plea. "Are you going to marry her?"

Still he did not look at her. "Don't be silly – I can't marry her. She's my brother's widow – it's against the law."

"But would you want to? If you could find a way, would you marry her?"

He turned then, and her first thought was that he looked tired, or would have done, if not for the feverish brightness still in his eyes.

"What do you think?" he asked, letting out a breath he seemed to have been holding for some time. "No, I don't *want* to marry her. All else aside, she's a miserably dull thing. But it would be better if I could – you do see that, don't you?" He managed the barest shadow of a smile – in it she fancied she could glimpse the ghost of the warmth it had once contained. "We can go to Istanbul next year. Once it's all been settled, I'm sure I'll be in dire need of a holiday."

Like a candle shut in a jam jar, all the air seemed suddenly sucked out of the room. Margaret had never needed marriage particularly – intention had been enough; partnership had been enough. And they had been partners, always. All through the blur of those years, through the parties and the laughter and the dancing and the wine, they had been partners. Even when there had been others, for curiosity and amusement, separate and shared, they had never been unsteady. They had understood each other, so that even when they had fought, on those rare nights of true anger, when he bricked his anguish up behind walls of ice and she drowned hers in a lake of whatever came to hand, it was in the knowledge that by morning, his bricks would have melted and she would wash up on the shore, and then they would sit together again and be fair.

But they had never fought like this. This wasn't even fighting, to Margaret's mind, but a change of the battlefield beneath her feet.

Or could it be that it had always been that way, only she had never noticed?

"Did you intend to come for me?" The question was out, there in the room before she'd even admitted it was in her mind. "That night, when you put me on the train, did you really intend to follow me?"

He'd been so angry with her for failing to write, scolding her like a child, insisting it was obvious that he'd meant her to. Perhaps it was, but now all she could think was that he'd never asked. And that she knew, now, that it didn't take a hired man six weeks to find a foolish country girl lost in London, not the sort of man Christopher Bancroft could afford.

"Of course I did!" he flared, just as she'd known he would. "And I did come for you, didn't I? I sacrificed everything for it!"

Whatever had been true at the time, Margaret saw that he truly believed his own words now. But it wasn't enough. "Then come to Istanbul with me and let Nora Bancroft use her miserable dull rope to hang herself."

"Meg…" He came towards her, arm outstretched even as his brow darkened, pulled between tenderness and frustration. "You know it's not the same—"

"*How* do I know?" The question exploded out of her. "You don't tell me what you're doing, you've barely said two words to me since Antwerp – how could I possibly know it's not the same?"

The hand dropped away, along with any suggestion of warmth, as he squared himself against her. "You know because I've told you so."

She knew it at once, that look: cool, collected, confident of its rightness, unassailable in its entitlement to be so, with that very same imperial highhandedness which had persuaded the *haut monde* of Europe that a disgraced English boy and his below stairs lover not only belonged among them but were worth making room for. It was an effective look, a powerful one, and never had she thought to find it trained upon herself.

There was horror in it, but it was a cold kind, a sluggish, glacial mass creeping over her insides, freezing everything in its path and trapping them beneath its enormous inevitability. Somewhere within that frozen calm, it occurred to Margaret that she had never said goodbye to Mrs Stovell. The old woman had been the only true friend she had made in London, a lifeline in her kindness and her currant buns both, yet when the moment had come, Margaret had left without a single word, without a note even, like a thief in the night. *Or a whore.*

She had thought of it of course. How could she not? But they had been vague thoughts, quickly dismissed as being uncomfortable just when a world of never-ending comfort was opening itself before her. In the face of it, the whole of her time in London had made her uncomfortable. She thought it legitimate enough to prefer to forget the way the fleas from the rags she sorted at the pulping plant had got into her hair and up under her sleeves, becoming her constant companions into the night, their little black bodies scurrying over every inch of her as they sank their vicious little jaws into the most fanciful of places until in the darkness she longed for a light and was thankful to have none; the way the matchstick factory had seemed innocuous enough, the work of filling match boxes oddly satisfying and even pleasant compared to the reeking, filthy rags, only making it all the more unbearable when one day a skilled woman, one of those who made the matches, had entered the boxing room and Margaret had seen for the first time what was meant by the term "phossy jaw".

In the hotel which cost more for a night than a month's wages together, the thought of such things had been awkward, a juxtaposition as unnatural as it was untenable, dizzying to hold in one's mind. The thought of speaking it aloud had been absurd, shameful to think on, and so she had not. If she had, she might have come to the conclusion that she would not want Kit to think of her in those circumstances, to know of her lack of faith. To speak of Mrs Stovell, to tell him she wished to pay a visit to Waterloo, or to write a note he might casually ask about would have been to admit to both. So she had not, and he had not asked about her weeks in London nor she about his time in Hampshire with his father, and thus an unspoken agreement had formed between them to leave well enough alone.

It was an agreement which had served them eminently, and only now did it occur to Margaret that it was not the entire truth. Saying goodbye to Edna Stovell would have meant telling Kit about her, true; equally, it would have meant telling Edna Stovell about Kit. It was to admit to giving up independence for something as nebulous as love. It was to invite Edna Stovell to blow past feeling and into practicality, to look at her the way her own mother had, the way Paul had imitated without understanding, the way she would be looked at out of the corner of her eye in ballrooms and salons across the Continent, no matter what light Kit had tried to cast upon her. It was the way Margaret had caught herself looking at that woman in the gutter.

Yet she could not regret. If, once, six weeks apart had aged them, ten years together had preserved them. Bounding about in a fairyland of their own making, abandoned by any power which might force change upon them, they had remained as they were, boy and girl in love. Had they stayed in their exile, they might have been so still. But like the knight returning from Avalon, they had found the years waiting for them on the white cliffs, ready to clobber them into the shapes they were always intended to take. In the blink of an eye, he had grown to be the man his father had raised him to be, and she – well, she had to face the natural consequences of being a village girl unable to accept a village girl's lot.

And yet fairyland had not been without its lingering gifts. She could see now, and she could object. And if she was never to be free from that look for the rest of her life, she could at least refuse to turn away from it. She could – she must – meet it square on and let it do what it would.

"I won't be your mistress. Not like that." There was a calm in her voice which surely must be shock or else understanding. She met Christopher's gaze and saw both reflect there.

"You understand she holds all the cards, don't you?" he tried. "She'll leave us destitute if she realises it."

"Then let her. We'll manage."

Margaret watched and hoped, even now. The tendon in his throat twitched once, twice, but no other sign came. She had not really expected it to. Even as he looked at her, she knew he did not truly see. She was no longer his object in life. The prospect of being *the* Mr Bancroft dangled before him, the Mr Bancroft his father had wanted and his brother had failed to be, and he could not look away. In his eyes, there was no longer room for anything else, for Margaret or decency or even pity, for the poor mad widow he proposed to trap by whatever means he could.

Margaret packed as much as she could carry, choosing the best dresses, the most expensive shoes, every bit of jewellery she could find. And why not? Was it not her due as an ersatz lady, a discarded gentleman's whore, to take her earnings when she went? And he would not begrudge her, would not even miss them. She understood now that it had never been about the money.

Only when she was at the door did he find his tongue. "What will you do?"

Margaret shrugged. "Sell flowers in Covent Garden," she said lightly, jokingly, believing herself that she didn't know and then realising immediately that she did. "Or help those who can't. Those whose great crime has been to have worse luck than me."

She glanced back once, just in case, but he had turned away, back to his paperwork, as though the sight of her leaving might be a distraction.

The rain had stopped by now, and the evening was fresh and bracing. Hansom cabs rattled over the cobbles, and all around her, bundled-up pedestrians stepped over puddles with varying degrees of grace and success. The air smelled of smoke and rain, and of chestnuts roasting in a brazier on the corner. Margaret bought a bag, pulling off her gloves to peel the nuts, hot and sweet beneath the crusted salt.

She'd told herself once that she'd only experienced one kind of happiness in this dank, dour maze of a city – the happiness of knowing she would shortly be leaving it. That wasn't quite fair she realised now. It might not have been happiness precisely, but there had been something before then, a satisfaction, even a harsh kind of joy. Again the woman in the gutter appeared before her, and even as the head drooped in shame, Margaret saw the shoulders which held it straight and proud, promising to remain so for as long as they possibly could.

Margaret had seen enough of the world to know there were causes aplenty in every great city. Even the visitor could not help but see them, whether they wished to or not. But she knew now for the first time that this was her city and those shoulders her cause.

Ahead, the triple brass orbs of the pawnbroker's sign gleamed, wet in the flickering light of the gas lamps. Margaret passed it by. She knew the value of what she had and would find a more promising buyer. Then, where St Nicholas had given his three golden balls to poor girls in order that they might marry, she would arrange her own wealth to help them do whatever they bloody well pleased.

XV

Her dress scratched at her, even in sleep.

Only gradually did Nora become aware of her eyes having opened. They fixed on some point beyond the open window, a black speck against the white swirl of sky, meaningless until it turned its gleaming eye to look at her.

She watched absorbed as it circled, wide and careless, spreading its wings until it became a bird, feathers sleek in the silver light. On it came, beat by beat until the air pulsed in time. It circled the cornice, stark black life against the dead white, swooping lower, ever closer. So effortlessly did it glide about her that Nora was seized by the impulse to join it, to spread herself out and rise up alongside it, to play, to compete, even to fight, for the sheer joy of movement. She thought she might have done it, had her wings not been bound up in the scratching, hateful dress.

Though she spoke not a word, moved not a muscle as she lay prone, immobilised beneath her own unnatural weight, her distress cried out and was heard. The swoops became measured, grew tighter as the creature came down, wings beating about her face as it circled, close enough that she saw it was not its eye gleaming at all but a silver pendant hung about its glossy throat.

With a strength she had not known until that moment yet had been conscious of always, she reached up to take what was hers.

At her touch, it slipped through her fingers like so much water, and she only succeeded in pulling the bird down on top of her. The points of its talons dug into her chest as it shifted and balanced upon her, cocking its black head to one side as it considered her with jewelled eyes.

Without warning, it lunged forward, plunging its beak like a sabre into the stuff which bound her, pecking around whalebone and pulling with all its might at the choking lace at her throat. It made no difference: still she was trapped. She lay prone, her strength spent, unable to lift her own limbs.

They knew it, all of them, and one by one they came. The crows settled upon her shoulder, tearing into her sleeves with single-minded determination, not so much as glancing up as the rooks joined them, and the ravens, and even the flash of a magpie's white and cobalt blue. The whole of her was covered in them, a teeming, cawing mass, feathers ruffling, shifting together as they pecked and pulled and scratched as one, the weight pressing her down, holding her in place until it grew more burdensome even than the awful dress. In their ardour they forgot to let her breathe, and though she could not move, she remembered her will and summoned it: "ENOUGH!"

The storm of their wings blotted the room as they left her alone in the darkness.

She caught her breath in time for the opening door, starting at the cry which followed. "My good heavens, what in the world happened?"

McNeal set down her tray and carried the lamp over as Nora lifted her hand to her face.

"I had a bad dream." She stared in fascination at the cuff which dangled from her wrist, utterly decimated. "I suppose I must have scratched myself."

About her on the bed, her dress lay in a tatter of rags, shredded beyond use even as humble dust cloths. Nora did not need to see McNeal to feel the housekeeper's incredulity as she took in the scene, but her own disorientation would not let her spare it any mind. The windows of her bedroom were closed, she saw, shuttered and nailed as they should be, as they had been for weeks. As she had ordered them. Everything floated around her, or perhaps she was the one floating. She groped about but could not find what day it was, whether it was day at all or dead of night. The word she had cried still hung in her throat, though she was certain she had not spoken, and anyway—

"Why did you wake me?"

The housekeeper bowed her head in apology, yet there was about her an air almost of gratitude, as though even an uncalled-for upbraiding was preferable to having to look at Nora's shredded skirts for a moment longer.

"Your pardon, madam. I thought I heard…" McNeal gave her head a sharp shake, as though dispelling something unwelcome. "And a letter came for you, madam, hand delivered from Mr Vascelles's office just now. I thought you would wish to see it immediately—"

She broke off as Nora stepped past her, reaching for the silver tray McNeal had set down on coming in. An envelope lay upon it, and she tore it open with such ferocity that the housekeeper started and looked up from her task of collecting the remains of the gown. It was so disintegrated that Nora had stepped out of it without popping a single button or undoing one solitary clasp.

The envelope contained a note wrapped around an article seemingly cut out of a newspaper. She read the note first.

Dear Madam,

Came across the attached in the course of our enquiries re your great-aunt and thought you might be interested. Evidently the name recurs.

Sincerely,
Hugo Vascelles

The crackle of the newspaper bespoke its age, but the print was clear as she held it to the lamp:

Miss Jennifer Morrow for the Hillside Express – *1 March 1871*

FIRE DEVASTATES ANCIENT HOUSE – On the night of 28 February 1871, fire raged through Bridde Place, claiming the lives of Mr and Mrs Stephen (36) and Alice (28) Dallaway, as well as of Mrs Dallaway's father, Lloyd Michael Carswell (62). Only one survivor has been reported, being Miss Nora Dallaway (3), daughter of the aforementioned. The child is believed to have hidden herself in the stone stairwell and thus escaped with only bruising around her collarbone. The child is believed to have sought out the stairwell by instinct, finding the strength to wrench open the weighty door through fear and, this publication suggests, the grace of God. She was found wandering the ruins of her erstwhile home shortly after dawn by the housekeeper, arriving to begin her day's work.

Bridde Place is known to be the oldest house in the district by far and is likely familiar to readers through its association with local legend, the so-called Beast of Bridde Place immortalised in 'The Bridde Lament', a popular folksong. The Beast, described as a cloven-footed hellhound of gruesome aspect, with blackened wings and jagged horns shadowing eyes of flame, is said to curse the house, driving every third daughter born into nearby Bridde Pass – known locally as Devil's Pass – before her twenty-first birthday. In the time preceding this tragedy, the creature reportedly stalks the surrounding countryside, killing stock and frightening those unlucky enough to see it wholly out of their wits.

Even in the modern age, belief in the tale persists among the local population, to the extent that the local reverend blames the so-called Beast for the dwindling population of the village. "There used to be an accord," Mr Magnus Duinne claims. "But how can anyone abide by it, when there's none above ground as remembers what it was?"

As with many local superstitions, investigation suggests that a kernel of truth may lie at the heart of the tale: Miss Virginia Herron fell to her death in 1796, at the age of nineteen. Indeed, Miss Herron being the older sister of the late Mrs Dallaway's mother – unusually, Bridde Place is entailed on the female line – the present Miss Dallaway, as the third daughter born in the house since Miss Herron's tragic demise, would be next in line. Therefore, whether readers will take Mr Duinne's opinion at face value or consider that economic factors are more likely to be responsible for the desertion of the area, they may be relieved to know that Miss Dallaway will be taken in by her paternal aunt in Kent, with the remains of the property to be sold to provide for her future.

Nora had thought the light bright enough to read by, but now the print blurred before her eyes and her head reeled with the effort of making it out.

McNeal noticed her mistress sway just in time to help tumble her into the nearest chair. "You're unwell, madam. I'll have Mr Alcott send for the physician, or perhaps you'd like to take one of the draughts he sent?"

"No." Nora held her muddled head, shaking it as hard as she dared, as much to clear away the fog as anything else. "No more draughts." Hugo was right of course: it was simply a coincidence, a family name. It must be.

Abruptly, purpose seized her. "Fetch a walking dress – the black silk will do – and my coat. I'm going out."

The housekeeper, good woman that she was, was unable to quite master her expression. "Out? But, madam, it's near enough nine o'clock, and the weather—"

"The rain has stopped." Nora got up, folding the article. She felt strong now, determined in her quest.

McNeal bowed her head in acquiescence. "Very good, madam. I'll have the landau brought round—"

"No need." Nora put the folded article in the rack, the trembling of her hand fluttering it against the stiff card of the Brucknell invitation. The ball was on the following night, she realised dimly, and still she had not declined. "I intend to walk."

~

The night was a damp one. With no sun to warm it off, the rain lingered where it had fallen, penetrating every crack, soaking into every pore. Occasional hansom cabs and private carriages clattered over the wet cobbles, but on the pavements she was alone, the blustery wind pushing her along even as it nipped reproachfully at her cheeks. The rhythmic clip of her heels rang in her ears, echoing through the streets.

She walked with purpose and asked no questions of it, indeed did not so much as glance at it, for to look was to doubt. She only felt it there, compelling her, driving her, removing all need for thought, and was grateful.

Through the dowdy grandeur of Kensington she went, past neat, modern Chelsea terraces separated with innumerable tiny parks, her path revealing itself only as each new turn appeared on the horizon. Finally, at the very edge of Knightsbridge, on a street of which she had never heard, she found a façade of unpretentious white stucco at the end of a genteel terrace, and though she had never before laid eyes on its door, black and no different to any other black door in any other white house for a mile at least in any direction, she knew it innately for the one she sought.

By now she knew better than to question; that way lay madness. She only mounted the steps, rang the bell and asked for Inspector Ritter.

~

By the time Ritter was on the stairs, Annabelle was already at the door.

"Are you sure we can't persuade you to stop in, Mrs Bancroft?" he heard her ask, all concern. "It's such a dreadful night. A drop of something by the fire to warm you while you speak to my husband…"

It was kindly meant and entirely pointless. The moment he laid eyes on the widow, Ritter could see she heard not a word.

Even knowing her, he was shocked by her appearance, the sallow skin pulled so tightly over her sharp bones that it was a wonder they did not break through, her eyes at once bright and unfocused, seeming to roll with every move of her head, like diamonds loose in their fittings.

"I wish to see Inspector Ritter," she repeated mechanically, as though she had learned the words by rote, unconscious of their meaning. Indeed, Ritter was quite prepared to believe her unconscious of anything much at all, until the moment she caught sight of him.

The change in her demeanour then was nothing short of alarming, vagueness giving way to a fixation so fervent that Ritter found himself pausing instinctively in his descent and shifting his weight to his back foot, as though preparing to flee an assailant. He caught himself immediately, knowing the foolish trick of his mind for what it was. Nevertheless, with the way those strange eyes fastened on him, savage in their desperation, he would not blame himself entirely.

Annabelle withdrew as he came to the door, leaving him alone with the widow. He faced her and noted that some of the fight seemed to go out of her then, if fight it had been. It was as though, having successfully pounced upon her prey, she was at a loss as to what to do next.

He found himself thinking of Annabelle's fairy tales suddenly, only he was unable to decide which role belonged to each of them. As she stood there, hovering like a lost soul unable to come in, Ritter found himself preparing to dart out to catch her should the need arise. The way she swayed gently with every gust of the persistent wind, it did not seem unlikely, and yet he could not be comfortable with her, not until she stopped looking at him like that.

"Mrs Bancroft," he prompted, when at length she did not speak, "to what do I owe the pleasure?"

The question seemed to throw her. Again her eyes unfocused – strange, diamond eyes – as though she were looking inwardly for an answer she had hidden even from herself. When she saw him again, and he could name the precise moment she did, it was with the face of confusion.

"I only wanted to know if you had found my necklace yet," she tried, offering it up plaintively as a child offers a stick-figure drawing, knowing it has not succeeded in depicting what it really means and hoping against hope to be understood nonetheless. "It's important, you know."

Pity came upon him unexpectedly – a deep, echoing sadness that made him want to offer her more than he had.

"Not yet, madam, but rest assured we have our best men looking. Now please do come in and warm yourself while I send for your carriage to collect you."

If the empty street behind her had not been enough to tell him she had come alone, the state of her hair torn up by the wind would have done so.

It was only when she stepped back that he realised he had been about to reach for her arm. About to.

"No," she said with sudden determination. "I thank you, no. I… I only wanted to see about the necklace. I'll say good night."

"As you wish." Ritter was sorry for her, and sorry that she would not accept help, but evidently she was in no state to be quarrelled with. Better to simply send to her home once she had left and let her staff manage her as they would.

"Just one question before you go, madam, if you'd be so good? Might I know who gave you my address?"

It was a reasonable question, he'd thought – most senior policemen did not like their home addresses to be widely circulated, for reasons precisely like the one before him, and worse – but the widow's reaction gave him pause for doubt: though she had no colour to drain, her whole being seemed to stiffen at the question, almost to convulse. Her eyes twitched and then clenched shut, her fists curling in on themselves until Ritter was horrified to find a single drop of red splattering on the step below. Her mouth pressed together as her throat worked furiously, though whether to get something out or keep something in, he could not tell.

It came to Ritter that what he was witnessing was not a fit but a war, some internal battle of which he at his distance could only detect the smoke of cannon fire.

Just as he feared she would be bowled over by the force of it, she righted herself and was still again, opening her eyes to regard him with that unfocused gaze which seemed to see nothing at all.

"Goodnight, Inspector," she said, nodding at him as she turned away, entirely as though he had not spoken.

Ritter stared after her as she swept down the steps, too astonished to remember that he had.

Nora walked as on the edge of a dream. Fragments blew about her, and though she knew each to be true in its turn, it was beyond her power to pull them into any kind of sensible whole. Every step seemed to take place in the moment of waking from deep sleep, and she moved between the dim amber pools of the gas lamps as between puddles of her own consciousness, wishing for light one minute and longing for darkness the next.

She became aware by degrees that she was shivering, not with the cold nor the damp, but with the exhaustion of disused muscles in the first hours after the brace was removed. She needed to go home, she needed to rest, but home was, well, where?

The darkened streets stretched in every direction, streets she did not know and had no business walking. She was alone, but the drone of the city drifted in the air – carriages and trains and horses and dogs and people, the violence of their passions and the depths of their despair. She felt it all at once, and all at once she was afraid.

The spire rose, black and resolute against the night sky. She knew it at once, knew height, knew safety, remembered it in many-coloured rain falling from ebony wings. Knew frustration too, when she found the iron-studded doors barred against her, her unhappiness turning it to bitter resentment, for were not shelter and kindness, answers and understanding promised in places like this?

She banged the question on the doors, making them feel it, making them groan and creak under the force of her misery, until they finally gave way with a crash.

～

Mr Quince, rector of All Souls Church, Knightsbridge, was closing up his satchel in the vestry when he heard the commotion in the nave. So loud was it that he knocked the bag to the floor in surprise before realising that it must be the doors, blown open by the gale which had kept him company all through evensong, howling through the belfry in accompaniment to the organ.

Retrieving the satchel, he dug out the huge iron key which locked the front doors, and then, after a moment's thought, a smaller one, thinking he had better check the crucifix cupboard as well. After all, had he not been convinced a moment ago that he had already locked the front doors after the service, as he always did? If he had been as distracted as all that, he might as well be mistaken twice as once, and if the earthly value of the plate crucifix and goblet were of no significance to the Almighty, he nevertheless would prefer not to have to explain their theft to the synod.

The nave was lit only by what little moonlight could manage to seep through the cloud cover and in through the stained-glass windows. He had made it to the choir when he froze, feeling the yawning space all around him, and watched the thing come out of the dark.

Under different circumstances, he thought he might have been rather proud of that phrasing and used it to tell the story to any future grandchildren he might be blessed with. But the circumstances made it not a story but the deepest dread of every man ever to take his orders.

In the first instance, he thought he might be mistaken. It had the shape of a woman, bedraggled and hunched over under the torment of weather and despair. And perhaps also, Mr Quince considered delicately, by other, more mundane substances.

She wore no hat, her hair all the wilder for being caught half within its pins and half without, and her coat hung open, slouching off her shoulders as though she had forgotten it was there. In the first she staggered, as though having applied her weight to a thing she had not expected to give way. Recovering herself, she looked about in an aspect of confusion, as though she knew not where she found herself and couldn't imagine why.

Mr Quince set out across the flagstones with due caution. His belief in the innate goodness of every human soul was unshakable but did not preclude his being conscious that drink might put the Devil in the very meekest character. Just as he did, however, her wandering gaze fell upon the baptismal font where it stood in the top corner of the nave.

Still curiously hinged at the waist, as though some great weight burdened her back, she made for it.

Quince watched in astonishment as she mounted the edge of the stone pedestal, as a child wishing to see over the edge might, leaning over it with her arms braced. She did not look into the font however. Instead, she craned her neck round over her shoulder, an impossible angle, and stared through the gloom at the arched window behind her, depicting St Peter with his holy key, as though waiting for something.

So long did she stand in that attitude that Quince's own neck ached in sympathy. Finally, she seemed to despair of whatever it was ever coming, her shoulders, indeed her whole body, slumping under the weight of disappointment.

So pitiful a figure did she cut that Quince called out to her across the empty nave: "My dear lady, are you quite well?"

Immediately, he knew his mistake.

She turned her head slowly, not as one startled by his presence but rather wondering what use it might be. She fixed him with a baleful stare, and in the half-light he saw that everything about her was slightly wrong: the angle of her head, the length of her back, the planes of her face.

It was the face that struck him most. It was a face for shifting, a face for shadows, a face to creep behind them and peer out from within, a face to be seen only in snatches of dread. In the fixed interior of the nave, it stood out in the gloom, a skull hung on a spine impossibly curved, twisted towards him as though it were nothing but cobwebs and silk. Her fingers curled about the edge of the font like talons carved in bone, and Quince found himself hoping absurdly that she wouldn't tear away the stone.

"There's no help for me here, is there?" she asked.

The question echoed against the silence, so forlorn and heard so often that Quince found himself speaking before he could think.

"There is help here for all God's children…" he managed, but as her eyes fixed on him, glittering with a light not meant for him to see, he faltered. He could not bear to look at them, yet he could not look away. What he had said was true, and of no use to her: he looked into those eyes and knew that, in the Church of All Souls, she was not one.

A primal terror like quicksilver filled him then, held at bay only by duty and the knowledge, packed deep in his spine, that in any case there was nowhere to run.

"I don't think so," he said instead, in a voice that trembled with the knowledge. "I should be grateful if you would leave now please."

She looked at him and did not move.

Quince found himself reaching for the gold cross always around his neck and took comfort in finding it where it always was, tucked away safe against his skin. He tried to hold it before him in thought as he searched for the words – the right, godly words to say – but already the quicksilver was infecting his mind, and when he opened his mouth, all he managed was a hoarse cry: "Leave now!"

"And go where?"

It was the incongruity of the question which gave him pause, enough to retake the barest semblance of composure.

"Why, back to—" Quince hesitated. "Back to whatever darkness bore you, I suppose."

Though he had been trying for heat, the words came out curiously uncertain. Quince was not by nature a ferocious man, and when he reached for that celestial store of righteous fury, he found it unexpectedly empty.

"And if I don't know where that is?" The question seemed posed in plea and challenge both.

Through the churn of his mind, the faint press of the cross upon his breast, small and neat, found Quince's attention. It lay warm upon his skin, a focal point, a calming force, the whole of it directed towards himself in comfort, none of it towards her in threat. He felt it, gentle but firm, reminding him not to take human frailty – human fear – for divine imperative.

When he did not answer her question, the creature took on an air almost of apology.

"I fear I'm most dreadfully lost," she said, and for a moment he might have taken her almost as the thing she was masquerading as, a genteel lady lost in the night. Then she cocked her head at him, as though she could see him better from that angle, and looking into those beseeching, resentful, maddening eyes, he was put all at once in mind of an incident many years before.

He'd still been at home in Surrey then, barely more than a boy. The mere fact of a jackdaw finding its way down the chimney was not so very exceptional: the birds had a habit, well known among country folk, of making use of human labour to heat their nests, and it was not unheard of to find a stray chick in the fireplace, generally dead from the fall.

What made the occasion memorable then was that the intruder had not been a chick but a full-grown bird. Emphatically alive, it had burst from the sitting-room fireplace chimney in a flurry, scattering the family from where they had been sat to enjoy Flora's playing. Frightened by its strange surroundings and furious at finding itself confined, the thing had flown about in a panic, knocking down pictures, overturning vases and getting into the ladies' hair. And yet, even in the midst of all the running and screaming which followed, Quince would wager that not one person present would have wished to harm it.

Rather, their instinctive aim was to drive it away, to return it to its proper place, the threat lying not in the thing itself but in the situation in which they found themselves with it. There in the house, it was an alien force, trapped out of its rightful place; it was disruptive, grotesque, even dangerous. It had torn Phoebus's cheek open, very nearly taken out Flora's eye, and more than one finger had been cut on the shattered glass it had left behind, the last fragment of which had not been found until months later. And yet no benefit would have been derived from harming it. The thing had meant no harm, had been too confused to mean anything at all, and while that had not made it harmless, bird and human alike would have been best served by calm, compassionate guidance, to help the creature find its way back to its own world with a minimum of upset to all concerned.

She was watching him, expecting an answer.

Firm in the knowledge both that there was a place for all and that this was not hers, Quince gave her finally the advice he wished he could have given that jackdaw: "Retrace your steps until you find something you recognise. Begin at the earliest beginning, if you must. That will lead you back whence you came."

She nodded slowly, as though to herself, and looked away from him into the depths of the font. Then, just as he thought she might be contemplating the horror of her own existence, she turned back to him.

"Do you think I can still make the train to Kent?"

THE YOUNG ELIZABETH

I

On the day she met Ambrose O'Rourke, Nora left the Gordon household after breakfast to take her walk, as she had done every morning since arriving in London. In the beginning they had been short walks to test her strength and then to build it, but the warm May weather saw her well enough to wander across the river and into the twisting backstreets of the South Bank. There, one theatre or another could generally be counted upon to provide rest and diversion in the form of a matinee performance, and as she preferred not to spend the allowance Violet generously provided for her amusement, it was often to the Young Bess that she turned her nose. She'd found the old crust in the ticket booth there did not consider it worth his pay to challenge a young lady well dressed, thus when she hurried past the peeling red-and-gold paint, clutching her hat in her best impression of a hurried governess left behind, she met with no argument.

Taking her place at the back just inside the door, she watched the curtain rise, trailing its ragged satin fringe over scenes as the murmuring audience settled and grew still. The hush of it was always her favourite part, that moment in which every person present seemed to enter into a silent agreement with the company and themselves, promising that here, away from the scrutiny of daylight, they were prepared to find wonder and hilarity in even the smallest token which might be offered to them.

On that day, lulled into the rhythm of the play, Nora did not notice the figure looming up behind her until a hand like a bear's paw reached out, grabbing her wrist in a vice-like grip. Startled, she began to yank her arm away as she turned, before faltering in sheer surprise as the sight of her captor.

By height and by width, Nora judged him on the upper end of humanity's range, and by everything else surely a character too immense to be contained on the narrow stage of life. From the dangling paste earrings whose lowest baubles almost brushed the broad shoulders, to the end of the gold tassels which trimmed the orange costume, neither dress nor tunic but some glorious improvement on both, to the face enhanced by as much powder as the whole company on stage combined, and far more intricately applied, Nora could not help but gape as the man leaned down and murmured, in a low husk which brooked no argument: "This way please, madam."

Nora, without ticket or the wherewithal to protest, allowed herself to be led out into the corridor through which she had come, and further still. To her surprise, her captor did not turn down the passage which led to the ticket booth and exit beyond but went straight past it and up a flight of stairs. Suddenly acutely aware that she had not the faintest idea of what the penalty for non-payment might actually be, she was distracted from the question on her lips by the realisation that the sparkle near the man's left temple was coming from a cluster of diamante in the centre of a pink silk daisy, half hidden under silver curls streaked through with henna.

"You're a fierce one," her captor began conversationally, noting her interest as they continued along the corridor. He gave a short bark of laughter, which contrived to be as warm as it was startling. "For a moment there I thought you were about to take my arm off. May one enquire what it is that makes daily viewings of *The Lady and the Goat* more appealing than home? The playwright is a dear thing, of course, but it must be admitted that—"

"Three boys under seven and their doting mother." The answer came in a burst, startling her so that she snapped her mouth shut in surprise.

Her companion turned to her, pencilled eyebrows raised, then laughed again at her expression.

"Ah, family, a familiar trial!" He winked a brilliant blue eye conspiratorially as the other twinkled in mirth, a wry twist coming over the scarlet mouth. "I had to put three hundred miles and the Irish Sea between myself and mine before I was comfortable."

Nora shook her head, hot with shame. "I didn't mean that – it's really very good of them to have me. And Violet is a wonderful mother, and the boys are terribly sweet really."

"I'm sure you are right, dear, and I'm sure they are very fond of you for it."

For just an instant, Nora thought she could just see a trickle of vulnerability bleeding through the paint, in a shade something like her own.

"I made my choice and I stand by it, but I don't say that there aren't times I miss them or wonder about them. I realised some time ago that I won't even know when my mother dies – that was a bit of a shock. She wasn't five-and-forty when I saw her last, you know, and already she could barely open her hands; ruined, they were, by all the stitching required to feed a growing family, even with my father breaking his back at the dock from before sunrise every day of his life. Poor man. Poor woman. Poor all of us, I suppose. Up this way, if you please – don't worry, if you fall, you'll land on me. I assure you I'm marvellously soft."

The corridor had been leading them on a gentle upward curve and finally ended in a rickety set of steps, more akin to a ladder than a staircase. For all the sorrowful words, Nora's companion seemed little the worse for wear as he indicated for her to climb, with a sweeping gesture which made the orange stuff billow enough to raise the dust on the floor.

Nora glanced sceptically from the ladder to her companion, eighteen years of feminine training coming to the fore.

Her companion gave her a look of comical disappointment. "My dear girl, do you really imagine that I am the slightest bit interested in what may or may not be up your skirt, even if it were remotely visible under all the petticoats and bloomers you are no doubt embalmed in? From anything other than a professional standpoint, I mean."

He smiled as he spoke, a bright, theatrical smile, but again there was that touch of something warm peeping out from behind, and Nora realised that no, she really didn't.

The steps led through a trapdoor into the theatre loft, all sloping ceilings and crude beams, though its arrangement was quite unlike any loft Nora had ever seen. It seemed to be at once sitting room, workshop and dressing room, though whose dressing room was harder to discern.

A sturdy table dominated the space, with a sewing machine in pride of place, surrounded by a litter of needles, pins, pencils, clothes chalk and spools of thread, an unrolled measuring tape winding itself through the debris like a lazy snake. At one end of the room stood a sofa, and at the other a dense brocade curtain was pulled across the width of the space. All around hung, stood or were scattered an inconceivable array of clothes, shoes, perukes and other accessories. On the rafters, from dressing rails, on worn-out chairs and upturned crates hung gowns, suits, hats, wigs, hats upon wigs, riding boots, high heels, painted staves, decorated crowns, coloured beads and paste adornments of every sort. The room appeared to contain clothes for an entire kingdom, from Bavarian prince to fairy queen to adventuring labourer, and every item, even down to the humble maid's patched pinafore, carried about it a spark of whimsy, a playful zest, an invitation to find joy in the meanest of moments.

"Welcome," said her companion, pulling himself up to his full height with a grand gesture, "to my atelier."

Nora turned to him with something like awe. "This is your work? I had taken you for an actor."

Her host laughed, and Nora realised that it was that very laugh, that twinkle, which was threaded through each and every garment in the room, as surely as if it had been stitched in by the needle.

"Oh dear no," he said. "I did have aspirations once, when I was young and beautiful, but it turned out that I enjoy being myself far too much to play at being someone else."

"I'm not sure I can imagine what that feels like."

She glanced up, finding him illuminated starkly in the light of the oil lamp above. With round blue eyes, a mouth faintly too small below a long nose sharp as a wedge of cheddar, and the barest whisper of a chin now pillowed in softness, Nora found it difficult to see how such a person might ever have been considered beautiful, yet at the same time, as he moved and laughed and looked at her with twinkling eyes, hard to understand how he was not considered so still.

"Do come and sit down," he said, leading her across to the sofa. Once it had been of brown velvet, but at some point somebody – and glancing at her companion, Nora thought she knew who – had begun to patch it with scraps of every colour and type of fabric known to man, so that by now the original upholstery was a mere dull shadow hinted at around the edges of infinitely more fantastical fabrics.

Her host took a seat on one side and patted a large heptagon of paisley brocade beside him. "Now, you've heard the trials and tribulations of clan O'Rourke; I do believe it's your turn. Tell Auntie Ambrose all about Miss...?"

"Dallaway," Nora supplied but distractedly: just in front of the sofa, a single floorboard had been removed, providing the sitter with a fine aerial view of the stage – and a potential deathtrap for the unsuspecting.

Nora stepped over it gingerly, shivering as a draught caught at her skirt. "Nora Dallaway. But I'm afraid there's not much to tell about clan Dallaway, other than that I'm the last of them."

"Even better!" Ambrose beamed. "What brings you to London, Miss Nora, last of the Dallaways?"

Nora bridled in spite of herself. "What makes you think I'm not a native?"

"Well, in the first place," Ambrose began, with the air of explaining to a particularly dull child, "a native – or even a tourist with a decent guidebook frankly – would know of far better ways to pass the day without spending a penny than sneaking into grotty little theatres. The *same* grotty little theatre at that, and for a whole week! Honestly, I don't know how you've stood it."

His amusement was infectious, and Nora found herself grinning through her embarrassment.

"I've been enjoying it, as it happens," she said, sticking out her chin in mock defiance. "And it's never completely the same anyway. There's always something new."

Ambrose raised an eyebrow. "They do forget a different line every time, I'll give you that. There can't be many shows where you're from, if that's all it takes to entertain you."

"Well, no," Nora admitted. "I'd never been to town until last month; I don't think I'd ever been to a play – a proper one I mean, not Punch & Judy. There's something about being closed off from the world like that, with only the story before you…" She bit her lip, but his eyes were warm and encouraged her to go on. "Truly, I've found it quite enchanting."

Ambrose put a large hand gently on her knee, the same hand with which he had caught and held her not half an hour prior. The nails, she noticed, were painted alternating poisonous green and deep, vibrant purple.

"That's because it is, dear," he said.

"Are you just visiting us?" he went on, rising to address himself to a tea urn half hidden beneath a pile of shimmering tulle. "Or are you to be a permanent transplant?"

Nora shrugged, then realised he had his back to her. "I'm not sure," she said. "Violet only invited me down to convalesce, but the idea of returning to the country is" – she hesitated, impulses coming too fast and making her dizzy before she could suppress them – "disagreeable, and London seems as good a place as any to seek my fortune."

"Ah, a fellow fortune seeker!" Ambrose spun round, a pair of daintily painted and entirely unmatched cups in his hands. "No place better, I can assure you. And what shape will your fortune take, Miss Nora, last of the Dallaways?"

Nora smiled wryly as she watched Ambrose try to coax more than a thin brown dribble from the spout. "I'll have to let you know when I find it. A job, I suppose, or a husband."

Ambrose, crouched on his haunches, left off wrangling with the urn to look up at her. "You don't sound entirely convinced by either of those."

His eyes were bright as they searched her face, and Nora looked away as she shrugged. "I suppose I don't know enough about either to convince me. Although I can't say they strike me as being all that different."

She looked back to find Ambrose still watching her, the tea things forgotten at his side. He looked as though he wanted to say something, but she cut him off with a question: "Did you find yours?"

Ambrose grinned as he spread his arms wide. "As you see."

"How did you know where to look?"

It came out smaller than expected, and she had the sudden impulse to pull her knees up like a child. She didn't of course, but some speck of it must have shown in her eyes, because he reached over the gap in the floor and took her hand. "I had help, my dear. We all need a bit of help."

His glance down was accidental and made him start. "Oh! Is that really the time?"

As he rose to his feet with an apologetic look. "I'm afraid I have to shoo you out, Miss Dallaway, delightful as your company has been. I am called to arms!"

He smiled at her confusion. "The curtain is about to go down and I must unhitch the company from my work, preferably before they wet it. But tomorrow you can come straight up and we'll discuss your predicament at length. Why, what's the matter, dear?"

Nora had a sudden urge to study her hands. "What about—" she began, not looking up. "Are you going to fine me? For the ticket?"

Ambrose's brows knit in confusion for a moment before he understood. "Don't be silly," he said, laughing. "No one cares about that! I only grabbed you so I could have a closer look at your eyes, to see if there was some trick to it. Professional curiosity, you know. I'd have thrown you out if you'd been tiresome, but you're not, so from now on you can be my guest. You can't imagine how dreary it is to sit through the same show day in, day out, for weeks on end, unable to leave in case someone tears something. It'll be nice to have a bit of company."

Nora smiled, because yes, it would, but one thing caught her attention. "What about my eyes?"

Ambrose looked at her, surprised. "Why, don't you know, dear? They glitter in the dark."

II

It was cosy to curl up on the patchwork sofa, watching the matinee performance through the gap in the floorboards with a cup of tea in one hand and Ambrose's commentary running continuously as he worked. The monologue, which appeared to be almost as much for his own amusement as for Nora's, consisted of a litany of anecdotes, philosophy, snatches of advice and fragments of thought. It was delivered in a wit now caustic, now charitable and paused only when he needed to summon her to come and stand model for this jacket or that petticoat. Though such summons were invariably couched in such beseechingly ostentatious terms as "dear Miss Dallaway" and "I would be monumentally grateful if", Nora soon learned that the additional syllables were purely to give her time to rouse herself. Failure to do so by the end of the sentence would result in being hauled bodily to the task in question, and even then she often found herself being tugged impatiently along. Though she complained as ferociously as laughter would allow, it was these liberties, taken affectionately amid the sprawling disarray of creation, which made the attic warm to her.

In spite of his initial promise, Ambrose never returned to the subject of their first conversation. There was something in the young woman's demeanour which did not invite it, something in the way she clung to the ordinary fantasy of his day to day which told him that this was where she felt at home. As she came faithfully at least thrice a week, he was content to leave her there, knowing that she would raise other subjects if she wished.

Thus, when towards the end of May she did not appear for a fortnight together, Ambrose knew to be concerned.

The plentiful and unexpected connections of theatrical types are well known, and Ambrose had had thirty years to cultivate his particular web. Sending out urgent enquiries, he soon learned that sickness had come to the Gordon home, and though the little boys had shaken it off easily enough, Mrs Gordon's young cousin was faring considerably worse.

On receipt of the news, Ambrose put aside Salome's head-piece and set to planning. He must call on Nora, that much was certain: though her cousin sounded kind enough, he could not help but feel the girl lacked something of a protective wing and found himself instinctively extending his own. Too, though she grew quiet at any mention of the illness which had prompted her removal to London, he knew it had not been a trifling one; a relapse could be serious indeed.

And yet, paying a call to his friend was not the simple task it ought to be. In the first place, he could not go in his own clothes. There were certain places in London where he would be welcomed as friend or even family, and others where he would be tolerated on the basis of being known as a good customer, or by his ability to throw his considerable weight behind a be-ringed punch when left no alternative. The Gordon household was located in neither such place. Indeed, it was doubtful whether he would even reach the street without being arrested or chucked in the river – the river being by far the preferable option – and even if he managed to reach the house, the mere suggestion of Nora being familiar with a person dressed like that would be fatal to whatever meagre prospects she had.

Calling on her in conventional masculine dress was equally out of the question. Apart from the fact that a call from a man unknown to her family would immediately lance her reputation, he possessed no such clothes. Even as a youth, straight-cut trousers and mannish waistcoats had seemed on him more of a costume than any theatre concoction, and these days he was not sure he could bring himself to even pretend to wear them, not even for Nora.

There was one solution, and only one, yet he hesitated. He did not think she would mind – he had told her enough, and seen enough of her reactions, to feel confident – and yet it was impossible to be entirely certain. Often, in Ambrose's experience, people themselves did not fully know how they would feel until they did, and by then it was too late. Still, surely good intentions must count for something; if nothing else, if she were truly troubled, it would be easier for her to disavow him as a stranger.

Dashing off a note to beg the landau for the afternoon, it took him the better part of the morning to prepare. He was not in the habit of dressing this way, except for the occasional laughter of the audience or the entertainment of friends, where everyone saw the costume and knew it was for the part he was playing. Now, no one must know. The slightest mistake, discovered at the wrong moment, could give the game away, spelling catastrophe for them both. He must inhabit the clothes as though he owned them, dress himself so as to become invisible within them. It had been years, many years, since he had been called on to do the like, and even as he worried he had forgotten how, equally he felt the dread of remembering.

To be certain no detail was overlooked out of habit, he began by stripping down until he was a blank canvas. Billowing silk pantaloons and a ruffled crimson shirt followed the Chinese robe with its embroidered dragons. Shoes with painted heels were tucked under the eaves, and the headpiece of violet tulle artfully strangling a miniature tri-corner returned to its stand. Rings and bracelets and beaded chains of coral and pearls piled in a sparkling mound – the paste majority enhanced by a few genuine glitters – and the paint was taken off flick by deft flick. Finally, all that was left was the face so familiar he couldn't remember the last time he'd seen it.

In the glass, he saw them all there in it: his mother's strength, his father's warmth, his brothers' pity, his sisters' confusion, and himself, the boy who did not yet know his name was Ambrose. He saw that boy's despair as he watched adolescence warp and twist his pretty child's face, pulling on the nose as though it would never stop and cruelly refusing to allow the mouth to keep pace, widening the jaw until he had no chin left, flaxen hair giving way to mouse brown and his own tears blurring the image, knowing that rescue only comes for beauty.

As he'd grown, he'd worn his brothers' clothes, but though they had not needed altering, they did not fit, but, on his character not cut of their cloth hung empty and absurd as long johns on a washing line. Obvious to all, and yet not a word was said. Seeing the boy on the cusp of a manhood they did not recognise, they had none to offer.

On the day he'd procured himself work loading a ship bound for Liverpool, his mother had given him the whole family's breakfast eggs with tears in her eyes and his father had pressed a coin into his hand without a word. The boy had been grateful to them both.

It had been a long time since Liverpool, and the boy. There he'd learned that, if not quite rescue, pretty eyes and a lively mouth could procure things almost as delicious, and a light-footed spirit could make the most of less promising situations. The discovery had been almost enough to persuade himself that the next stretch was not as daunting as it was. Almost.

"It'll be worth it," Ambrose promised the boy in the glass. "Not perfect, but worth it." Then he turned away, leaving the boy where he belonged.

Going to the rails, he retrieved the dress he sought and held it up to the light, looking it over with the satisfaction of the craftsman rediscovering the quality of his own masterpiece. And truly, there was no other word for it: something had got into him that night, and the result was a replica of the Queen's mourning attire which was possibly more accurate than Her Majesty's own.

At first it had been sheer spite – he'd been bullied into a cameo role by the entire company swearing hand on heart to the spitting resemblance between himself and good Queen Vic, in face and overall shape, if not in height – but then it had become something else, a desire to prove to himself that he could make something more than flamboyant confections not intended to last more than a ten-week run. It was a piece of work he might have shown his mother, knowing she would have understood the skill of it, the artistry, and been proud.

To date, his masterpiece had been seen only for a few minutes at a time, by crowds too distant, too ignorant and too drunk to appreciate her. That was about to change: with her entourage of cape, gloves and hat, today his masterpiece would get her proper debut.

He painted his face not as himself and not as a direct portrait but settling somewhere in between, that he might not be mistaken for his royal inspiration but rather a relative, some distant Prussian cousin visiting London for want of anything better to do.

All put together, the result pleased him, lacking only the final detail. With an ease belying his disguise – though not his six feet and proportionate build – Ambrose hauled the patchwork sofa back and, laying down a sheet to avoid dirtying his skirt, pried up a floorboard to reveal a large velvet jewellery box.

Wiping away the accumulated dust with a loving hand, he pulled it out and opened it to reveal a parure fit for a queen. Enormous sapphires edged with rows of diamonds caught the lamplight, as though the gems contained within them the brilliance and glamour of the night sky. In their presence the whole room seemed to brighten, so that even the paste pieces left lying about seemed to sparkle the more for it, as though knowing they looked upon that in whose image they had been made. For there could be no mistaking that the contents of this box were the genuine article, worked by the best Russian artisans until the result was not just fit for a queen but demanding of one.

Emil had called it insurance, the presence of the velvet case beneath the floorboard easing his mind when he left in the mornings. The sale of such a set would keep Ambrose in comfort for the rest of his natural life and beyond, thus absolving Emil of making more technical provisions in the event of his death. With jewellery already gifted, there would be no need for a public squabble in court over a will which would humiliate his children and grandchildren and end worse for Ambrose, when the clause providing for him was inevitably overturned and questions arose as to how it had come about in the first place. And if they should be parted by less lethal means, well then, Emil could return to his life of plenty and console himself with the knowledge that at least he had left something precious behind.

Ambrose knew from experience that gifts came at the height of the affair – gold bracelets and enamelled lockets, pretty trinkets whose sparkle reflected the eyes of each giver in succession – and over the years it had been a long succession. Those eyes were invariably lit up with expectation, and each time Ambrose had met it gladly, been profuse in his gratitude and admiration. And meant it too, on the day. If the bracelet strained to reach around his wrist, or the locket struggled to mark its presence on a chest much broader than the designer had anticipated, those poor beloveds could hardly be expected to admit the nature of the body they were shopping for after all.

And yet, after the inevitable end of love, it had become easier and easier to part with those items which had never fit in the first place. The first couple had found themselves at the bottom of the river of course, a monument to love's despair, but after that, when the young Ambrose had begun to realise that despair, like enchantment, eventually wore off, a mutually beneficial relationship with a friendly pawnbroker had developed, and he had found himself none the worse off for that.

Thus, the surprise of Emil's gift had come not from the mere fact of it, nor even from sheer monetary worth, though it was more together than Ambrose had ever beheld in his life. No, the true shock of it had come from the heft of the earrings, the weight of the brooch, the sheer regal stature of the necklace. It had come from the way the ring sat on his hand, heavy and proud, entirely in proportion, every bit as though *fait pour*. Most of all though, it had come from the way Emil had looked him over appraisingly and noted, with evident satisfaction, "Oh good, it fits," little realising perhaps that no one before him had ever troubled himself over that particular detail.

It was at that point that Ambrose realised he would be buried with every single piece. Emil called it insurance, but Ambrose called it something else entirely. Though sometimes, at night, listening to his lover's steady breath in the dark, he thought perhaps they both meant the same thing.

III

Her Grace the Archduchess Ambrosia von Schliesburg-Karlstein-Glücksbad of Brandenstrow called at the Gordon house at half past three – ten minutes after Violet Gordon was seen to depart – on a charitable visit for the benefit of the poor orphan understood to have been taken badly ill.

It was not a perfect ruse: the archduchess had no attendants, her carriage sported no coat of arms and her accent kept inexplicably drifting into suspiciously Irish tones. Nor would the housemaid perhaps have described Miss Dallaway in quite such terms. However, the sparkle of the jewels made their impression, as did the length of the name and the undeniable grandeur of the person bearing it. The poor maid being even less well versed in the minutiae of Prussian nobility than the person before her claiming it, she found it impossible to refuse entry.

Yet, though the nagging sense of being had remained, as she led the way up to the convalescent room, the young maid could somehow not find herself entirely ungrateful. There was something about the way Miss Dallaway screamed out the worst of her fever, the way she flung those grasping, bony hands about her that made one flinch away. Instinct it was, Nanny said, and no amount of Mrs Gordon's scolding would change it. Thus, archduchess or no, she was not displeased to close the door and leave the peculiar orphan creature to someone else's care for a time.

~

Ambrose waited until the maid's footsteps sounded on the landing below before breathing out in relief, making his stays creak. Nora lay on the bed, blanket thrown off and sheets twisted around her. A sheen of sweat glistened upon her forehead, and her breath came in ragged gasps. Every few seconds, a shudder passed through her frame, and though her eyes were closed, Ambrose could see them darting behind their parchment lids with a force so frantic they seemed liable to tear through at any moment.

As he approached her bedside, Nora's eyes flew open. "Marit?" she whispered as she struggled to focus.

"No, dear. It's Ambrose." Thinking that she merely didn't recognise him, taking him perhaps for some nurse or matron she had known, he leaned over to give her a better view.

So suddenly did she lash out that Ambrose had no time to avoid it.

"You must stay out of the woods!" she cried, the sheer force of her despair flinging her upright, clutching his wrist. "There's something. It's there – can't you hear it? The window!"

Hair clung to her face in black tendrils as she pulled him close with a grip which threatened to crush bone.

"The window!" she hissed, close enough to let him feel the words upon his skin. "The pane, it won't hold— Can't you hear it? The shutters – you must close them, shut it out!"

She released him then, as suddenly as she had taken hold, rolling her eyes towards the window even as she twisted her body away from it.

Rubbing the life back into his wrist, Ambrose went and peered out but saw no branch or bird which might have troubled her. He closed the shutters anyway, just in case.

With the click of the latch, her breathing quieted, as immediately as if a door had been closed upon it.

"Ambrose?" she asked as he turned to find her watching him. Though the effort of merely lifting her head from the pillow seemed to tax her, her eyes were clear now and her voice fluttered with hoarse amusement. "Is it really you in there?"

"Were you expecting a different Prussian noblewoman?"

With more than one kind of relief, Ambrose executed a combination curtsy-bow, making them both laugh.

"How are you feeling, my dear?"

Somehow, it was the wrong thing to ask: in the moment it took him to settle his skirts on the chair by her bedside, all merriment drained from her face. In response to the question, Nora gave him a look so haunted and miserable that he could not hide his alarm.

"Why, whatever is the matter?"

"Ambrose, I fear—" She groped for words, squeezing her eyes shut. When she opened them again, tears dulled that curious glittering effect he had become so fond of. "I fear I am an unholy thing," she whispered, almost whimpered, and there it was, the thing he had recognised without naming it the moment he had first seen her.

It was not the same of course, or he should have known it immediately. But hearing her now, he remembered with pity the boy cowering in a grey little Belfast church, that very same word driving him to his knees as he prayed it not be true. The sobs which wracked her exhausted body now were the same, or near enough, and all he could do was shift his bulk to the edge of the bed, so as better to catch them.

"Aren't we all, my dear," he murmured. "Aren't we all."

IV

The patient turned a corner in the days which followed, and no further demands on the archduchess's charity were made. Nevertheless, in that hour, in that room, a bond had been forged.

On her return to the Young Bess in time for a matinee performance of *King Herod's Trousers*, Nora found herself caught up in a hug like an iron vice, only to be thrust out to arm's length before she could begin to struggle and looked over with a sceptical eye. Only after repeated assurances that she was really, perfectly well, the wool shawl being only a token to satisfy Violet's equal scepticism, did Ambrose relent and issue an invitation – or command – to return the following Tuesday at three o'clock sharp.

Tuesday was dark day at the Young Bess, the day on which no shows would be performed. The theatre lay in stillness, save the rats in the stalls and Ambrose above, as well as any of the company making use of the secret places beneath the stage to enjoy their trysts, or sleep off the night's excesses without the aggravation of an unpaid landlord.

Nora had never visited on dark day, and she was unsure whether the unlocked door was for her convenience or a matter of general practice. After all, with the rather dilapidated state of the theatre, a good padlock might well be the only thing worth stealing.

Inside, the passage was silent, save the wooden echo of her boots, but beneath the ladder, she had a sudden sense of presence, the feeling of a conversation hushed only by her approach. Ambrose, she knew abruptly, was not alone.

It was unexpectedly and oddly jagged, this realisation that she was not the only person invited to visit above the stage, but she had not the time to parse the surge of feeling it brought. Already her feet were on the rungs, her head poking through the open trapdoor, impatient to know what awaited her.

On the sofa beside Ambrose sat a small man of middling years, neat and well dressed and looking nevertheless entirely at home in his odd surroundings, next to his even odder host. Or, Nora realised, seeing the well-shaped hand draped casually over Ambrose's, rather more than host.

Both men rose to greet her.

"Miss Dallaway," said Ambrose. "Allow me to introduce Mr Emil Vascelles." He glanced at his companion and added, rather less elaborately. "Em, meet Nora."

It was in that casual address that there lingered something, a sort of warmth, or pride perhaps, which gave a new importance to Nora's liking of this Mr Vascelles – or not, as the case might turn out to be.

"Pleased to make your acquaintance, sir." Nora curtsied, at once grateful for something to hide behind and irritated that formality was being imposed up here, amid all the familiarity of the atelier.

"The pleasure is mine, I'm sure." Vascelles returned a bow, and though he did so entirely correctly, Nora wondered if there wasn't just the faintest touch of mockery about it.

Immediately she was cross with herself, for seeking fault in a man she must – she *would* – find a way of getting along with, but then he straightened and removed all doubt. Tossing aside all suggestion of politeness, not to say common decency, he walked straight up to her with an air of such frank scrutiny that only sheer bloody-mindedness kept her from taking a step back in astonishment.

He was a handsome man, with a hard mouth and a shock of wiry coal-black hair, shot through with grey at the temple. His features tended towards the fine, but the mouth was pressed firm with the habit of half a lifetime, and the dark eyes which now bored into hers were nothing short of fierce.

Nora held her ground with outright obstinacy: if he would be intimidating, she thought, she would be rude.

As he came within breathing distance, she drew herself up to her full height, which was several inches taller than his. She knew it, and he knew it, and all at once she realised that one of them was quite spectacularly amused by the fact, as apparently by the world in general. It was not herself.

"So you're the sick little orphan who couldn't do without my landau, are you? I had to take a cab because of you, you know." He grinned up at her, an impish twinkle in his black eye. "You don't look so sick to me. Or so little."

It was at that point that Nora understood three things.

First, that Emil Vascelles belonged to that select group of men so entirely confident in the size of his own presence as distinct from his physical frame as to elevate the diminutiveness of said frame to a mark of character, a point of charm, thus rendering any suggestion of defect laughable in turn.

Second, that it must take an enormous strength of will to keep that agile, laughing mouth restrained as it had been for hours at a time, unable to respond to the world with its natural mirth – or, under the right provocation, she suspected, malevolence. When he grinned, it was almost impossible not to grin along with him.

And third, that she would be able to get along with him, very well indeed.

Ambrose, seeing the introduction satisfactorily completed, took his cue to chivvy things along. "Nora is here to seek her fortune," he announced before bending his head close to Emil and adding in a stage whisper. "That means she wants to marry a rich man."

That much Emil evidently already knew – it was clear to Nora that her situation had already been discussed, likely at some length – but he chuckled anyway, reaching up to peck a light kiss on Ambrose's painted lips with a fondness so entirely natural that Nora was only vaguely aware of it being anything out of the ordinary.

The couple settled themselves on the patchwork sofa while Nora perched on an overstuffed ottoman opposite. She knew nothing about Emil Vascelles other than what the past few minutes had taught her, but the Vascelles name was dimly familiar to her as being on the uppermost echelons of business. It was the businessman who faced her now.

"We've been discussing your situation," Emil began. "And we've concluded that a young woman who, through no fault of her own, is without connections is offered considerably less choice in life than one with better luck. Which, as I'm sure you'll agree, is really rather unfair. That being the case, Ambrose has asked me to connect you as well as I can manage, which, I flatter myself, is rather well indeed. It's too late in the season to bring you out properly – and frankly doing so would probably draw more attention than is useful – but acting in the capacity as a friend of your late father's, it is well within my purview to escort you about and make whatever beneficial introductions I can."

Nora felt her eyebrows meet her hairline. "*Were* you a friend of my father's?"

"Probably not," Emil admitted, grinning at her. "I don't know, I have no idea who he was. But I'm about the right age for it, and I can't say for certain that I *wasn't*, providing you don't tell me his name. And nobody else will be able to either, even on the off chance that they care enough to try, which they won't. As a device to explain our connection, it's entirely plausible, and that's as far as anyone will care to look. Ambrose wanted to dress you at first of course – you should see his sketches – but as much as I personally would enjoy that, I'm not sure London is ready for Maison O'Rourke just yet, so you've got an appointment with my daughter's favourite dress-maker tomorrow at ten. Just put everything on my account."

He twinkled at her as Ambrose smiled. "Well, Miss Nora, last of the Dallaways, what do you say?"

Nora looked from one to the other. "Thank you," she said.

V

The taking of Nora Dallaway into society would prove one of the few miscalculations of Emil Vascelles's life. His fortune and his existence both had been built on an uncanny ability to step between the raindrops, so that by middle age, he no longer remembered what it was to get wet. And indeed, by then those who might once have sought to soak him on principle had forgotten why they should bother.

Though his entry to their exalted circles had been through his wife alone, somehow her discreet withdrawal to the home of her childhood had only made him more appealing in the eyes of London's hostesses. Just as a single drop of ink can change the colour of a whole glass, a note of pity, though barely acknowledged in itself, now tinged Emil Vascelles so that a half-foreign, self-made man once considered entirely too sharp for his own good was transformed into little more than a convenient addition to a seating plan. And he made himself a useful one, a single piece able to be slotted in to fill any little gap, who could be counted on to be witty and charming, and to use his disarming irreverence to smooth over any little ripples arising between his less gifted neighbours.

He had become a fixture, and if he was an odd one, that genial smile – containing just enough of the rakish to please without threatening – made him acceptable. The hostesses thought him dear and the hosts did not think about him at all, preferring to forget that over the years he had amassed a great number of their secrets, while even now they knew none of his. In those halls of important, powerful men, Emil Vascelles was easily overlooked. Indeed, he had arranged it that way.

So he might have gone on indefinitely, had he not forgotten himself and broken the first rule of camouflage: no unexpected movements. By conceit or carelessness or some fiendish impulse to destroy his own creation – in truth he never knew which, but he knew which he would prefer to imagine – in his fifty-first year, Emil Vascelles moved. Appearing midway through a season he had been largely absent from, he set about introducing an unknown woman to circles in which he walked with an air of impunity, and in doing so reminded the circles that in fact he had no business being among them at all.

By the time he realised his mistake, it was too late, for himself and Victor Bancroft both.

Nora Dallaway first laid eyes on her future husband on the very first evening Emil took her out. He stood across the room, a young man in a cluster of other young men, well built with ruddy cheeks and large soft eyes which made him look younger than his years. It was none of that which drew Nora's attention however; rather, just as even now the more perceptive elements of the crowd were marking Emil out for his behaviour against the grain, so Nora marked the young man for his.

"Victor Bancroft," Emil supplied, glancing along the line of Nora's gaze as he helped himself to salmon. "Eldest son of Henry and Theodora. Family goes back to, oh, something about Cromwell, which is probably why there's no title. Absolutely pots of money though, own half of Hampshire, or rather *he*" – here Emil gestured with an emphatic bit of caviar-laden toast to make his point – "owns half of Hampshire. Old man kicked it last year. Not that he was that old actually." Emil made a face. "A year younger than me, I think. Hunting accident – nasty stuff. Honestly, I'll never understand the impulse to get on a half-ton behemoth with a walnut for a brain and force it to barrel through the undergrowth while you attempt to steer. Sheer lunacy if you ask me. Anyway, taken together with the fact that the mother has been underground a good few years already, what you are looking at over there, my dear Miss Dallaway" – here the remaining crescent of caviar toast made another appearance – "is arguably the most eligible bachelor of the season."

Seeing that Nora's attention had left him and wandered back to its original mark, he swallowed the toast and leaned over to add, in an exaggerated whisper: "That means he's too eligible for you."

Nora didn't know about any of that. No doubt Emil was right of course, but her interest had been piqued. As Emil went back to his flirtation with the Dowager Lady Peabody across the table, declining to acknowledge the glare from her fastidious young lord of a son, Nora returned to her study of the quiet young man who had struck her and then realised that that was it: he was quiet. Standing in the middle of a group of young men all laughing and talking and jockeying for position, with each other and with the cloud of young ladies pretending to ignore them nearby, Victor Bancroft stood quietly among them, somehow apart in the very centre, a position no doubt guaranteed him by sheer eligibility.

There was something intriguingly bovine about him, Nora decided. Nothing about his disengagement was proud or aloof. Rather, she sensed from him an air of boredom, of confusion, though whether he was bored because he was confused or confused because he was bored, she couldn't tell. Most of all he reminded her of a prize bull at the fair, wearing his rosettes politely and without seeing the slightest point in them, chewing his cud and allowing himself to be penned into the corral without fuss, knowing it from experience to be the easiest way back to his paddock.

Nor did the nights which followed do anything to change her impression of Victor Bancroft. As the young people on both sides engaged in their games, the dance taking place on the edges of the ballrooms as well as in their centres, the so-called most eligible among them was not so much found to have two left feet – judging by red faces and shattered glasses, Nora thought he would not have been the only one – so much as no feet at all. One or two of the more intrepid – or perhaps ambitious – young ladies made attempts, but there is nothing more dispiriting than an opponent who will not play.

One evening, honing her ears to conversations around the lavish room, Nora overheard a couple of diamond-dipped grande dames wondering which of the young ladies would be keen enough on the estate to be willing to make the best of the man. The elderly pair were charitable enough to hope that whomever she might turn out to be, she managed to get herself a taste of romance before her marriage, for certainly there would be none after. Old Henry had left a divided legacy, it seemed – all the looks, wit and warmth in one son, all the money in the other. There the conversation had ended, with laughter and deep pulls of champagne.

Nora wanted to ask Emil about it, but though he was all kindness and fun when his attention was on her, that attention seemed to be straying more and more.

She could not say when it had begun precisely. She had been caught up herself, in Victor and in this new life now on show. The way every distraction could be shut out with the mere opening of a gilded purse fascinated her. She had noticed, however, that after the first couple of events, he had ceased to introduce her except in passing. From dragging her round to half the tables on the first night, he now rarely rose from where he was seated. He no longer flirted with dowagers but met curious gazes with pointed grins. Comments addressed to him seemed now to have a prickle nestling among polite words, and he returned them with a relished barb. Few people approached them at all now, yet somehow they seemed under continuous scrutiny. Nora felt it from every corner as she picked up snatches of conversation she did not fully understand. It frightened her, almost as much Emil's gleaming new armour did.

It frightened her, but not half so much as the idea of leaving did. And as Emil made no move to leave, she set aside what she did not understand and focused on what she did.

First, she understood that she would stay in this world of light and artifice. Cost what it would, she would cling to it, and woe betide him who tried to wrest it from her hands. Second, she understood that she could never do so by joining the other young ladies in their game: not brought up to it and lacking the vivacity to learn on the fly, she would be soundly beaten without her opponents even noticing that she was trying to play. Third, she understood that, if she lacked the necessary skill to win, Victor Bancroft barely grasped the rules. His character was so singularly unsuited to its purpose in life, which made it so eminently suited to hers.

She watched him from corners, across rooms and over lantern-lit lawns, until at last he turned towards her willingly, recognising the choice which would demand only what he had to give – no more than a place by his side, safe in his gilded cage forever.

VI

"How?"

It was a small word, and it sounded even smaller in the darkness, hanging in the air beneath the eaves.

Emil shrugged, feeling the horsehair of Ambrose's mattress shift beneath his bare shoulders. "Does it matter? Someone saw me I suppose, or Briggs made the wrong comment to another driver, or, hell, maybe someone had me followed, I don't know. What difference does it make?"

Ambrose didn't reply; it made none. "Why didn't you tell me?"

Emil started to shrug again and then stopped: it was an awkward position to shrug in. "I wasn't sure, at first. Didn't see any sense in worrying you."

That was part of the truth. He made himself add the other part. "Suppose I didn't want to admit it really. It's embarrassing, getting caught out with the ice cracking beneath your feet like that."

"*Embarrassing?*"

The way Ambrose hissed the word sounded as though he found it almost obscenely inadequate, and also as though he hadn't taken a proper breath since the conversation began. Emil knew himself to blame, for starting it in the dark. He hadn't meant it to be an unpleasant conversation. He'd already had that one with himself, in dribs in the carriage after taking Nora home and drabs as he lay awake in the cold early mornings, and had come out of it knowing exactly which way he wanted to swim when that ice finally broke.

Reaching for the matches under the pillow, he fumbled with them until the lamp flared to life. The light bathed the sleeping pallet in a cosy red glow reflected from the drapery which curtained it off from the rest of the attic.

"Let's go somewhere warm," he said, wanting Ambrose to catch up. "And sunny."

Ambrose blinked against his suddenly bright world. "What?" he said, but at least now he had enough breath to say it. "Where? *When?*"

"As soon as possible. A fortnight, or sooner even. I'll square it with Hugo and then we can go anywhere you like, anywhere at all. Only say you'll come."

Emil felt the giddiness bubbling up at the thrill of adventure and the relief of escape so very near, but he swallowed what he could of it as Ambrose opened his mouth only to close it again, glancing around the room with wide eyes, as though realising for the first time that it was there.

"What about…?" he managed at last, gesturing not only to the small space behind the curtain but everything beyond it. Work, friends, memories; twenty-five years of a life.

Emil softened. "I know it's sudden, but honestly what's keeping you here, other than sheer habit? I mean really?" He hesitated, taking a large hand between his own. "And look, it's not as if it's transportation. London probably won't crumble the minute you leave. You can come back in a couple of years, if the world doesn't suit. Ships sail backward as well as forward."

Ambrose caught his gaze, and though his mouth was still tight from the shock, a tiny smile was nudging itself into place.

"I think you'll find they sail forward in both directions, dear," he said, making a little circling motion with one finger. "They turn around at either end."

Emil chuckled, a little exhale of relief. "Yes well, you'd know better than me. At any rate, you're not going to be trapped on a desert island with me."

"I could think of worse things." The hand Emil held began to twine its fingers with his, and then stopped. "You said if *I* want to come back. What about you?"

Ambrose looked at him, two bright eyes peering carefully from beneath the remains of a painted brow, knowing full well what the answer would be and searching now for Emil's feelings about it. He offered them up willingly, tasting each word himself to make sure it was true.

"The funny thing is I can't imagine I'd ever want to. There's the children of course, but I hardly see them now they have their own families, and under the circumstances, it'll be better for them to keep it that way. I'll miss Hugo, but taken against the weather, the traffic, the people, the pretence... And I need something new. Every problem which has come across my desk this year I solved twenty years ago or more. It wears me down in a way it never used to. Honestly, I can hardly wait to leave it behind. I hadn't planned it this way, but now that it's come about, I can't imagine why I didn't think of it before."

Ambrose nodded slowly, as though in time to a familiar tune he had not expected to hear outside his own head. When Emil finished, he smiled, all trace of uncertainty smoothed clean away. "So we're retiring, then?" he asked, with a sudden contentment which needed no response. "A retirement in the sun?"

Emil leaned in close. "Retirement is such a dull word. Let's say we're turning to the next chapter," he said. "In the sun."

Ambrose's echo was all but lost in the depths of the kiss. "In the sun," he murmured happily.

VII

On strict instruction, Nora had not been back to the Young Bess since the game had begun, Emil fearing that even to be seen walking across the river would be a mark against her at this stage. Yet, when the invitation came – exhorting her in neat hand to make up a tea party with her friends, that she might have something to read aloud to Violet – her feet found their path through the maze of corridors like a comfortable old groove.

The theatre had baked the July heat solid, a dense, dry weight which seemed to warp and swallow everything within, so that the cheerful bickering of excited voices waxed and waned in the dusty air, punctuated by brisk metallic taps and solemn, considered thuds, like wooden crates having their lids nailed down before being set aside.

"Dear heart." Emil's voice drifted down through the trap-door as Nora made the final climb towards it. "Is it your intention to take the company's garderobe in its entirety? Won't they miss it?"

"I made it, so it's mine." Another thud emphasised Ambrose's reply. "And anyway, I'm leaving them enough to be getting on with. I hardly expect the old man is going to pursue us across the high seas for the sake of a few bits of old taffeta and some mottled feathers."

Putting her head through the hole, Nora found Emil sitting on a closed packing crate. He kicked his heels against it as he surveyed the growing stacks with a bemusement bordering on mild alarm, looking very much as though he would like to ask, if that was all it amounted to, what all this effort was for.

Catching sight of himself in a stray mirror, he pulled a comical face before almost toppling off his perch at the sudden appearance of Nora behind him, staring wide-eyed about the room. Half of it had been stripped and left bare to the rafters, only the odd snatch of coloured thread and stray feather left to suggest that there had ever been anything bright there at all. The old patchwork sofa stood forlorn in the gloom, as though knowing itself a relic of a past already distant. It gazed disconsolately towards the other end of the attic, where the entire content of its own half was now divided into three disorderly but distinct categories: the precious, packed carefully into crates; the discarded, heaped in a pile of cracked beads, stained dresses and ratty wigs; and that still to be sorted, over which Ambrose hovered, inspecting each item with professional attention.

Nora barely recognised the room, and yet she knew immediately what it meant. "You're leaving," she said, leaving the *me* hovering unsaid.

Emil, having recovered himself, gave her a gentle smile. "'Fraid so," he said, but though the look on Nora's face might make him sorry, it could not make him regretful. "We sail in eight days."

The words hit Nora just exactly in the centre of the solar plexus. "I see," she said, feeling it bore in and tighten like a screw. "And your work?"

"I am going for my work. At least, that's the official line. Expansion into some far-flung corner of the globe and all that. My brother will manage the London business. He knows I'm involved in a scandal, that it'll be better for everyone this way."

He glanced fondly at Ambrose, who had turned from his work to watch the exchange. "My own scandal," Emil added playfully, but though Ambrose smiled, his eyes were on Nora.

"But this is your home!" With every word, the screw made another turn, pinning her front to her back and threatening to squeeze out everything between.

Emil frowned, not unkindly. "If I stay in England, the whispers will soon become open jeers. Then I will have to choose between destroying the future happiness of my children, and all my family, or destroying my own. I might even face the Reading Gaol for the crime of having touched it. On the other hand, if I take myself abroad now, the whispers will die away for lack of fuel, and I can spend the rest of my life in the sun, watching Ambrose flutter his feathers among the other birds of paradise, instead of hiding away in a dreary old attic to avoid offending the pigeons." He smiled – a small, sympathetic smile probing cautiously for a response.

Nora was beyond seeing it. She found herself *needing* suddenly, in the way a child needs, in a way she had never had anyone to need as a child. "Can't you just stay?" she burst out, with such force that Ambrose flinched.

"Em…" he murmured, inclining his head towards the open hatch.

Emil hesitated but, seeing his lover's determination, gave him a quick kiss for luck and was gone.

Nora was looking at the boxes, brow creased as she tried to make sense of the room, once so full and now incomprehensibly empty. "This is your home," she repeated.

"My dear girl." Ambrose started towards her, but as she turned to look at him, something in her eyes stopped him in his tracks. There was confusion there, yes, but even as he watched it was being frozen, crushed, crystallised by what was forming around it. She met his gaze with something he did not recognise, hard as diamonds and just as bleak.

"Is that what you want to be?" she asked, and for the first time, Ambrose realised how cold that glitter really was; mocking, like a chattering magpie. "A scandal?"

Taken aback though he was, Ambrose did not flinch. Since his earliest youth, it had been a point of pride to take the most unexpected blow in stride, and so he took Nora's. "I was born a scandal, my dear, and I will die one. If in between Emil

Vascelles is willing to claim me as his own, then I will thank my lucky stars and be glad."

The jut of his chin made her a challenge, should she choose to meet it. Nora did not.

"This is your home," she repeated for a third time, with a doggedness that made him wonder what precisely she meant by it. "You belong here! You would cast yourself adrift…?"

Ambrose raised his painted eyebrows. "I know myself far too well to be lost in other people's tides, my girl, never fear on that score. I am my own anchor. As for home…" He sighed. "Sometimes a place offers what one needs, and sometimes it doesn't, and when it doesn't, one has the choice of building it oneself or going somewhere it already exists, that's all. I have done both in my time, and building is hard work. Sometimes it's worth the effort, particularly when nowhere else promises better, and sometimes it frankly isn't. London has been kind to me in many ways, but I won't apologise for wanting more."

"You're leaving me!"

The explosion was so sudden that it stunned both of them. The force of it shattered the diamond shell, and through the tear-blurred shards, Ambrose glimpsed the girl he knew.

"Please try to understand," he begged. "Before I met Em, I hadn't dared hope I ever would. You are young, and clever, and stronger than you think. You will find your way, and Em won't leave you high and dry – he'll set something up for you—"

"No need. Victor Bancroft is going to propose to me, and I intend to accept. I will be 'anchored', as you put it, before the summer is out."

It was the way she said it as much as what she said which filled Ambrose with a sudden chilling dread. Though she spoke calmly, there was something in it, something beneath the surface of her absolute certainty which struck him as gruesome, horrible in a way which he could not fully grasp.

"Nora," he began carefully, trying to find words that might reach her, a warning she might understand. "No one else can anchor you, no one in the world. If you try to make them, you will either lose yourself or become enmeshed, and either way you will drown."

"Oh, I think the Bancroft purse will keep me quite dry." Her smile was an ugly one. "Never fear on that score."

"It's not—" Desperately, Ambrose turned his mind out in search of words he knew he didn't have. Even to himself, he couldn't name what he feared, nor even for whom he feared it. He could only watch in dull horror as the tears receded, the shattered fragments reforming before his eyes, fusing piece by jagged piece until his own odd girl was gone, the woman left behind a stranger.

She turned on her heel and left without another word.

~

The hot air leaped about her with the promise of a storm, crackling through the empty streets and tearing at the bare branches of the plane trees until they howled like winter woods. Their shadows writhed and shivered on the baked cobblestones, and as Nora stalked between them, she did not walk alone.

The knowledge nipped at her, worrying the edges of her consciousness, whining in demand of recognition as the thing padded along just beyond the edge of sight, breath furnace-hot on her ungloved hand. Reflexively, her fingers swung back, drawn by the promise of that familiar heat, but just as the tips were about to brush iron-grey bristles, the red of the Gordons' front door came into view, bright and galling in the low light. Nora snatched her hand up to wipe away the stinging tears, refusing to shed another. Going in, she slammed the door behind her, and thus shut out the most loyal companion she had ever known.

Violet, writing letters in the front room, could not help but take fright at her cousin's appearance, but Nora would not be drawn into explanation.

"Won't you play for me?" she begged, indicating the little upright piano with its sweet worked runner. "My head is full of such a dreadful howling, I can hardly think for it."

And so Violet played, until at last the sky outside cracked open, and Violet ran out to the garden to bring the older boys in before they caught their deaths.

Nora did not wait for the landau that night but went on foot through the streets still damp with rain. When finally the lantern-hung garden of the Piermont home came into view, the hem of her dress was dusty and splashed, her satin shoes held together by little more than the cobbler's last will. Had they come apart entirely, Nora would scarcely have noticed. Victor Bancroft stood on the terrace, and she approached him with such determined intention that he turned to her even before she expected him to.

Before that night, they had never spoken a word one to the other – still he saw what she offered and did not fight it. He did not wish to fight it. Peace in his mind was surely better than love in a woman, or money, or name. The match suited him as it suited her, and thus they were agreed. On this basis, Victor Bancroft offered Nora Dallaway his arm.

VIII

"I get the impression your host doesn't like me very much," Emil informed her, by way of greeting. The maid had left the parlour door ajar behind him, whether out of propriety or in the hope of gossip, and through it Harold Gordon's footsteps could be heard clomping up the stairs with emphatic vigour. Violet's lighter ones scurried behind, and the clatter of curious little ones came down from above, until the whole family was installed on the landing in a hush of worried scolding.

Nora set her book aside. "He suspects me of being your mistress," she said, not rising to greet her guest. "I think Violet does too, come to that, but she disapproves less or, at least, cares about my feelings more.

"The poker is behind the credenza, if that's what you're looking for," she added, watching him hunt around. "The boys have a tendency to get carried away with their fencing games otherwise."

"Ah!" Emil retrieved the rod with a triumphant flourish and used it to stoke the anaemic fire into something like life – in spite of the season, there was a damp chill in the air which would not let up. He settled himself in the wing chair across from Nora, his feet on a worked footstool, entirely as though he visited every day of his life and had a perfect right. "Won't they be surprised when you make your announcement?"

"The one you're here to talk me out of?" She felt defensive, and it came out in shards of irritation.

Emil gave her a searching look. "Now why would I want to do that? Even supposing it would make the slightest difference, which I have no reason to expect it would."

In spite of herself, Nora felt herself softening. The argument with Ambrose had been all the more distressing for being so unexpected, so entirely incomprehensible to her. The need for approval, for encouragement in doing what she could to protect herself, overtook her.

"You mean to say you don't agree with him? That you don't believe I am making my life's mistake by doing what every woman in my position would be pleased, even grateful to do?"

Emil's dark eyes studied her for some time before he answered.

"I don't believe you are every woman," he said at last. "Indeed, I do not believe that any woman is every woman, any more than any man is every man. Whether or not our canvasses are cut of equal shape at birth is a question for learned men like your Mr Gordon upstairs. What I do know is that, by the time we are of an age to chart our own courses, each of our maps has already been painted by our own individual experiences, and the strengths and weaknesses they have given rise to, so that what may be an eminently sensible path for one is entirely impossible for another, even when their present positions would appear to be quite the same. Ambrose's experiences inform him that to give ground is to lose categorically. To relinquish even the smallest part of himself would be a mortal blow, not survivable unless the same can be retaken somehow. He cannot conceive that it might be different for other people, least of all those in whom he recognises himself."

"But you disagree?" Nora leaned forward, drawn by her eagerness to hear him sanction what she would do regardless, cost what it would.

"You know that I of all people am exceedingly fond of all of Ambrose's parts. I will never be anything but grateful that against the odds, he managed to keep them intact long enough that I might come to know them and grant them what protection I am able to afford."

Emil smiled – a small, private smile – before growing thoughtful. "That being said, even his approach can be stifling, in a way: he keeps all of himself and on full display, it is true, but at the cost of mounting a constant defence and having to restrict his path accordingly. Whereas others, like myself, may decide we would rather travel a more significant distance than carry every single part of ourselves with us at all times. Everyone sacrifices something in the end, you see. The only question is what is easiest for each to bear, and for what reward are they willing to bear it."

Nora's laugh sounded hollow over the crackling of the fire. "It sounds so simple, when you put it like that. How can one ever know?"

"I'm not sure one ever does." Emil gave her a wry look. "One takes stock of all the routes open to one, makes one's choices with the knowledge one has and then one hopes for the best."

Nora nodded glumly, staring into the fire. It had not taken much to knock off the summer chill, but though the room was rapidly warming beyond the comfortable, contemplating her own "open routes" put a deep cold in the pit of her stomach. "How did yours turn out?"

Emil snorted. "Ask me again when I'm dead."

Glancing at Nora, he went on more gently: "I can't pretend to know much more now than I did when I began, but one thing I have learned is that a choice which seems ideal at the time may go very wrong but may also come right again, in ways one never expected. Take my wife and I. We were not a love match – she needed my money; I needed her family – but we were not so very far from it. Both of us were pleased with the other and willing to do our bit, which made it all the more disappointing when it became apparent that our temperaments and modes of life were miserably unsuited. Frankly, by the time our eldest was ten, the smallest interaction seemed to take years off each of our lives. It was dreadful, feeling that we had doomed ourselves and each other, yet there seemed no way out. And yet now, ten years after that, we are both happier than we've ever been. She is back in her ancestral home, now with the money to restore it and keep all the horses, dogs and country mud she could want besides. I, on the other hand, have had the liberty to stumble across what I never knew I wanted, now with the experience to know him for what he is and the acumen to put together a life of relative comfort and security for both of us. So you could say that Antonia and I each wasted twenty years of our lives, or you could consider that we invested twenty years in order to hopefully spend the next twenty enjoying what we could not have had without them."

Nora gave him a level look. "So, in my place, you'd marry Bancroft – a man you said you'd jump in the Thames rather than sit within range of at dinner – and hope for the best."

"I don't know what I'd do in your place – I've never been in it." Emil looked thoughtful. "But for my part, I think you could make a worse choice. Bancroft might have all the wit of a boiled potato, but at least he has the temperament to match. I wouldn't wish to dine with him, but I doubt his wife will have to do so more than occasionally. Once the children are born, likely even less. He doesn't strike me as a man to ask or even want very much in the way of coddling, though I expect you already know that. After the honeymoon is over, be attentive when you see him and otherwise leave him to his amusements, and don't discourage him from taking a mistress. In the meantime, you spend his money and your time on whatever gives you pleasure. I suspect you may find it quite as pleasant a way to live as that love match upstairs, with only the study door between them."

He glanced up, and Nora instinctively followed his gaze. Muffled sounds of prickly conversation drifted down, punctuated by the occasional mysterious thud or running feet on carpeted floor, as Violet attempted to wrangle all the elements of her family at once.

"And as an early wedding present," Emil went on, the Gordon family having made his point for him, "since I will miss the happy event, I've taken the liberty of doing a bit of investigation on your behalf. I'm please to confirm that it's all quite sound, and relatively uncomplicated for such a significant estate. And no entail, which was a nice surprise – just in case, you understand."

Nora withdrew her gaze from the ceiling and managed a smile. "Thank you," she said, rising. "For coming, and for…"

She faltered as Emil rose with her.

"You are most terribly welcome, my dear," he said, taking her hand and kissing it before pulling her into a paternal embrace. "I do hope we'll see you before setting sail. I know Ambrose wants it. He's absurdly fond of you, you know. You are his particular pet. Promise you'll try."

Nora nodded, pressing her lips together as the cold mass tightened in her stomach. "I promise – I promise I'll try," she said, pretending she did not know already what the result must be.

XVI

Croftsend had not changed since Nora had seen it last. Slung low and comfortable in the morning light, it nestled at the end of the drive, the mottled red brick bright against the green of the rhododendrons, lush even at this time of year. The same paisley curtains edged the windows, their frames painted in the same shade of cream, and there on the windowsill of the good sitting room was the same Ridgway vase, a wedding present from Captain Lindup's sister and treasured by his wife out of all proportion to her attachment to that lady.

The lowing of cows drifted down from the fields, followed by the yelp of the farmer's dog, just the same as on that day many years ago when Nora had first laid eyes on the house, sitting wide-eyed and silent as they drove up the same lane she walked now, her uncle beside her on the seat, a stranger then. Only the air was different: it had been early in the year then, and though the branches overhanging the nursery window remained stark and brown, they had been covered in tiny buds, little brown knots of promise. Now though, in December, the year's promise had been spent, and there lingered over the place an air of contentment in resignation, acceptance that, for good or for ill, there was no more to be done.

The same air which touched her house seemed to hang over Judith Lindup; indeed, Nora wondered whether her aunt might not be the source of it. Now a grandmother seven times over, the matriarch had long since sloughed off the mere mother's fastidiousness, receiving Nora over breakfast in her canary-yellow wrapper, the edges of the sleeves stained with the watercolours which Nora suspected now filled her days entirely. She glanced down as Mills, greyer now yet bustling no less than ever, fussed over the trail of country dirt Nora had brought in with her, but the only reproach was of a morning interrupted.

"I was not expecting company this morning, but do please join me. Mills, leave that and lay a place for Mrs Bancroft directly. My most sincere condolences."

"Thank you, Aunt." Nora took the chair indicated. "Do forgive the intrusion."

Judith demurred in a murmur, but Nora barely heard her. The room came to her in sections: the scalloped edge on the tablecloth, the tastefully painted roses on the tea set, the alabaster bust gazing vacantly down over Judith's head. Everything was the same, just the same as the day she'd left.

Judith was even failing to meet her eyes in just the same way.

"You haven't replied to my letters." A plate had appeared before her, and tea in a painted cup, but Nora had no use for them. She wanted only what she had come for and no more.

There was something satisfying in the tremor which ran through Judith's shoulders at the remark, culminating in a cough into her cup. Evidently, her aunt had not expected the obvious to be raised so soon, nor so directly. Nevertheless, she was composed as she replied, "I haven't replied because I don't understand what it is you expect."

Nora did not try to contain her frustration – no, her fury – at being denied even now. "I expect you to give me my aunt's address. You have no right to keep it from me."

"I'm sure I can't imagine what you mean. I am your only aunt."

"My great-aunt then." Nora pronounced the words one warning at a time. "On my mother's side. Virginia, who wrote to me when I was a child."

"No one by that name has ever written to you."

Across the table, Judith seemed to have shrunk in her chair, but Nora had the curious impression that it was not the conversation that oppressed her but rather some unspoken thing hanging in the air between them, the very same thing which had hung there through every interaction with her aunt Nora could remember. Even now she could not grasp it, and in the attempt lost hold of the last of her self-control.

"You're lying!" she burst out, surprised at the tears starting in her eyes. "She wrote to me every birthday and when I was ill, and you know she did because you took her letters from me. You had no right—"

"I did what I thought best for you!" The cry seemed to come from somewhere even Judith had not been fully aware of, stunning them both into silence. "I always tried to do what was best for you," Judith repeated shakily.

Nora could only stare. "'What was best for me'," she repeated, sheer incredulity putting a momentary lid on her fury. "You stole my letters, you stole my inheritance, sent me away to the middle of nowhere—"

"Your inheritance?" Judith's voice still trembled but now with the laughter she struggled to repress. "You mean that burned-out ruin sitting on some godforsaken cliff in a place no one can even pronounce? It's yours, my dear, entailed upon your mother's female line from now until kingdom come. By all means go and claim it, I entreat you."

Still her aunt's shoulders shook, so that the wrapper shivered with laughter – or with something else entirely. Nora couldn't tell and was past caring. "Why did you never tell me—"

"Because it was unbearable! To think my poor brother travelled all that way, poured what little our own wretched father hadn't drunk up into that evil house, only to have it kill him. To know that while he is dead and gone it remains, laughing at him, at all of us, unable to be sold, incapable even of being rented, because no sane person will go within five miles of the place. Do what you please with it, still there it will sit forever more, until that cursed cliff finally caves in and takes it back to Hell!"

Shaking off whatever cowed her, Judith vented twenty-five years of pent-up resentment over the breakfast table. "As for sending you away, I kept you when it counted! When that so-called expert wanted to take you, to lock you up in his asylum after you maimed him, I stood for you! I kept you here, *I* did, because you were Stephen's blood and mine too, whatever else you may be, and I couldn't bear the thought of you in a place like that! And children do go to school, you know! St Clare's has an excellent reputation, and with Violet gone, what else was there for you to do? It might have been different if you had made friends in the village, if you'd ever shown the *slightest* inclination, but you needed – you needed—"

Spent, Judith's anger trailed off, leaving her to deflate in a series of gulping breaths, tears dripping onto her toast.

Nora watched her, an old woman clutching her handkerchief to sagging lips moistened by grief, and realised with a distant sense of surprise that she was right: she had done everything she could for the niece she did not understand, and it had not been enough, and now that Nora knew both statements to be equally true, suddenly neither mattered a jot. A curious sense of calm descended on her at the thought, the soothing of a wound she had not realised she was suffering with until now.

"You said 'whatever else you might be'," she said as Judith collected herself. "What did you mean by that?"

Across the table, Judith lifted her eyes, looking directly at Nora for the first time since she had arrived, and though Nora had a sense that she immediately wished she had not, she did not look away. She looked tired.

"They're in the attic, your letters. The physician at St Clare's insisted you shouldn't be allowed to see them once you were out of the delirium. He thought it might set back your recovery." She smiled, small and tight, as at a joke she couldn't quite bring herself to laugh at. "Go along and take them now – you might as well."

~

The south window illuminated the attic room, as well as the layers of dust and cobwebs which covered it. Outside, the chestnut tree waved the tops of its branches, their skeletal shadows falling upon the old hatbox tucked in at the end of its shelf, blue and pink stripes faded with the years. Something sharper than nostalgia tingled in her fingers as Nora lifted it down, settling herself on the very same window seat where years ago she had watched the sun rise; a bittersweet compromise, needed because good little girls did not go outside at dawn.

She brushed the dust from the lid with more of a caress than a wipe, running her fingers along every dent and crease in the battered cardboard, the ones she remembered and the ones she did not. It was stiff to open, a decade of alternating damp and dry having swelled the walls to seal it tight. As she worked the lid carefully, it creaked and grumbled with the strain, and when it finally gave, it was with a crotchety puff of musty air which filled her nostrils and made her cough.

The contents were yellower than she remembered, the writing faded and blotted in places, but otherwise all was as she had left it – two dozen thickly packed envelopes one on top of the other, not so much piled as scattered within a confined space. Among them, a forgotten ribbon poked out its forlorn head: in her fever, she had had no thought of trying to tie anything up.

She picked an envelope from the pile at random, the paper dry and crackling under her careful touch as she drew out the letter and unfolded it. And froze.

The first page and every one behind it was covered with a close-cribbed scrawl which seemed to have been put down by a person in a disturbed state of mind. The words grew and shrank at random, as though the writer had not been in full control of the hand holding the pen, or else unable to see what they were doing. The letters crawled here, sprang there, leaped off the edge of the paper and were lost, and yet through it all there was a consistency to them, to the sharp wedge of the N and the sweeping curve of the R, which marked them undeniably as the same hand, a hand Nora recognised instinctively.

As if propelled by clockwork, she set the letter aside and mechanically reached for another, and then another. Each was the same, in form and in substance, a substance she suspected she could only decipher because that horrible demented hand was so awfully, dreadfully familiar. Silently, easily she mouthed the sentences, and though some distant part of her pleaded frantically that children copied what they saw, that after all the hours she had spent reading and rereading those letters it was really no wonder, it was in vain: even the most confused scribblings were clear to her, and they were clear to her because the hand they were scribbled in was undeniably her own.

Her first impulse was violence, to shove the box and all it threatened physically away, to cry and distract herself with panic, and yet she did not move.

Somewhere in the house, a clock struck the hour. Some time later, it did it again. Nora sat still, barely breathing, watching and not seeing the winter sun chase the sprightly dust motes across the room. Snatches of memory tumbled through her mind. Misinterpreted, misunderstood, misfiled, they clamoured and cried out, struggling – *fighting* – to set themselves right in relation to the others, so that at long last they sorted themselves out and what she had always known took shape in her mind.

The apricot sun was low in the sky by the time acceptance overtook her. When she looked up, it was with purpose, gazing into the corner of the room where the shadows of the chestnut branches still waved and knowing exactly what she would find.

The thing sat on its haunches, watching her with amber eyes of flame. It was not a wolf nor a stag nor yet a great falcon, yet contrived somehow to be all at once, separately and combined, a creature incomprehensible to the human mind, forcing mankind to turn away or brave certain madness. It watched Nora, and Nora did not look away.

She knew it now as she had known it then, the very first time it had come to her. As the flames spread around her and her parents lay where they had fallen, it had clamped its jaws around her tight enough to bruise and dragged her, crying and choking, to the last remaining sanctuary in that burning house. There it had comforted her until morning, and might have done so until this very day, had she only kept faith. But her head had been turned by the thoughts and fears of other people, people who confused their own legends with hers, who repeated folksongs and wrote articles, people who meant no harm but did not understand that if indeed that eldritch house was cursed, then the curse was not on the daughters but for them.

As the creature, invited now, padded loyally to her side, Nora looked into the shadows whence it had come and knew them for her own. If there was a Beast of Bridde Place, it was herself.

XVII

Ritter would console himself, half-jokingly, that at least it was his own creation who had joined the parts together. He'd brought Wilcox into his office and was reading the morning's sentry reports to him, partly to watch his reactions and partly to distract the boy from what gnawed at him.

They'd come to the section in which Mrs Sharpe had made her daily appearance. The sentry on duty reported that, on being turned away following Ritter's new orders, the good woman had "threatened to knock [his] block off", and from the look on her face, for a minute he had feared she might.

At the constable's snort, Ritter glanced up to find Wilcox grinning darkly. "Bet she could too – and worse. Don't you think, sir?"

Here, Ritter might have expected himself to grin, or agree, or perhaps even reprimand the young man for making light of so serious a matter as threatening a police officer. But for reasons not at that moment known fully even to himself, Ritter did none of those things. Instead he asked very carefully: "What do you mean, Constable?"

Wilcox shrugged, ducking his head as though embarrassed that his thoughtless remark was receiving such undue attention, but he answered: "Well, with her being a butcher's wife and all. I bet she'd know exactly where to cut with that big knife of hers. Remember, sir?"

Ritter did indeed remember Mrs Sharpe's big knife, and he remembered her husband's profession, and he knew from experience that, in family businesses, gender was typically less of a concern than the ability to work. And Mrs Sharpe, he did not doubt, could work. He thought of those huge shoulders, the powerful forearms, and knew that in them must surely be the strength to separate flesh from bone, the power to crack a joint as well as any man.

He was tempted to claim that the connection had eluded him, but to own the truth he had turned from it. He had done in fact the very thing he had been at pains to teach Wilcox not to do, relying on his own notions of how things ought to be even when they were not borne out by the facts in front of him. A woman as accomplice he could imagine, accessory to man's brutality, particularly a woman like that. But when he thought of Victor Bancroft's mangled corpse and tried to make a woman responsible, even her...

Well, he must learn his own lesson, that was all.

"Wilcox," he said, rising from his chair, "go and get the Bancroft weapon out of the evidence room and meet me downstairs. We're going to have another little chat with the kitchen staff."

Mrs Sharpe had not been at home all day, which in the first instance suited Ritter fine. Conjecture, after all, was nothing without proof, and in the suspect's absence, he was at liberty to find it in the form of Millie Chapel, senior kitchen maid and second in command to Mrs Sharpe. When presented with the knife retrieved from the garden path that bloody morning, its blade still stained with spots of rusty red, Millie did not hesitate.

"Mrs Sharpe's filleting knife!" she exclaimed. "Why, sir, wherever did you get that?"

Beside him, Wilcox drew a sharp breath, reaction enough for both of them.

Ritter looked at the girl. "Have the goodness to look again, Miss Chapel. It is of the utmost importance that you are not mistaken. Take your time. No one will think the less of you if you prefer to withdraw your previous statement. Are you absolutely certain this is Mrs Sharpe's knife and not merely one which looks like hers?"

Millie looked first at the knife and then at Ritter, one eyebrow cocked as though wondering if he was having a joke on her. "I'm certain, sir," she said, turning over the handle to show him. "Look, one side's darker than the other, from where Sue put the kettle down on it. Ever so careless she was. Mrs Sharpe gave her such a smack as I never saw and well deserved I'm sure – Mrs Sharpe said she'd have scalded herself for life if it'd gone over. But she was always careless, Sue was."

Ritter was beginning to feel slightly lightheaded. "Miss Chapel, please show us where Mrs Sharpe keeps her filleting knife."

The knife store in which Ritter had once watched Mrs Sharpe put away another knife was locked of course. The cook still not having been heard from, the housekeeper with her key bunch was summoned to open it.

All four of them gathered around to hear the well-oiled bolt slide back. The plain door opened to reveal a notched bar hung with a row of dangling knives, gleaming fearsomely side by side like crocodile teeth.

Millie's hand was already going to the place she had been asked to show. "There, sir— Oh!"

Faltering, she turned to Ritter, for the notch to which she had been pointing was already occupied, by a knife of remarkably similar size and shape to the one wrapped safely in Wilcox's hand.

"S-She must have got a new one," the girl stammered, embarrassed. "Only I never noticed, there not being much call for filleting these past weeks…"

"She did get a new one."

McNeal's voice was such that Ritter found himself turning to see if she was all right. He found her staring at the knife where it hung benignly in the cupboard, as though its very existence was a horror to her.

"It's brand new," she said in that same distant voice. "Only look at the handle."

Ritter looked, and indeed, though the blade had already been worn down by many a turn on the whetstone, the handle was impeccable, clean and still glowing with the oil it had left its maker with, bearing none of the marks of life in a working kitchen.

The housekeeper's face had turned an unwholesome shade of grey. "And," she added, "I can tell you exactly when she got it."

It was as they were on their way back to Whitehall, Ritter listing all the resources he thought he might be able to muster on short notice to locate the fugitive and bring her in, that Wilcox made his suggestion.

"I was thinking, sir…" he began tentatively. "It might be worth me going down by Shoreditch. They hear things there – you never know…"

Ritter thought about it for a moment. No doubt the population of Shoreditch did hear things, and indeed, you never did know. That being said, Ritter felt fairly certain that they were unlikely to have heard of the movements of a cook not yet known to be a fugitive, and even if they had, they would be unlikely to tell Constable Wilcox about it. Nevertheless, Ritter estimated he would shortly have half of Scotland Yard on the prowl, and there had been something shifting in the young man since the encounter at the hospital. Ritter was curious to see where it might lead.

XVIII

It was five o'clock when the train pulled into Charing Cross. The cold hit her bones, and Nora smiled at it like an old friend who ought to know better. She ignored the waiting cabbies, their horses stamping impatient hooves as chill air froze their steaming nostrils, and walked out beneath a sky like a whirl of flossed lead.

London smelled delicious.

The lamplighters were out in force, illuminating the city at the peak of its evening tumult: all around people rushed, following the day into evening as though afraid to miss it. Wheels clattered over cobbles, chimneys belched soot as coal was heaped on fires below and the evening damp caught in wool coats, bringing out the waft of distant herds to mingle with the odours of humanity.

The city opened before her a wonder, exhilarating, a vast stage upon which she might do anything she liked, perform any dance she pleased, without consideration for an audience whose opinion did not concern her. That she had never noticed this before came to her as nothing short of incredible, but it did not suit her mood to question it. She knew only what she knew now, and that was enough. Every line was clear, every corner sharp in its distinction, every object full of life and every life luminous. She saw it all and danced with it, saw herself and twirled about her own shadow, intoxicated, dizzy in the rising moonlight.

The scent caught her on the doorstep, a heavy musk lingering there as though in wait, threatening in its despair. The knowledge of it ran through the house, unconscious yet irritating, like the periodic twitch of an over-taut muscle. It hung about the footman on the door, chased the chambermaid down a corridor, yet it was not until Nora reached her bedroom that she was able to place it. The pile of unanswered cards greeted her, a looming stack white and accusing in the gloom, and suddenly the odour took shape, gained a figure, a face. A name.

She reached for the pull and tugged, and knew immediately she needn't have bothered. Even before the jingle of the bell in the distance, footsteps were approaching, short and measured, McNeal on her purposeful way before Nora had even thought of her.

With a knock, the door opened. Nora did not bother to look round. Her eyes were still on the pile of cards, the odour which clung to them filling her head, sparking in her stomach. "I take it Mr Bancroft has called again?"

The housekeeper was hesitating, thrown off by a question so entirely unrelated to the information she had come to relate. "He has, madam. He hoped you might be persuaded to dine with him this evening."

Nora felt the corner of her mouth twitch as the spark in her gut caught flame. "Persistent, isn't he?"

The hesitation this time was rooted in delicacy. "As you say, madam. Mr Alcott declined on your behalf."

Nora turned sharply. "On whose authority?"

The housekeeper inclined her head, setting about lighting the Argand lamp to avoid showing her expression. "I believe he thought it best, madam, under the circumstances. Mr Bancroft was... well, suffice to say he did not appear to be himself this evening."

Nora had no patience for delicacy. "Out with it, McNeal."

"Well, madam, the fact is that he appeared to be drunk. He was in rather a dishevelled state – not even a hat – and Mr Alcott says the smell of strong drink was plain upon his breath when he – when he…"

"When he…?"

"When he threatened Mr Alcott, I'm sorry to say, with physical violence," the housekeeper finished in a rush. She bowed her head as though she truly was sorry, as though the behaviour of the scion of her employer's family somehow reflected upon her own character.

Nora was too distracted to pity her. All around the room, bright things flickered in the lamplight, catching her attention, so that she turned now to watch the play of it on the back of a silver hairbrush, now to inspect the glow on the curved brass below the dainty orb of the lamp itself.

It was as she was admiring the inky gloss of her own hair in the glass that McNeal lit the lamp on the dressing table, and in doing so illuminated the polished corner of the letter rack. Hugo Vascelles's article was where Nora had left it, folded neatly in front of the stiff card of the invitation she had never answered. The date on it sang out to her, every curling letter speaking of the music, the gowns, the food, the decorations being prepared even now, of the splendour and delights to be offered not an hour hence. She felt her lips curl in response, thrilling with anticipation.

"Send a message to Mr Bancroft. Tell him I'll see him at the Brucknells' ball tonight, about nine or so."

"The Brucknells' ball, madam?" McNeal repeated. "Tonight?"

"At nine," Nora reminded her. "One wants to enjoy the sights a bit before getting down to business, doesn't one?"

For a moment, protest flashed across the housekeeper's steady face, bobbing up on a current of sheer incredulity that she, Geraldine McNeal, should be called upon to participate in such unseemliness. Nora could practically hear it – *Not two months a widow and going to a ball, the very idea*! It was only a moment, however, before it was swept away, pushed down by duty weighted with sheer exhaustion, the burden of worries Nora had not cared to ask about, compounded, Nora suspected, by the look on her own face.

"Very good, madam," was all she said. "I will order a bath prepared."

When the housekeeper returned, it was with a quilted silk robe over her arm – the same quilted silk robe she had wrapped Nora in that fateful morning . Nora wondered whether she realised it hadn't been washed since then, having evidently been overlooked in the commotion. It seemed impossible that the old woman genuinely did not know it reeked of old blood, that she did not feel the way the heavy garment carried a fraction more weight on the left side as she draped it over Nora's shoulders, or hear the faintest chink of metal emanating from the depths of the pocket there.

It fell against Nora's leg, and suddenly she could not be still.

Heedless of McNeal's attempts with the sash, she stepped out of reach towards the shuttered window. Unable to bear her confinement a moment longer, she threw open the curtains so that the brass rings sang on their rails and yanked at the shutters until they gave way.

Reflected in the windowpane, McNeal had not moved a muscle. "What dress will you wear, madam?"

Nora looked at her own reflection, smiling at her own grin. "The black, I think. It's only appropriate."

~

Some distance away, although not so far as might be expected from the change in scenery – not to mention smell – Margaret

answered the knock at her new front door not without trepidation. It was not that she was afraid precisely, but the idea
that absolutely anyone could walk up to it, without footmen or
clerks or even a lock with a functioning bolt to stop them, was
taking a bit of getting used to. It was the first such knock she
had received in her new lodgings, so it was perhaps as well that
the sight of the face on the other side chased away those nerves
she swore she did not possess in a rush of frustration.

"What do you *want,* Paul?"

On the other side of the threshold, her brother shrugged. "I
heard you were living here and thought I'd come by. You know,
to say hello."

He looked over her shoulder into the room beyond as he
spoke. It was easy for him to do – the top of her head barely
reached his chin. A little of her irritation abated as she noted
the hat held politely in his hand, but even so…

"How did you find me?"

Another shrug. She remembered it, the noncommittal
answer which was safer to give when the right one could not be
made certain of – or like as not did not exist.

"I asked around. Elsie Smith says you helped her."

"We helped each other," Margaret corrected. "She found
me this room. And anyway, someone had to."

Paul flushed. He still flushed so easily. Margaret supposed
she did too. She thought he looked faintly sheepish.

"Inspector Ritter says it's our job to look after people like
her. Like them. Like—"

Like you, Margaret suspected he had been about to say,
but something stopped him, whether some internal scruple or
purely the frank challenge in her eye.

"Well that's a lie," she snorted and was surprised to find her
brother looked genuinely stung. She softened. "It's a nice idea
though."

"Yes." He seemed to consider it. "I thought so."

Margaret, who had been the courted wit of salons across the Continent, could think of no reply to that.

Silence closed about them, straining at the walls of the dingy stairwell, pressing against the confines of her sparse rooms behind. In so restricted a space there seemed no room for the bitter rancour of their last meeting, the threatened explosion, but equally there seemed nothing else to fill it with, neither of them certain what they might wish to place there instead.

"Mother has had locks put in," he tried, casting back to their sole shared topic. "Proper iron ones with keys, from Guildford. I do feel safer about her, knowing it."

Margaret was about to laugh, to point out that the greatest threat to the little whitewashed cottage on the green was standing in front of him, safely many miles away, when she realised that was exactly it: safe many miles away.

She would wonder, later, whether he at that moment had come to the very same conclusion, whether he had realised it long ago and knew what it had brewed, or whether he even now chose not to see it, truly believing that he was stating only fact when he said: "I was alone with her, after you left."

Margaret could do nothing but acknowledge the truth of that. "Yes, you were."

Something on his young face quivered at that, the merest shiver escaping before he buttoned it back up. Though more might have been said, Margaret knew then it would not be and felt the guilty relief, for though she could acknowledge the truth of it and wish it were not so, she could not pretend she would have done anything different.

The weight of the past settled all around them, and yet the shifting of it loosened things too, made it possible for Margaret to look her brother up and down, gentle mockery covering the stirring of genuine pride: "Plain clothes, eh? You are coming up in the world."

Paul flushed again, but any fraternal retort was cut short by the appearance of the runner. Gasping, he clambered up the fourth and final flight of stairs, and as soon as his eyes alighted on Paul, he wasted no time in relaying his breathless message: "Telegram received... Bancroft implicated... Meeting widow... Br'ckn'll res'dence... Inspector wants... arrest outside... no scene."

Message relayed, Margaret half supposed the lad was going to expire on her very own landing, but some internal stubbornness kept him upright as Paul turned to him, suddenly all duty. "And the cook? Has she been located?"

The runner replied in the negative, already on his way back down the stairs, but Margaret barely heard him, responding in a daze as Paul took his hasty leave and followed. For a moment, the world seemed to stop on its axis, momentum sending Margaret reeling as she fought to keep from losing her balance completely. Kit implicated? In what? Should she warn him? And was it truly he who needed warning?

Beat by beat, Margaret found her footing again and knew the answer.

XIX

The invitation was the last straw.

No, not the invitation; the *summons,* for that was what it was.

*Mrs Bancroft begs to inform that she will be attending the
winter ball at the residence of Sir Lionel and Lady Brucknell
this evening and will see Mr Bancroft there at nine o'clock.*

Will see. Not *requests to* see, nor even *hopes to* see, but *will*
see; summoned, like an errant child. The words on their card
pricked like acid, burning a hole through his pocket until he
could feel them hot against his skin, getting into his veins and
strumming through his body until they were all he could hear.
They ate away even the wherewithal to hire a coach, so that he
went pounding through the gaslit streets, trying to stamp the
worst of it off on the damp cobbles.

But the note was not even the worst of it. No want of cour-
tesy towards Christopher himself could compare to the utter
lack of respect she showed her husband, the absolute indignity,
Victor not two months in the ground and his widow attending
a bloody *ball.*

Well, Christopher only hoped she would enjoy it, for he
intended to make sure it was her last.

The Brucknell residence glowed like a great Christmas present, every window gilded in streaming light and merriment,
each one a picture, teasing glimpses of glittering ladies and

extravagant gentlemen in stone frames as they talked and ate and laughed and danced. To and fro they passed, from one window to the next, until it seemed that all of London's most superior crust must surely be gathered within.

Already, the heat of the principle rooms had driven a number of the revellers into the comparative cool of the marble entrance hall, so that Christopher was met with a fragrant blend of sweat, aromatic waters and pots of wilting hothouse flowers as he entered. The perfume was wafted along by fans and chattering hands, and with it ran a murmuring undercurrent which fell silent as he passed.

He ignored the heads which turned to follow him, not sparing so much as a nod even for those he recognised, but he could not ignore the face which accosted him at the end of the hall. Framed in a gilded mirror, it glowered back at him from under hair matted and damp with the drizzle outside. His cheeks were mottled with the cold, the exertion and the anger he clung to. Even his collar was already beginning to wilt.

He grinned at himself and an ugly thing, almost a snarl, met him in the mirror: on top of everything else, she had made him forget his hat.

Inside the ballroom, he caught sight of her almost at once. Indeed, he could hardly have done otherwise. She wandered among the ice sculptures, a tall figure in black gazing at the gently melting faces of swans and cherubs and the majestic Christmas angel as though she had never seen the like, while all around her the crowd parted to give her a wide berth, some looking pointedly away while others stared in open disdain.

Christopher was among those who stared. Whatever he had expected, whatever he had feared, this was worse. In the weight of it, he found relief, knowing that no doctor told of such a spectacle could possibly fail to be convinced – and sign what was in front of him accordingly.

Her dress was technically black but of such ostentatious luxury that it might as well have been scarlet. Faceted jet and diamond beads ran in streaks from the silk bodice down through the skirt, glorifying every twitch of her limbs. Worse still, her eyes seemed to catch the light in the same uncontrolled manner as the jewels, looking neither here nor there but everywhere as she wandered like a child in a summer garden, treasuring each splendour equally, as though they appeared entirely for her personal amusement. Her head swivelled as she walked, drawn now to the sparkle of a crystal champagne flute on a waiter's tray, now to the diamond glitter of a trembler on the shoulder of a marchioness immobile with fright. Mesmerised, the widow's eyes glittered back.

At the end of the room, the massive Christmas tree held its lofty court. A murmur rippled through the crowd as she not only curtsied before it, folding her long body together in an order which was not quite the right one, but, rising, seemed to be listening to the great tree, craning her neck towards it like a devotee hoping to catch the last words of her dying master. Christopher could not tell whether she had been successful or not.

In the next moment, a young lady had the misfortune to bob her turquoise ostrich feather just close enough to catch the line of the widow's sight, and thus she was off again, pursuing the poor girl with the purposeful amble of the predator, through a crowd which parted in instinctive revulsion.

It did not part so for Christopher. He soon found that catching sight of her had been the least of it; catching any other part promised to be a battle in itself.

In their efforts to avoid her, the assembled company pressed themselves into all those places where she wasn't, so that everywhere he turned, a polished plate or mound of piled hair seemed to block his way. He took a step, two, and found himself hemmed in on every side, unable even to retrace his steps and turn back – not that he had anything to turn back to.

The air was close, stifling, tangling around him like sweaty sheets on a muggy summer's night. His collar had by now given up the ghost entirely, and he could feel the colour burning his cheeks, heat and shame both, growing hotter with every moment's delay. Left with no choice, he forced his way through, trusting that once all was said and done, those he left in his wake would understand; indeed, in his position, would do the same. It was simply what one did, that was all.

He found her at the edge of the room, having abandoned her feathered quarry in order to admire the top of a particularly fine buffet. She was running her ungloved fingertips over the polished green marble with an air of the greatest luxury when he snatched her arm and dragged her without a word through the nearest door.

They found themselves in a small sitting room currently in use as a serving base. Upon their entry, a liveried footman started up, caught in the incriminating act of polishing a tray of crystalware.

"*Out*," Christopher snarled.

Taking one look at his face, the young man very nearly dropped the glass he was holding in his haste to obey, scarpering through the servants' door without pausing even to close it behind him.

Christopher forgot him the instant he rounded on his sister-in-law, who stood with her head cocked to one side, regarding him with infuriating curiosity.

"What the Devil do you mean by this? What on earth can have possessed you to do this – to have—" Anger made him splutter, which only made him angrier. He wrenched the arm he still held, yanking her close to him and holding her there.

She did not appear to notice. "The Devil?" she repeated with the thoughtfulness of one turning a necessary word over in their mouth, trying to reconcile themselves to the bitterness of it. "I suppose it must be, mustn't it? For what it's worth, I did my best."

The question in her eyes was real, but he could not hear it over the blood thundering in his ears. "Your best? Your *best*?" The words came out spitting, undignified. The force it took him to close his mouth produced an audible snap which echoed in his back teeth, forcing air through his nose.

"I will take you home now," he said, once he trusted himself to speak. "I will pass the night, and in the morning, we will travel to Hampshire. Dr Mumford can come down to assess you there. His reputation is beyond—"

"Oh, I'd forgotten about that. You still mean to have me locked away then?"

It was not the words so much as the way she said them: playful, even flirtatious – the tone of a woman making a silly jest, a deliberately foolish joke, to see whether her beau was besotted enough to sacrifice his dignity and laugh at what was not the least bit funny.

It was that, the realisation that even now she wanted more, when she had taken so very much already, which snapped the last fraying thread of Christopher's self-control.

With far more force than her bird-boned weight required, he hauled her up close enough to feel the heat of his breath reflected off the angles of her face.

"More than ever, my dear," he hissed, taking a savage satisfaction in the way the flesh of her arm yielded beneath his crushing grip. "More than ever do I intend to keep you under lock and key while I attempt to repair the damage you have done to my family's standing. I swear to you, if I have to drag you by the hair and forge the signatures myself, I will remove you from society until you have learned the responsibilities which come with the name you swindled your way into, even if it takes the rest of your life. And what's more, you will learn to be grateful for the opportunity to pay off some small fraction of the debt you have accrued. If you had any idea what I've sacrificed to save this family—"

Feeling overtook him entirely then. Words momentarily lost to him, he shook her violently and might have gone on doing so and more had not the noise from behind startled him.

It was hardly anything – the faintest intake of breath from a person who should not be there – but something in it made him still his hand as he glanced over his shoulder. Sure enough, there was the worn heel of a woman's boot, disappearing through the door of the servants' staircase with a speed which rivalled the hapless footman. Just for a second, Christopher fancied he knew that heel, that it was the same heel by whose side he had walked mile after mile of cobbled backstreet and dusty riverside, which had sprawled comfortably next to his own shoes in borrowed rooms across Europe and beyond. The idea that the owner of that particular boot might have glimpsed the scene was enough to sicken the pot of his stomach.

It could not be of course. He knew that but had no time to find relief in it, for in the very next he knew also that it didn't matter. It didn't matter who else had seen the affair, for in that momentary distraction he saw it himself, and the ugliness of it took his breath away.

He saw himself standing over a defenceless woman, his own sister-in-law, handling her as he would loudly object to any dog being handled, however disobedient. He saw the purple blush which must be forming even now beneath the cruel press of his thumb into her flesh. He saw his own face hideously contorted, unrecognisable in rage, the rage he himself had built to burn off the pain of loss, the guilt of it, the rage which he had stoked and built up and stoked and built up until the blaze of it consumed all his attention, so that he no longer noticed what he threw on it.

He had needed to of course, needed to do all that work himself, because this woman could never have done it for him. No awkward sister-in-law, no matter how conniving or mad or indecent, could by herself have produced anything so great. What was she, after all, but a poorly chosen wife, unable to live up to the expectations of her role, either in life or in death? And for that matter, was he himself any better? Had he not chosen his mate just as poorly in the converse? And had he lost her and been expected to adhere to a complexity of rules while confining himself alone with his grief, was his sanity not likely to be just as much in question?

Of course, he had not lost Meg. She was not among the things he had thrown on the pyre he'd named Duty. No, Meg had gone of her own volition after seeing him wilfully burn those parts of himself she valued most, those parts he had valued first, those parts he had first seen the worth of in Dot Sharpe's kitchen, taking refuge there from his mother's death and his father's agony then permeating upstairs life. And now he had burned them all, to distract from another death, from his own guilty conscience. He had named it Duty, but what duty had he done?

He had not gone down to Hampshire to speak to the tenants and do what he could, bring her back a list of what else needed to be done. He had not offered his sister-in-law help in a way which she might have felt able to accept. He had not, in fact, done anything actually useful to anyone at all since the day he'd set foot on English soil. Even the name, that lifeless, feelingless Bancroft banner he'd chosen as his mantle, even that he'd dragged through the mud and left in tatters with his evening's performance thus far. Through no one's fault but his own, he was left with the cracked shell of his father's dignity in which he had once held all the rest. Empty, it was a worthless thing, devoid of warmth and meaning.

It seemed a burden suddenly, and suddenly he saw it could have but one earthly use: perhaps, if he threw it on the pyre in just the right way, the flames might be induced to give up a few charred remains of decency – of kindness – which could form the foundation of something new, something entirely his own.

All this passed before him in the moment he caught sight of that cruel hand wrapped around the unresisting flesh. It seemed suddenly incredible that it should belong to him, and yet he could feel clearly the ridge of bone pillowed beneath ripples of muscle. The feeling appalled him suddenly, and it came to him in that moment that perhaps the solution might be as simple as to just let go.

The fingers so determinedly locked in place sprang open all at once, so that she all but dropped out of it. He felt her stumble, and as he moved to help steady her found words already on his lips.

He would never know what they were to be.

Looking down, Christopher found himself staring into the face of his brother's end, bright and alive and entirely without human feeling, the eyes cold as diamonds, sparkling in too many places and without any colour of their own.

They were not looking at him.

Nora pushed past him towards the servants' staircase, following the vanished boot. In the moment before the fog rose about his mind, Christopher had the impression she was enjoying herself immensely.

By the time the older Brucknell boy appeared to lead him discreetly down to the waiting officers, Christopher was thinking about nothing much at all. It was really rather nice.

XX

Nora hunted.

She did not use the word. She used no words at all; there were no words to use. All existence was in the purity of pursuit. It got into her blood and made it jump, invaded her senses, exhilarating and expanding them into their natural shapes. It filled her and lifted her, the power and the pulse of it, *her* pulse, strumming with the heady lust of newfound strength. Ahead, the hatred glowed hot and bright in the darkness, as pure and intoxicating a feeling as any ever directed towards her. It drew her on, goading her to give chase. She wanted it, as instinctively and powerfully as she had ever wanted anything in her life, wanted to catch it and pin it and snuff it out.

Nora hunted, and Margaret fled.

~

The stairs were taken in a clatter, then down the passageway and out into the Mayfair night Margaret went, feeling the widow behind her by the pricking at the back of her neck as much as any sound the creature made as she gave chase. The air was sharp with the promise of frost and heavy with the musk of good coal which drifted down from the chimneys of elegant houses. With each front door they passed came a gasp of sweet resin, the musk of dying pine newly nailed above polished knockers, but the doors remained closed: if, somewhere within, someone had happened to peek out in time to see Margaret running as though the very darkness itself were at her heels, they kept their curiosity to themselves.

Marble Arch rose up and was behind them in a flash, stone paving giving way to hard-packed earth as they passed into Hyde Park, on and on. Margaret's thoughts were no more than a collection of disjointed images knocked about with every jolt of her boot upon the unforgiving ground; every empty, gasping breath. Mrs Stovell was there, and Elsie, and friends she had known in her exile. She did not think about them, or even want them, only held them up, a distraction, that she would not be tempted to remember why she ran.

But holding them up cost precious resources, already dwindling dangerously.

As the darkening edges began to close in, the image turned to Kit, first at his best and then shifting into his worst, so that in her anger she found a few more steps, spurred on to spite him. Her mother had the same effect, appearing in the only way Margaret could remember her, which made her ashamed when she was sober and spiteful when she was drunk. Though she had not had a drop of liquor in hours, she was drunk now, and spite spurred her on.

It could not last. Another few faltering steps and her mother was joined by Paul, the man still with his little boy's face, and then all she knew was sorrow, and regret, and finally peace, that strange peace which comes with knowing that there is quite simply nothing more to be done.

The path curved left and Margaret did not. Lacking the strength to even turn, momentum carried her staggering onto the grassy verge and into the shrubbery beyond. She had no thought of hiding, knew deep in her marrow that there was no hiding. Black spots flickered before her eyes, obscuring thought and blotting out the night. Her boot caught on a root and there followed a moment of blissful nothing before the impact of the ground. Then the shock to her knees and the grit in her palms brought her back, brought everything back, and something in her would not let it end in defeat.

She could not rise, could not run or fight or even speak, but even as the world flickered and she suffocated in the stranglehold of her own bound-up ribcage, she found a last crumb of strength.

With a final effort, she rolled onto her back, pushing herself up onto her elbows, and though every muscle in her body shook and threatened to give way at any moment, Margaret Ann Wilcox met Death with defiance.

Death, crouched behind her ready for the pounce, sat up on her haunches and blinked.

∼

It is a strange thing to find one has rules which carry no punishment and yet cannot be broken.

The hunter's impulse was not created to manage complexity. Hunt is hunt and prey is prey: the prey hates the hunter and the hunter kills the prey – that is the way of things. The concept of anything more – of prey as fearful, prey as angry, prey as regretful and grieving events passed – is liable to muddle even the dullest dog, if it can grasp it. And Nora was no mere dog.

She looked upon Margaret sprawled in the undergrowth, her body prone, her throat vulnerable, glaring up in full knowledge of what inevitably came next, quivering with useless, helpless rage at the prospect. That all that anger, all that passion, all that life should be snuffed out simply because that is how the hunt ends...

Nora cocked her head, the spring going out of her body as she found no justification for it. She was not hungry; she was not threatened. Looking within herself, she found she was only curious: "Why do you hate me?"

~

Margaret laughed, incredulous, then choked as the laughter ate up air she did not have to spare. She turned onto her side, coughing violently in her determination to regain control of her lungs. When she turned back, there was no Death but only Mrs Bancroft, and it was suddenly unaccountable to Margaret that she should have thought anything different. Indeed, the whole of her most recent existence was fading fast, like an uncomfortable dream not to be looked at too closely upon waking. If that put a considerable gap between her present situation, sat among rotting leaves in the dead of night with a woman she last remembered seeing in a brightly lit sitting room, well then, it was preferable to the madness of the alternative.

"I don't hate you," Margaret said when she trusted herself to speak again. "How could I possibly hate someone I've never met?"

She almost believed it. She might have done, had Nora not sat so still, watching her and waiting patiently for the truth.

"All right," she admitted. "Perhaps just for a moment. I came to warn you, but when I saw him with you, I just—" She made a vague gesture which she hoped evoked the notion of honourable intentions shattered in a single moment of absolute heartbreak.

"Warn me? About Christopher?" Nora cocked her head, thoughtful. "He's very angry with me, you know."

"Oh?" Margaret could not conceal her surprise and was only half successful in repressing the flare of joy she no longer had any right to be feeling. "I thought you must have come to an arrangement, the way you were standing. I saw you smiling at him – I'm sure I did."

"Well in my defence, he was being rather ridiculous," Nora said, and something in her grin brought the moment back to Margaret. Now stripped of blurring pain, she saw the details more clearly – Kit with his back turned, the widow pulled up against him, the curl of her thin lip revealing white canines as glittering eyes fixed on Kit's exposed pulse—

The thought made Margaret's heart stutter and her head swim. She dropped it from her mind as though burned.

"I don't know what he's so upset about," Nora was saying, a note of the sulking child creeping into her thoughtfulness. "Money doesn't make the difference, you know. There's no joy in it, no real satisfaction."

"Not the way you spend it certainly."

The words were out before Margaret could regret them, and she forced herself not to shrink from that horrible gaze as it turned on her. But there was a sort of prickly hurt in it now though, oddly pathetic and uncomfortably familiar. It was in the spirit of solidarity that she went on.

"I know, you see. I've tried it. And it's true that after the essentials are paid for, the rest can become a bit of a golden froth, thrilling in the moment and not much more. But as to money not making the difference, after two weeks in Shoreditch, I can assure you that any number of differences could be made for the price of even one of those beads."

She nodded at Nora's dress, at the gems sparkling even now in the little moonlight filtering through the bare canopy, conscious even as she did of how much it would have pleased her to wear a thing of such beauty, of such opulence. Even now, if—

Nora shook her head. "It's a millstone," she insisted. "The work of it, schools for the children, provision for the widows – it's never-ending—"

She still sounded sore, so Margaret tried to infuse her reply with kindness: "Why don't you give it back then?"

Nora only looked at her. The ghostly face was smooth in the darkness, and Margaret could read no expression there.

"You said you came to warn me this evening," Nora said at last. "Why?"

It took Margaret a moment to recall. "He – Kit – Christopher, I mean – has got hold of some of your old medical records, from a doctor we met in Antwerp. He intends to use them as evidence of incapacity and have himself appointed your guardian."

Nora smiled, not unkindly. "Yes, I had rather gathered that. But why did you wish to warn me?"

Margaret shrugged, awkward suddenly. "I don't know. In the spirit of fairness I suppose. In the last few weeks I've had this idea, a sort of impulse, that I could help some of those who suffer worst in this town – who suffer as I might have done, had I not happened to be exceptionally fortunate. You know, he's really not that…" Margaret trailed off, unsure of what she wanted to say, whether she had any right to say it, whether it was even true. "Anyway, it struck me that few suffer more than those held against their will, even if the cage happens to be a gilded one, so when I heard you were to meet tonight—"

"I'm grateful to have been thought of," Nora said, and there was a touch of warmth there which lit her eyes from within. "You know, I've enjoyed this evening, more than I've enjoyed any evening for a long time now."

The dead leaves whispered beneath her skirts as she picked herself up. She looked impossibly tall against the trees.

"Where are you going?" Margaret heard herself ask, feeling herself a child suddenly. The cold was catching up with her, raising the hair on her arms and making her shiver.

Nora did not look back, but the warmth was still there as she replied, "Home."

~

Telegram sent by Christopher Bancroft, Esq., Antwerp Station, Belgium to Victor Bancroft, Esq., Kensington Park Square, London, England on 31 October 1896, 8:42 p.m. local time. Message reads: V. Coming home. Know about yr wife. Meet at KPS tomorrow 10 a.m. to discuss. C.

Ritter read the transcription aloud, keeping one eye on Christopher Bancroft seated opposite to gauge his reaction.

It was not what he had been expecting.

Indeed, Ritter was half beginning to wonder if they'd got the right man or instead picked up some other Bancroft scion by mistake, one with the same face and none of the expression. Knowing how these families got about, it was not impossible, and Ritter could think of no better explanation. Anything seemed more likely than the man seated against the dingy backdrop of the interrogation room being the same Christopher Bancroft he had met six weeks ago.

His evening finery was in a bedraggled state, and there was a friendly but slightly dazed look upon his face, his long limbs sprawling as politely as possible, as though he wished to be courteous while not being fully master of all his own parts. All told, Ritter might well have persuaded himself that the man sat in that mean chair was an entirely different person to the one who interested him, were it not for the fact that, as Ritter came to the end of the message, Bancroft closed his eyes and drew in a breath, as though some tender spot were being prodded.

"Yes, I believe that's what I wrote," he said, exhaling. "Feels a lifetime ago."

Ritter might have been inclined to agree – surely nothing less could produce such a change – but the whole thing galled him beyond belief. The calm, even pleasant way the man spoke, that faint smile playing across his face, as one associating the conversation with bittersweet memory, as though he himself were not responsible for consigning his own brother to that sphere of existence, not to mention well on his way to frightening a poor widow quite literally out of her wits.

Ritter knew what was in the hospital files by now, but he wanted to hear Bancroft say it.

"You accept you wrote this then? You admit you threatened your brother and his wife?"

Across the table, Bancroft shrugged. Even in his dishevelled state, he somehow contriving to make the gesture look unreasonably expensive. "Yes, I suppose I did." He gave Ritter a sheepish look. "Seems rather ridiculous now, doesn't it?"

With every word, Ritter felt his footing slip, the footing he'd been so sure of when he'd entered the room. Once he had seen the telegram, what little doubt had remained in his mind had evaporated. Combined with the psychiatric reports and the man's own behaviour, surely there could be no other explanation. Only there was no trace of that behaviour in the man now before him, no trace of ire which had caused him to storm into his brother's house the very morning of the murder, of the seething resentment which had run under every civil word he'd spoken to Ritter at the hotel, of the mania which had kept him holed up day after day, emerging only to pursue his sole objective of tormenting his sister-in-law.

And not only was there no trace of that single-minded fury, but it was almost impossible to imagine that it had ever been there. There was something so complacent about the man now, almost docile. He seemed in a daze, as though he had received a great blow which had unexpectedly knocked away some even greater burden he had been carrying, so that now he looked about him in wonder at the lightness of the world, even as he winced at the air touching pressure sores left behind.

Frankly, it was rather disconcerting, and Ritter did not enjoy being disconcerted.

" 'Ridiculous' is not the word I would use, Mr Bancroft," he said, aggravation crisping the edge of his words. "I prefer 'evidence of intent'."

It was further evidence of Bancroft's state of mind that he had to mouth the sentence back to himself before he could grasp its meaning, and even then his first reaction seemed to be genuine perplexity.

" 'Evidence of...'?" he repeated, his face a question.

Ritter did not answer it, preferring to let the penny drop on its own. When finally it did, Bancroft shot up in his seat with a violence that made his coat tails flap against the legs of his chair, lamplight bouncing off the silk lining.

"You can't seriously mean you think *I*—?" He stared at Ritter wide-eyed, as though it was only just occurring to him to wonder why they were both there. "For God's sake, Vic was my brother! And anyway, what on earth *for*?"

There was no guilt in the question and no guile, only a flash of that arrogance Ritter recognised, a man exasperated not with what he thought wrong but what he thought stupid. The sight of it was comforting in a way, to know that it was still there, regardless of what enchantment might have come over him on this particular night. Still, Ritter only enjoyed being thought stupid at times convenient to him and this was not such a one.

"I'm sure I couldn't say what for, sir. Why don't you begin by telling us why you decided to threaten him?"

Bancroft was already sinking back into his seat, as though he lacked the vigour to sustain any level of passion for more than a few seconds. He shrugged.

"I don't know," he admitted, and Ritter found himself almost believing it. "It was only, we'd been away from home for so long, and it gets tiring, you know, never being able to properly settle, but Vic never answered my letters so one just got on with it, only then we happened to be introduced to this physician in Antwerp, this children's analyst who it transpired had seen Vic's wife when she was a girl. I thought the threat of embarrassment if the fact were made public might be enough to get his attention, but then we got back and Vic was dead and the last thing he'd heard from me was a childish threat, and then—"

Bancroft broke off with a helpless gesture, as though it were all the explanation he could furnish.

Ritter did not find it sufficient. "And then?"

"And then…" Bancroft seemed to search for words, then deflated into his chair as he found them. "And then I suppose you might say I got a bit carried away. I'm afraid things got rather out of hand."

Well, that was certainly one way to put it, Ritter would give him that. "And at what point did your conspiracy with Dorothy Sharpe begin?"

"My *what*?"

Indignation propelled Bancroft up in his seat again. Under different circumstances, Ritter thought he might have found it amusing.

"You needn't trouble to deny it, sir," Ritter said, because the circumstances were not different and he was increasingly far from amused. "You were seen speaking intimately with her at your brother's funeral and leaving Great Ormond Street Hospital with her on…" Ritter shuffled through his notes, pretending to look for the date as Bancroft scowled.

"I believe the law permits me my personal attachments, Inspector, even still."

Ritter raised his eyebrows. "I can't say I recall much of an attitude of attachment at the time."

"Yes, well." Bancroft's scowl grew sheepish. "As I said, I haven't been myself recently, and in any event, she and I haven't seen eye to eye since she took against— Regardless, that stubborn old woman half raised me, and I have no desire to see her catch her death for the sake of a bit of cab fare."

"A noble impulse, I'm sure. Do you have a similar one to account for your behaviour towards Mrs Bancroft? Since returning to England, our intelligence suggests you've sent her upwards of eighty cards and letters – none of which have been returned – and called upon her unadmitted no less than—"

"I wanted to protect what was left of my family." Bancroft's temper flared again, this time defensively. "Of my brother. To see the whole of that legacy in the hands of a woman entirely unequipped to manage it, who might marry again and lose even the name—" He scowled again, though this time it seemed directed inward, as though hearing them spoken aloud forced him to face the ugliness of his own intentions. Still he persevered.

"I admit it, I intended to use her medical records against her, to force her into retirement, under lock and key if need be. And yes, I would have pressured her into marriage if I could have possibly found a way around the law. If my behaviour was unworthy, and I accept now that much of it was, I can only assure you it has been at great personal expense. If Meg—"

It was at that moment that Ritter remembered Wilcox at his post in the corner.

"Meg?" he repeated.

Though it was posed as a question, something in the weighting of it sounded to Ritter more like an answer, the key to the cogs of a conundrum long puzzled over. He almost turned to look at Wilcox, to watch the ponderous rotations play out and ask what the result might be, but before he could, he was caught by the look on Bancroft's face opposite. The man was staring over Ritter's shoulder at the constable, as though noticing him for the first time, and on his face was the wide-eyed, unfeigned dismay of one desperately wishing to put his own words back in their box.

"Ah," he said. "I take it you didn't know then."

XXI

Night was on the wane by the time Nora mounted her own front steps. The promise of daybreak contrasted with the remaining night, leaving the darkness deeper still, barely dented by the hall light shining from within.

Alcott slept by the door, awaiting the return of his mistress in a high-backed chair, his neck lolling back with surprising elasticity, putting a kink in his snores. All around that nasal note the sounds of the house rose and fell upon her en masse, each clamouring for attention. Every creak of wood, every settling of stone, every scrape of every tiny claw upon the stairs or behind the skirting boards, every thump of every heartbeat, the tremor of every breath – the chorus of every life the house contained washed over her, through her all at once, until she had to wince at the racket and turn away.

Immediately, she turned back again. She would learn, she would master it, or perish in the attempt. She had no alternative.

She did not wish the butler to awaken and so he slept on, safe in dreams.

From behind the door of McNeal's makeshift bedroom came the tussle of a sleep restless and wretched with worry, but she settled as Nora passed; there was no need for that, not now.

In her own temporary bedroom, Nora changed out of her ballgown and into the more comfortable black walking dress, finding with no great surprise that she needed no help but could stretch her limbs and twist her joints to the necessary angles with ease.

As she worked, her eyes fell on Marit's old book, languishing on the gaming table by the tray still overflowing with cards. It distracted her for a time and she paused in her dressing, one arm in its sleeve and one left bare, to flip through the pages with a faint smile of recognition. The mystery words did not interest her, only the faces, which were no longer mysterious at all: one did not need names to enjoy an album of one's foreign cousins, knowing them for kin for all that one might never meet.

The robe hung on the wardrobe door, and as Nora finished dressing, she brushed against it so that a silvery tinkle rang out through the silence. For a moment she froze, the old trepidation snarling up her limbs, but it passed as quickly now, shaken off with the recollection of all she had learned since that night. It was with a sense almost of nostalgia then that she reached into the left pocket and withdrew the necklace from where it had lain since the moment she herself had placed it there, unable to look upon it, and thus made of it a secret to herself and thus to the world.

She lifted it before her, the curved pendant catching the moonlight as it turned slowly on the end of its chain. Lifting it to her lips, she held it there but did not blow. The whistle was to help the child; as an adult, she no longer needed it.

She left it lying upon the book, proof if any should be needed, and closed the door behind her for the last time.

~

Hugo Vascelles awoke to the knowledge that Mrs Bancroft was outside, waiting to see him. It was entirely clear to him, as certain and uncontroversial as the fact of his own foot, even as he held within his mind the equal knowledge that beyond the curtains the sky was yet more dark than light, presiding over no more than the nightman's cart clattering over frozen cobbles, a few straggling revellers staggering home – or, at any rate, on – and a pair of tomcats quarrelling noisily across the way.

And Nora Bancroft, waiting outside to see him.

He did not trouble to wonder how he knew: he had no objection to seeing Mrs Bancroft again and helping her with her business; consequently his only thought in lighting the lamp and pulling on his dressing gown was that they must go to the library rather than the sitting room, to avoid disturbing Julia.

His guest was waiting for him just beyond the portico, her pale eyes luminous as she scratched her dog absently between the antlers. The sight of it caused Hugo the barest whisper of consternation – Julia's love of the brutes was matched only by the appalling extent of her allergies – but the beast slunk back into the shadows as his mistress approached the door, and so, just as easily, the subject slunk from Hugo's mind.

The lady's requirements, as she recounted them, were entirely straightforward to accomplish, and yet so unexpected a request that he found himself peering at her by the light of the candle, trying to find the reason in it. It was there, he knew, there in his mind, within reach but hidden behind a veil he could not draw, a veil which whispered kindly but insistently at him not to try. Hugo was a man of mettle however: he knew his fiduciary obligations and took them seriously. He must at least ask the question.

"And you are certain that this is what you wish? It will be a most exceptional situation—"

"It is already a most exceptional situation."

The widow regarded him with perfect composure, and yet there was something behind the glitter in her eye, a tightness of regret, of things rued which can never be fully mended. Hugo found himself having to drop his gaze, his eyes falling instead on those long hands, curling around each other in her lap, talons glowing white in the lamplight.

"I do not pretend to know my choice is the right one," she admitted at length, recalling him. "But it is the best I can come up with under the circumstances."

Hugo nodded. He believed her and knew somehow that, even when she was gone and the veil she had hung disintegrated and fell away, he would believe her still.

Drawing up the will she required was a simple matter, though the witnessing requirement necessitated waking Julia after all. Pulling her wrapper tight about her, she greeted Nora with bleary eyes and every kindness her half-waking state would allow, and still refused point-blank to sign any document she had not read.

Leaving her to it, Hugo had intended to offer their guest what refreshments could be mustered without waking the staff but found himself instead drawn into a discreet corner out of Julia's hearing. The shadows concealed Nora's face there but could do nothing to hide her eyes, peering out at him with an almost childish hopefulness he found himself wishing to gratify.

"Have you news of your brother?"

"Not very recently."

Watching the proud shoulders sag, Hugo was abruptly sorry to have disappointed her.

"The post is awkward at this time of year," he added, hoping to lift them. "The weather you see. No doubt I'll be wished a merry Christmas in January, postmarked in August. We correspond more regularly in the spring. He is well, I believe, or he was in July. The life out there seems to agree with him."

"He—" She chose her words deliberately. "I believe he went out with a friend. A close friend?"

In the darkness, she kept herself very still, as though afraid to spook the answer and turn it against her.

Hugo found he had to be careful also: there was no veil here, but there were risks to everyone concerned.

"You may be right," he agreed slowly. "I can't say I'm overly familiar with the details of his personal arrangements. Our correspondence is mainly business."

Prudence made him pause, but she looked at him so plaintively that he found himself offering a little more.

"That being said," he went on, "judging from those small personal remarks which inevitably slip in between brothers, it is my understanding that he has built what he set out to, in the, ah, private aspect. Reading between the lines, I believe his home is a happy one."

The shadows let out a breath. "I had a letter – that is to say a few – early on," she admitted, dropping her gaze as one ashamed. "But I'm afraid I... I misplaced them before I had a chance to read them. I am glad to know that they— that he is well. Very glad." She hesitated. "Perhaps you would be kind enough to include a note of my own with your next letter?"

Hugo was surprised. "Certainly, though I'd be happy to give you his address straight away if you'd prefer?"

"Thank you." Nora smiled. "But I'd rather it went in the spring, when it's more likely to get through."

She looked at him again, eyes luminous and lacking any definable colour, and Hugo quite forgot to wonder why she could not simply post it herself.

～

It was a bad habit of girlhood to leave the most difficult job till last. Perhaps, Nora thought, if she had never developed that impulse to ignore the pressure, to hold off, to see if Violet would finish her own work quickly and come to her cousin's aid, to see if the clock might not tick down to teatime, perhaps things might have been different. If she had never learned to push the unpleasant task so far away that it was almost out of sight, so that she could claim not to notice when rather than shrink it festered, growing, swelling, putrid like an unlanced boil, perhaps then she might have learned to control it, perhaps it might not have come to— But it had of course. It had, and now she could only bandage it as best she could and try to make the best of the mess.

Great Ormond Street was as dark as any hospital ever is, with floor upon floor of dimly lit corridors, dotted with plaintive cries and the swish of lonely nurses hurrying between rooms, as though afraid of what they might meet if they paused.

Nobody spoke to Nora as she entered. The night porter dozed fitfully behind the reception desk, and those nurses who saw the figure, tall and dark except where her skin caught the feeble light, turned from it at once, their minds refusing to remember it during waking hours. Even the sentries at their posts stood aside without comment, every bit as though they had been expecting her. Perhaps they had; she was not quite sure of the specific mechanics of the thing yet.

There was no lamp in the room, but the blind had not been drawn and the moon peeked in, blue against the paling sky. A beam fell upon the unconscious form of Joan Fletcher, kindly, protective, so that Nora had to stand and contemplate the withered face of consequence, or that of it still above ground.

The shape beneath the sheets was so slight as to make the narrow bed look all but generous. Strands of limp hair fell across the forehead, touched silver by the moonlight. Nora reached down to brush them aside. When she withdrew her hand, its retreat was watched by wide eyes, still blurred by dreams but open now for the first time in weeks.

"Your hair, madam…" Voice hoarse from disuse, Joan struggled to raise herself as she reached instinctively to tidy the head which had been her crowning responsibility.

Nora tried to brush the little hand away, but her refusal only produced a whimper of insistence, the distress of a muddled head clinging to a single point of clarity. Submitting, Nora perched upon the edge of the bed to allow the girl access.

From beneath the door came a sliver of light, sufficient to create a reflection in the window and show Nora the tempest around her head which distressed Joan, thick black loops standing out against their pins like a bramble crown. There was an element of wildness about it, less untamed than crazed, a creature straining hour after hour against a bond which may loosen with time and exertion, shift but never quite break. It looked worse, surely, far worse than if it had never been pinned at all.

Nora watched with something like marvel as Joan's deft fingers calmed the storm, lock after lock settling and falling away to curl easily down her back, the fearsome pins left to chink harmlessly in the maid's hand.

When the last pin had come away, Nora turned to her. "Thank you," she said, looking into that dreaming gaze. "What do you remember, Joan?"

Joan's brow creased at the question, as though anything beyond the present instant taxed her fragile mind almost beyond the bearing. Finally, though, a vague smile came over her face as some dreg of memory was thrown up for her to clutch.

"You were kind to me," she murmured. "You let me come and work upstairs, and sleep in my own room. I liked that, even if I was frightened alone sometimes."

Guilt twisted in Nora's gut, but she managed to turn her grimace to a smile – almost.

"Perhaps it's better this way," she said. "It will return, in time, and you will be yourself again."

Joan smiled back at her, entirely content now that her mistress's hair was in hand, and without the slightest idea that there had existed a time which was not now.

Nora frowned. "Or I think you will be, at any rate. If not— Well, I've made provision for Mrs Sharpe to look after you, until I can find you and..." She trailed off, wanting to avoid making a promise she did not yet know if it was possible to keep.

She sighed. "I am sorry, you know."

She was almost at the door when the little voice arrested her, still faint but already stronger than before. "Where will you go, madam?"

Nora turned to find herself watched by eyes beginning to recover some semblance of focus, and relief made her answer easy. "I believe I need to spend some time at home, at Bridde Place," she said. "There perhaps things will come clear."

~

Sergeant Jameson had been pleased to inform Ritter that Dorothy Sharpe had been located. He had been less pleased to admit that the reason it had taken the force the better part of ten hours to do so was that they had not thought to look within their own house, where indeed Mrs Sharpe had been located since even before the search had begun; indeed, ever since she had been turned away from Joan Fletcher's hospital room on Ritter's orders and had gone directly to make her complaint to him. As she would consent to speak to no one else, the clerk on the desk had followed standard procedure in such cases, taking her to a bare interview room deep in the catacombs of Scotland Yard, smelling just enough of damp to be subtly but actively irritating, and leaving her there until she dispersed of her own free will.

Procedure had not accounted for a will like Dot Sharpe's however, and so there she had stoically remained until discovered by a young constable looking for a private place to further inspect the exceptionally well realised illustrations of a tract he had confiscated on his recent rounds of Green Park.

Ritter left Wilcox to finish dealing with Christopher Bancroft and went down, trying not to let eagerness quicken his step. The last interview had caught him off guard: it had been difficult not to believe Bancroft's account but harder still to accept that the investigation had been circling the wrong tree for near enough two months now. The idea was uncomfortable, but Dorothy Sharpe promised to be the antidote. If he had been wrong about the money, Ritter was certain he had the muscle. Once she confessed, it would merely be a case of working his way up.

On his way down, he stopped at his office to retrieve the knife still lying on his desk, yet even with the murder weapon in hand and the confirmed owner before him, he still felt a moment of discomposure as he entered the room. Even after the better part of a day in that mean, dank little room, Dorothy Sharpe's back remained straight, her massive shoulders squared over the flimsy table. The chair was too small for her – it was too small for most people: that was the point of it – and though by now it must be exceedingly uncomfortable, she sat with an impassive dignity Ritter suspected the Queen herself would have been pleased to possess.

When she looked up at him, it was not with surprise and certainly not with gratitude, but rather as though he had kept her waiting for some paltry length of time, and though she had every right to expect better, she was willing to overlook it out of the depths of her own magnanimity. It was not the look of a murderess left with time to examine her own conscience.

"Inspector Ritter," she began, even before he had closed the door behind him, "thank you for finding the time to see me. I found myself surprised today to hear you have given new orders concerning Joan, when I believed I had your word that I—"

Ritter sat down and placed the wrapped knife on the table between them. The woman might be as haughty as she pleased – it changed nothing, and indeed the cook fell silent as he met her eye and held it. Slowly, deliberately, he unwrapped the paper until the blade caught the dull light around those rust-coloured stains which were all that remained of Victor Bancroft above ground.

Her eyes widened at the sight, the heavy brow rising to reveal pinpricks of fear in the small bright eyes beneath. Ritter might have felt sorry for her, were it not for those stains.

"I understand this belongs to you," he said, to ram home what he could see beginning to sink in.

Mrs Sharpe looked up at him then – and burst into tears.

"I'm sorry," she sobbed. "I'm so terribly, terribly sorry. I only gave it to her so's she'd feel safe. I never thought she'd be so daft—"

Gulping for air, she fumbled with her sleeve for her handkerchief. Ritter could see the bulge of it lurking just behind the cuff.

"The *silly* thing," she went on. "And now look—"

Her face was growing increasingly pink and wet, and still the sleeve would not yield. Finally, able to bear it no longer, Ritter pulled out his own handkerchief and handed it to her.

"Mrs Sharpe, do kindly pull yourself together. You do yourself no favours, carrying on like this."

With the second interview in what had already been a very long night rapidly veering into uncharted territory, Ritter struggled to conceal his frustration.

Through her tears, the cook nodded, and as her great shoulders quivered with the force of containment, she looked at him apologetically. That made it worse.

"Now please," Ritter said, once she had quieted, with only the odd intermittent wheeze to interrupt the conversation, "from the beginning: what did you give, to whom, and when?"

"That knife, my filleting knife." Mrs Sharpe indicated the knife on the table. "I gave it to Joanie—"

"Joanie?" It was not the answer his subconscious had been expecting. "Joan Fletcher, Mrs Bancroft's maid?"

The cook squeezed her eyes shut, pressing her lips tight to stop their trembling as she nodded. "Yes sir."

"When? And, for God's sake, why?"

The cook swallowed thickly before she could answer. "Every night, after she moved into the big room. So's she'd feel safe, you see."

Seeing Ritter's questioning eyebrow, she went on: "You must understand, sir, we took Joan straight from the workhouse to train up as a scullery maid. Cots and attics was all she'd ever known. She had ambition aplenty, and I don't say as she mightn't have achieved it, but workhouse to lady's maid is not a leap to make in a couple of years, not for a girl like Joan. But of course she wouldn't hear it, and when the last one left, she managed to persuade the mistress – Lord knows how, but the mistress knew no better – and I don't say she didn't do the work well enough, but it's a lonely position, sir. Not with the kitchen staff, not with the house maids... It takes a certain self-assurance, a certain independence, and Joan didn't have it yet. And how could she?

"That first night in the big room by the mistress's was the first time she'd ever slept alone in all her life. It was too much for her. She started coming down to the kitchen to wake me, saying she heard things, knocking at the window and a dog walking in the halls, though she knew as well as I we have no dogs in the house, the mistress not caring for them. So I lent her the knife to quiet her, so's she could sleep—"

The cook pressed a large hand to her mouth. "She must not have recognised him that night, with it being late and him not being in the habit…"

Ritter felt his mouth tighten as what he was being asked to believe sank in. He knew when he was being had.

"Mrs Sharpe, having been a butcher's wife, you will know better than most the force required to disembowel a large animal, and I see no reason to imagine that the presence of a human soul would make the difference. Do you really expect to persuade me Joan Fletcher, a girl weighing barely seven stone, would be able to summon the strength to do what was done to Mr Bancroft, even in a fit of terror?"

He glared across the table, showing her his irritation at being taken for a fool. "No, Mrs Sharpe, you murdered Victor Bancroft, you used that knife, and when Miss Fletcher awoke in the next room and caught you in the act, you panicked and threw the knife out of the window, pocketing a trinket at random to make it look like robbery. Your personal attachment to Joan Fletcher prevented you from killing her too but not from standing vigil to keep her quiet when she woke up. You did it for money, to buy your longed-for bed and breakfast, and now you will be so good as to tell me who paid you."

He had expected protest. He had expected denial. What he had not expected was quite so righteous an indignation.

"Inspector Ritter," she said, pronouncing every syllable as though she were dragging it over her whetstone, "I'll have you know that I have worked every day of my life since my Harry died – and before too – and I can account for every penny I own, every single penny, sir, to you or anyone else who may care to ask. When I hand in my notice – not long now,

God willing – I shall go to the sea and be proud that through my own sweat, I have the ability to give Joanie a home, even if—"

Here a violent trembling of her lip forced her to break off. She pressed Ritter's handkerchief against her mouth to compose herself.

"As for the rest of it, I admit I threw the knife out of the window. When I found her there, insensible, covered head to toe in gore with my filleting knife in her hand, I took it from her and threw it as far as I could. I acted foolishly, I own it freely and will take whatever consequences the law sees fit, but I did it out of fear for a child out of her senses. And if it's further proof you require, I ask you, why would I kill the master in front of his wife, knowing she might wake up at any moment? Why not wait until he returned to his own room?"

If there was more, Ritter did not hear it. That was the question, wasn't it, not just for Mrs Sharpe but for any potential killer? Except, of course, that it wasn't.

I know about your wife.

As the words arose in his mind he became aware of an inkling he had not realised was there, an awful memory of glittering eyes and a threat he had not realised existed until this evening—

Christopher Bancroft had threatened his brother, true, but who had really felt that threat? In his mind's eye, Ritter could picture with cold clarity the image of Victor Bancroft receiving a telegram so worrying that nothing would do but that he must deal with it immediately, returning home in the middle of the night to confront his wife and she, waking from deep sleep to find her position, her whole mode of existence threatened by exposure of that which she had kept even from her husband...

Ritter offered Mrs Sharpe his arm as he escorted her outside, finding unexpected solace in her stately dignity, her composure now fully regained in spite of her tear-stained cheeks and puffed up eyes.

When he had seen her into the safety of a passing cab, he felt the loss of her. Alone on the pavement, feeling the darkest part of night seeping into his bones, there was nothing between him and the inevitable, awful conclusion.

He had felt guilty over the time it had taken him to connect Mrs Sharpe to the knife, guilty over the prejudices which had blinded him to the obvious. He felt no such remorse now. It was simply not a conclusion anyone sane could be expected to arrive at. Still, as he saw those glittering eyes before him, soulless as diamonds and twice as sharp, doubt evaporated and he was left with only one question: if the knife had been in Miss Fletcher's hand through the whole episode, what on earth had *she* used?

XXII

The train all but emptied at Newcastle, leaving Nora to watch the dwindling hamlets in virtual solitude as she carried on. The station she finally alighted at was no more than a weatherworn platform topped by a tumbledown shack, yet the stationmaster was no less gracious for his meagre quarters. For the price of a shilling, indeed, he was pleased to take charge of her letter to see it safely returned to London, and in addition was able to point her in the direction of Mr Thomas Cochrane, at that moment engaged in taking delivery of a batch of bovine worming draught. The farmer raised a woolly eyebrow when he heard Nora's intended destination, and a second one as he took in her fine kid boots, designed with no more than the occasional loose cobble in mind, but he made no effort to dissuade her.

"Aye, I'll take you up as far as I go," he said, with a tolerant air that suggested she was not the first London eccentric to pass his way. "From there six miles across the hills will take you to the old village, and another mile or so will show you the house, and the end of your path."

The presumption rankled, Nora was aware, more than it perhaps ought to. Nevertheless, she frowned. "What makes you so sure of that?"

Cochrane shared a glance with the stationmaster, and Nora had the distinct impression he was hiding a grin behind his grizzly beard.

"The ravine." He chuckled. "Near enough a hundred yards across it is, and twice again as deep. Standing on the edge of Bridde Pass will make a man sure of many things, most of all that he's best off staying on the side he's on. I'll wager the same goes for women, unless you're hiding a pair of wings beneath that coat."

"But surely there must be some way across? A bridge?" She had only planned as far as the house, but the idea that anything must end there cut deep.

Cochrane went about hitching a bored-looking cob to his waiting cart. "I reckon you'd have been right once, mistress," he admitted. "There's posts on the near side that's matched on the far, and a path leading from the old house straight down between them. But it's long gone, even when I was a lad, and better that way if you ask me."

Nora found herself suddenly breathless. "You've seen it?"

At the question, something in the words or in her voice, the man stiffened, as though realising he had opened a thought he would have preferred to keep closed.

He turned away from her, busying himself over a buckle. "Once, as a lad," he told her gruffly. "Don't know why anyone would want to cross anyway – naught but forest on the far side, miles and miles of it, too dense to be of any use. Now, mistress, if you'll climb up and not mind holding this box here on your lap, you should have my gratitude. It cannot go in the back, you see. The roads round these parts are not what you'll be used to, and in the back, the bottles would rattle fit to break."

The box in question was more properly a small wooden crate, crudely fashioned with bits of yellow straw poking out through the gaps. On the side was stamped the arms of the Royal Veterinary College. Nora settled it on her knees as Cochrane smacked the reins across the cob's broad rump, and so they set off into the pale winter sun.

The raw hillside rose before them, the road a fraying ribbon snaking through a landscape made of coarse rock jutting out of patches of virulent green. Coming from London, where even the grime and the grit were entirely manmade, it seemed impossible that people could live in such a place, yet Farmer Cochrane sat beside her, sturdy and sure as a mountain goat.

"I've heard it said the village is dwindling," Nora said, recalling the article.

"Say rather abandoned, mistress. Last man died near enough a score year ago now."

"Did something happen?"

Cochrane shrugged, not taking his eyes from the road. "Poor land, mostly. Always had been, but by the time I was a lad, what little goodness there had been was worn out. And then there's too much rock up there to be laying decent roads, and nothing to get to beyond that can't be reached by easier means. The fire at the old house sped up what was already happening, reminded the old folks of their superstitions. Can't say I blame them – terrible thing with the gentleman and his wife so young, and then the little girl taken so far away. Stirs up any grandfather's heart, a thing like that." The thickening of his voice suggested the old man spoke from experience. "Still, if the land had been better, I reckon the younger folks would have accounted differently. As it was, the sharp ones looked around to find new places to call home, and the duller ones soon followed in their wake."

The cartwheels bumped and skidded over the rocky path, so that Nora had to clutch the crate tightly to keep it from rattling. "And the man who stayed? Was he sharp or dull?"

"The old reverend." Cochrane's voice was flat, as one who was beginning to regret entertaining his subject, but he went on nevertheless: "Or so the people called him anyway. Truth is, I don't think he ever went away to be 'ordained' or any such.

Simply, there'd always been a Reverend Duinne in Bridde so long as there'd been such a place, passed down father to son, or so they say. Only the last one, the one who stayed, he was a bit funny like. His great-grandfather died young, y'see, and our Mr Duinne was haunted by the idea that, on account of his early death, he'd failed to pass on some knowledge to his son. After the fire, our Mr Duinne was what you might call obsessed with discovering what it was, claiming it would restore something lost."

The sun was setting in earnest now, a December apricot ripe for the plucking. Nora stared into it. "And what had been lost?"

Cochrane snorted into his beard, or tried to: it had grown cold now, truly cold, and all he managed was a violent shiver. "Your guess is as good as mine, mistress. Lot of old superstition around that place, but then I'll wager that's why it interests you."

~

Driving along, something had been pricking at Thomas Cochrane. At first, he had dismissed it as the cold, drawing his wool cloak tighter about himself as he grumbled sternly to his old bones. Then, thinking of his passenger's polished footwear and evident lack of any provisions whatsoever, he had taken it for conscience – and the less noble but equally weighty desire not to have to explain to the authorities why he had allowed a woman of obvious wealth and equal foolishness to wander off alone into the freezing dark, with nothing but treacherous terrain and an eventual sheer drop ahead of her.

It was at the moment he had made up his mind to bring her home and give her a meal and a bed for the night that she turned to him.

"Actually," she said, "I'm interested because I was born there."

There was nothing in the words really. Rather, it was something in her eyes, the way they glittered as they fixed on him. The cart bumped over a rut, enough to rattle the bottles in the crate he had naively asked her to hold, and yet her head remained absolutely perfectly level, defiant of the rules of God and nature – as understood by man anyhow.

Thomas Cochrane was a practical man, and one whose continued life on earth had depended from his earliest boyhood on being able to anticipate and manage the impulses of the shying horse and the stamping bull. He knew that in those moments, thought could be fatal. Instinct alone counted, instincts bred and honed by generations of forebearers eking out their existence among creatures able to strip a man of life by mere accident.

Thomas Cochrane relied on those instincts now. He made no effort to put what he knew into words, nor did he think of turning to see what sat beside him. He declined to recall that he had chuckled at her ignorance – it could not be helped now – and if his heart pounded in his chest, pushing frantically at veins turned to ice, he did not trouble to feel it. Rather, keeping his mind as clear as a mountain stream, he allowed the Rules to bubble up, those Rules learned by every little girl and boy in the county before they could count to ten. In that clear mind, a creaking voice he recalled as his grandmother's reminded him of how one dealt with the Neighbours: one followed instructions, one was unfailingly polite and one never, ever admitted obligation.

In light of the Rules, Cochrane considered his options. They did not make an appealing spread: for one thing, none of them involved pushing her from the cart and driving old Fred hell for leather in the opposite direction until sunrise.

Equally, it was too late now to apologise for laughing at her, or for insisting she dirty herself with the crate. The best thing he could do, Cochrane judged, was drive her to the point where the route to Bridde was shortest and least treacherous, and pray that she asked for nothing more.

The rest of the journey was undertaken in silence. It formed the longest two miles of Thomas Cochrane's life, though his nerve faltered only once, at the moment he remembered that he had named himself a grandfather. Then it trembled fit to break and was steadied only by the recollection that he had not spoken of Daisy by name, nor indicated her being only three months old. He could only shudder then and thank mercy he had not offered to bring the creature home.

When finally the road began to fray and dissolve into the coarse grass of the sloping hillside, Cochrane almost broke his neck in his hurry to hand her down. Bowing as deeply as fear would allow, he declined her offer of a purse for his trouble, taking care to be scrupulously courteous and never once use the words "thank you", by which she might consider him in her debt.

Departing, Cochrane kept his head until he knew himself out of sight, and then he could keep it no more. Applying the whip as never before, he drove the terrified horse not home but down to the river. With the vigour of a man half his age, he wrenched open the crate to reveal the narrow glass vials, four rows of four.

Ignoring the splinters in his hands, he methodically uncorked each in turn, emptying the contents into the rushing water before dashing the bottle against the stony banks, until there was nothing left of them but smithereens on the riverbed, glinting in the dying sun.

When there were no bottles left, he broke up the crate as well and threw it in.

As it floated away, he felt his knees give out beneath him. Sitting on the bank, he allowed himself a minute of great sobbing breaths before hauling himself to his feet and turning the trembling horse towards town. He could fill the beast's trough with oats in apology; he could order more draught for the stock. He could even move the family if it proved necessary, somewhere outside of the creature's sphere of influence. But before anything else, he had to fetch the vicar, that Daisy might be baptised this very night and thus kept safe from reaching shadows.

As they rushed through the night, Fred's old hooves kicking up the stony road as though he understood the urgency, the creature's parting words rang in Cochrane's ear.

Turning from the cart to the slope ahead, she'd picked up her skirts and said, not to him but to the wind whistling down through the scrubby trees, "All right, I'm coming now."

~

When Kit turned up at her rooms towards the end of the afternoon, Margaret was not surprised. She could not say whether she would have been under normal circumstances, and neither could she quantify precisely why the present ones were not so.

"Miss me yet?" he asked.

Margaret looked him up and down where he stood in the doorway. He was still in his eveningwear from the night before. Based on the degree of rumple in its folds, Margaret judged the night had been an eventful one, followed by a distracting day. Yet the smile he met her with was anything but tired.

Margaret turned away from the door. "I did at first. Then Elsie got me a buttonhook, so I was all right after that."

She too had passed an eventful night and a peculiar day, and if he wasn't tired, she certainly was – too tired to have this conversation with herself, never mind him. Nevertheless, she left the door open as she went to the sagging easy chair, and he followed her on the invitation she was not quite ready to admit it had been.

Yet tired was not quite the word, or at least, it was not the sort of tiredness a single *nuit blanche* would produce – and Margaret had enjoyed enough of them to know. Rather, she had the sense of an exhausting return to herself, as after sickness, only she could not remember falling ill. And while she could remember the base events of the night – going to Mayfair, speaking to Mrs Bancroft in the park – they hung unconnected, floating in isolation like scenes in a troubling dream, so that she did not care to dwell on them.

Kit took a dining chair – she had no room for more than one easy chair – and sat down opposite her. She thought she recognised something in his face, something beyond the mere familiar fact of it. The same mist which still hung over her eyes was clearing from his, and yet it was more than that. As he gazed around the dingy room, there was a sort of lightness about him, a weightlessness, a man momentarily relieved of all expectations, even his own. It was the relief of having tried one's hardest and failed, only to find that already the lustre of the goal was beginning to fade against the potential of all the rest of the future.

Margaret recognised it, because she had felt just the same.

"I've sold it all," she said, to recall herself from straying down a path he had not given her concrete inducement to tread. "The jewels and the dresses. They brought a tidy sum."

He took it easily enough. "What will you do with it?"

"For the moment, buy some bonds, while I determine the details."

To distract herself, she rose and went to put water on to boil. The accusation was all her own: for a plan which had been so vivid she could taste it the night she'd walked to Shoreditch, the truth was that the details continued to elude her.

"But it must be here?" He came to her side, retrieving a couple of cups from the claw-footed chiffonier with the gaping crack down the far side.

Watching him wipe them out with his handkerchief, she could not tell how much of his help was the instinctive product of long unity and how much was a deliberate attempt to return to it. She wondered whether he knew the answer any better than she did.

"I think so, at least for the time being."

She poured out a measure of tea from the tin caddy and followed him back to the sitting area, the teapot warming her hands. The conversation, once begun, was comfortable, like an old coat.

"What about you? What will you do?"

Accepting his cup, Kit looked for a moment pleased that she'd asked and equally as though he wished she hadn't.

"You made the flower industry sound rather appealing," he said, quirking an eyebrow. "Could start small, violets in Covent Garden and so forth. What do you think?"

Margaret looked him frankly up and down. "Too tall. You won't sell much if you can't look plaintively up at the punters."

Kit shrugged. "Ah well, back to the drawing board then."

He made a face, something like amusement at his own ineptitude, and she saw with a start that he truly had no idea. She had known from the moment he appeared that something had happened to put him off his plans, but she hadn't realised it had stripped him quite so bare as that. Whatever had passed between himself and his sister-in-law, it must have been momentous.

"I thought I might go down to Hampshire," he said, after a time. "Just for a visit. Pay my last respects to the old man, tell him and Mother about Vic. Though I suppose they must already know." He frowned, as if it were only just occurring to him that, of the family he had known, he at not yet thirty was the only one still above ground.

He glanced at Margaret. "You could come, if you like. And you brother too." Seeing her face, he hesitated. "He told me where you were. I wasn't sure if that meant…"

Margaret shrugged. She wasn't sure either. But that was more than she had been only the day before. "Perhaps," she said.

They lapsed into silence for a bit, lost in their own thoughts, sipping their tea as dusk deepened to twilight beyond the windowpane. It was a still night, stiller than any she could remember since they had arrived, as though the storm they had brought over had finally blown itself through.

Allowing herself to contemplate him, she realised that in the wake of it, Kit had been left as he essentially was: still young, still agile, still capable. Still with an individuality of character flexible enough to withstand the rigidity imposed upon it, if he had a reason to.

Yet even so, it was quite a leap he would have to make. She had made it only just, and she was lighter by far – for though he might have divested himself of all that he could, it would be foolish to pretend that at least some of the weight of the past was not grafted to his core, in ways he himself perhaps was still unaware of. That would take a far more concerted effort to dispense with, if indeed it could be dispensed with at all. And yet, it was not impossible. Whether by nature or by the life he had chosen before he knew better, he was now as much an anomaly as she was. And if she still felt the edge sucking at her now and then, she had made it nevertheless, and would go forward fortified by the knowledge. He might do the same. For herself, she must go forward. She could not turn back to help him make the leap, nor wait for him if he dithered. But if he made it across, and his path brought him close to hers, she saw no reason to deny them both the company.

At length he rose, rolling his shoulders back in a stretch. "Fancy a walk? She's probably cut me off by now, but I reckon I can just about still afford a bag of chestnuts."

"All right." Margaret rose too, fetching her purse. She liked chestnuts.

XXIII

A whispered suggestion of the forest floor drifted in on the crisp hillside air, the sweetness of leaves mouldering into new growth mingling with the acrid soot which even so many years later still lingered about the ruined house. So had Nora found it, charred beams and tumbled walls collapsed around a central stairwell of granite, a squat square structure dug into the ground, built long before more elegant walls had enclosed it and standing long after they had fallen, impenetrable in the inferno they had not been able to withstand. It was to this spot the Beast had dragged her, jaws clamped around fragile young bones, bruising the delicate skin in their mutual panic. Flames had barred every exit, but here in the centre they had been safe, curled up on flagstones cooled by the chill of deep earth.

It was to this spot Nora had gone the night before, instinctively, as though it called her. Through the ruins she had known it exactly, and curled up on the dusty floor and slept as she had then, to wake as she did now, to a presence strange and familiar. The question was in her throat before she'd opened her eyes: "Why didn't you take me?"

Virginia stood in what had once been a doorway, her long hair silver in the dawn. Tall and still, there was something cadaverous about her, not like a corpse but like a tree, passing through the life and death of seasons over so many years that the Reaper had become an old friend. Behind her, a narrow path snaked away down the hill, barely discernible amid the overgrown thicket, the remains of what had once been a garden.

"It was not yet your time." There was a certainty in the way she spoke, serenity in the face of the inevitable, but it was softened in the next by a small smile touched by sorrow. "We were beginning to worry about you, my girl."

The notes of her old voice scraped and ground, as though long out of use. They reminded Nora of Joan, lying in her hospital bed, speaking for the first time in weeks. With the thought of Joan came the rest.

"I don't know why – I wasn't the one in danger." Nora could not tell whether it was the old woman's mistake or her several own which pricked her, but the question came out sharp as she rose: "Are we cuckoos then?"

She was quite sure that, with her youth and heeled boots, she was at least of a height with the old woman if not the taller, yet as she stood, Virginia still seemed to tower over her, precisely as she had in the memory of the child.

"Did you eat the food off your cousin's plate, and throw her weak and starving from the nursery window to break her neck?" Virginia scoffed. "No, we are not cuckoos."

Nora did not try to stop the snarl which came over her lips: Victor had seen it – it was only fair that her blood relations should see it too. "I'm sure my husband would have been gratified to hear that. I understand the coroner's first question was not who killed him but what. I suppose that must be my question too."

Virginia sighed, but though it was an impatient sigh, it could not mask the regret filling the lines of that proud old face. "You do not need me to answer that, any more than a hawk need be told it is a hawk, or the chicken to fear it."

Nora did not answer. Her anger had lodged itself in a lump in her throat, but she could not tell who it was there for.

"I did what I could for you from afar," Virginia went on. "But at such a distance I could only tell you what you were inclined to hear. And then you stopped being inclined to hear me altogether."

The old woman smiled – it was regretful but tinged with something like pride. "I'd trusted to that stubbornness of yours, that tenacity to see you through. I never dreamed you'd turn it against me, let alone against yourself. And to keep it up for so long—"

"I thought I could keep myself together, if I only pulled the laces tight enough and lived a life where nothing and no one could startle me. I managed it for a while, but then..."

Nora looked away. Hot breath moistened the back of her hand in comfort. In spite of her turmoil, she smiled, scratching the bristling grey skull. "What about him?"

Virginia followed her gaze to the great shaggy creature sat at Nora's side. "A little bit of company, and a bit of guidance to lead you to what you already know."

Nora grimaced. "I'm afraid I got rather turned around."

Then something occurred to her which made her forget all else. "I won't be wicked, you know."

She glared at the ancient creature, bracing for a fight. It didn't come. Indeed, Virginia looked perplexed at the very notion. "Then I suggest you not be. You are as you choose to be, and you must live with the same, just as any other creature."

Somewhere in the back of Nora's neck, a knot she had not realised she had tied tightened and then released itself. That was right, she knew, and could not comprehend that she had ever been unaware.

Virginia was watching her, pale eyes uncanny in their familiarity. "You know your way, now?"

Nora found herself nodding.

"Then I will see you soon, my girl."

Left alone, Nora stepped out of the ruins which would never be called a home again. The path led through the wilderness of the garden and out into the open, cresting the hill before dipping down the other side, ending at the edge of the chasm which cleaved the world from the endless forest on the other side. Twin pillars of stone marked the drop, mirrored on the opposite side, like sentinels tasked with keeping the outside out – or the inside in.

As Cochrane had warned, the bridge which had once hung between them, spanning the gap, was long gone, but the idea no longer distressed Nora. In the fathomless depths, the wind howled, calling her home.

~

Ritter was struggling to collect his thoughts. Along with every bone in his body, they seemed to be shaken loose by the jerking gait of the pony as it clambered over the treacherous hillside, picking its way through the rocky landscape.

It was a good pony – Ritter did not say it wasn't: a little native type, it trod surely where a finer horse would have broken all four legs and its rider's neck into the bargain, and Ritter had not a word to say against it. Which was just as well really, as it had been the only one available, thus forcing him to leave Constable Wilcox behind, warming his hands over the stationmaster's stove.

Privately, Ritter thought that was perhaps for the best. The constable had been preoccupied for days now, his distraction only increasing after the Bancroft interview. It was the sort of distraction which bespoke a fundamental shift of mind, and though Ritter was not against it – indeed, he took some satisfaction in seeing that the lad possessed the sort of mind able to manage it – nevertheless it was not a state generally conducive to the sort of delicacy Ritter suspected would be required in the coming hours.

It was for the same reason that he found himself quietly relieved to discover that none of the local police forces who had been sent telegrams detailing the fugitive's expected route and required apprehension had been able to do more than meet the Metropolitan team at their respective stations, to confirm that she had indeed passed through shortly before they were notified. It was also why Ritter had just passed a night of sleepless frustration on a bench in the stationmaster's lodge, having arrived to a darkening sky and a terrain too dangerous to consider crossing by night.

Self-preservation had held him back, but only just. When at the first light of day, the promised guide had not appeared, Ritter had commandeered the only pony in sight and set off with nothing but a map crudely drawn by the stationmaster, leaving Wilcox to follow once the guide arrived.

As the ruined house came into view, Ritter was beginning to regret his solitude: ever since he had left the road, crossing onto a hillside once worked and now abandoned by human hands, he had felt a pricking on the back of his neck, not quite as though he were being watched but as though something was aware of his presence – as if it were permitting it. But there was no turning back now Ritter knew, clinging to the pony's mane as the creature scrambled over the unforgiving landscape with all the lopsided agility and cheery confidence of a mountain goat. Then they crested the next hill, Ritter forgot everything but the figure below.

The figure – and the drop behind her.

Leaving his mount nibbling contentedly on a particularly prickly gorse bush, Ritter climbed off and began his cautious approach. The widow stood on the edge of the cliff, her back to the empty space as she turned towards him, smiling as though she had been expecting him. In the pale sun, her strange eyes sparkled like lakes in the midst of a joyful gale, bright with anticipation – of what he dared not consider.

"Mrs Bancroft," he called, once he was within earshot.

"Inspector Ritter." She nodded pleasantly, as though they had crossed paths in the park. "I'm glad you came. I've left a letter with the stationmaster – I should be grateful if you could undertake to bring it back to London and give it to Hugo Vascelles. He is expecting it."

"By all means, madam." Ritter spoke slowly, playing for time. The howling of the wind within the gorge was almost deafening, and Ritter had to suppress a wince every time it crept out of its lair to tug at her skirt or play with her long, loose hair. One strong gust and—

Ritter took another step, watching her carefully for any objection. "Of course I should be pleased to carry it for you, when we both go back together." Another step. "If we set out now, we may yet catch the sleeper from Newcastle."

He was very nearly within grasping distance – very nearly, but not quite.

A certain narrowing of her eyes stopped him. The fatal consequences of a single wrong move hammered in his skull like blood pounding with every heartbeat, yet it did not seem to be suspicion she regarded him with, but rather… Was that amusement?

The crying wind whipped her loose hair about her, veiling her face. She peered through it, as though waiting to see what he would do, and Ritter realised that this was his chance, the only one he'd get.

"Come along home now," he said, gently and without hurry, drawing out the words so that she wouldn't notice the subtle shifting of his bulk. "Then you and I can sort all this out together."

He managed a fraction of a step; she did not blink. "Wouldn't you like to go home, Nora?"

Her smile told him his mistake, too late, and the way her eyes fell to half mast, as though catching some distant tune. Ritter watched as her skirt flowed back, not at the caprice of the wind this time but to allow her leg its passage into thin air.

"Yes," she said. "I would."

He was too far away – Ritter knew that. Time moved like treacle, glued together by his own powerless horror. He could not possibly reach her, and yet nothing could stop him putting every ounce of his being into the attempt: throwing himself forward, his outstretched hand grasping desperately at the slippery edges of silk falling too far, too fast—

It was too late, and then it was not.

Though not a religious man, for that one moment of his life, Edmund Ritter believed himself the instrument of a miracle. The silk, which had been sliding so cruelly from the hold he had never quite managed to take, caught suddenly in an updraught, reversing its natural trajectory and flowing up, up and over his hand.

Reflex alone made him clutch the black stuff which now willingly filled his grasp as he flung his weight backward, lest the momentum send them both over the edge.

Misjudging the counterweight, the force of the fall knocked the wind from his lungs, so that it took him a moment to realise what had happened and understand that he had misjudged the counterweight because he did not know what it was.

The dress, lying in a limp black heap before him, no longer held the woman it had a moment ago.

And yet it was not empty. Ritter watched in dreadful fascination as the heap began to move. Petticoats flapping in the wind, the black stuff twisted and bulged, pulled about by some unseen force, until at last, a head was thrust through the neck hole. The size of his fist, covered entirely in dense black feathers with a polished beak to match, it belonged to the largest jackdaw Ritter had ever seen. So large was the creature that it had to extract itself from the useless dress one gleaming wing at a time, all the while watching Ritter's astonishment with an amusement he could not persuade his brain to recognise.

Finally freeing itself, it hopped onto the cliff edge then glanced back at Ritter, cocking its glossy black head with a look so expressive it was hard to believe it had only a beak to grin with. Then it turned away and, spreading its great wings, took flight, soaring upon the wind towards the eternal forest beyond.

Ritter watched as it crested the treetops, a cloud of black shapes rising from the canopy to greet it. Still he saw its eyes before him, with their glitter as pale as day.

EPILOGUE

They were quiet on the train home. Alone in their carriage, Wilcox gazed out of the window, full of thoughts of his own, while Ritter stared at the letter in his hand. He felt muddled, scattered, as though some of the pieces shaken loose by the pony's gait had not quite slotted back into place yet. Turning the envelope over, he tore open the seal.

12 December 1896

My Dearest Friend,

It is ironic that, having spent the past weeks confiding myself in letters you will never read, now that I have reason to hope this may one day reach you, I hardly know what to write. The challenge is all the greater for knowing this will be my last letter.

No doubt by the time you read this, some fragments of what has happened – and what is about to – will have reached even your distant shores. I will not attempt to assemble them for you, nor make clear what I lack the words to explain. I beg only that you will not distress yourself or think of me in grief. I do not say that there is no truth to what you hear, only that it is necessarily incomplete. How can it be otherwise, when I myself do not fully understand what I now know?

The first thing I must tell you is that I am sorry. I am sorry for what I said to you, sorry for how I left it and sorry I threw your letters in the grate unread. Most of all, however, I am sorry I did not take your advice.

You know it perfectly well, but no doubt you will enjoy me admitting it: you were perfectly right. I understand your choice now, as I think perhaps I did then, only I hated you for it, having not then the courage to make it for myself. For it is true that I have always heard it, that call, a hum like water on the cusp of boiling, ever on the far side of hearing. All my life I have been afraid to turn towards it, afraid of what I might find. That was what I truly sought in London, not fortune or marriage or even happiness, but sanctuary, a place whose own thrumming activity would drown it out. And so it has, for a time, but drowning out the sound of the river does not make it wear any less upon the rocks in its bed. You knew that, and tried to explain, not because you had any obligation to but because you wanted me to know.

And yet, you were not right about everything. You said a poor choice would hurt me most of all, but that has proven not to be the case. I have stunted myself perhaps, been bent out of shape, yet even now I may yet grow true. The privilege of time, of life, allows me that, as it allows me to sit and write to you. It is a privilege Victor will never have again, for I took it from him.

Yes, I do not deny it. For the longest time I could not face it, but now I accept that to turn away is worse. It was not intentional: he appeared where he ought not to have been, and with the dream still around me, I knew only the disturbance in his eyes, the distress in his voice, felt the weight of him upon my shoulder bidding me to wake. The flash of the knife was in the distance, and in that instant I knew only my own preservation. To defend myself against forces I did not understand, I reached in a panic for what I could not sanely acknowledge, and in doing so left my husband dead in my bed.

My poor husband. I cannot say that I loved him as a wife should, nor even as a friend. I believe he looked upon me in the same light, and in that light we loved each other with a sort of ferocious gratitude for the other's identical feeling. It kept us safe from the expectations of the world while imposing no expectation of its own but of that continued mutual protection. And then he died for it, and I have nothing to offer for it but my everlasting regret.

And if he had not? If he had waited till breakfast to discuss whatever it was which troubled him, would I be writing to you now? I confess I do not know. Always it has been a struggle to hold the parts of myself together in such a way as to allow myself to know but half of them. Every day I seemed to have to lace myself tighter, to keep from catching sight of the disintegrating edges, yet every day I did it.

I think perhaps that's why I banished all thought of you the moment you were gone. You raised too many questions it was dangerous for me to answer. Teetering on the edge, the slightest thing might have sent me over. And yet now that I am falling, I wonder only that I did not jump sooner.

I do not know where I will land – or how. I do not pretend that even now the worry does not come over me that, in my ignorance, I will break my own neck or worse. The difference now lies in the knowledge that the risk of going is better than the suffocation of staying.

To those left behind, who choose to stay and improve, I have made the best amends I could think of. I recognise that my brother-in-law, though I do not pretend to like him, is right when he says that the estate houses many people whose happiness depends on an effective squire. To him I have left the Hampshire estate, along with what Hugo claims is enough capital for him to make a success of it, if he proves as clever as he thinks he is. And last night I met a lady who expressed such interesting views on the state of London that I could think of no one better to leave the house and the remaining capital to, saving provision for any care Joan might need, trusted to the hand of Mrs Sharpe. I hope Christopher will see the sense in this and not fight it in the courts – based on the last moment I spent with him, I dare to think he might.

I do not pretend to know whether I have done right, but equally no more can I wonder over it: I only know I have done what seemed best to do and no more. I have now only left to send you both all my love, and to assure you that I am, and always shall be,

Ever Your Nora

IS *THE BEAST OF BRIDDE PLACE* BASED ON A REAL LEGEND?

This was often the first question I was asked by people reading the manuscript. The answer is no but also, in many ways, yes.

There is no such place as Bridde, nor is there to my knowledge any real legend which mirrors the Beast's. However, the concept of a fairy child being left to be raised by unwitting humans is a common theme of British and other Northern European folklore. Historically, before modern imaginings added dainty wings and a sparkling wand, fairies were known in an altogether darker light. These days, characters like Rumpelstiltskin and the evil fairy Maleficent in Disney's *Sleeping Beauty* hint at a nature which was once common knowledge.

They were considered powerful, unknowable beings, amoral tricksters with ambiguous motives and desires beyond our ken, and while an encounter with a friendly fae might occasionally give a boon to the person who pleased them, more often interactions between humans and fairies ended badly for the human one way or another. Even great romances tended to end in bittersweetness, with the beloved human eventually wishing to leave the fairy kingdom of plenty to visit their human loved ones, only to find that time passes differently in Fairyland, and while they have been away only a few years, hundreds of years have passed meanwhile at home, everyone they loved long dead and all they knew crumbled to dust.

So determined were our ancestors to avoid interactions with fairies that some would go so far as to refer to them only by euphemisms such as the Folk, the Good Folk or the Good Neighbours, in order to avoid drawing unwanted magical attention to themselves by speaking the name of the feared ones.

To my mind, nothing illustrates the reason for this fear better than the legends of changelings, which recur in many forms throughout folkloric history. While the details and especially the cause change – sometimes the parents were said to have done something to offend the fairies; sometimes the fae just saw an opportunity, wanting human babies for reasons of their own – the core remains remarkably constant: a human infant stolen from its cradle and replaced with a fairy child outwardly identical in every way but soulless and sinister – inhuman – within. Baptism was often said to protect a child from being taken in the first place, but once snatched, remedies varied. They almost always involved violence to the imposter, however, on the understanding that even creatures as strange and remote as the fae would not be able to stand seeing a child of theirs suffering.

In more recent times, it has been suggested that such legends originally arose to explain certain types of disability in a world with no understanding of conditions the cause of which they could not see. Conditions such as autism, which may only manifest outwardly years after birth and then markedly change the behaviour of a child hitherto assumed to be typical, would have baffled and frightened parents who had no way of explaining what had happened.

Although these days the original fairy tales have largely been forgotten or hidden behind a flimsy cartoon veneer, the idea of the *not quite right* child continues to capture our imagination. Doris Lessing's *The Fifth Child* and Lionel Shriver's *We Need to*

Talk About Kevin both deal with the mothers called upon to raise them, and the loyalty their very humanity gives them to their inhuman sons.

Such stories tend to be told from the perspective of the mothers or wider families, however I have always been drawn far more to the child's own. These children elicit my sympathy because, however monstrous their appearance or behaviour, that is ultimately what they are – children needing what their human carers simply do not have to give. As well as that, that duality of characters as villain and victim both at once has always fascinated me, and it was through a combination of this that Nora was born, the adult result of a changeling stuck making the best of an inhospitable human world, intrepid heroine and horror in the attic in one Gothic package.

And yet, for all that Nora is ultimately the monster in the book, her story is a very human one – the story of finding your true path in life. This was entirely unintentional, but I wrote it while attempting to find a way out of a career which was destroying my mental health, and such things generally come out in the wash. Nevertheless, I was surprised and pleased when some of the advance readers related it to their own diverse struggles to break out of the moulds imposed upon them. As I write this, I don't know how *The Beast of Bridde Place* will be received once published, but if this is what readers take from it, I will consider it a success.

– A. L. Waters

ACKNOWLEDGEMENTS

The Beast of Bridde Place began its life in 2017 as a story I wanted to read which did not exist yet. The process of bringing it to life has been somewhat ramshackle, full of twists and turns, ups and downs, and one of the most rewarding experiences of my life. It has also been supported by a great many people. In particular I would like to thank:

Mehitobel Wilson, who has edited, supported and mentored my writing since my very first attempt at a novel.

The advance readers Steve, Jan, Sihan, Gapsun, and others, who took time out of their lives to read the manuscript at various stages of development and whose feedback gave me so much to think about when refining it.

Jackie Tee both for her incredible artworks and for her patience with me while making them, and Laura Kincaid for combining it with the manuscript and using her skills to create a single beautiful whole.

Maria Bishop, who helped with the hardest part of any book – the blurb!

David Haviland, who arrived just at the moment when I couldn't decide between self-publishing and traditional, and who offered a third option, and Kirsty Long, whose enthusiasm helped make it a reality.

And finally my parents, who have supported my writing from the beginning, and my partner Chris, who was not on the scene during the writing of this book but who has been so supportive during the publication of it.

Special mention to Mr Davey who was the first person to say he could see me writing a book some day.

ABOUT THE AUTHOR

A. L. Waters studied Law at Cambridge and spent thirteen years in financial services before leaving to pursue a career working with horses which would also allow her time to write. When not at the yard or at her computer, she enjoys walking and reading, and is currently trying to learn how to garden.

The Beast of Bridde Place is her first published novel, the culmination of a lifetime love of folklore and all things that go bump in the night.